Dire Crossing

By

Patrice Leary

Courtney —
My great friend and
great golfer.
Patri

ISBN: 1-4140-2849-0 (e-book)
ISBN: 1-4140-2848-2 (Paperback)

Library of Congress Control Number: 2003098545

This book is printed on acid free paper.

Printed in the United States of America
Bloomington, IN

1stBooks - rev. 01/06/04

Dedication

To two great showmen . . .

My father, Ed Leary, who always strived for the best, and Little
Lito, comedian extraordinaire.

. . . May they both smile down on me from heaven.

Acknowledgments

I must be one of the luckiest people on earth to be surrounded by such talented friends and family. First and foremost I need to thank my parents Ed and Wilma Leary for traveling around the world with four children and never losing their sanity. My sister, Linda, and my brothers, Todd and Eddie for their input, memories and humor. Brianne, thank you for letting me use your beautiful name.

Hopping from the ice rink to the computer was quite a leap, but I didn't do this alone. To Cheryl Lopanik who helped me through my early days of editing and all my friends I used for testing ideas and who happily read early drafts, I salute you.

I turned to specialists for parts of this novel and I owe a special thanks to Mark E. Chariker, M.D. for his expertise and help. And to Linda Leary-O'Brien, RN, BSN; CCRN: not only for her nursing suggestions, but also her knowledge regarding horses, of which she owns a blue-ribbon winning Hanoverian.

My children and stepchildren along with their spouses, were a world of information, and support, you are all in my thoughts and prayers everyday. To Marty, Charlene, and Jessica Durham — an extra thanks with hugs all around.

To the extraordinary person who helped me every step of the way in the final editing process, Robert Berens. What can I say? I will never be able to thank you enough for all your inspiration, tough judgments and guiding hands. You taught me so much about writing.

To my wonderful husband, Ed, a big kiss of thanks to my best friend, my golfing buddy, my fishing guide, and the love of my life.

Thank you all.

ONE

D r. Robison Murphy was ready for the vacation of a lifetime. She'd earned a break from the stresses of surgery and the professional nuances that kept her in a strait jacket of propriety. Yes, a well deserved rest was the perfect prescription.

After arriving home, Robison turned on the computer to check her e-mail. She and Wade were eagerly awaiting news of their upcoming vacation in the Dominican Republic. Scanning through her incoming mail, she spotted the e-mail from Brianne, her best friend and the planner of their trip. They never quite knew what Brianne would come up with, which is why Robison eagerly opened her e-mail now. It read:

In the event someone feels the need to interrupt our holiday in the Dominican Republic, they can reach us at the following number: 809.423.3000. The villa is on Cerezas #57. We supposedly will not smell the odoriferous horse trail; at least that is what they keep telling me, however, you never know for sure until you get there. Thanks to the advice from Evelyn and Richard, I have <u>requested</u> a non-horse villa. So keep your collective fingers crossed. The great news is the villa comes with its own maid and butler! Now that's what I call a vacation! Tom says not to get too used to it!

Our tee times are as follows: Sept. 15 2:36 PM- Teeth of the Dog
Sept. 16 10:09 AM- The Links
Sept. 17 8:02 AM- Teeth of the Dog

Once again Richard has recommended that we take plenty of one-dollar bills. From what I understand, this is to pay the caddie for recovering any lost water balls! (Richard's swing was obviously not "on" during his last stay.) Tom shall carry his dollar bills in a separate duffel bag attached to the wing of the plane. We girls will only need to take one dollar or at the most two!

The restaurant times are as follows:

Sept. 15	*8 PM*	*Tropicana - Continental*
Sept. 16	*8 PM*	*El Pescador—Seafood*
Sept. 17	*8 PM*	*Casa del Rio—French Gourmet*

The Casa del Rio is in the 16th century village of Altos de Chavón and will require a short shuttle ride to the restaurant.

A passport or birth certificate is necessary to enter the Dominican Republic. However, Tom knows someone named "Jose" who may assist us in getting over any little hurdle should one pop up (yeah, right). There is also a $10 fee to get in the country (they call it a tourist card) and a $10 fee to depart. I just hope we aren't willing to pay more than $10 to leave when the time comes! Just kidding.

Here's to a great weekend of golf and drink, eat and drink, sleep and drink! Say, I think I've taken these "holidays" before!

The word for the weekend is...rum!

Don't forget:	*Sunscreen*	
	Sun Glasses	*(girls)*
	Blinders	*(guys)*
	Hats.	

Here's to a fun time and I can't wait to see you guys.

Love, Brianne

———————————

Robison Murphy printed out the e-mail, answered a couple of others, then signed off the Internet.

Amused with Brianne's e-mail, Robison thought about how they'd teased her many times about being a tour guide instead of an attorney. Robison had never been to a place where a butler and maid came with the accommodations. The idea was very appealing. Now this really would be a vacation!

Both she and Wade were looking forward to this time away. The weather in Murrells Inlet was supposed to turn cold, plus they'd both been busy working and moving into their new home. Robison was still making a few last-minute arrangements with the decorator so he could continue working on their ideas for the new house while they were gone.

Tom and Brianne Winstead, their closest friends, would be flying down in their King Air from Hickory, North Carolina, stopping in Myrtle Beach at the small private airport to pick up the Murphys tomorrow after lunch. The weather was going to be cold but sunny, perfect for flying, according to Tom. He only flew in good weather, even if it meant delaying a day or two. It was a precaution both Wade and Robison appreciated.

Tom and Wade had been roommates at Duke in North Carolina. Tom Winstead and his brother owned and operated a large successful furniture manufacturing plant in Hickory. Handed down from their father, the business was on its way to becoming a multimillion-dollar worldwide company. Private planes were a company expense and when company executives weren't using one of their eight planes, they leased them to the various race car drivers and pit crews North Carolina was so famous for. Lately, they'd often had the problem of not having one of their own planes available for personal use. Now Tom was seriously thinking about purchasing another plane and keeping it out of the leasing "pool." Since he was a longtime pilot, he could fly it himself. On this trip to the Dominican Republic, however, Tom would be copilot.

Brianne was always the "hostess with the mostess," planning, arranging, and organizing everyone and everything right down to the smallest detail. Every year the four of them would decide where to take a trip and Brianne would do the rest. This was perfect for the other three, since none of them wanted to handle details, nor did they have the time.

The decision to fly to Casa de Campo resort in the Dominican Republic was Brianne's pick and it would be the first visit for all four of them. Mutual friends, Evelyn and Richard Franks, had been down to the island several times and had suggested such a trip.

Brianne was the only one who was unemployed. Well, that wasn't entirely true; she worked, but not for compensation. Brianne had a law degree, but she preferred to ignore her income potential and instead volunteered her legal services to women in "need." This also allowed her to be available to fly with Tom whenever he went on a business trip or golf outing, either of which could happen at the drop of a hat.

All four of them were excellent golfers and neither couple had children, so they were free to go once they cleared their business schedules. Of the four, only Robison's schedule was truly difficult to work around.

Laying the e-mail on the kitchen counter to show Wade later, she picked up his grocery list. Wade was into cooking with exotic spices and using recipes he'd read about recently, and then he expected her to understand his grocery list when often she didn't have a clue. Robison usually took the ribbing quite well since she really didn't care much about cooking. Glancing at her watch, she saw that she barely had enough time to get the suitcases out of the attic, select some clothes, and get to the store before Wade returned.

Robison and Wade Murphy's home in Murrells Inlet, South Carolina, was a large, white antebellum house with huge pillars in front and back. Because they lived directly on the water, their house required a "front" on both the street and water side. Lacking only moss-laden oak trees lining the driveway, their home was a picturesque reminder of the "Gone with the Wind" era. One almost expected Rhett Butler to come bounding down the front staircase, an effect Robison sought to achieve when she and Wade designed the house. Situated on the north end of the inlet, the panoramic views from every room were a spectacular treasure.

A quarter of a mile north of their neighborhood in the heart of Murrells Inlet was the old fishing village lined on the east by the salt marsh creek. Deep-sea fishing boats that anchored in Murrells Inlet journeyed daily to the Gulf Stream, returning with fresh catches. From any of their rooms facing the water, the Murphys could see the big shrimping boats leaving the inlet and heading for the ocean.

Returning from the store and unloading the groceries, Robison glanced at her watch again. Wade, her...not-so-famous chef...wine connoisseur husband, would be home within thirty minutes or so. She would tease him about his exotic grocery list, of course, and hope she hadn't overlooked anything.

The phone rang. Seeing the number displayed, Robison answered, "Hi, honey. Are you on your way home already?"

"Yep. I should be there in just a few minutes. Did you get all the stuff on my list? I wasn't sure you understood everything, but since I didn't hear from you I guess you did okay."

"Yes...I'm not totally cooking challenged, you know," she said with a laugh.

"Oh, you're not? That's right...I remember now. You made cereal with sliced bananas this morning. A real epicurean delight!"

"Very funny! By the way, I received an extremely interesting e-mail pertaining to our trip. It's quite enlightening."

"Great. No doubt it's from our favorite Hickory tour-director-attorney. Anyway, I'll see you in just a few. Love you, babe."

"Love you, too."

Wade had designed the kitchen with beautiful handmade maple cabinets, granite countertops, along with the latest industrial appliances, all of which he knew how to use. Tonight, the entrée would be grilled marinated filet mignon of tuna, caught earlier on an offshore fishing trip he'd been on.

Wade cut each tuna fillet thick and round, similar to a filet mignon, marinated them in teriyaki sauce blended with fresh spices before grilling them over a hot charcoal fire. Lastly, he topped each with Japanese pickled ginger and added a side of eggplant mashed potatoes. He selected the perfect wine to accompany their meal, a Pinot Gris, which was a full-bodied Alsace white Robison loved.

Shining so brightly it lit up the entire sky, a full moon slowly rose over the water. Seated in their breakfast nook rather than the large dining room, they dimmed the lights to better take in the moon casting a wide beam of light across the inlet. The luminescence reflected off the water like tiny sparkling diamonds. Wade proposed a toast, saying, "Here's to the beginning of a beautiful vacation."

"And here is to kicking your butt at golf!" Robison said, smiling as they clinked their wine glasses together.

They consumed the gourmet meal and polished off the entire bottle of wine, before pushing away from the table.

"It's a wonder we don't weigh three hundred pounds each," observed Robison.

"Well, there wasn't anything really fattening, plus I didn't make a dessert. How bad could it be?"

"Oh yeah! Like those eggplant mashed potatoes weren't fattening."

Wade cooked, and so Robison cleaned up…a "deal" that suited both of them. As Robison wiped down the granite countertops, her beeper went off.

Frowning, Robison dried her hands and went into the study. Sitting at her desk, she opened the top drawer and pulled out a pad and a pen as she returned the call to her answering service.

"Dr. Murphy returning your page," Robison said. "You know, I just want to remind you that I'm not on call for the next week. The doctor on call is…(she looked in her daytimer)…Dr. Gasque."

"Yes, I see the notation about that now, Doctor."

"Okay. What's up?" Robison inquired.

"Sorry, Doctor, but it seems one of the nurses at the hospital needs to talk to you concerning some medication. I believe it is for a Mr. Morrison. Anyway, it's the patient you operated on this morning."

"Okay, thanks. I'll call right away."

Robison called the hospital and prescribed a different pain medication for Mr. Morrison, who was having side effects to the morphine pump. She said to tell him that she would be in to see him first thing in the morning.

Even though it had been a small problem, she suddenly realized how tired she felt. Of course, drinking all that wine with dinner only magnified the fatigue from her long day in surgery that had begun at six in the morning. Surgery was stressful, of course, but she still loved every minute of it.

Her appearance belied the responsibilities she assumed daily as a medical professional. With silky long blonde hair, blue eyes, and a few freckles running over her nose, Robison looked more like a twenty-year-old than an accomplished surgeon in her mid-thirties. Being on the golf team in college had made her more of a jock than the debutante type. Her tomboyishness had totally flustered her "southern belle" mother.

Medium in height but small and petite, Robison appeared feminine, though definitely not the type to bother entering beauty contests. She was into sports and intellectual activities, pursuits

Wade loved. Wade, too, was attractive, with boyish good looks accented by dark red hair and a nice physique. In appearance, Wade and Robison were the quintessential "Hollywood" couple.

Wade was calling from upstairs, sounding desperate. While she had been on the phone, he had started packing. He couldn't figure out what to take so he had clothes strewn over the bed, the floor, and closet door—enough to last a year or more!

Robison went up the long winding staircase to their bedroom. In the back of her mind she was already designing the Christmas decorations she would put up this year. Robison loved the Christmas season with the planning, shopping, wrapping and celebrating with friends. This would be their first Christmas in the new house. She made a mental note to begin designing invitations for a party as soon as they returned from the Dominican Republic.

Robison entered the master bedroom and burst into laughter at Wade's helplessness.

"I'll make a deal with you," she said. "You get our golf shoes and golf stuff organized and I'll pack everything else."

"I knew you would come to my rescue, dear damsel," he said, kissing her cheek. "I'll return momentarily." Abruptly he asked, "Any problems at the hospital?"

"No, just a change-of-medication order. I'm going in early tomorrow morning to check on my patient. I'll enjoy myself more knowing everything is okay."

After returning half of his clothes to the closet, she packed what they would take, into the suitcases. Although they wouldn't leave on the plane until after lunch tomorrow, she hoped to depart from the hospital early. She and Wade had planned to play a round of golf before they left for the airport—at least nine holes. Highly competitive, Robison wanted to "tune-up" her game for the matches against the Winsteads.

This trip to the Dominican Republic was going to be a great vacation…she could just feel it!

TWO

The magnificently landscaped front entrance to the lavish Forest Hills subdivision displayed meticulously manicured flora. Flowers were strategically planted against the backdrop of rich green shrubbery to partially hide the high stone wall surrounding the elegant neighborhood. A set of ornate fifteen-foot-high black and gold painted wrought iron gates featured a centered crest emblazoned with the initials "F H" in gold leaf. Inside the tall gates stood a quaint little ivy covered guardhouse with twenty-four hour security guards to greet residents and guests or turn away any unauthorized vehicles. Not nearly as pretentious, the back gate was used only by the residents and had no security guards. Each resident was given a private code that changed annually.

Louis Ramundo waited near the back entrance, making sure there were no oncoming vehicles or passersby to spot him. The way was all clear! Pulling up to the electronic arm, he punched the five-digit code into the small silver box. The arm slowly lifted to let him pass, then it lowered quickly behind his inconspicuous white van. Louis checked his rearview mirror one more time; no one was following him and no one was leaving in the oncoming lane. According to his plan…this was perfect.

Turning right onto Forest Lane, he wound his way through the tree-lined street of the posh neighborhood. Deep estate lots displayed huge homes barely visible from the quiet two-lane road. A young woman passed him in a new blue Jaguar convertible while he made his way around the next small curve. She didn't notice him; she was too busy talking on her cell phone and checking her make-up in the rearview mirror.

This splendid gated subdivision in Charlotte, North Carolina, boasted a totally private eighteen-hole luxury golf course that annually held a nationally televised PGA Tour event. Tickets to the golf tournament were hard to come by, unless a person was on a certain list or privileged enough to be an acquaintance of a Forest Hills resident. With an initiation fee set at two hundred fifty thousand and no monthly dues, members were billed for whatever the club's expenses were; only the wealthy need apply.

Were these residents demanding and persnickety? Absolutely—
and proud of it!

It was midmorning on that sunny September day when the
Centurion Locks & Security Systems van Louis Ramundo was driving
pulled into the driveway of the preselected estate.

Centurion was one of the most respected electronic security
companies in Charlotte. Being an old family-run business it had been
in operation for over seventy years. Louis had been an employee with
Centurion for the past six. He was well-liked, a trusted employee.
He'd never been "written up" nor were any "red flags" raised during
the background check Centurion performed on all new employees.
Louis Ramundo was a model employee.

Pulling around to the side of the house in front of the triple garage
doors, he came to a stop and put the van in Park. Stepping out, he
went around and opened the side door, then reached inside for his tool
kit. Warily, he watched and listened for any human movement.
Deciding it was all clear, he pulled the sliding van door closed with a
gentle "click"…opposite his usual manner of slamming it shut with
full force.

Born in the Dominican Republic, Louis' parents had immigrated
to the United States when he was very young. His first language was
English and he spoke very little Spanish. He was short and not
particularly good-looking. Although Louis had the stereotypical dark
hair and brown eyes, he didn't look anything like his dashing and
handsome cousin, Carlos Alvarez, whom he'd met only twice.
However, according to the plot, Louis would be seeing Carlos again
very soon.

Louis went to the front door, put on his rubber gloves, rang the
bell, and listened as the tones reverberated off the marble in the large
open foyer. He waited just to be certain—no answer. When Louis
punched in the eight-digit code, the light on the security panel turned
from red to green. From a large ring of keys, he selected one and
inserted it into the ornate brass lock, but it didn't turn the tumblers.
Selecting an almost identical key, he slid it into the lock and turned it
to the right—silently the huge oak and beveled glass door swung
open. Picking up his toolbox, he stepped inside. Quietly closing the
door, he heard it lock automatically behind him. He was now in the
home of Mr. and Mrs. Henry Barnes, III.

He looked at the bottom of his tennis shoes to check for dirt or moisture; tracks might show up on the white marble floor so he needed to be extra careful. The recent rain was one reason he had waited until today. He made a mental note to discard his tennis shoes after he'd finished here.

Henry Barnes was a steel manufacturer who had inherited the plant, along with several million dollars, from his deceased parents. Henry was a genuine blueblood through and through. Valuable family antiques strategically placed throughout the foyer flowed into the adjoining room and beyond. The house had been professionally decorated to the nth degree, probably done before Marianna, Henry's new wife, entered the picture.

When Louis had met her on an emergency call, he thought she was a bit wild. She definitely had that "come-and-get-me" attitude. He couldn't quite visualize her and Mr. Barnes together as a couple. She must have bowled him over by her youth and vibrancy. Or perhaps, Louis chuckled...she was "screwing his brains out."

As the "newest" Mrs. Barnes, Marianna had just been named "Volunteer of the Year" by the Women's Club of Charlotte. The Forest Hills Country Club, especially the ladies locker room, was buzzing with conversation about her new award. Marianna thrived on the attention, of course. However, members also snickered behind her back because she was so young and very fashionably thin. The old biddies were just jealous—viciously jealous. They were certain Henry must have paid someone off for his bimbo bride to win such a prestigious award. How else could she have won?

Louis took the long winding staircase up to Henry's master suite two stairs at a time. It wasn't really the master bedroom; that was on the ground floor. Louis knew something that was not common knowledge: old Henry and young sexy Marianna had separate bedrooms. He wondered how she rated the "real" master suite when it was Henry's house, but Louis dismissed it as Henry being ruled by a young pussy.

Henry enjoyed flaunting his sexy bride wearing braless tops and midriff shorts in front of every man who came into view, including the burglar alarm man, Louis. Henry was on the verge of looking ridiculous—like there was no other man on earth that could handle her. Yeah, right!

Louis quickly navigated to the end of Henry's walk-in closet where a full-length mirror was attached to the wall. To the left side of the mirror were over two dozen expensive suits. Pushing aside the silk jackets revealed an alarm keypad with a glowing red light. Louis punched in the code he had written on a small piece of paper, and watched the light turn green and the mirror retract into the wall. Lights automatically snapped on with the opening of the door. Louis stepped into the walk-in vault, which he had installed four years ago while the house was under construction—and before the new Mrs. Marianna Barnes had secured her position in old Henry's life.

The hidden room was plain but it was filled with cubbies and drawers. Lights shone down on several oil paintings hanging in various places on different walls. Henry had positioned a chair at the opposite end of the small hidden room for the sole purpose of admiring his art. To the side of the wingback chair sat a small decanter on an antique end table. Louis removed the heavy crystal top and smelled the contents, cognac. Louis chuckled as he imagined the pompous old fart sitting in a closet, sipping cognac and staring at a bunch of pictures on the wall. Ironically, copies of these originals were hanging in the library downstairs; however, Henry wanted to admire the real thing whenever he felt the impulse.

To his complete surprise, Louis discovered three small "peeking" windows down to Marianna's bedroom. One was over the king-sized bed, another was over the Jacuzzi, and the third was in her closet. So that's how the old coot got his rocks off, concluded Louis. A video camera stood on a tripod near the window over the bed. Louis thought about stealing the tape but then he came to his senses. He needed to stick to the goddamned plan!

Pulling open several shallow drawers, he finally found what he was looking for. Louis gently lifted the pretty gold box out of the velvet-lined drawer. He opened it to reveal a smaller box with a brass enclosure. Carefully unlatching the second box, he lifted the lid gently—what he saw took his breath away. There it was…the diamond and ruby necklace with the matching bracelet and earrings; estimated worth—three million dollars. The platinum bejeweled ensemble had originally belonged to Mrs. Henry Barnes II, Henry's mother.

Louis smiled to himself. If Henry's mother wasn't spinning in her grave over her new daughter-in-law, loss of her prized jewelry would surely send her into a whirling dervish.

Louis placed the contents into the small cloth bag hanging from his belt. Then he carefully closed the box, relatching it securely. He slid the box back into the larger gold box and returned it to its original position in the velvet drawer. Well, at least old Henry had brains enough to keep the family jewels in his safe under his constant watch—not Marianna's!

There were other trays of jewelry, but taking them was not part of the plan. It was Louis' intent that Henry not miss anything for weeks or months. After all, how often would the new Mrs. Barnes III actually wear this ostentatious necklace? Closing the drawer, Louis looked around to make sure everything was in order.

It was so quiet...so still...he needed to hurry. But curiosity got the better of him. Instead of stealing the videotape, he turned on the television and pushed the Play button on the VCR. On the video she was making passionate love not to Henry but to another woman. Marianna was truly gorgeous nude. Louis watched for several minutes then thought about where he was. Hurriedly he rewound the tape and turned off the television. Too bad he wasn't in the blackmail business. Perhaps Henry was impotent and this was how he got his kicks. Who knew? Better yet, who cared?

He passed through the door, then turned back towards the keypad. He punched in the proper sequence of numbers that allowed the retractable mirror to close, then pulled the clothes back over the tiny glowing red light.

Moving on to his next target, Louis quickly maneuvered down the back staircase leading to the butler's pantry. He hurried through the granite and stainless steel kitchen into the dining room, progressing towards the library.

Louis smiled, remembering how he and Mr. Barnes had come up with the idea of putting the safe not behind a picture, but built into the wet bar. Soon he was dialing the combination code of Mr. Barnes' safe. Taking out several stacks of one-hundred dollar bills (neatly wrapped in bank wrappers) Louis opened the small toolbox he'd brought along. He and his girlfriend Felicity had meticulously cut newspaper-size dollar bills, which he now inserted between the real bills he'd taken from the middle of each wrapped stack.

With latex gloves on, it took more time than Louis had estimated to stuff the newspaper bills between the genuine bills. Tossing the real money into the toolbox, he repositioned each fake stack exactly as it had originally been. Then he closed the safe. Perhaps good ol' Mr. Barnes wouldn't need any cash for awhile either. At least that was what Louis was counting on as he gave the combination dial a final spin.

He made his way out the back, taking no chance of being seen by exiting through the front door. He reentered the burglar alarm code, turning the light from green to red.

Driving out through the rear gate, Louis rode through town to Centurion and parked in a preassigned space near the office. After opening the van door, he replaced the keys under the front seat, unloaded his bag and toolbox, and closed the door with a final "thud." He wasn't going inside the office, nor would they be expecting him. His two-week vacation had begun the day before, so Centurion would never realize he had taken another employee's van this morning instead of his own. Louis knew the other guy was out sick; "prostate surgery," someone said.

Walking briskly, he removed his gloves and placed the bag and toolbox in the back of his newly purchased pre-owned station wagon. It was lunchtime and he was heading over to pick up Felicity from her work at Ionosphere Tour and Travel, which was conveniently located only two blocks from the front entrance of Forest Hills.

A month ago, Marianna Barnes had come into Ionosphere to buy tickets to Hawaii for a ten-day vacation. The visit had started the ball rolling for the Barnes jewelry heist.

"There you are, Mrs. Barnes," Felicity had said. "Two first-class tickets to Maui, your hotel pass for your penthouse suite, and the voucher for the rental car."

"Oh, Felicity, this is going to be wonderful! Henry has been working so hard lately, and this will be such a great surprise for him. It's our anniversary tomorrow, you know; that's when I plan to give him the tickets."

13

"How romantic, Mrs. Barnes!" Felicity exclaimed. "You are so lucky. Oh...and of course he is, too," she added in her effervescent style.

Only a few weeks before, a picture in the *Charlotte Observer* had shown Mr. Barnes escorting his lovely Marianna, adorned in the diamond and ruby ensemble, to the Heart Ball. Now while they were in Hawaii was the perfect time for Louis to heist the precious jewelry.

Pulling up to the side entrance of Ionosphere, the side that didn't have any windows, he patiently waited for Felicity to come out. Meanwhile, he decided to open the back of the station wagon and began rummaging through his suitcase, until he came out with a new pair of tennis shoes. He put them on, and placed the old ones behind his seat.

It wasn't long before the door opened and Felicity appeared, hurrying to get in the station wagon. Hers eyes were red from crying.

Backing out onto the street, he inquired, "How did it go?"

"I told them my mother had a stroke. I cried and the whole bit. I should get an academy award! Anyway, they all felt so sorry for me. I told my boss I didn't know when I would be able to return. He said for me to take all the time I needed," she explained.

"How about a lifetime?" he laughed.

According to the getaway they'd worked out with Carlos, the two of them would head directly for Myrtle Beach, South Carolina to spend the night.

"How do the pictures in our new passports look?" Felicity asked.

"Great! We are now Mr. and Mrs. Luís Gomez. Notice the new Spanish style of spelling my name."

"Well, that's one way of getting married. I hope I can remember our last name is Gomez. Have you contacted your cousin to tell him to be ready to fence the jewelry?" she asked.

"Yep. Well, he didn't know we were going to hit the place today. He just knew it was going to be sometime this week. He also gave me instructions regarding the next set of passports that will be in San Juan when we arrive."

"Do you feel bad about stiffing Centurion?" she asked.

"No. I should have been making more money all along. Anyway, we'll be long gone from this country by the time they miss me."

"I still don't know why we have to spend the night in Myrtle Beach. It's such a waste of time, I'm scared. I think we need to get on a plane and out of this country sooner than tomorrow," said Felicity.

"We have to follow our plan. Listen, no one even knows anything is missing; they might not discover it for weeks. Besides, I love my cousin Carlos and all, but I don't trust him. So we're going to stay and take a little extra time to set up a few precautions. Better to be safe than...poor," Louis said. "You'd better get some sleep while I drive. We have a lot to do when we get to the campground."

Alone on a deserted stretch of highway, Louis threw one of his tennis shoes out the window. After about forty miles, he threw the other out. Now there would be no traceable tracks. As he drove, Louis thought about other shoes he'd seen in the past on various highways. What story could they tell?

Driving the rest of the three-hours from Charlotte to Myrtle Beach, Felicity slept. As she did so, Louis contemplated his not overly attractive accomplice. Felicity was not fat, but not thin. She had red hair, green eyes and a personality to die for. She'd never met a stranger she couldn't win over with her charm. She was exactly the type of person he needed at this time. Did he love her? He wasn't sure.

With his eyes on the road, Louis reveled in thoughts of his newly acquired wealth. Now he'd get anything he desired—even a new girlfriend if he tired of Felicity. Yep, things were looking up for Louis Ramundo as he headed towards his new life in the Dominican Republic.

THREE

Tyler Kelly turned left onto Kanner Highway in Stuart, Florida, where he was going to exit onto I-95 south towards Miami. With such a gloriously sunny day, thoughts about having to spend the whole time inside a theater taking out an ice rink were not setting well with him. Ty wanted to be working in his yard or sitting by his pool, anything but stuck in this heavy traffic.

He enjoyed his ranch-style home when he was there, which hadn't been very often lately. Ty had just finished a tour in the States and another in Europe, which had ended in Miami. Normally, the show would take some time off after such a grueling schedule, but the opportunity to do a show in the Dominican Republic had popped up at the last minute and he wasn't about to turn down good money. Besides, he sensed this show would face unique circumstances and he liked that prospect.

The Dominican Republic was an interesting place—politically intriguing to say the very least. Culturally, it had certain charm and, of course, the Dominicans loved ice skating, a rarity among Caribbean sports enthusiasts. Ty was confident that the show would be a big success and he could manage the downside nuisances readily enough. Always had, so why would things be different this time?

But first, Ty literally had to get his "show on the road," and that was always a complex challenge. He talked on his cell phone the entire trip, attempting to verify the presence of a crew to work the "load out," and to double check with a tractor driver he'd hired from a local company. The driver would haul the two containers, one with the rink and the other with show equipment, to the docks in Miami this afternoon. The schedule was tight, but nothing new about that.

Ty's ice show company had its headquarters in Stuart, just north of West Palm Beach. It seemed odd to many people that he had housed his company in a warm weather locale, but being close to Miami was convenient for shipping ice rinks, costumes, props, lighting, and sound equipment worldwide. A location such as Minnesota wouldn't work because trucking containers to the nearest port would cost a fortune.

He finally arrived on the outskirts of Miami, although he felt like he'd just left there. Last night, the cast had performed the final show for this venue, so after the skaters packed their costumes into aluminum crates designed for the traveling wardrobe, they went about their merry way. On the other hand, crew members still had a lot of work to do, and Ty would see that they did it.

In the sewing room, the washer and dryer were humming with last minute cleaning, and drying. Nothing was packed wet; otherwise it would mildew during transport. The washer and dryer "lived" in a rolling, wooden crate carried with the show all the time. The hoses and cords extended through a hole in the back for quick and easy hook-up. It even included a little "cubby" to store detergent and bleach.

The wardrobe lady packed the larger costumes, sewing equipment, and supplies, and ultimately dismantled three dozen rolling costume racks.

With the help of two local crewmen, the sound controller packed all the audio equipment and miles of cable. The stagehands lowered the set that hung from electrical winches, folded all the curtains and packed them in rolling canvas crates. (Canvas was used instead of wood or aluminum so the curtains could breathe.) Crewmen gathered all hand-props, and packed them with the larger magic props.

Finally, the crew took apart the set and overhead lighting grid. By morning, all the scenery, costumes, lighting, sound equipment and road boxes were in the "show" container ready to go. Still, Tyler hadn't gotten to his home in Stuart until four in the morning. He could have stayed at a hotel, but there was nothing like his own bed, thus the long drive to Stuart and back.

At five minutes to eight, Ty arrived back at the theater. Twelve men hired to help with the rink "load-out" were waiting at the back roll-up door. With that many men, Ty knew they should be loaded into the container by lunchtime.

After the last show, Ty's ice engineer had dropped the antifreeze solution to two degrees, which made the ice colder and harder. This also kept the ice "dry," enabling the stage crew to roll the heavy crates around without slipping. That the brittle ice cracked under the weight of some of the crates didn't matter; the real nightmare was trying to load out on wet ice. Dropping curtains and not getting them

17

wet would be impossible. Then too, crates wouldn't stay put on the ice when they were being crammed full with gear.

The ice was now frosty white, hard, and ready to "break out." Several men took sledgehammers and began tapping the ice and breaking it into large pieces. A front-end loader scooped up chunks, then carried the load outside and piled it over a drain. Even in the Miami heat, it would take two or three days to completely melt this mountain of ice.

Soon neighboring children discovered the frosty heap and began making ice balls; most of them had never experienced such fun before. The local newspaper was "johnny-on-the-spot" and took pictures of kids throwing snowballs in Miami, for tomorrow's edition.

A reporter spotted Ty. "Excuse me, sir. I'd like to ask you a quick question."

Ty stopped what he was doing and said, "Okay. What can I do for you?"

"Why not simply let the ice melt?"

"If I let it melt there would be thousands of gallons of water flooding the theater," Ty explained.

"Wow. Well that makes sense. Oh, I didn't get your name."

"Tyler Kelly. And thanks for your interest."

Once all the ice was outside, the engineer turned off the compressor and unhooked the hoses. Then the workers took apart the serpentine pipes that made-up the ice floor and loaded them into a container. Lastly, they folded and packed the rubber liner that protected the floor from any moisture. With that, Kelly Productions had an entire ice rink neatly loaded into one container.

By one o'clock, Ty had paid the workmen and was on his way to the shipyard in Miami, following the transported containers. He made a quick detour into a fast-food restaurant to pick up a burger and a coke. Now if he could get through all the red tape by four this afternoon, the containers would leave tomorrow morning for the Dominican Republic. It would take two to three days for the ship to reach the island's port of embarkation. There a rented chassis trailer was supposed to be waiting to take the containers to the next venue, Altos de Chavón.

Today was Monday. The rink would arrive in the Dominican Republic by Thursday...maybe. Friday was an extra day in case something went wrong at the shipyard…which usually happened. The "load-in" of the rink was scheduled for early Saturday morning in the charming little village found on the Chavón River. Rather than inside a beautiful theater, this time the rink would be installed in an amphitheater on a temporary stage built by the local promoter, Raúl Armada. Ty had faxed the "specs" for the stage to Raúl earlier in the week along with a list of other requirements for the show.

Indoors, a "skatable" ice surface normally took twenty-four hours to freeze after the "load-in." This time Ty would be dealing with a foreign country, setting up outdoors, and he was already certain they wouldn't have the electrical requirements for the rink, even though they insisted they would. Anyway, Ty left a two-day window for the set-up, just in case.

He'd already checked with Raúl concerning local work habits. It was good to know the men would work all day, and only take an hour for lunch, not like other countries where they wouldn't come to work until nine and then lunched at noon; followed by a traditional two-hour nap. Quitting time, of course, was six. "Frustration" best described Ty's feelings in such circumstances.

The technical crew was to fly down to the Dominican Republic the middle of the week, with the cast flying over the day before the opening. They all knew the routines since it was the same show just performed in Miami. Ty didn't need a bunch of bored ice skaters wandering around Altos de Chavón, driving him crazy or eating at the wrong places and ending up too sick to skate. Their egos needed catering to, but only to a point. Tyler Kelly ran a tight ship.

Making the final turn into the Miami port, Ty headed towards the U.S. Customs office. Tens of thousands of containers stood six high, running in rows and rows for what seemed like miles. How they were able to keep track of every container, its location, its destination, when and on which ship it was coming from or going to, was inconceivable. Rusty brown, newly-painted, or shiny aluminum, it was an elaborate labyrinth of stacked metal boxes.

Ty followed his chassis trailer to U.S. Customs and Port Authority where they pulled up and parked. U.S. Customs' officers would probably inspect the two containers and if everything was in order, including all of Ty's paperwork, the U.S. Customs agent would affix the official seal. This seal was to remain unbroken until the container arrived at the appointed destination and had cleared Customs on the other end.

Leaving the truck driver in the cab, Ty walked over to the Port Office and presented his manifest. With all papers in order, he picked up directions to his assigned cargo ship before leaving the office. Ty left his SUV parked where it was, walked back to the chassis truck, and climbed in on the passenger side.

"Okay, go down to the right, then bear to the left and it's the fifth ship. We'll see its name painted on the side. It's the *La Lucia*," Ty told the driver.

After passing through the narrow aisles of containers, they came to a row of ships. "There it is," Ty said pointing to *La Lucia*, spelled out in large red letters on the side.

A large crane was already loading containers onboard. As they watched, it grabbed onto the next container to load and lifted it high into the air. With a dozen or more chassis trailers in front of theirs, he and the driver patiently waited in line. As the crane lifted each container onto the tanker, they watched the massive ship sink a bit closer to its waterline. Ty had made this trip dozens of times, yet the maze of containers, many of which were being lifted by awkward cranes never ceased to fascinate him.

When they reached the front of the line, Ty hopped out as the crane picked up his first container. The massive machine lifted it fifty feet into the air, swung it out over the water, across the deck of the ship, and onto one of the stacks. Then the great arm swung back, the huge jaws opened and plucked the other container off the truck as it rocked from side to side.

"I'll never get over being nervous when I see my containers swinging out over the water like that," Ty said to the driver.

"I wonder if they ever drop one in the ocean," the truck driver said.

"Well they'd never tell us, I bet," Ty responded.

They hopped back into the truck, navigated back through the maze of containers and stopped beside Ty's SUV. Opening the back of his truck, Ty took a check from his briefcase and paid the driver. The driver signed the paperwork, then "swooshed" his air brakes, and eased into the exit lane of the shipyard. Ty was right behind him.

With any luck at all, he'd be home in time for dinner...if the traffic flow kept at a steady pace up through West Palm Beach. An hour and a half later, he exited I-95 at the Stuart—Indiantown exit, turned left onto Kanner Highway, and sped west past the Florida Club towards home.

When his cell phone rang he was walking into the house. "Ty, here."

"Señor Kelly?"

"Yes, sí."

"Sí, this is Señor Armada (he rolled his r's as though there were at least ten in his name), calling from the Dominican. I was just...uh...how do you say? ...checking...yes, checking to see if you shipped ice rink today?"

"Sí, everything is in transit...on the boat. It should arrive in three to four days on the *La Lucia*. I will fax you a copy of the manifest."

"What else must I do? Only get the chassis truck big enough for two containers?" he inquired in accented English.

"Yes. Or two chassis trucks if you can't get a large one," Ty replied. "Don't worry. I'll be there when the *La Lucia* arrives in the Dominican. Did you take care of all the electrical requirements and the supply of water?"

"Oh sí, sí. Believe me, Señor Kelly, I take care of everything...you have no need to worry."

"So, you got them to put in two hundred twenty volts, three-phase with two hundred amps per leg?"

"Oh yes, yes, no problema. And the stage is complete as well. I also have two block buildings cleaned out to use for dressing rooms."

"Can they be locked? Secured?" Ty inquired.

"Sí. Sí."

"Good. I will call you when I know what time I arrive at the airport. By the way, how are ticket sales?"

"Oh, Señor, the ticket sales are excellent. We are selling out for many of the performances."

"Glad to hear it," Ty said.

"Adios, mí amigo," Señor Armada concluded.

"Adios," Ty said.

From experience, Ty knew foreigners usually only told him what they thought he wanted to hear. Shit, by the time he got there, it was a distinct possibility that none of the specific requirements and equipment he needed had been taken care of by ol' Señor Ar...r...r...mada, exactly like all the others in the past. Ty shrugged, preferring to be optimistic about Raúl Armada, promoter extraordinaire; perhaps he would be different. Of course, Raúl would be a lot more cooperative, if as he said, ticket sales were good and he'd make a pile of money from promoting Ty's show.

Ty went to the refrigerator, grabbed a beer and headed down the hall to the master bedroom. Changing into a bathing suit, he stepped outside to swim in his beautiful outdoor pool.

Refreshed after a few laps, Ty checked his e-mail messages. There were several, but one from Russia confirmed the deal between Ty and a Russian ice show. The show would perform in Greece for three weeks, and it needed one of Ty's ice rinks. The Russians didn't have any ice of their own. Strange that the Russians would put so much effort into a traveling show, but not have any ice. All the better for Kelly Productions, however.

He e-mailed back to confirm the rental of the ice rink, including an ice engineer. Ty planned to fly over to Greece right after the show closed in the Dominican. As prearranged, the Russian company would wire the first payment to arrive tomorrow and promised to e-mail the schedule with dates, times and locations. These shows would also be performed in outdoor amphitheaters; no problem for Ty or his rink. As soon as the wire transfer was confirmed at the bank, he would ship the container to Greece. The biggest hurdle was his scheduled flight to the islands tomorrow. There was a lot to do and not much time to do it in. Welcome to show business!

He spent the next hour on the phone getting shipping schedules from Miami to Greece, trying to get a head start on the details. If the transfer didn't come through, he could always cancel but right now he needed to reserve space on one of the cargo ships ASAP. With this development, Ty realized he might be delayed a day arriving in the Dominican, but that's why he had left a "window" with a couple spare days. Because travel time for the transport ship to get from Miami to Greece was too long to use the ice rink from the Dominican, Ty scheduled another rink he had stored in Stuart to leave as soon as possible. Thank goodness the Russians only required the rink and not the whole show, which made Ty happy.

Next he needed to get in touch with Sam Holden, one of his ice engineers who lived in Tallahassee, and from the schedule it looked like he was available to work the two dates in Greece. That Sam had been to Greece before was a big plus. It was short notice, but Sam being a single, carefree kind of a guy, was usually ready to go at the drop of a hat.

Ty dialed Sam's cell phone number. "Sam, Ty here."

"Hey, man, what's up?" Sam asked.

There was a tremendous explosion in the background...then a second...and a third.

"What the hell was that? Where are you?" Ty inquired.

To be heard over the clatter of falling debris, Sam hollered, "I'm working up at the Crazy Horse Memorial in South Dakota. They just did a series of blasts. We're working on the horse's head and neck at the moment."

"The Crazy Horse Memorial? What are you talking about? I can hardly hear you...a Memorial in Tallahassee?"

Now things had quieted down in the background. Sam replied, "No, man. In South Dakota, I said. I've been coming up here since I was a boy. I'm just fascinated with the size of this gigantic monument. It's even bigger than Mount Rushmore. Of course, I'll probably never live long enough to see it completed. But...I love it."

"Well, to each his own. Does this mean you won't be going to Greece?"

"Is the Greece gig still a go?"

"Well, I have e-mail confirmation. I'll know for sure tomorrow, but it sounds pretty solid."

"Sure, I'm always ready to roll," Sam said excitedly. "You're going to be there, too, aren't you? I'd prefer not to deal with both the Greeks *and* the Russians on my own. Wow...now there's a mind-blowing thought."

"Don't worry; I'll be there. Anyway, I'll talk to you later when I have more details. Just plan to get back down here in a few days or so. Oh, by the way, I didn't know they allowed a horse's ass to work on a horse's head," Ty joked.

"What are you talking about? Man...they love me up here. You've got to come here and see it for yourself. It's awesome."

"I bet it is. Maybe one day I'll be up that way…you never know. Hell, for that matter, I never know from moment to moment where I'll be going next," Ty laughed.

It had been a long day by the time he headed inside for dinner. His regular phone started ringing. It was his mother. "My icemaker isn't working again, dear."

"But, I just fixed it."

"I don't understand how you can install huge sheets of ice all over the world and I can't get a few ice cubes. Can you explain that to me?"

"No, but that is an interesting point of view," he said. "I'll be over tomorrow."

"Aren't you leaving in the morning?" she asked.

"No. I've got to make some shipping arrangements, so I'll be over tomorrow morning. I had to delay my flight to the Dominican by a day and get all this Greece stuff together."

"Okay, dear. Thanks."

Tomorrow, as soon as the wire transfer arrived, he would start lining up another chassis trailer to pick up the container in Stuart and haul it to Miami. Then he would call the Port Authority to confirm container space on the cargo ship to Greece. He also needed to check on the type of visas he and Sam would need to enter the country. Another long day on the phone, but this time it would pass while he soaked up some rays out by the pool…after he fixed his mother's icemaker, of course.

FOUR

At four o'clock, alias Mr. and Mrs. Luís Gomez pulled up to the tropical entrance of PirateLand Family Camping Resort in Myrtle Beach, stopping short of the security guard. Luís parked the station wagon, while Felicity went to check in.

"Welcome to PirateLand. How may I help you?"

"We have reservations…Mr. and Mrs. Luís Gomez."

"Oh yes, I believe you wanted to be across from the Lazy River?"

"That's right. We enjoy watching the kids and all the excitement," Felicity lied.

"That's the place to be for that. By the way, we're having a barbecue and a reggae band on the pool deck beginning at six. It's free to our guests."

"Wonderful! This is better than we expected."

Felicity took the receipt, a brochure of the campground, and a map to locate their site near the Pirate's Oasis Water Park. She regretted they wouldn't have time to enjoy the Lazy River or the mile and a half of beach during their short stay at PirateLand. A month ago she hadn't used any of the amenities either, because they'd departed Charlotte after work and drove hurriedly to Myrtle Beach. They erected their new tent, scouted out the campground, spent the night and returned to Charlotte the following morning. That's when they'd decided the Lazy River site was their best option in carrying out their scheme.

Guided by the map, they found their campsite directly across the little street from Pirate's Oasis Water Park. There was plenty of action and, best of all, plenty of noise—exactly what they needed. They unpacked the large tent from the back of the station wagon, quickly erected it before unloading everything else, including the toolbox with the jewelry and one-hundred dollar bills.

"I'm exhausted!" Felicity said plopping down on the ground inside the tent.

"Well, just think how much more tired you'd be if we hadn't practiced putting this tent up and down in your backyard. Remember how long it took us the first time?"

"I hated that day. Oh, there'll be a reggae band starting up at six tonight."

He looked at his watch. "That's only twenty minutes from now. What a break! We couldn't ask for better sound cover than that."

Luís pulled back the canvas covering the floor and began digging a deep hole with the small shovel he'd brought. Without the noise of kids screaming and yelling, and the music playing…someone would have surely heard the digging. Then too, he needed to dig while it was still daylight; otherwise his illuminated silhouette would have been visible from outside the tent. So far, so good! Everything was on schedule just as they'd planned.

Taking the necklace, bracelet and earrings out of the cloth bag, Felicity gasped at the sight of the huge sparkling diamonds and rubies. "Oh! My, God! These are beautiful! And this necklace is so heavy!"

"Just stick to the plan," Luís grumbled as he tossed the shovel to one side. Picking up a towel he wiped the sweat from his face. The hole he had dug was over three feet deep—deep enough that some camper's metal detector wouldn't pick up the mother lode after they'd gone.

Wrapping the bracelet and earrings in a piece of velvet, Felicity placed it in a plastic bag, then into another plastic Ziploc and put the double-bagged jewelry inside a waterproof plastic jar. While Luís (he now insisted on using the Spanish pronunciation of his name) rested, she opened the toolbox and counted the cash: three hundred fifteen thousand dollars! She packed one hundred fifteen thousand into plastic bags and then put it into a different jar. After putting both jars into a square waterproof container, Luís placed it into the freshly dug hole.

"There. All done," he announced.

"You need to cover it up while the band is still playing," she carped.

"Easy for you to say," a sweating Luís retorted.

After covering the container, he placed the surplus dirt into a plastic trash bag and loaded it into the back of the station wagon. He'd toss it on the way to the airport. Replacing the canvas floor, he unrolled two sleeping bags. He stepped outside to have a cigarette while she showered at the bathhouse. The reggae band gave the water

26

park a Caribbean flavor, no doubt about it. Kids were still squealing as they rode inner tubes around the Lazy River. "Enjoy it while you can," he thought to himself. It was supposed to turn cold tomorrow, poor kids.

It was another hour before the water park closed down for the night. Extinguishing his cigarette, Luís reentered the tent. He lit the lantern, fluffed his pillow, and got ready for a good night's rest. Felicity returned from the bathhouse smelling sweet and sexy but he was too tired to "fool around." Luís snored soon after his head hit the pillow.

Pulling their first heist had been stressful and exhausting—but so far successful. However, Felicity was nervous about what was ahead of them. So far everything had gone way too smoothly, in her estimation.

The next morning they dumped their belongings onto the floor of the tent. Luís pulled back a false bottom in each of their suitcases, in his briefcase, and in her purse and strategically apportioned the two hundred thousand among the various pieces. The necklace, he gingerly placed in his own suitcase. It would be risky putting the cash and necklace in the luggage to be checked, only to see them being whisked away on the conveyor belt—but there was no other way. At least they had some of the cash with them in a worst-case scenario. At one point he even considered having Felicity wear the necklace under her blouse, but with security so much tighter since September 11, 2001, he didn't think it wise.

"Remember, don't use the stolen cash," he reminded her. "Use only the money we withdrew from our bank account."

"Hey, I'm not stupid!" Felicity shot back, as she repacked clothes on top of the hidden stash.

Luís put the suitcases in the car, and then they took down the tent. After folding it neatly, he placed it in the back of the station wagon. Next he went to shower at the bathhouse, while she watched their belongings. When he returned, she took a small bag of clothes and cosmetics with her to the bathhouse.

The breakfast pizzas at the arcade smelled delicious, so Luís bought two. What a life! Once he fenced the necklace, he would never have to worry about anything again. After a few weeks, he would return to South Carolina and dig up their stash. Then he would fly back to the Dominican Republic, fence the earrings and bracelet for another tidy little sum, and live on "Easy Street" the rest of their lives.

He was in a good mood when he pulled through the gate, waving to the security guard as they left. They were off to the airport for a flight to Puerto Rico where they would change identities yet again. Then on to Santo Domingo in the Dominican Republic, just as his cousin Carlos Alvarez had arranged. Life was good!

Mr. and Mrs. Luís Gomez landed at the airport in San Juan, Puerto Rico. They had no problems going through customs; their fake passports worked without so much as a second look from the custom agent. They collected their luggage, which hadn't gotten lost, and took a cab straight to the address of a small jeweler in a seedy section of Old San Juan—following instructions Carlos had given Luís earlier in the week. The streets were narrow, full of potholes and littered with trash. Obviously, this wasn't the tourist section of Old San Juan he'd heard so much about.

Entering the small shop, the two of them and their luggage, filled up most of the space in front of a dilapidated counter. A small, elderly gentleman approached from somewhere in the back of the shop, and swept aside the filthy curtain covering the doorway.

Looking up, the old man asked, "¿Sí?"

"We are Sr. and Sra. Gomez," Luís announced.

The old man seemed puzzled.

Surely, he had been told in advance of their impending arrival by Carlos. Otherwise, Luís wasn't sure what he would do; this was most unsettling.

Then the man nodded his head, and held up one finger indicating to them he'd be just a minute. He turned around and went back through the greasy cloth curtain without saying another word. They waited a few long minutes. If this didn't pan out, plan "B" would be to get a hotel room in San Juan and call Carlos. Luís' confidence in Carlos was waning with each passing moment they spent standing in this fleabag store. He felt Felicity clutching his arm a little tighter; she was nervous, too.

The old man finally returned, this time with a young boy holding a manila envelope that looked cleaner than either the man or the boy.

The boy said, "My grandfather does not speak English, so I will translate. He has this for you." He handed the envelope to Luís, then continued, "That will cost you four hundred American dollars."

Luís hesitated, knowing the contents supposedly had been prepaid. Ultimately, he shrugged his shoulders and reached for his wallet. Luís was being ripped off, but right now he just wanted to get out of this place. Felicity opened the envelope and checked the contents—two new passports and other documents that would make them citizens of the Dominican Republic.

The boy spoke again. "My grandfather says he is supposed to take a picture of the necklace to fax to Carlos so he can 'shop the goods.'"

Luís and Felicity looked at each other nervously. Then Luís said, "Okay, but I'll take the picture."

"No problema," said the grandfather, who obviously understood more English than he had pretended.

Luís unzipped his suitcase, tossed things aside until he reached the false bottom, and pulled out the jewelry. Then he fastened it around Felicity's neck after she removed a scarf and pin. He wanted to make certain her face would not appear in the photo. In any case, he felt safer with it around her neck than having either of the two locals handling it.

Felicity wondered how this decrepit old man could know anything about fax machines. What must this Carlos guy be like if he dealt with such people? Suddenly the flash of the camera jerked her back to the task at hand. Good! Now they could get out of this rat hole!

After Luís took the picture, she hurriedly adjusted the necklace beneath her mock turtleneck and replaced her scarf and pin. There was no time to waste. Luís repacked the suitcase. Then he and Felicity hauled their luggage out to the curb and hailed a passing taxi. Once inside the vehicle, Luís wanted to inspect the passports. He opened the envelope and inside found two tickets to Santo Domingo along with new passports. Now they were Sr. and Sra. Luís Manolo and their flight would leave San Juan in two hours. He told the cabby to take them to the airport "pronto." As the driver darted in and out of traffic, Luís kept glancing back to see if they were being followed. Seeing nothing suspicious, they began to relax a bit. Surely, the crummy little jewelry store with the filthy old man was out of their lives for good.

After all, they had a rich new life to start living…as soon as they found Carlos.

FIVE

The servants and employees could hear the small private helicopter in the distance. With the sound getting ever louder, they busied themselves getting ready for the arrival. Several men in dark suits walked briskly towards the landing area. Shading their eyes, they looked towards the sun. Clearly, their boss was sitting in the passenger seat as they expected. One of the men radioed to the main house announcing the arrival. The helicopter hovered momentarily over the small designated landing area. Then it set down delicately on the tiny pad in front of the boss's sprawling vacation home at the Casa de Campo in the Dominican Republic.

The fourteen-thousand-square-foot, two-story house featured a gorgeous thatched roof. Parts of the second floor had open-air spaces, with large bamboo fans hypnotically circulating at low speed. The south side of the mansion faced the ocean. The second floor open-air bar, on the eastern side of the house, looked onto the eighth green and fairway of the famous Teeth of the Dog golf course. Accentuated by ocean waves crashing against the huge boulders near the base of the lush green, the vista had captivated many a visiting spectator.

The flowering fauna and tall swaying palm trees made this large estate a tropical paradise. The impeccable manicuring of every bush, tree and flower was magnificent. In all directions servants were diligently at work. Clearly, vast amounts of manual labor were not a problem here.

A wall fifteen feet high covered with red and yellow flowering vines completely surrounded the house on three sides. Four rows of barbed wire were strung along the top. The wall and barbed wire, deceptively disguised with the flowers, made it attractive and inviting rather than ominous and guarding. Intentionally, it had been made to look like a lovely vacation home rather than a top security fortress.

At the driveway entrance near the gates to the house stood a tiny guardhouse manned by a twenty-four-hour armed guard. Only the side of the house facing the ocean had a clear unobstructed view, but then, on closer scrutiny, armed guards protected it from any intruders. Discreetly placed video cameras sat atop the fence, guardhouse, guest quarters, on the corners of the main house, plus all the entrances.

The helipad consisted of a small flat boulder with a white painted circle surrounding the "H" in the middle. It sat about twenty-five feet out into the sea with a rock pathway leading back to the shore. Slightly more elevated than the other boulders, the waves still crashed against the helipad with abandon, occasionally washing over the landing insignia.

Two armed guards stood on either side of the pathway onshore that led to the house, waiting for their boss to emerge from the helicopter. When the rotors halted, the small door opened and a squat, heavyset, Spanish man in his early sixties emerged and started up the rocky path towards the house. He passed the two guards, silently nodding to them. They nodded back as he made his way up the curving stone stairway carrying his briefcase. At the top, he paused to catch his breath. Then he crossed the terrazzo patio surrounding the large pool and Jacuzzi, went past the entrance to the small guesthouse, and headed towards the French doors that led into the side of the house. He didn't bother going to the front door…that was the long way to get to where he was going, and he was in a hurry.

Momentarily stopping beside the pool, he glanced up at the open-air thatched covered balcony off the master bedroom to see if she was there. Another guard opened the French doors and stood waiting for him to enter.

"Good evening, Señor Alvarez," the guard said.

"Thank you," Juan said stepping inside, handing the guard his briefcase. "Where is my Bibí?"

Before the guard could answer, Bibí flamboyantly rushed down the wide staircase, her kimono trailing behind her. A sensual aroma of gardenias permeated the air swirling around the lovely young woman.

"My darling, Juanito," she gushed, hurrying over to plant a juicy kiss on the lips of her lover.

Now smeared with lipstick, he started wiping his reddened lips with the back of his hand. Noting the stain, he reached for his handkerchief to wipe both his mouth and then his hand. Smiling broadly, he caressed her face, and then gently kissed her while stealing a "feel" inside the top of her kimono.

"My little pumpkin, how I've missed you," he said in Spanish.

"I've missed you, too."

Slinging his jacket over a nearby chair, Bibí loosened his tie then slid it off and unbuttoned his shirt at the top.

With his wife safely tucked away at her sister's in Miami, Juan felt free to enjoy the company of his young and sexy mistress. After all, he deserved a vacation, and Bibí *was* his vacation. She was wild...free...an untamed tigress.

He and Bibí had been an item for the past three years. Juan had promised to divorce his wife, but then there would always be excuses. Now Juan had the best excuse of all: he was running for president of the Dominican Republic. He was the candidate of the Dominican Liberation Party and was presently the Minister of Finance. There was no way he could weather scandal, especially a divorce. In fact, his relationship with Bibí was pushing the limits now. How could he have this lusty creature for his wife? Why she might fuck half his cabinet before he could move into the presidential mansion! As it was, he had trouble getting her to wear clothing around the house; her spontaneous nudity was driving every man within range insane.

The other problem was the media—not to mention his opposition—who were always trying to dig up the latest dirt on Alvarez. But he was doing exactly the same to his opponent, just hoping for some bit of scandal that he could use in their upcoming campaign. Lately it had become a mudslinging contest, so Bibí was definitely a dangerous liability. However, Juan Alvarez was reluctant to admit it and most of the time pushed thoughts of breaking up with her out of his mind. He was addicted to her sexual charms, and there would be no voluntary disengagement on his part.

At least his vacation home was obscure, difficult to get to, and completely secure. This was the only place he and Bibí could be together without the danger of discovery by the opposition. Critics might think she was there, but they had no proof.

The situation was not entirely pleasing to Bibí, however. She felt their relationship changing and she planned to have it out with Juan towards the end of this weekend vacation. As matters stood, she was wasting her time and needed to get on with her life. Who was he kidding anyway? He would never leave his wife, so if Bibí was on her way out she wanted money to live on—even if it was "hush" money. After all, she had given the old fart three years of her young, vibrant life, and certainly deserved compensation. Yes, she would show Juan the time of his life—and then hit him with the deal.

When a meek-looking maid stepped into the room, interrupting the lovers, Bibí's head snapped around. "Bring a pitcher of martinis and keep the ice separate. Make it snappy!" She ordered in rapid Spanish. Always rude and demanding to the servants and bodyguards, Bibí was your basic "bitch-on-wheels."

Juanito had what he wanted sitting in his lap, so he didn't care about her rudeness. Besides, adding a great martini would be all the better.

When his cell phone rang, Bibí suggested he not answer it.

"It is, Carlos," he said as he looked at the number displayed on his cell phone. "Don't worry this will be the last call tonight."

Bibí persisted in trying to interfere; however, Juan was not in the mood for this game so he stood up and let Bibí slide unceremoniously to the floor...just as the maid reentered with the pitcher of martinis. When the maid smirked, Bibí glared back, got up, brushed her kimono back into place, and took the tray. Under her breath Bibí sneered. "Get the hell out."

Bibí had grown to loathe Carlos, Juan's only son, and everything he stood for. The feeling was mutual, as Carlos did not approve of Bibí either. But so long as she kept Juan Alvarez sexually satisfied, she was in control. Or so she thought. She, of course, would never admit she resented Carlos and his interruptions. The current scene was typical. Juan had just arrived, was all hers, and then that damn son had to spoil everything! She believed he did it on purpose— asshole!

Carlos was getting closer to convincing his father that Bibí-the-bitch had to be dumped because of the upcoming campaign. Perhaps this would be their last weekend together. He already had come to the realization that his father would have to pay her off, but Carlos had not yet broached this new plan with him. But he would this weekend, for security advisers and public relations people were pressing Carlos to get rid of the bitch. Bibí had to go!

Bibí poured two martinis, placing in each glass two olives skewered on a sterling silver toothpick. She plunged the glass pitcher back into the bucket of ice. She handed one glass to Juanito who was still talking to Carlos; he saluted her with his glass and took a swig.

Turning his back to her, he continued to talk in a quiet voice. He stopped talking for a moment and walked outside by the pool, out of earshot. Now she was seething. She watched him give an order to one of the guards, snapping his fingers in a "get moving" gesture, even as he continued talking to Carlos. Looking out towards the ocean, Bibí saw his helicopter take off, which made her furious. If he thought he was sending that helicopter to pick up the "asshole," she was going to blow her stack. She paced while she watched him through the glass doors. Snatching up her cigarettes she lit one, and forcefully exhaled a cloud of smoke.

Still talking on the cell phone, Juan's mind was racing. With the prospect of Carlos arriving in a few hours, Juanito would have to pacify Bibí one way or another. He'd wanted to be alone with her this weekend, but a business deal had come up and had to be dealt with. Money before mistresses—even before the tantalizing Bibí!

Obviously, with no love lost between Carlos and Bibí, Juan figured Carlos would start the "time-to-dump-Bibí" speech again as soon as he arrived. Juan knew the time was coming…but not quite yet. He had explained to Carlos that screwing Bibí did not affect the bond with Carlos' mother. Bibí was a play toy, nothing more. But with the presidential campaigning beginning in earnest, Juan knew that Carlos was right. Juan also suspected his public relations department was pressuring Carlos to "handle" his father's mistress. Juan also knew his PR people would never have the "balls" to talk to Juan themselves. They had no choice but to go through Carlos.

Turning towards Bibí, now pouring a second martini, he cooed, "Darling, I have an idea. Why don't we adjourn upstairs, shower, and go for a lovely dinner at the El Pescador?"

He wanted her out of the house before Carlos arrived, and he wasn't exactly certain when that would be. Juan knew Carlos had a six o'clock meeting, but had no idea how long it would last. In their phone conversation a few minutes ago, Carlos indicated the meeting would not last long.

Abruptly, Juan began to feel old. He couldn't keep up with Bibí's vivacious energy, sexual or otherwise. Who was he trying to kid? He certainly wasn't fooling himself. So maybe this would be his final weekend with her. And if so, why not succumb wholeheartedly?

The problem at the moment was that he was too tired for any confrontations, especially between Bibí and Carlos. If this weekend would bring the crescendo, why not hold it off for as long as he could.

Still seething over Juan's long conversation with that son-of-a-bitch Carlos, Bibí fought to regain her composure. She needed to follow her plan through the weekend. So she took a deep breath, and turned towards Juan, her kimono opened to reveal her lovely breasts.

"My Juanito," she said, strolling over to kiss him. "I think we need to go for a swim first."

The kimono dropped to the floor. Carrying her martini, Bibí walked to the pool and slipped into the water. Swimming over to the edge she leaned against the side of the pool. He watched her swallow the last sip of her drink. She took the silver toothpick, and licked the olive seductively...before devouring it whole.

Slamming back the rest of his drink, he dropped his clothes and followed his mistress. With raving red hair, deep brown eyes, and gorgeous figure, Bibí excited him like no other woman he'd known. She would do to him what no other woman could. It didn't bother her that the guards might be watching; in fact, she rather liked the idea. In her mind Bibí had a power that the guards would never attain. Forcing them to watch, garnered respect from all the guards and house servants alike. In her self absorption Bibí never realized the guards and servants scoffed and made fun of her behind her back. Earning respect was a task she knew nothing about.

Diving into the water, Juanito swam towards her from underneath. Coming up for air where Bibí floated, he first caressed her breasts then ran his hands all along her sleek body. She playfully dipped beneath the surface then wrapped her arms around his neck and her legs around his waist. She took him there in the water until he came with groans of ecstasy. Even at that climactic moment, she winked at the guard standing nearby.

After a while Bibí walked slowly up the pool steps, knowing Juanito was watching. She dried her hair with a towel and then wrapped it around her long red mane. Only the setting sun covered her glistening body. With a sly but knowing glance towards the guard, she strolled into the house with her tanned and toned physique on full display.

She poured two more martinis, before calling for the maid in a loud and garish voice. When the butler arrived instead, she ordered him to take away the tray. Not only was she nude but the cool breeze had hardened her nipples. So embarrassed was the elderly butler that he kept his eyes cast down upon the floor.

Impulsively she grabbed his chin and raised his head saying, "You don't like what you see?"

"No, no, you are very beautiful," he blurted, trying to turn away from her.

She took his hand and placed it on her tit, but he jerked away, as if burned. She laughed a loud, haughty laugh. Humiliated, he hurried from the room.

Juan finally made it up the pool steps and walked towards the house, wrapping a towel around his paunchy midsection. During the minutes it took to maneuver inside, he'd missed the entire "butler" ordeal.

Leaving their clothes strewn all over the floor, Bibí took his hand and gently led Juanito upstairs. He watched her bare derriere all the way up, every step of the winding marble staircase. It excited him so that he decided to take a tepid shower—alone. Besides, they needed to get ready for their dinner engagement at the El Pescador, for which one of his security men had made reservations. He wondered how many of the guards Bibí had slept with, for all of them eyed her lasciviously. Maybe he would ask the butler. Better yet, he would review some of the security tapes tomorrow.

As Bibí finished her makeup, a self-satisfied smile crept over her lips…everything was going according to her plan. By seducing Juan with her charm—basically screwing his brains out—she was going to get everything she had coming. She just had to keep it up!

So when Juan emerged from the bathroom freshly shaved, dressed and ready to go, he was detoured by Bibí stretched out on the bed naked, wet and ready…

⌢⌢⌣

Sr. Raúl Armada drove to the newly constructed airport near Casa de Campo. The old airport had cut a runway through the middle of one of the golf courses, bisecting a hole about a third of the way down the fairway. Golfers frequently had to wait for an arriving or departing plane before making a shot across. It served as an interesting topic of conversation, but held up play, making the head golf pro unhappy. Time was money! The new airport was about fifteen minutes away by car, even less if Juan used his helicopter.

Raúl parked his car and headed inside through the new glass doors. The airport had been open only one day, so chaos seemed to be the word of the moment. Raúl watched the hustle and bustle of employees trying to figure out where and how to arrange their customs desk, with others trying to organize ticketing procedures. Why hadn't they gotten organized before opening? He guessed that would have been too simple. Now everyone was barking orders, no one was listening, and tempers were flaring.

Raúl continued strolling around the small airport lobby, waiting to ask someone about arriving flight times. But it was impossible to pin anyone down. How could anyone know? The "arriving" and "departing" signs were all blank.

He noted that no expense in the architecture or in the decoration of the new terminal had been spared. The marble floors and high ceilings were impressive. The bright, vivid colors of the sofas and original paintings decorating the two sitting areas were beautiful. Large tropical plants gently swayed with the breeze as it flowed through the open-air terminal. But then, this airport was catering to the rich vacationers flying in on their own airplanes or jets.

Settling down on one of the ornate, overstuffed couches under an electric ceiling fan, Raúl looked at two Lear jets parked to the left of the main runway. Both were sleek, white and had armed guards on the tarmac near the engines. The guards sat on stools when they weren't pacing the immediate vicinity. They had to be hot out there sitting or standing all day long; Raúl was sweating just sitting on the couch.

Raúl Armada was here to pick up Tyler Kelly from the one daily commercial flight from Miami to Casa de Campo. Ty had already mentioned on the phone that he would go directly to the amphitheater to inspect the staging area, electricity and water availability. Raúl had reserved rooms at a small hotel near there for Ty and the other cast members who would be arriving in the next few days.

When he saw the airplane approaching, Raúl left the couch and exited through the glass double doors. The airplane touched down with a big puff of smoke billowing up from the landing gear when the tires hit the hot tarmac.

As he waited outside the terminal, Raúl Armada took out his handkerchief and wiped the sweat from his brow. When the airplane door opened, a staircase rolled towards the opening. After several people deplaned—all of them looked like tourists—Raúl saw a man he knew had to be Tyler Kelly.

Ty was putting on the sunglasses that had been hanging around his neck. With briefcase in hand, he talked on his cell phone while descending the stairs. Wearing blue shorts and a silk flowered shirt, he waved at Sr. Armada. Raúl concluded it was the briefcase and no camera that set Ty apart from his fellow Americans on the flight. This fellow was no tourist.

Ty readily spotted Raúl, the only man dressed in a suit and tie.

"How's it going?" Ty shouted as the engines wound down.

"Bueno, bueno,…good," Raúl answered as they shook hands.

"Wow, this new airport is pretty spiffy compared with the old one," Ty said, looking around.

"Yes, it just opened yesterday. You will see how confusing everything is. Hopefully going through customs won't take very long."

"I hope not. I need to get to the rink," Ty said as he glanced at his watch. "What time are the laborers arriving?"

"They should be at the theater at eleven this evening," Sr. Armada said. "So, we have plenty of time."

Ty knew not to hold his breath. One hour in the islands somehow converted to two or three. If they actually showed up by midnight, it would be a miracle.

"They seem to be having difficulty getting things organized. But we will see," Raúl informed Ty, pointing towards the chaotic desk.

"Sorry, I couldn't be here when the cargo ship arrived, but I was trying to get another rink shipped to Greece before I left Stuart. I'm glad everything went all right with the manifest, getting through customs and hiring a chassis trailer."

"No problema. Everything is in order," Raúl Armada assured him.

Raúl went to a small drink machine and bought ice-cold cokes while they waited for an official-looking lady to process Ty's passport. The open-air airport became quite stuffy with so many people in such a small space, even though several large ceiling fans whirled away.

Ty retrieved his luggage, paid the ten-dollar fee for his tourist card, got his passport stamped, and was ready to leave. It did indeed take a bit longer, but it was nothing serious, plus it gave Ty time to catch up on all the messages left on his cell phone.

"Okay, Señor, let's get to the amphitheater first, then I'll check into the hotel. No?" Ty said throwing away his coke can.

"Sí, sí,…we go now. My car is very close." They walked towards the car and Raúl continued, "So, you send another ice rink to the Greeks?"

"Something like that. I'm sending a rink to Greece for the Russian government. They are doing their Russian ice show there, only they didn't have any ice. So, once I'm finished here, I'll get this rink shipped back to the port in Miami and probably fly from here to Greece or back to Florida first. But, anyway, I'll be in Greece for about three weeks."

"You do this alone?"

"No. I have one of my ice engineers flying over too. His name is Sam. In fact he's been to Greece a couple of times; it's always good to have someone who knows something about the country, even if it's as simple as ordering at a restaurant. Personally, this will be my first trip over there."

Ty threw his luggage and briefcase into Raúl's trunk, slamming it shut.

"Why don't the Russians have their own ice rink?" Raúl asked.

"Beats the shit out of me," Ty replied.

Raúl looked puzzled.

Ty added, "I really don't know why. But in any case, I'll make some good money."

"It sounds exciting. All the traveling and getting to see different countries, and money is always good, too," said Raúl, as they both got in his car.

"Well, it may sound exciting, but it usually turns out to be nothing but a big headache before it's over," Ty said, with a grin. "The

Greece trip ought to prove quite interesting with all the different interpreters we'll need. I'm afraid Spanish is the only foreign language I can handle, so I'll be in the dark over there."

Ty didn't mention that he needed to concentrate on one show at a time. One headache at a time—namely, any headaches connected with *this* show. Then he'd worry about those in Greece: the language barriers between Russian, Greek and English, combined with the finicky, egotistical ice skaters' temperaments. Ty shook his head; if he started thinking too far ahead he'd work himself into a full-blown migraine.

"Why don't you take that jacket and tie off?" Ty asked Raúl. "Aren't you about to die in this heat?"

"I wanted to make a good impression," Raúl replied sheepishly.

"Well, take it off, man. You've made your impression! And don't wear it again. I wouldn't want you to die of heatstroke on me, or some damn thing."

They both laughed. Yes, they would get along very well.

Felicity and Luís landed in Santo Domingo and passed through customs without any problem. While waiting for the luggage, Luís was sweating bullets—even though no bags had been lost on any of their flights so far. But then, they had never had so much hidden inside, either!

"There they are!" Felicity squealed with delight as she pointed at the conveyor.

Luís was not so much delighted as he was relieved; almost immediately the airport felt cooler and his sweating diminished. His blood pressure plunged at the sight of the luggage.

With belongings in tow they hailed a taxi by the curb, loaded up, and sped away to their prearranged hotel. Exhausted by their ordeal, they were both ready to crash for the night even though it was only four in the afternoon. While checking in, Luís was given a message from Carlos with instructions to bring the "present" to an address at six sharp. So much for "crashing" for the night.

Up in the room, Felicity unpacked while Luís took a shower. They ordered two sandwiches, a beer and a bottle of wine from room service. He brushed aside thoughts of a nap; as tired as he was he might not wake up in time.

They ate quickly and Felicity kissed him goodbye. "I'll probably be asleep by the time you return," she said. She was glad to see him leave. He really seemed edgy…and she wanted to relax in a hot bath with a nice glass of wine.

Felicity locked the door after he left, and settled into the sweet smelling bubble bath. Noting her reflection in the mirror, she lifted her wineglass in a toast to her own good fortune.

"Here's to my boyfriend….Oh, yeah…alias husband," she said, taking a sip.

"And to my new life as a wealthy woman…who can buy anything her heart desires."

She savored her new-found status for a few silent moments. Then holding the glass on high, she proclaimed, "I'm the luckiest woman on the face of earth."

SIX

Two dozen candles of every size burned brightly, casting a warm glow across the cream-colored walls of the small room. A pungent odor of eucalyptus permeated the air. Soft piano music in the background mingled with the sounds of waves crashing on the shore. The ambiance was as relaxing as it was meant to be.

Nude except for the sheet covering his body; Carlos lay face down on the table. Alicia entered the room. The masseuse carefully placed two hot towels, one around his shoulders and the other squarely on the small of his back. Her fingertips drifted lazily down his thigh…then over his calf to the bottom edge of the sheet. She lifted the cloth and tucked it between his legs—gently.

Well-moistened hands began kneading, pulling and massaging every muscle from the top of his leg to his heel. Finding two small knots in the bottom of his heel, she noted, "You've been having some lower back pain lately, I see."

He grunted, trying not to pay attention. He wanted to concentrate on the music, on the relaxing atmosphere, on the shadows dancing across the walls. But mostly, he didn't want to get a hard on…in vain.

After re-covering the first leg, Alicia uncovered the other…again tucking the sheet around the sensitive area between his legs. Deftly she worked her way down to his other heel and back up to the top of his thigh.

Carlos had just spoken with his father who was at Casa de Campo. Carlos had closed on a business deal and needed his father's signature on the papers. But that wasn't the big news he'd given his father. Carlos told him of the impending meeting with Luís and the "fence," outlining the plan in detail. Juan suggested that he have the family helicopter pick Carlos up from the airport following his meeting with Luís. Carlos agreed. It was nice to have a rich and powerful father.

Carlos was just over six feet tall with jet-black hair, large brown eyes, and a slim, but muscular physique. In addition to the masseuse, his personal trainer was an absolute must, for Carlos had an image to uphold: he was single, wealthy and very available.

Alicia readjusted the hot towels and lowered the sheet from his shoulders to his buttocks. His muscles glistened in the candlelight as she kneaded, pulled and worked her fingers along his spine. Pressing down firmly with the palm of her hand, she massaged his buttocks in circular strokes, and then began kneading the small of his back. Her busy fingers poked, prodded and caressed their way up his spine to the base of his skull.

"Okay, time to turn over," Alicia said ever so softly.

He dreaded this moment no matter how often he came for a massage. His hard on was evident as she held up the sheet to let him turn over, gathering the folds over his midsection to masquerade what they both knew protruded beneath. Covering his eyes with an eye pillow, she then pulled back the sheet to his waist. She worked the muscles in each arm, extending down to each finger. Then moved up his neck and onto his head; rubbing his scalp, massaging his face and earlobes, turning his head from side to side, stretching…pulling…gently, vigorously.

She was so close. He could smell her lotion, not what she was using on him but one that had a sweet apple-scented aroma. Perhaps what she used after showering, or perhaps it was her shampoo. His erection throbbed.

Uncovering one leg, she started at the top of his thigh pulling downwards in long smooth strokes towards his feet. Then Alicia worked his foot, instep and every digit. Carefully she folded back the sheet to uncover the other leg.

After she had finished, Alicia covered him completely. "Stay as long as you wish. A little quiet time will be good for you," she said, slipping from the room.

Resting was the furthest thought from his mind as he exploded into a towel. He needed a shower. The candles still danced to the soft music playing in the background as he turned on the water in the shower stall.

Fifteen minutes later, Carlos Alvarez emerged from the small room, ready for his meeting, before catching a plane to Casa de Campo. As he departed he whispered in Alicia's ear, "You're the only woman who can get away with making me hard and not finishing me off, you know."

"My job is to relax, not excite you."

He stuffed fifteen hundred pesos in her pocket and winked. "See you next week."

Outside he walked swiftly to the waiting car and driver. He explained to the driver that there had to be a change in plans. He had a quick meeting scheduled with his cousin, Luís and the "fence" before going to Casa de Campo. He looked at his watch. It was almost six. Perfect!

～～

Luís paid the taxi driver after it pulled to a stop in front of the small, seedy hotel. He checked the address on the message he'd received. Yes, this was the place. He gazed up the filthy sidewalk where trash clung to every crevice. Then to the entrance where someone had taped over a large crack running the entire length of the hotel's front door. The foreboding that came over him was not good. What had Carlos gotten him into? Never having fenced anything before, Luís fought to control his emotions.

When the taxi abruptly pulled away from the curb, Luís jumped. Shit! Why was he so jumpy? What was wrong with him? This was supposed to be exciting…the moment he'd been waiting for. He told himself to calm down.

There was a bar inside the small hotel. Not many patrons though, and Carlos easily spotted his cousin in the back booth. After greeting Luís and a bit of small talk, Carlos tossed the barmaid a few pesos and stood up to leave.

"Do you have the 'present' with you?" Carlos inquired as they walked away.

"Yes," Luís replied.

"Good. I have a room upstairs. Our friend should be waiting for us there by now," Carlos said, glancing at his watch.

"What's the guy's name?" Luís inquired innocently.

Carlos scowled. "No names. That's always the deal."

Luís felt stupid. Of course, there would be no names in this kind of transaction. Luís hoped he wasn't "in" over his head. Thankfully, he had his cousin to lead him through this ordeal. He couldn't imagine how he would have done this on his own.

They took the elevator to the third floor, riding in silence. Luís couldn't quite put his finger on his uneasiness as they walked down the dimly lit corridor. He hoped it was only nervous anticipation.

Carlos tapped on the door of room 306 and walked right in, not waiting for the customary invitation. Standing by the window, was an elderly man dressed in a sweaty pinstripe suit. The collar of his well-worn shirt was greasy around the edges. Luís felt nausea in the pit of his stomach, but he got over it when Carlos began speaking rapidly.

"Let's get down to business. Where is the necklace?"

After hesitating briefly, Luís pulled the prize from his pocket and handed it over.

"Very beautiful," Carlos exclaimed, fingering it gently.

The fence rolled out a piece of black velvet on the table top. He snapped on a small light he'd brought with him. Carlos placed the sparkling diamond and deep red ruby necklace on the cloth.

To the side of the cloth was a pad of paper and a pencil. Luís watched the fence carefully as he inspected each stone through a jeweler's loupe, recording several notations about each stone on the pad lying nearby. Since this was going to take awhile Carlos turned on the television, but Luís sat in a chair opposite the man handling the necklace, and never took his eyes off him.

"I'm about to die of thirst. What do you say we order up a few drinks?" Carlos asked.

The man working so diligently did not answer. Luís felt hot and thirsty.

"I could go for a beer or two," Luís said. "It's stifling in here."

Carlos ordered room service from the bar which arrived quickly, probably because there weren't many patrons downstairs. Carlos unscrewed the top on a beer, and handed it to Luís. Nervous, Luís turned quickly, and knocked it out of Carlos' hand. The bottle landed with a foaming thud on the carpet.

"Goddamn it!" Carlos cried.

"Sorry, man. I'll clean it up," Luís said, jumping up from his seat.

"Hell no! Just keep your eyes on the necklace over there. I'll get a goddamned towel and take care of it."

Carlos dropped a towel over the mess, pressed it down with his foot, and then returned to watching television.

After downing a couple more beers, Luís was glad the old man seemed to be nearing the end of the inspection. Making notations on the last stone, he put away his loupe, turned off his lamp, meticulously folded his little black velvet cloth, and packed it all in a small, well-worn suitcase.

"Well, how much?" Carlos asked. "Don't keep us in such suspense."

Luís was glad Carlos was here to handle this part of the negotiation. This was the moment he had been waiting for...even dreaming about. His stomach was churning, his heart was fluttering, and his blood pressure was rising.

The little man handed the necklace back to Luís and said to Carlos, "No deal. There's not one stone in the necklace that's real."

"What?" Luís shouted, jumping up. "What the hell is he talking about?"

Carlos took one giant step and grabbed his cousin by the shirt. "You dumb son-of-a-bitch! You put me through all this because you stole a fake necklace. You asshole!"

Not wanting to get involved in this unpleasantness, the fence took his small suitcase and slipped out of the room as inconspicuously as possible. Carlos' chauffeur escorted the tiny man down the hall and outside, then handed the fence a sealed envelope. It was payment for his services.

"There is no fucking way that it's a fake!" Luís shouted. "Why would Henry Barnes keep a fake in a big walk-in vault?" Beads of sweat popped out on his face.

Carlos let go of his cousin and crossed the room.

"Did it ever cross your stupid, idiotic brain that maybe he'd already sold the real jewels?" Carlos asked. "Maybe he needed the cash and didn't want anyone to find out. Hell, how should I know?"

Carlos paced back and forth. "Do you know how much time and effort I put into your fake passports, the airline tickets and setting all this up?" he demanded. Before Luís could respond, Carlos marched to the door, turned around and sneered, "You stupid son-of-a-bitch! I don't want to see or hear from you ever again. Just get the fuck out of my life!" He slammed the door loudly behind him and stomped down the hall.

Luís was stunned...shocked!

He couldn't move. His legs were too heavy to lift; they were planted in concrete. In angry frustration he threw his beer bottle violently against the wall, shattering it into a million pieces.

No, he decided; he wasn't shocked or stunned…he was fucked!

Tom and Brianne would be arriving at the private Myrtle Beach airport in their King Air shortly after one in the afternoon.

Earlier that morning, Robison had made her rounds at the hospital and was on her way home when her cell phone rang. It was Wade. "Baby, are you on your way home already? And how is your patient?"

"Yes, I'm on my way home. I just turned onto Hwy. 17, Business. Mr. Morrison is doing very well this morning. He's in some discomfort, but that's mostly from the physical therapy."

"Since we're all packed, what about playing golf?"

"How about if I meet you at True Blue for a quick eighteen holes?" Robison asked.

"Darling, have I ever told you that I have to be the luckiest man on earth to have a gorgeous, smart, great golfer for a wife?"

"You can just stop gushing! I still get two shots a side from you no matter how much flattery you use!" she laughed.

"Damn, you're a tough negotiator. I thought you'd give *me* shots."

"Slip into your pajamas, baby, because you're dreamin'," she countered. "See you there."

Situated on a beautiful tract of land that was once an indigo and rice plantation, True Blue was a real test of golf. Fortunately, this bright, mid-September morning was kind to them; it was up to fifty-six degrees when they arrived at eight-thirty. A cold front had come in and the Weather Channel had predicted a high of only fifty.

Even with the windshield up in the cart, they found it a bit nippy as they sped along.

"Just think, by this time tomorrow we'll be wearing shorts or a bathing suit in a tropical paradise instead of freezing our asses off," Robison said as she blew on her hands to warm them.

"Yeah, and we'd better enjoy it while we're there, because we'll only be gone a few days," he said. "Besides, what's with you? It's not cold here; it's fifty-eight degrees. You act like it's going to snow or something."

"I can't help it. I love warm weather," she said.

"So, I take it you won't be leading any expeditions to the North Pole then," he joked.

At the end of the eighteen holes, Wade was pulling the car up to the bag drop when his cell phone rang.

"Tom, here. We're at the Hickory Airport and I'm filing our flight plan. We'll be in the air in a few minutes. That'll put us there a little ahead of schedule, around twelve-thirty, I'd guess."

"We'll be at the airport waiting on you, ol' buddy."

"What have you been doing, playing golf this morning?" Tom asked, hearing the bag boy in the background.

"Yeah, Robison beat me out of fifteen bucks and she still insists on two shots aside. But those days are officially over after the butt-whipping she just gave me," Wade laughed.

"You know, I don't feel sorry for you one bit. Some of us have to work for a living, in case you forgot."

"Oh yeah, and my heart is breaking for you. Anyway, you and Brianne have a safe flight and we'll see you shortly. We'll stop and pick up some lunch and snacks to bring on the plane."

"Sounds great!"

Tom the workaholic would work at the furniture plant until the day he died, and although he talked about retiring all the time, the three of them were sure it would never happen.

Short, with receding brown hair and bad eyesight, Tom looked more like an accountant than an owner of one of the largest furniture manufacturing plants in the southeast. Brianne, with her effervescent "never-met-a-stranger" personality, was the balance in his life. Clearly, opposites did attract…they were the perfect couple.

Tom and Brianne had been trying to get pregnant for the past two months, but time was running out in her estimation. Her favorite phrase when the subject arose was, "We just need more practice." Tom would roll his eyes and shake his head at her brashness, but he loved it nonetheless.

Wade drove out onto the tarmac of the small private airport, where he and Robison would wait until the plane arrived. Traveling was easy with the Winsteads. Of course, anything was easier with a lot of money. Wade spotted Winsteads' airplane approaching the runway.

"Right on time," he said, pointing east.

The plane parked near Wade's car. Brianne deplaned first. She was only a couple inches shorter than Tom, cute with a new pageboy haircut that emphasized the blonde highlights she'd added to her dark blonde hair earlier in the week. Tom soon followed and they greeted the Murphys joyously.

"Let's be on our way!" Tom shouted as he turned back to the plane.

The pilot loaded the suitcases and golf clubs, while Robison carried two large grocery bags of food onboard. Brianne quickly secured everything before takeoff. Wade parked the car in the adjoining lot, while the pilot was inside filing a new flight plan. Soon they were ready to continue the next leg of the journey with Tom acting as copilot. Wade relaxed, sat back, and read a golf magazine.

After a ten-minute delay, they got the go-ahead to takeoff. The pilot headed for a private airport in Fort Lauderdale at an altitude of twenty thousand feet and speed of two hundred eighty knots. They arrived on time, went through U.S. Immigration and Customs, refueled and picked up a Life Raft Kit—an FAA requirement for overseas travel. It contained five lifejackets and one inflatable raft. The rented "kit" would be returned when they refueled on the way back.

Airborne once again on their nonstop flight to the Dominican Republic, Brianne was the first to speak. "I don't know what the raft and life preservers are going to do for us if we fall from twenty or thirty thousand feet. Do you?"

Tom pretended not to hear, so Wade answered instead: "They're orange, so if we go 'splat' and become chum for the sharks someone will be able to spot where we went down."

"All right, that's enough of that kind of talk," chimed in Robison, who didn't like the direction the conversation was going. After all, this was a vacation, a happy time. Settling back, she announced, "Let's have the time of our lives!"

At the end of the two-hour flight, they landed without incident at the new airport near Casa de Campo. A tail wind had shortened the trip a bit, usually a good omen.

Airport employees scrambled around trying to find the proper paperwork. Tom was clearly not happy with all the pandemonium; the other three were more philosophical. Wade wandered over to the drink machine and brought back four cool drinks, since all were already perspiring.

"Well, is it hot enough for you now?" Wade asked Robison. "Or is the North Pole expedition looking better?"

"Oh, hush," Robison whispered in mock exasperation.

A young girl named Angelisa arrived in a shuttle van and orchestrated the loading of baggage and golf clubs. No one "official" examined their luggage or belongings—or even counted bags. So with people scurrying everywhere, Brianne kept her eye on the bags and golf clubs. What a terrible trip it would be if someone stole their clubs! Clothes were one thing, but clubs! God, she'd never hear the end of it from the others.

After forty-five minutes of confusion, Wade, Robison, Brianne and Tom had loaded into the shuttle van and were heading towards Casa de Campo. At the security gate leading into the resort, they waited in line until a guard examined villa reservation documents. Then at the entrance to the small neighborhood of eight stately villas, another armed guard stood inside a tiny shelter.

Robison wondered why so many guards were needed. And she wasn't alone.

"My God, that guy had a gun on his hip!" Wade noted. "Brianne, what have you gotten us into?"

"He had a gun?" Tom asked. "For Christ sake, what's going on?"

"Oh, just be calm," Brianne responded. "They're here for our protection." However, she looked over at Angelisa.

Angelisa, reassured them as she drove. "It's only a precaution. We are close to Haiti here, and we want to make sure that all of our guests are comfortable and their valuables are safe."

"Great! In that case I feel much better," Wade growled, crossing his arms over his chest as he spoke. Tom continued to scowl at Brianne, wondering if she really knew what she was doing. So far, not so good!

Angelisa turned right at the small guard gate—not bothering to stop—and proceeded down a street lined with beautiful Spanish-style villas picturesque enough to be in a travel magazine. She even slowed so they could get a better look at neighboring villas. All were similar: tropical, with tiled roofs…but each was different as well. The view was especially interesting to Tom who was fascinated by different architectural designs. Already the unpleasantness of the armed guards had been forgotten.

"Brianne, if our villa looks this good you'll be off the hook," Tom said, as they turned into the driveway of a beautiful single story unit with beige stucco walls and a dark red tile roof. When they came to a standstill under a huge portico, a maid, with a butler standing behind her, opened the front door in welcome.

"Hey, you weren't kidding about a maid and butler!" Robison exclaimed. "Wade, we may never leave this place."

Brianne was pleased and a bit overwhelmed as well. "Oh, my gosh! I've never had a butler before, have you?" she asked.

"Are you joking?" Robison replied.

The butler hurried out to unload the luggage while Angelisa issued instructions in Spanish to the maid, who then disappeared into the kitchen.

Brianne and Robison scouted out the bedrooms—four master suites in all. Furnishings were all ornate antiques. Colorful area rugs were placed around the room to accent the unusual tiled floors.

"Look, the windows are wide open with no screens," Robison noted. "I guess bugs aren't a problem here."

"At least not the flying kind," Tom quipped.

Each room had one or more slowly revolving ceiling fans; only the bedrooms had air conditioning. The window in the Murphy's bathroom—above the mirror over the sink—had no glass at all. Robison assumed that rain came right in. However, with exquisite floor to ceiling tile, she supposed it didn't matter. In any case, she decided to keep the bathroom door closed when the air conditioning was on at night. No sense in cooling the outdoors, right?

The panoramic view from the rear of the house, overlooking the pool and golf course was breathtaking. Palm trees lazily swayed in a light tropical breeze. Very romantic! Of course, the guys had something else in mind. They watched four passing golfers hit shots to the green. Beautiful!

"God, I can't wait to get out there!" Tom said. "Wade, let's walk up to the green and look it over."

Wade didn't hesitate. "Honey, we'll be back in a minute," he said. "We're going to take a look at the putting surface."

However, the women were otherwise occupied by then.

After overseeing the butler carrying the luggage and bags of golf clubs inside, Angelisa showed Brianne and Robison around the house. When Wade and Tom returned, Angelisa seated both couples at the dining room table. There she described the facilities;

"First, I want to give you each a key to the villa and a separate key to your bedroom. Always lock your bedroom when you leave. Only the maid has the key so she can clean it. Here are keys for the two golf carts on the carport. Use them to get around the property; for instance, to the golf course, to the restaurants, or to any of the attractions here at the Casa."

The villa keys were attached to heavy brass rings, the size of a donut.

"Well, we won't lose these things," Brianne noted. "I just hope I don't drop it on my toe and break it....My toe, I mean!"

Unfazed, Angelisa continued, "If for any reason you want to leave the property, like to go to Altos de Chavón, please call me and I will arrange a shuttle for you."

"Let's do that right now," Brianne interrupted. "We have plenty of time tomorrow morning before golf."

"Brianne, let her finish," Tom scolded, looking over his reading glasses. He was already studying a map of the resort, figuring things out on his own.

The maid entered at that point with a huge platter of fresh fruit, a bottle of rum with various fruit juices and mixes.

Angelisa continued: "Your maid will prepare breakfast for you every morning and it will be served by the butler. The day before, you must decide from this list of items what you choose for breakfast and at what time you want to eat. There are plenty of snacks and other food items in the kitchen when she is not here. She and the butler will leave at approximately three o'clock every day. If you have any special food or drink requests, please give them to the maid and she will stock it in the kitchen for you. Also be sure to never drink the water, not even at our restaurants. Always get the bottled water. We want you to have a pleasant vacation and the water from the tap may make you ill," she said, smiling. "Are there any questions?"

Tom whispered to Wade, "She means Montezuma's Revenge!"

"Tom, be quiet and let her talk. Do we have any questions for her?" Brianne asked.

A bit overwhelmed at that point, they asked for Angelisa's phone number, just in case. Angelisa also left a map of the resort with directions drawn to the Tropicana restaurant where they had reservations for this evening's meal.

After Angelisa left in the shuttle van, and the maid and butler said good-bye in broken English, Tom made rum and fruit drinks to celebrate their arrival. The preliminaries were over; the party was on!

"Well, I don't know about you folks," Wade said, raising his glass. "But with the private plane ride here, a maid and a butler…life is good!"

"Cheers!" all said holding their glasses in the air.

"What time is our dinner reservation tonight?" Robison asked.

"Eight o'clock," Tom answered. "We'll need to leave in our golf carts at about seven forty-five."

"Wow, I'd better get unpacking," Robison said as she headed to the bedroom with rum drink in hand. While passing Wade she gave him a kiss on the forehead and said, "Love you, honey."

"Love you, too, babe."

Carlos also landed at the new airport where his father's helicopter waited to take him to the Alvarez estate at the Casa. It was not necessary for him to go into the terminal; the pilot had made it quite clear who his passenger was as they were approaching the airport— and who owned the airplane. The short helicopter flight put him at his father's house at about seven-thirty.

"¿Donde está mí, Papá? (Where is my father?)" Carlos asked one of the guards upon his arrival.

"He and Señorita Bibí are at the El Pescador for dinner. Do you want me to take you to them?"

Carlos snapped at hearing Bibí's name. Shit! He took a deep breath, trying to regain composure. The mere mention of her name made his skin crawl. Come hell or high water, he wouldn't put up with her tonight!

"No, get me a table at the Tropicana for eight forty-five," he told the guard.

"For one? Or is someone joining you?"

"Just for me."

Pouring himself a stiff drink, Carlos walked upstairs to take a shower and change clothes. Knocking his drink back in one swig, he poured another from the upstairs mini-bar, walked into the bathroom and set the glass down near the bathroom sink. He started the water in the shower and undressed. He couldn't wait to get the stench of that seedy hotel off his body. Ugh!

Dinner alone tonight would be better than sitting through an excruciating session with the two of them pawing each other. Having to see Bibí around the house for the next couple of days would be punishment enough. His relaxing massage had already been wasted after hearing about that gold-digging bitch!

Well, he would bring up the subject of Bibí with his father tomorrow. With his father's upcoming presidential campaign, she had to go! Bibí would probably take a payoff to keep her mouth shut and not sell out to the tabloids, but that was not a guarantee. There really was only one way to ensure she wouldn't speak to the tabloids or the opposition. But that was another matter altogether. Either way, she was a big fat thorn in their side, whether his father wanted to admit it or not.

Finishing his second drink, Carlos placed a last business call for the evening. He concluded with a question: "Do we have a deal?"

"Sí, Señor Carlos. Everything is ready."

"I'll call you tomorrow," Carlos said.

He allowed his mind to wander for a few minutes while he lay upon the bed, under the influence of his two stiff drinks. No doubt about it, Bibí had a gorgeous body, and he'd seen it plenty of times. Hell, she hardly wore any clothes around the house day or night. Even he was constantly telling her to cover up when someone was visiting. It was a shame to eliminate such a lovely creature, but he had no choice. Then he snapped back to his senses. Gorgeous she may be, but she was still a bitch-on-wheels. And he was just the man to "wheel" her right on out of this world when the time came.

Still Carlos fantasized. Maybe he'd get one last "blow job" before he had his guys do away with her. The thought made him smile. She despised him, but that was his price for erasing the videotapes of her screwing the guards while Juan was away. Carlos enjoyed having Bibí under his "control."

His reverie was interrupted by a phone call.

"The car is waiting out front, sir, whenever you are ready to go to the Tropicana."

"Gracias—thank you. I'll be down in a minute," Carlos said, putting his empty glass down beside the phone. After taking a last glance in the mirror, he walked out the door and down the stairs—leaving his bags for the maid to unpack.

SEVEN

After a thirty-minute action packed ride from the airport, Tyler Kelly and Raúl Armada entered the village of Altos de Chavón. Raúl found a parking space at the end of the parking lot amid all the tour buses. Erratic foreign driving was never easy to get used to, so Ty was thankful they'd arrived in one piece.

"The amphitheater is over in that direction," Raúl said, pointing down one of the cobblestone streets when they emerged from the car. "As you can see, this is a very quaint village and it has many…many tourists that come to visit."

"We like tourists. That's what pays our way, isn't it Raúl?"

"Yes, yes, Señor Ty," the promoter smiled brightly.

Actually, Ty really was happy to see tourists busily scuttling from shop to shop. He liked good crowds and, even though he'd received his fee for the show up-front, he still wanted the promoter to make money as well. If so, chances were good that the ice show would be brought back again soon.

While they walked towards the amphitheater, Ty noticed all the buildings looked several hundred years old. Built out of handmade bricks, complete with turrets, old tile roofs and cobblestone streets, the village appeared to be from the sixteenth or seventeenth century, but actually construction hadn't been that long ago. A businessman built it, hoping to make a profit off all the tourists staying at the "Casa" and surrounding tourist areas. Apparently, it had been a very good moneymaking decision.

Back to business, Ty's real interest was in seeing the layout of the amphitheater and making sure the containers that had arrived the day before had been placed in the right positions. He wanted to tackle any electrical issues immediately, not later when they were trying to start up the ice rink in the middle of the night.

"So, Raúl, tell me, did they get the two-hundred amps, three-phase power in?"

"Yes, Señor. Just like you specified."

"Terrific!"

Ty still had his doubts, but kept them to himself for the moment.

After arriving at the top entrance of the amphitheater, they made their way down the steep steps of the outdoor theater. Ty took a good look at the temporary wooden stage erected for the ice rink. The bracing underneath the three-foot-high stage looked very sturdy and well built.

Ty hopped up and walked around. So far so good!

"Nice stage, Raúl. Whoever you got to do the construction did a good job. You know, when this is over, you could probably take this stage apart, sell the lumber and get your money back. It'll still be like brand-new," Ty said, jumping back down to the ground.

"Oh, Señor, that is a good idea...a good idea," Raúl said, scratching his chin.

"Where's the water, Raúl?"

"Oh, right over here. We had to run some pipe to get a, umm, how do you say? ...A three-quarter inch bib within a hundred feet of the stage. I believe this is what you told me."

Ty looked over the water connection and was satisfied with everything he saw...so far.

"Are those the two block buildings for the dressing rooms?" Ty asked the promoter.

"Yes. Yes."

"Let's take a look inside, mí amigo," Ty said.

Raúl flipped on the light in the first building. They could see it was fairly clean and well lit with tables and chairs positioned against one wall.

"This looks good. It doesn't leak, does it?" Ty inquired.

"Oh, no sir. No water leaks," Raúl assured him.

"I mean, any leaks from rain?" Ty asked again.

"No, no. It is dry all of the time."

Ty turned to him, "So, since it is only six twenty-five, how about let's get me checked in at the hotel and then go to eat? I have to be back here by nine-thirty or ten o'clock to get ready to start putting in the ice rink."

"I don't understand why you don't start in the morning when you are fresh and rested."

"It's a hell of a lot cooler at night, and I can sleep tomorrow." He glanced at Raúl, smiling. "Don't worry, mí amigo, you don't have to stay here with me all night. You can go to bed, no problem. Let's get going. I'm starving. Where are we going to eat?"

"I reserved a table at the El Pescador. It is a very nice seafood restaurant over at Casa de Campo."

"Perfecto; let's go," Ty said, patting Raúl on the back.

Luís was pounding on the hotel room door. After the hot bath and polishing off the entire bottle of wine, Felicity was passed out in bed. Finally hearing him yelling, she sleepily came to her senses and turned on the light.

"Just a damn minute! I'm coming, so stop hollering."

After she turned the lock and removed the chain, Luís burst through the door almost knocking her over.

"What is the matter with you?" she asked completely surprised by his demeanor.

"We're fucked! That's 'what's the matter.'"

"What are you talking about?"

"This piece of shit!" He threw the necklace across the room. It hit the couch and fell on the floor.

"Piece of shit? What do you mean?"

Luís was pacing, with sweat pouring from his beet-red face. Felicity thought he might have a stroke.

"It's fake that's what that piece of shit is. *Fake!*"

Felicity gasped, grabbing the side of the bed to steady herself. She sat down; her hands flew up to her mouth. She began trembling and started to cry.

"What are we going to do now? I don't understand. Why would Barnes keep a fake necklace in a safe?" Her voice trailed off, her mind raced and tears streamed down her cheeks.

"Carlos thought old Barnes probably sold the real jewels years ago and just didn't bother to tell anyone."

"What are we going to do now, Luís? How are we going to live? We can't just go back to Charlotte and forget the whole thing, you know."

"No, I couldn't but...you could. Think about it. No one knows you haven't been visiting your mother. You could go back, check it out, get the other cash and jewels from the campground, and come back. What do you think?"

Felicity sat silently staring into space, trying to slow down the thoughts racing at break-neck speed through her mind.

Finally looking up, she said, "I could wind up walking into a trap. What if the police already know about us? Besides, how am I supposed to erect a tent and dig up that money by myself?"

Luís shrugged his shoulders, and replied, "Okay, let me think. God, I'm so tired I can hardly organize a sentence. Let's sleep on all of this. It will be clearer in the morning. We can't afford to make a stupid decision now."

He went into the bathroom, showered and slipped into bed. They both needed a good night's sleep to begin a new day of re-plotting their future. His head hit the pillow and he was soon snoring. Felicity remained wide-awake, her mind whirling at a hundred miles per hour. She smelled a rat. The trouble was…she didn't know if the rat was Luís or Carlos. What if they'd plotted together to eliminate her from the deal and this was just a ruse to get her out of the country? She was trying to figure out exactly who had been "fucked"…Carlos…Luís…or…her.

The scene as Bibí and Juan Alvarez entered the El Pescador became tumultuous. First, two guards entered the restaurant, and gave all of the patrons the "once-over," not any too discreetly either. One of them whispered something into the hostess's ear. She smiled and began walking towards the corner table at the back of the restaurant, which was near an exit door. She rearranged the chairs, and laid down two menus. Next she began issuing orders to a waiter, who then began arranging the place settings on the table so both parties could sit with their backs to the wall. Juan had to have a view of anyone approaching. He didn't like surprises.

A second, smaller table nearby was for two guards who would sit with their backs to Juan and Bibí. They, too, had to see who was approaching, especially any reporters. When all was in order, the hostess left the guards on their own. A third guard went in and out of the exit door near the table, checking and rechecking. Finally, he brought in Señor Alvarez and Señorita Bibí. They had been spared a "parade" through the crowded restaurant. Of course, the commotion drew the attention of dining patrons who now watched very closely. And even though there was a long line waiting for tables, two empty ones near Juan would stay that way. No one was allowed to sit too close to Juan Alvarez, presidential nominee, and his mistress.

Bibí loved the attention they attracted. Everyone stared as they swept in and a buzz of conversation rolled across the room. Although she acted nonchalant, she took note of the excitement she and her lover created. She was important!

Juan held her chair as she sat down. When both were seated the two guards sat at their own table, while a third man was posted outside the exit. The guards weren't there to dine, although they made a pretense of doing so. They knew their parts well in this "dining-out" charade.

Placing two preordered drinks on the table, the waiter rattled off the list of nightly specials. Juan ordered for both of them, which pleased Bibí immensely. The numerous martinis were clearly taking effect. She could only giggle profusely…but still appeared somewhat poised.

Entranced by Bibí's presence, Juan had "control" problems of his own. He still smoldered from their afternoon escapade in the swimming pool and then again after he'd showered. He could hardly wait to get her back home after dinner; however, the thought occurred to him that he might not be "able" to perform again after so many drinks. But he'd worry about that later.

Most of the patrons were American tourists, who didn't know how important Juan was in the government; many assumed he was Mafia. Who else would come into an upscale restaurant with gun-toting bodyguards? Of course, the waiters kept silent about anything they knew, or thought they knew, regarding Sr. Alvarez and "company." Any one of them would be fired if they crossed the line of silence. Good paying jobs on this small island were few and far between, so pretending not to understand usually fended off questions from American tourists regarding the self-absorbed, contentious Juan Alvarez.

Juan glanced at his watch, anticipating Carlos' arrival at any moment. In a way, Juan was hoping his son would not come to this particular restaurant for dinner tonight. Bibí and Carlos would no doubt start arguing as usual. Juan was certain Carlos had every intention of bringing up the Bibí thing as soon as he found an opportunity. On the other hand, Carlos might prefer a relaxed meal after the intensive business closing that had taken most of the day. Juan was anxious to hear about the jewelry deal that had gone down at that seedy hotel he loathed so much, too.

A lot was happening in Juan's life right now. He couldn't let his mind become too clouded by booze and sex. However, on second thought…this was his last vacation before the campaign really began in earnest. So,…what the hell?

As if the guard could read Juan's mind, he came and whispered in Juan's ear. Carlos would not be joining them; after arriving by helicopter, Carlos had opted to eat at another restaurant.

What a relief!

Bibí reached over to Juan's lap and began discreetly fondling him. Soon his thoughts about the tensions between Carlos and Bibí vanished. She specialized in re-focusing his attention, and he loved the way she managed to do it. God, he would miss her!

Half an hour earlier, Ty and Raúl had been standing at the entrance of the same restaurant when they were told there would be a fifteen-minute wait. Embarrassed, Raúl whispered into the ear of the hostess who immediately took them to a table. Raúl hoped he had pulled it off without Ty seeing him slip her a few pesos, but ol' Ty had seen the transaction.

"You must have whispered something really hot to that hostess to get us seated so quickly," Ty teased, not wanting to burst Raúl's bubble.

"Oh, Señor Ty, when you whisper beautiful things to a woman, you can get anything you want," Raúl said casually, half-smiling.

"Is that how it is?" Ty chuckled. He dare not tease Raúl too much for a flamboyant Raúl would be more useful in the upcoming days then an embarrassed one.

The open-air restaurant featured a variety of seafood delights in a pristine tropical setting. Ty and Raúl sat on the outer edge of the eatery, where they were partially protected from rain by a thatched roof; otherwise their table was under the starry sky. A cool yet tropical breeze blew in off the ocean. A quaint wooden boat moored not far from shore added to the ambience, even though the boat looked too weathered to be sea worthy. Still it was a nice theatrical touch. The sound of waves crashing in melodic tempo completed the scene.

Their table overlooked a small beach and tidal pool lit up by huge spotlights. Beyond the tidal pool was an open-air art market featuring paintings, handmade jewelry, and sculptures by "acclaimed" local artists. Tourists were snapping up souvenirs, haggling over the prices of these "one-of-kind" paintings and hoping to make "deals of the century."

The scene was entertaining especially to diners waiting for their drinks to arrive. Ty cynically concluded a flock of villagers probably painted the pictures by the dozens and then hauled them in every night to bedazzle gullible tourists. In any case the tourists loved it and in the end, that was all that mattered.

The arrival of Juan's bodyguards had interrupted the mood and ambience.

"What the hell is going on over there?" Ty asked Raúl, nodding towards Bibí's table.

"Oh, he is Juan Alvarez. I don't know the woman, but she's not his wife. She's probably his mistress. And those are his bodyguards at the smaller table next to him."

"So what's the big deal? Is he a drug lord or a godfather?"

Raúl shook his head and whispered, "Shhhh, he is very powerful in the government. Better we say nothing, at least not here. He has spies everywhere."

"Well, if he's such a big man in the government what difference does it make if we talk about him?"

"Shhhh! Please keep your voice down. You don't understand. He is the Minister of Finance and running as the PLD candidate for president. A powerful man; a very…how can I say this…?"

Ty chimed in, "A very dangerous, unscrupulous man on the take? Is that what you are trying not to say?"

Raúl nodded his head and added quietly, "Now you get the picture. But you did not hear it from me, okay?"

"Okay. But what is a PLD candidate?"

Raúl looked both ways and said quietly, "Translation is Dominican Liberation Party."

"Oh. Well, is that the candidate you want to win?"

"He will probably win. I guess he will be okay."

Raúl shook his head and put one finger to his lips as the waiter approached with a gin and tonic for Raúl and a beer for Ty.

"Did you need a glass for your beer?" the waiter inquired.

"No, gracias. I only drink out of the bottle," Ty said. When Raúl seemed puzzled, Ty continued. "I learned a long time ago, the hard way I'm afraid, that when I'm in a foreign country, any country, not to single out yours, I only drink three things: bottled water, bottled coke, and bottled beer. That way there's no ice cubes involved, no local water. I've managed to avoid 'Montezuma's Revenge' many times. I always tell the ice skaters that, but do you think they listen? Hell no! Anyway, I carry pills for it...just in case."

Raúl smiled, "Very clever, Señor."

⁓

"Come on, Brianne. You look fine!" yelled Tom from the golf cart.

"I'll be ready in a minute! And besides, you can't see how I look from out there," she shot back. She wanted to add that for once he had to wait on her, usually it was the other way around—but she didn't.

Wade and Robison were already in their golf cart next to Tom. Robison seldom put as much effort into beautifying as Brianne did; she'd rather be involved in activities. For instance, now looking over the map, she was telling the men which roads to take to the Tropicana. "First, we take a right at this guardhouse. Then we..."

"You mean the one with the gun-toting Barney Fife?" Tom kidded.

"I'm trying to be serious here," Robison scolded.

"I am, too," countered Tom. "I'd hate to break the speed limit for golf carts—only to have Barney gun us down."

Brianne appeared, and they all clapped.

"Time well spent!" Tom announced. "Looks good, even from way out here."

"Very funny....Ya'll think you're so damn amusing!" Brianne said, as she plopped into the seat next to Tom. Wade and Robison were already turning onto the main road near the guardhouse. It was dark, but the cart's tiny headlights were quite sufficient. Occasionally, cars came up behind them, checked their clearance, and then roared around. Some drivers—probably golfers—were more considerate than others.

Wade and Robison caught up to nine or ten other golf carts full of tourists. Apparently, they had already enjoyed rum fruit drinks, for they were all giddy and obnoxiously confused.

Wade followed Robison's directions and located the restaurant where he pulled up to "cart" parking. There they waited for Tom and Brianne to catch up, as Robison brushed her long blonde hair back into place.

"I thought they were right behind us," Wade said.

"Well, I thought they were too, but I may have mistook headlights from a different cart as theirs."

Wade shrugged and said, "Brianne is the hostess of this trip. Surely, she can read a map so let's go inside and wait."

Surrounded by tropical charm, they sauntered along, window shopping and chatting until they arrived at the entrance to the Tropicana. Their friends were not so enchanted, however.

"I can't believe you didn't bring a goddamned map!" Brianne said angrily. "Instead of sitting outside and hollering at me to hurry up...you should have been studying a map!"

"Well, it didn't look all that hard to find. We must have made a wrong turn."

"For crying in a bucket!" Brianne growled. "Now we have to go back to the villa and get a goddamned map! That is if we can find the villa!"

They turned about, and ended up back where they first discovered they were lost.

"Now what do we do, 'oh great leader' from the north?" Tom asked.

"How about...duh...we ask for directions?"

"Either that or sit here until someone sends the cavalry," he quipped.

When they waved down a passing car and asked for directions the driver didn't understand English. However, the window in the back lowered and the passenger spoke in English. Thank God! While Tom listened to the directions, Brianne, still in the golf cart, noticed the driver was alone in the front and the man in an aqua shirt speaking English, was alone in the back. "Hmm, must be someone mighty important," she mused.

Tom got back into the golf cart and they proceeded to the villa. After they passed Barney Fife, Tom stopped and ran inside the house to get a map. Brianne followed, having decided to call Robison and explain what had happened.

"You want to hear something really stupid?" Brianne asked Tom after the call.

"What?"

"Why didn't we just ask for directions to the restaurant instead of coming all the way back here?"

"Why didn't you say something earlier? I swear..."

Wade and Robison had ordered a drink after waiting for several minutes. They hadn't noticed a tall, dark, slim man dressed in white slacks and an aqua, opened-collar shirt come in and sit at the bar. After ordering a drink, Carlos went to the restroom.

"I'm going to the ladies' room," said Robison, picking up her small purse.

Paths crossed when with an outward swing of the bathroom door, Carlos knocked Robison's purse out of her hand. Her heavy brass key ring tumbled onto the floor with a loud clattering sound. Curious patrons turned to see the commotion.

"Oh, I am so sorry, Señora," Carlos said, bending to pick up the key and the purse. "You're staying at the villa on Cerezas, I see. That's very nice." He handed Robison the key and purse with a dazzling smile. "I do hope you enjoy your vacation here," he said.

Then he was out of sight...and he never heard her murmured "thank you."

Robison was more than a bit flustered as she continued into the washroom. What an attractive man! And polite, too! He must be a native, with that black hair and those dark penetrating eyes. Yes, his eyes had definitely perused her, she'd decided. She touched up her hair, added a bit of lipstick then surveyed herself critically before leaving the restroom. She hadn't been that intent on her appearance in a long time.

When the bathroom door swung open Robison came to her senses. It was nice to be flattered, but she loved Wade and that would never change.

Back at the bar, the bartender answered the phone, then placed the receiver down near Carlos. "Is there a Dr. Murphy in here? ...A Dr. Murphy, please?"

Wade turned to look at the bartender. Well, Robison was in the bathroom. Thinking it must be Tom, Wade walked to the bar and picked up the phone. "Hello?"

"Hi. It's Brianne."

"Brianne, where the hell are you?"

"We had to come back and get a map. We got so damn lost you wouldn't believe it. We'll be there in a second. Order us a drink, will you? We both need something strong about now or we'll kill each other." Then jokingly she added, "And if we aren't there in ten minutes, send a search party...along with drinks."

Wade hung up, and pushed the phone back towards the bartender. He lightly brushed against Carlos' sleeve; however, neither of them noticed.

Wade began walking back to the table just as Robison was coming out of the ladies' room. Carlos, having overheard the conversation, followed this intriguing American woman with his eyes as she walked to her table. He figured she was the wife of the doctor. Very interesting! He couldn't recall ever romancing a doctor's wife. Perhaps he would run into her again.

Tom and Brianne arrived at the table in a fluster just as their drinks arrived. The waiter also set down a huge bottle of water in the middle of the table.

"I'm sorry, guys," said Tom, shaking his head and rolling his eyes in Brianne's direction.

"Let's not go over the whole thing again," she said, taking a long swallow of her margarita. "We all know whose fault it was that we couldn't find this place," Brianne added, motioning towards Tom.

Brianne licked some salt from the rim of the glass and then replaced her drink on the cocktail napkin. Calmer now, she turned to another topic. "Listen, our tee time isn't until two thirty tomorrow. So what do you say we get up early, call Angelisa, and arrange for a car to Altos de Chavón?"

"What's an Altos de Chavón?" Wade asked, in all seriousness.

"Very funny, smart ass! Remember Angelisa suggested we go there during our little 'info' session at the villa this afternoon? It's a quaint little village with shopping and stuff like that."

"Sounds wonderful to me," said Robison. "Let's do it."

"God, help us!" Tom winked as he spoke. "We couldn't even find the restaurant; so how are we going to get to a quaint li'l village and back with Brianne leading us?"

"Up yours!" Brianne retorted, smiling. "Besides you need to look at it like…like we're on an adventure."

"Being your husband is adventure enough!" Tom said, as they all laughed.

"Okay, I'm starving," announced Wade. "Let's order."

"Since you're the gourmet cook, Wade, I'll have whatever you order," said Tom, closing the menu.

Robison piped in, "You'd better think about what you just said. Wade's already interrogated our poor waiter about every recipe on the menu, so you might end up with something quite exotic."

"Oh? So what are you having?" Tom inquired.

"Well, as Robison said, it might be a tad exotic, but I'm having Coconut Grouper with Mangu."

"Okay, I give up. Explain it to me in lay terms."

"Well, the Coconut Grouper is sautéed in olive oil and cooked in a coconut milk sauce with spices. And the Mangu is the Dominican Republic's answer to mashed potatoes. Basically it is plantains with a little onion and cheese. You know…those little cooking bananas," Wade explained.

Tom slapped his menu. "Sounds like a plan to me. I'll give it a try. When in Rome, do as the Romans. After our ordeal just to get here, I'm too pooped to think!"

Brianne gently tapped him on the shoulder. "Honey, I hope you won't be too pooped later this evening," she said coyly.

Pursing his lips and closing his eyes, Tom groaned, "God, give me the strength to keep up with her, and I'll surely try." They all chuckled.

Wade raised his glass in a toast to their vacation. All joined in "cheers."

A cool but smitten Carlos still watched…still yearned.

⌒⌒

Felicity had been awake for some time listening to Luís snore…trying to sort out her thoughts. Now she decided to get up and sit on the couch. If she read awhile, perhaps she would become drowsy and be able to sleep. Taking her pillow, she quietly got her book out of the suitcase and situated herself on the couch. She put the pillow behind her back and pulled the floor lamp closer.

With her mind racing so, she couldn't concentrate. She repositioned the pillow and crossed her legs in the other direction. Her left leg cramped, quickly she stood up seeking relief. As she did so, she kicked the necklace further under the couch. Walking back and forth in the dark, she eventually worked out the charley horse.

Felicity decided to retrieve the necklace before she forgot where it was. Down on all fours, she could barely touch it with her fingertips. Straining, straining…it was no use. She backed out and went to find a coat hangar. Again on all fours, she managed to snake the necklace out from under the couch.

Shit what a hassle…for a piece of worthless crap.

She sat on the floor leaning against the couch, trying to figure out what could have happened…for the umpteenth time. She fingered the necklace, concentrating. Minutes ticked by…

"Holy, Mother of God!" Felicity blurted out in a loud voice.

From a dead sleep, Luís shot up to a sitting position.

"What the fuck are you talking about? What the hell is the matter with you? Are you crazy?" he asked.

Felicity ran over to sit on the bed beside him. She turned on the bedside lamp.

Her heart was pounding; she was out of breath. "Luís, this isn't the same necklace."

"What the fuck? How do you know?" he asked.

"The real necklace had the initials M. L. B. on the clasp. Look! There are no initials on this. It isn't even the same clasp!"

Luís grabbed the necklace from her. "Are you sure?" he asked, squinting to look at the clasp.

"Yes. I'm positive."

"How could this happen? I watched the guy with my own eyes the whole time! And, besides, when would they have had time to make a duplicate? They wouldn't have known exactly what it looked like before our meeting."

"From the picture you took in Old San Juan, that the old man faxed, stupid. Except the photo didn't show the clasp because it was on my neck!"

"God Almighty!" He whipped the covers back and stood up. He thought he was going to puke, but maybe Felicity was on to something.

"Think Luís! Wasn't there even one instance when you might have taken your eyes off the fence with the necklace? Not *one* split second?" she demanded.

"No. No, I had my eyes on him the whole time. Carlos even told me to watch him." Luís was pacing from the couch to the bed and back. "Well…"

"Well, what?"

"I did knock a beer out of Carlos' hand, but it was an accident."

"Think again, genius. That's when he made the switch."

EIGHT

After leaving the El Pescador, Raúl Armada dropped Ty off at the amphitheater where a crew of fourteen men waited to unload some five miles of serpentine one-inch pipe. Before unloading, workers spread a waterproof rubber liner across the surface of the temporary wooden stage. With the pipes eventually in place, the crew constructed a wooden frame bordering all four sides; "boxing" in the rink. Then the serpentine pipes were connected to a main "header" pipe leading to the compressor unit located out of sight of the audience. The compressor pumped the antifreeze, pumped it through the pipes and then back for rechilling. The goal: drop the temperature of the pipes to below zero. It was this constant recycling that kept the ice frozen.

Once hooked up, the men covered the surface with crushed ice, packing it between the pipes and around the inside edges of the wooden frame, known as the "header covers." A thin layer of water sprayed every two hours sealed the rink. In twenty-four hours, the ice would be smooth and ready for skating...*if* the electricity stayed on! Unfortunately, power interruptions occurred frequently in foreign countries. Hopefully, this time it would be different.

An alarm on the compressor unit beeped Ty's cell phone if there was a power outage. Ty had a walkie-talkie from his hotel room to inside the refrigeration trailer. To "lose the ice," because the watchman didn't notice the electricity had gone off during the night, would lead to a costly crisis—perhaps forcing a show to be cancelled. Thus Ty could alert the night watchman regarding any electrical problems.

The last step: raise the temperature of the ice to between thirteen and sixteen degrees, the ideal temperature for figure skating. Skaters were finicky about ice temperature because it affected their ability to do jumps and spins. There was a fine line between good and bad ice. If the ice was too hard (the temperature too low) the ice lost its "spring" for jumps. On the other hand, too soft (the temperature too high) the ice became wet and sluggish. When it was too wet, the wardrobe lady would complain because costumes would get soaked.

Only certain items could be put in the dryer, just another one of the vagaries Ty dealt with on a regular basis.

Ty, as always, came dressed in a freshly pressed shirt and shorts with his Oakley's hanging backwards from his neck. In his late thirties, Ty's boyish looks were accentuated by closely-trimmed, dirty blonde hair with a hint of graying at the temples. His big blue-gray eyes sparkled, and his good nature belied toughness within. Ty had a knack for soothing tensions arising from the many "egos" that inhabited the entertainment world. A dry wit added to the magnetism of his personality. More importantly, Ty Kelly was a man of integrity…a man you could count on through thick and thin.

When the show was setup outdoors, Ty used a shallow canvas tent to shade and protect the ice rink from wind. (He would remove it shortly before show time.) Wind was the enemy that could quickly melt the rink by "sweeping" away the cold layer of air that hovered over the ice. Wind was much more devastating than the sun.

Raúl had not stayed to watch the load-in of the ice rink. However, he reappeared around six in the morning with a small sack of croissants and coffee. He and Ty sat on the steps of the truck leading up to the compressors and ate.

"Did everything go okay last night?" Raúl asked.

"Pretty good. It took awhile to get my point across to the local electrician, but once he got the power hooked up correctly, the compressor purred like a kitten," said Ty. "By the way, thanks for the breakfast. It just hits the spot."

"You're welcome. Coffee wasn't on your list last night, so I also brought bottled water."

Ty laughed, "Coffee's fine. I guess it's either the boiled water, or the fact the coffee in this part of the world is so strong it kills everything…including germs."

"Are you ready to go to bed at the hotel?" Raúl asked. "I'll give you a ride."

"Surely you're pulling my leg," Ty said.

There was a pause. Then Ty added, "Pulling my leg,…joking,…kidding."

"Oh…oh, now I understand. No, I no pull nobody's leg," Raúl said, shaking his head.

"Listen, my friend," Ty explained. "The next crew arrives in thirty minutes to start hanging the show. I have a cot in by the compressor and I'll catch a few winks...a nap...a siesta...before they arrive. But I'll have to hurry." He turned and started up the stairs, taking the bottled water with him.

"Hang the show? There is only sky. What is there to hang on to?"

Ty paused on the steps. "It's just an expression, it means put up the scenery, lights and sound speakers. Actually, we have a grid that holds things up; you'll see."

"Very interesting. Anyway, when will I see you again?" Raúl inquired.

"I'll finish around two this afternoon and then I'll go to the hotel and get some real sleep. What do you say we meet for dinner? ...Around eight o'clock? You decide where...my treat. Oh, by the way. Tell the powers that be *not* to turn off the electricity even though nothing is going on in the middle of the night. We have to keep the ice frozen."

"You no worry. I told them before...but I will tell them again. Have a good siesta, my friend."

<p style="text-align:center">~~~</p>

Up early, Carlos jogged down the back staircase to the kitchen. This was his favorite time of day at the vacation house. The maid was setting the morning table for breakfast.

"Is my father up yet?"

"No, Señor Carlos. But he said to have breakfast ready for him and Señorita Bibí in about twenty minutes."

Carlos picked up a couple of pieces of freshly fried bacon and stuffed them into his mouth. Then he picked up a hot biscuit. Slicing it open, he spread unsalted butter all over it. He placed bacon, a scoop of scrambled eggs, a slice of tomato and added a dash of Tabasco on the bottom part of the buttery bread, then topped his "breakfast sandwich" with the other half of the biscuit.

"Well, I'm not sticking around," he said. "I'm off to the stables. Tell my father I'll meet with him later in the afternoon. Fix me some coffee in a cup that I can take with me."

"Sí, Señor Carlos."

While waiting for the coffee, Carlos called the stable. "Get my horse ready, will you? Gracias."

The maid handed him the large cup of hot café con leche. Carlos also picked up a banana, an apple, two sweet rolls, and walked out the backdoor. No way would he sit down to breakfast with that bitch. No sexy body on earth was worth her bullshit.

Arriving at the stables just as dawn was breaking, Carlos saddled up his Hanoverian mare, Skyesrun. He fed her the apple and patted her neck. The mare pawed the ground with her great hooves, anticipating the ride.

Skyesrun, an unusually large German horse standing almost seventeen hands high, was chestnut in color and feisty in temperament. She had been a gift from his parents a few years back, a very expensive gift! Carlos loved her, cared for her, nurtured her. No one could handle her like Carlos.

He stepped onto the mounting block to reach the stirrup and then swung astride the trembling animal. Skyesrun trotted her way to the horse trail that wound through the Casa de Campo resort. He gave her a nudge and she broke into a gallop, something Skyesrun loved. When they neared the golf course, Carlos reined her back and patted her on the neck. They pressed forward in a slow trot through the early morning fog. Now he had time to think…to formulate a plan away from everyone and all the problems. Skyesrun, too, felt free and bolted into a gallop, veering off the trail. Pleased with her spirit, Carlos smiled and let her run.

The maid was clanking dishes while the smell of strong coffee began to permeate the rooms of the villa. It was early, but Robison always got up early to make her rounds at the hospital or to prep for surgery. Wade was still asleep when she wandered into the kitchen. The maid and butler were busily peeling fruit and preparing the breakfast items that they'd chosen the afternoon before. Robison said good morning in her best Spanish, which delighted them both.

"What is your name?" she asked the maid, who looked bewildered. "¿Como se llama?" Robison inquired.

The maid grinned, "Oh....My name is, Rosa." She pointed to the butler and said, "My name is, Alphonso."

Robison smiled at the misuse of the word "my" and walked over and shook both of their hands.

"Café for you, Señora?"

"Sí, gracias," Robison said still smiling and nodding her head. She'd already used her complete vocabulary of Spanish and to good effect, it seemed. She was pleased she'd tried, which is more than Wade or Tom would do.

Since no one else was up, Robison asked to have her coffee sitting out by the pool. The butler brought a huge urn of the steaming hot beverage, another urn of hot milk, and a fruit platter. Enough for ten people at least and there was only her...so far. She sipped the black coffee cautiously—a prudent move. It was so strong it took her breath away, sending a shudder up her spine. The butler handed her the hot milk container and placed the sugar within her reach; this was not the first time he'd seen such a reaction from a "turista."

Once her coffee was fixed up with hot milk and sugar, it was really quite good. Robison walked over to a lounge chair and settled in. She adjusted her robe and closed her eyes, delighting in the tranquility of it all. The pampering by the maid and the butler was comforting and luxurious.

Robison looked out onto the fairway. It was still too early for any golfers to be this far along on the course, but it wouldn't be long before some would come into view. The morning mist was beginning to burn off the fairway directly behind their villa, although fog still hovered just above the ground. She closed her eyes, breathed deeply and listened to the quiet for several minutes.

Her reverie was interrupted by the sounds of distant hoof beats. Wasn't this a "non-horse" villa? The idea of being near a horse trail bothered Tom who was a cleanliness freak and didn't want to step over "piles" to walk on the golf course.

She listened...sure enough there it was again. Hoof beats!

She sipped her coffee and then reached for the small plate of fruit sitting next to her chair. She stared at some of the unrecognizable fruit. Reaching for a fork, she decided to be daring and try all the fruit...or at least one bite of each.

The hoof beats were louder now. She sat up and looked around. Squinting into the rising sun, she made out a huge silhouette approaching through the fog. The horse appeared first, its nostrils flared and ears laid back. Then she recognized the handsome man atop the breathtakingly gorgeous animal—the largest horse she'd ever seen! The mist spiraled and swirled behind the charging beast. The sun glistened off its sleek chestnut coat. She could hear the horse snorting…and snorting.

Robison caught only a glimpse of the rider as he passed, but she was certain he was the man who bumped into her at the restroom last night…the tall dark haired man in the aqua shirt. She gasped when she spotted a holster with a gun strapped to his leg.

Robison was certain that he recognized her. He tossed a two-finger salute when he saw her, but he never hesitated in his gait. Still, he knew she was staying here from the information on the key, didn't he? Had this "visit" been just a coincidence? An ominous feeling came over her.

She felt relieved when the rider and horse vanished into the fog, out of sight and out of earshot. Especially when she no longer heard the horse's great hooves pounding upon the earth.

The sliding glass door suddenly opened behind her, startling her.

"Oh, you scared me half to death," she said to Wade.

"Sorry, darling. Why didn't you wake me?" Wade said as he poured himself a cup of coffee.

"You'd better put a lot of hot milk in your coffee or it'll make your hair stand on end," Robison warned, ignoring his question.

Wade looked into her cup and noticed that she wasn't drinking it black. He did as she instructed. He studied the golf course as he stirred his coffee, revealing where he'd like to be headed.

"Don't you think you should go get ready?" Wade asked. "Brianne and Tom will be ready to leave for Altos de Chavón in about thirty minutes. I believe Angelisa is bringing the shuttle then, too. By the way the phone rang a few minutes ago. Didn't you hear it?"

No response.

"Hey! I asked you a question!" Wade said with a hint of annoyance in his voice.

Robison swung her legs around, stood up and stretched her taut frame. Indeed, she had been deep in thought about the stranger she'd seen twice. "Sorry, I must have been daydreaming when it rang. And yep, I better get a move on," she said, giving him a peck on the cheek. "I love you," she reassured him. "And I love our vacation."

"I love you, too…and, no, I'm not giving you more strokes on the course this afternoon."

She playfully slapped his bottom. "Oh, you're onto all my tricks…. I'd better figure out some new ones…and soon."

"I'm way ahead of you, don't waste your time," Wade teased her playfully.

Setting her cup on the table, she glanced to her left, and then to her right—up the intriguing path where the handsome stranger on the beautiful horse had just vanished like a mirage. Why did the thought of him distract her so?

The load-in was going slower than Ty had expected, but then it was always slower in a foreign country with its language barrier to deal with. Plus, they couldn't roll crates on top of the ice when they were outdoors due to the tent, which always made it time consuming. Often they had to circle the ice to get to where they were going. It was much easier to set up indoors than outdoors, so "grin and bear it" was Ty's motto.

The amphitheater area was abuzz with men shouting to one another as they pushed and pulled crates filled with cable and lights everywhere. With the lighting grid now assembled, crewmen were hanging Par Cans, Fresnels, Lekos and color scrollers. Others were replacing colored gel where needed.

Ty cautioned two men carrying parts of a spotlight up to the top tier of the amphitheater. "Go slow,…despacio por favor (slow please). Don't drop it and break the mirror inside the lamp."

Ty's wardrobe lady interrupted saying, "I need two men to help me assemble the costume racks and unload the costumes. I also need to find out where I can set up the washer and dryer. I have a lot of laundry to do before we open."

As Ty turned to address the wardrobe lady's problem, his cell phone rang.

Taking his phone off his belt clip, he said, "Hello, Tyler Kelly here....Hold on a minute, will you?"

Turning back to the two men working with him, he said, "Hey, you there…. Go with this lady and help her. Then come back here to me…pronto. ¿Comprende?"

"Yes?" Ty asked when he returned to his cell phone. It was a call from the Russian ice show coordinator, Olga, who wanted to know about a chassis trailer in Greece to pick up the containers.

"Can't you just put some tires inside the containers for them to ride on when they arrive?" she asked.

Good God Almighty! What the hell was he dealing with here? Visions of disaster flashed through Ty's head as he tried to explain. "No, Olga. You don't understand. Picture a box coming off the cargo ship, and then loading it onto a truck that is flat so someone can drive it to the amphitheater. Understand?"

"Ohhh, yes, I understand now," Olga said in a thick Russian accent. She immediately hung up without saying good-bye.

The phone went dead in his ear.

"Well that's one good thing about the Russian company…there isn't a lot of idle chitchat," he said aloud.

He turned to see if his two lighting guys had returned yet. They had a knack for disappearing. At such times, Ty would usually find them smoking marijuana in the men's room. This time, however, the wardrobe lady had them busily hanging up heavy show girl costumes on the racks they'd just assembled. Well, he'd wait until she was through to finish his spotlight set-up.

The larger costumes hung backstage during the show. When the time came, the girls would put the "body" part of their costume on in the dressing room. Then a stagehand would help them into the large skirt or backpack just before they stepped onto the ice. Sometimes they needed help adjusting the large feathered headpieces.

If lighting was involved, an electrician would plug their headpieces into a battery hidden within the costume. After every performance, the costumes were covered and rolled into one of the dressing rooms. All dressing rooms had to be locked, and Ty carried his own locks since the costumes were worth hundreds of thousands of dollars.

The soundman was beginning to do checks, as indicated by the sporadic static on the amplifiers. The speakers blared varied parts of the show music...stopping (relief)...rewinding...and then replaying as the soundman ran around the amphitheater to check the quality. The sound went from barely audible to ear splitting. All this commotion combined with exhaustion gave Ty a headache and tempted him to go into a less stressful line of work. Yeah, right!

"Tired" didn't describe Ty's energy level; he hadn't slept in a real bed since Florida. His head hurt, his legs ached, and his back was strained from being on his feet for so many hours.

Walking toward the ice, Ty asked a crewman, "How is it going, anyway?"

"Good, but you look like hell. I think you need some shut-eye."

"God, that's an understatement." Ty said, checking his watch. "Maybe I'll get out of here in an hour or so...if I'm lucky."

He returned to the front of the amphitheater to finish the job he'd started when the wardrobe lady stole his two spotlight men. With the intense heat, Ty was fading quickly.

Raúl returned and saw Ty wiping the sweat off his face with a rag. Raúl had brought him several bottles of ice-cold water. Ty drank one of the cool drinks, then wiped his mouth with the back of his hand.

"Thanks, man. That hit the spot! How did it go at the airport?"

"Fine. I had two minivans for the ice skaters and a small truck to carry their luggage to the hotel. I've never seen so much luggage!" Raúl exclaimed. "And you know how confused the airport people are."

"Oh yes, I remember," answered Ty.

"Well, the comedian, Little Lito, made everyone laugh."

"That's why I brought a Spanish speaking, ice skating comedian here," Ty said. "By the way, I'm going to head over to the hotel to shower and get some sleep. Do you think you could stick around here for awhile in case some of my guys need help translating? And if any of my stagehands are suddenly missing a few local crew guys, they'll probably find them in the restroom smoking a joint."

"Yes, Señor, no problema. I take care of everything," Raúl said with a "thumbs-up."

Ty grimaced, but he was too tired to say anything else. Surely Raúl couldn't screw anything up by just translating. Dog-tired, Ty couldn't wait to hit the hay.

After Felicity's discovery that the necklace in their possession was a fake, she and Luís sat up most of the night trying to figure out what to do next. Where could the real necklace be? It was easy to conclude the fence was in cahoots with the filthy, little man in San Juan. But had they acted behind Carlos' back? Or were all three plotting together?

"I don't think the fence acted without your cousin being in on it," Felicity said. "I've never trusted Carlos from day one."

"You don't even know Carlos. You've never even met him. And besides, you needed to be there. The beer spilling was a pure accident. I was the one who whipped around knocking the bottle out of his hand. Not the other way around."

"So what are you saying? They didn't make the switch? ...Or just not at that moment? And what the hell difference does it make *how* they made the switch? It's done and we're fucked...unless you get it back. And don't think for a moment that Carlos is going to say, 'My mistake, cousin dear. Here's your three million dollar necklace back.' You idiot!" Felicity shouted, as she pulled the covers up over her head.

Luís got in bed as well, but his mind still wandered. He had to admit she was probably right. He'd have to try and get some answers in the morning. But hell! It was already morning and Luís had no way of contacting the fence that had switched the necklace any more than finding the man on the moon. Carlos was their only answer. But what if he was in on the switch? What kind of a plan could they devise to outwit Carlos? He probably would lie, telling Luís he knew nothing about it. They fell asleep from sheer exhaustion just about the time the sun was burning off the morning mist.

At noon they were both slow to rise. Luís ordered room service. Felicity whipped the covers back not saying a word and went into the bathroom. From her attitude, it was clear that she was furious and not speaking to Luís.

Felicity had a hangover from drinking that whole bottle of wine, so she was in no mood for more unsubstantiated calculations about a necklace they would probably never see again. In fact, she was trying to figure out whether it was in her best interest to leave…or to follow Luís to God only knew where. When should she tell him she wanted her half of the money hidden in their bags, so she could go back to Charlotte?

She turned the shower on. Stepping in, she let the warm water soothe the top of her hurting head. It felt wonderful, but tension was running rampant.

Luís appeared at the bathroom door once he heard the shower go off. "I'm going to try to call Carlos. I really don't know what else to do, Felicity," he informed her with pathetic remorse.

She continued to dry her hair; she wasn't yet in a speaking mood.

Luís sat down on the bed and slowly picked up the receiver.

NINE

Angelisa arrived at the villa on the shuttle bus with a driver. She first wanted to make sure everything was in order before they left since the driver didn't speak English. The transportation was right on time which no one at the villa was expecting—least of all Brianne.

She scurried around trying to get it all together at the last minute. Tom was sipping coffee with Wade, and Robison was reading a magazine. All were waiting for Brianne to alight somewhere, anywhere. She was a bundle of nervous energy. If Tom could figure out a way to bottle it, he said he'd make a zillion dollars. It was Brianne's mother who said her daughter needed "a shot of tired blood." In any case, Brianne always had "one more thing to do."

Tom yelled from the living room. "Brianne, we're all waiting for you as usual!"

"I'm coming. Hold your horses!"

Hurrying into the kitchen, she deposited her coffee cup and rushed in to sit at the dining room table. Angelisa said she had some helpful hints, although what she had to say wasn't exactly what they expected to hear.

"It's not far to Altos de Chavón and no matter what might happen, do not leave the village without your driver," Angelisa advised. "You will need to leave there at least an hour and a half before your tee time. It's only a twenty-five minute trip, but you don't want to miss your tee time. The golf courses are booked solid, and they will not wait."

She continued, "Do not under any circumstances, stop and get off the bus between here and there. Sometimes, there are bandits on scooters or motorcycles, pretending to need help and then rob you. Another scheme is to have a raggedy woman holding a baby begging for help. You stop, then they rob you and get away on a scooter they've hidden in the bushes."

"No problem," said Brianne, rolling her eyes. Did Angelisa really think they would actually get off the van in the middle of nowhere?

"Shouldn't we get going?" Brianne asked impatiently, hoping to end the little speech.

"Yes, yes. I will tell the driver you are ready," Angelisa said, turning and exiting through the front door. She was still issuing instructions to the driver as Brianne climbed into the front seat; the others got in the back. All buckled in, the driver backed out, and they waved good-bye to Angelisa.

"Remember to watch the time," Angelisa added, as they drove away.

The driver made a few turns on the way to the big front gate to the resort. The guard asked some questions, looked over the foursome, and then waved them on.

"Can't we even go *out* the gate without a gun-toting Barney Fife looking us over?" Tom complained.

"Calm down, Tom," Brianne said matter-of-factly.

As they were heading east out of the Campo on the small, two-lane road, Brianne began to read aloud. "Okay, listen up this is your personal tour guide speaking."

She then read from the brochure: "One of the country's greatest wonders is Altos de Chavón, translation: 'City of Artists.' A re-created sixteenth century village overlooking the Chavón River, it was built in nineteen seventy-eight by an Italian designer named Roberto Copa. Artists from all over the world live and work in this beautiful village. Altos de Chavón has an archaeological museum, an amphitheater, exhibit halls, superb restaurants, shops and a church. The Pre-Hispanic Art Museum boasts the valued collection of Mr. F. Pion from the internationally renowned Altos de Chavón School of Design. There are also amazing views of the mesmerizing Chavón River. You can find magnificent caves at the Rio de Chavón's delta, and there are daily boat tours along the Chavón River for fishing and sightseeing."

Her little dissertation finished, she looked at the other three. They all appeared to be sound asleep, then Tom let out a big snore. Brianne twisted her lips in exasperation before letting them have it. "Very funny, butt holes."

They all laughed, including the driver.

"It sounds kind of artsy fartsy to me," Tom declared.

"Tom, we're on shopping trip, for gosh sakes. So get with it!"

To change the conversation, Brianne read about the different shops located inside the small village.

Still bored Tom announced, "I need to seriously think this scootering bandito thing over....If this trip doesn't fulfill our expectations, we may consider dropping Brianne off on the way back!"

"You couldn't live a day without me,...Tom Winstead!"

A long line of cars and shuttles stopped them short of the quaint little city.

"Another guard gate, God Almighty, Brianne!" Tom exclaimed.

"I didn't make this 'gate thing' up just to piss you off, Tom, so stop being such a horse's derrière."

"Well, it makes me a bit squeamish to know we're under such armed security. What's really going on here on this island?"

Their driver managed to find a parking place, way in back near the amphitheater. All agreed to meet back at the bus by noon, in case they split up. Brianne pointed at her watch and gestured to the driver so he would understand the noon departure time. Nodding his head and saying "Sí, sí, sí," the driver departed.

"We are going to be shit out of luck if he didn't understand that noon was our departure time," said Tom.

"Never fear when Brianne is here," she said.

"That's exactly what I'm afraid of."

Loud noise and the sound of horrible static pierced the air as the ice show worked out bugs in its audio system.

"Goddamn! What the hell was that?" Tom asked.

Pointing towards the amphitheater, Wade said, "It's coming from that direction. Let's go take a look-see."

They stood at the top entrance of the amphitheater, where they saw men setting up the ice show. When they moved closer for a better look, little kids began begging them to buy chewing gum they were selling. They ignored the kids, who eventually drifted away to latch onto other tourists.

"That's where the ice show is going to be," Tom said. "See, they cover the ice with a small tent. I read about it in one of the tourist magazines at the villa. It's an American company, out of Florida, I believe."

"You'd think ice skaters came from Alaska or Minnesota," Wade speculated.

"Apparently not."

Robison looked at the miles of electrical cable strewn about on the ground and observed, "Sure is a lot to sort out."

"How do they keep that ice frozen?" Tom wondered.

"I have no idea," answered Wade.

They were entranced by all the people scurrying around. Two men were hauling a large spotlight up the steep stairs to a platform at the back of the theater. Others were erecting the top part of a grid on which they would hang the lights and curtains.

"He must be in charge," Wade said, pointing to Ty. "Looks like an All-American type of a guy."

Ty was talking on his cell phone while gesturing to two workmen to go with a woman carrying an armful of costumes.

"He must speak Spanish," Tom ventured. "Can you imagine what a pain in the ass it would be trying to set up with Spanish workers and not be able to speak the language?"

"Enough of this sidewalk engineering," Brianne said. "Are you going to stay here or go shopping with us?"

"Darling, we can't wait to go shopping," Tom said in a singsong voice, as he put his arm around her.

"You are full of horse hockey, Tom Winstead," Brianne responded.

Dodging cars, vans, and tour buses, they managed to cross the cobblestone square towards the retail area. The quaint little shops were filled with native artistic objects. Several art shops displayed large paintings and sculptures. Some of them were modern and others were traditional. All were expensive.

They slowly made their way from store to store. Tom and Wade found the architecture of the village interesting, and noticed all the nuances down to the smallest detail. The owner had spared no expense and it was evident from the huge number of tourists, that he was making tons of money.

In one tiny jewelry store, Wade found a trinket he thought Robison might like. It resembled a small ancient coin about the size of a nickel. These oddly shaped coins were called "Cobs," a term derived from the Spanish phrase "Cabo de barra" meaning, "The end of the bar." The genuine article was extremely rare. The store owner told Wade, that striking a piece of silver cut from the end of a silver bar and weighing and trimming it until it achieved the proper weight ensured that no two Cobs were exactly alike. This particular Cob was encased in a gold coin holder with a small dolphin at the bottom. It was meant to hang from a chain worn around the neck, and Wade thought it would look great on Robison, but he decided to see if she would like it first.

Robison was happy with the find as he described it, so Wade went back to the tiny jewelry store to "work out" a deal. Tom went along, noting his expertise would be needed to haggle the price down. Wade suspected Tom just wanted an excuse to avoid going through stacks of handmade linen tablecloths and napkins with Brianne.

They all met for lunch on the upper level of one of the stone buildings at eleven. From the veranda they had a view of the Chavón River, and magnificent it was! They were above a sheer drop of some six hundred feet straight down to the wide curving river. Or they could look farther out and see the tranquil bluish-green water flowing amid the palm trees and dense foliage until it disappeared.

After ordering, they showed off their "bargains." Robison showed Brianne her Cob and Brianne displayed all kinds of handmade linens. The guys were unimpressed with linens, but jewelry was more to their liking…and the Cob had been the extent of their shopping.

A water sport was a different matter. Off in the distance, Wade watched a fisherman hook his catch. Wade knew the technique: reel it in part way; let the fish take some drag; then reel it all the way to the boat. This particular fish put up quite a fight, holding Wade's attention throughout lunch. The table conversation, mostly about certain shops went right past him.

"Fishing must be fantastic in that river," Wade announced. "Too bad we aren't staying longer. I'd like to go on one of those fishing tours Brianne talked about."

"So…you were listening to me after all," Brianne said as she checked her watch. "But alas! …There's no time to dilly dally…we must be off….Back to the bus, so Robison and I can whip your butts at golf."

"Hey, better talk nice or we may just put your butt off the bus on the way back and let 'scooter-man' have at you like I mentioned before," Tom countered.

The girls had to make a quick stop at one of the stores on the way back to the van, while the men paid the bill. Brianne smiled as they approached the shuttle. She had reason to: the driver was leaning against the side of the tiny bus smoking a cigarette. Brianne couldn't let this pass so she turned towards Tom, pointed to the driver and said, "I told you he'd be here!"

The trip back to the villa took little time; all traffic was going to the old city, not from it.

❧

After his ride—and the chance meeting with Robison—Carlos cooled down Skyesrun before going to the house for lunch. He cherished this quiet time with this magnificent beast. Even though there was a groomsman for this chore, Carlos brushed Skyesrun and made sure she had fresh water and hay. He loved doting on Skyesrun.

Afterwards, Carlos returned to the estate and made his way through the kitchen and out to the patio. To his dismay, his father and Bibí were still lounging by the pool. Carlos wasn't about to go out and join Bibí-the-bitch, so he took the opportunity to catch up on business calls.

❧

Golfing had been the real reason behind this trip in the first place, so Wade, Robison, Tom and Brianne were anxious to get to the course. They changed into golf clothes, loaded their clubs on carts and headed, with map in hand, to the Teeth of the Dog course. They wound their way around the streets with Tom following closely behind Wade.

At the clubhouse several people were ready to tee off. Caddies were roaming around, trying to drum up business for themselves. The driving range was crowded, with people waiting in line to warm up. The practice green, too, was crowded with people trying get in a few putts on the undulating surface. Both courses started near the same spot, with a starter calling foursomes to the tees over a loudspeaker.

"Good thing we got something to eat before we arrived," Wade said. "I'm not sure we'd ever get to the snack bar by the looks of that line."

87

Tom and Wade went to the Caddie Master's shed to check in. He appointed them a "forecaddie," which was one caddie for the foursome. The forecaddie didn't carry the golf bags; he was there for pace-of-play, or to help them find the next tee. All golfers rode in carts; the caddie walked. The arrangement they'd decided, was designed to garner additional income for the club.

After hitting a few practice balls, the foursome was called to the first tee on the Teeth of the Dog course. This world famous course was highly rated in all the golf magazines, both for its layout and its scenic ocean-side holes.

By the end of the fourth hole, the girls had the guys down by five bucks. However, at that point they turned into the wind and moved to the ocean side of the course, which would prove a lot more difficult. At least, the guys were counting on this perceived disadvantage to overtake the girls.

The vacation homes lining the golf course were breathtaking. In most cases, several landscapers worked in the yards, and through the windows Brianne and Robison could see maids cleaning, dusting, and straightening up. The girls had to fight distraction from the surroundings. What a way to live!

"Everyone must have servants galore here," mentioned Brianne. "It's probably one of those countries where the people are very rich or very poor with no in-between."

"Sure looks like it, all right," said Robison. "Hey, we better keep our minds on the game!"

The fifth hole was a par three and they all broke even.

Ocean waves lapped at rocks bordering the fairways as the foursome passed. The blue sea gobbled up Tom's ball that he accidentally hooked far to the left. They all stood on the edge of the fairway and watched it disappear. Fantastic! Again they resisted getting caught up in the ambience instead of concentrating on the game.

"I can't wait to play this course again," Robison remarked. "I sure hope nothing interferes."

"Well, after Tom and I whip your butts you won't be so eager to play here again," Wade needled.

"Yeah, right! Keep dreaming, honey," Robison shot back.

At the green on the eighth hole, the wind was picking up noticeably. The guys now had the girls down by two dollars and they could expect no mercy. Holing out her putt, Robison walked to the edge of the green to get a better view of the sprawling mansion nearby. It was the biggest yet!

"Look, you guys,...look out in the water. There's a helipad! Have you ever seen anything like that in your whole life? ...Out in the ocean no less!" Robison gasped.

All gathered on the rise behind the green for a better view. Tom let out a low whistle. "What an incredible place! Can you imagine that being just your vacation home? I wonder what this guy's regular house looks like. So who lives here?" he asked the caddie.

"The Minister of Finance. He flies in and out on his helicopter." The caddie pointed to the boulder out in the ocean with the circle "H" painted on it, just in case they'd missed it. "He is also running for president. That's why there are guards everywhere. If you look closely, you will see them."

"President of the country?" Tom asked.

"Sí."

A foursome was approaching from behind so they hurried along. The cart path ran beside a tall, vine-covered wall that surrounded the mansion on three sides. As they were about to cross the road, Brianne said, "The guy even has his own armed guard and guard gate."

"Well, he is running for president, you know," replied Tom. "I guess he needs protection."

They craned their necks to look as the carts moved along, the guard was speaking to someone in a car waiting to enter the estate; the guard was impressively armed.

"Everybody wears a gun around here," observed Wade. "Wouldn't you feel weird wearing a pistol in a holster all the time?"

"Well, it might get in the way of my golf swing," Tom jested.

"Not to mention that your shorts could fall down due to the weight of the gun," Brianne added.

"I'd wear mine under my arm," Tom said seriously. "You know like secret agents and stuff."

"Hello, may I speak to Carlos?" Luís asked the receptionist.

"I am sorry; he is not here."

"Can you tell me how to get hold of him? This is Luís, his cousin."

"I recognize your voice. He went to the vacation house at the Campo. I'll give you the number."

After several tries, Luís got through to the butler who didn't speak English, but managed to indicate that Carlos was indeed staying there.

Felicity was packing suitcases. She wanted out of this relationship and out of this country! Perhaps she could go online and check out flight schedules. Although, on second thought, she'd better check out the newspaper and see if anyone was onto the robbery yet. Or onto her!

This whole situation was getting creepier by the minute. And if Carlos made the switch in such a "cloak-and-dagger" way, he could well be a dangerous man who knew dangerous people.

How had she gotten mixed up in all of this? Stupid is what she was. She still had nagging doubts about Luís. What if he was trying to get rid of her so he wouldn't have to split the money? Her head hurt and this was way too much thinking with a hang-over. Besides Luís was about to leave.

"I'm going down to the front desk, pay our bill, then see about renting a car to go to the Casa de Campo," Luís told her, opening the hotel door. "I'll be back in a minute."

She was pondering whether to take her half of the money they had stashed in the room, tell Luís to drop-dead, then catch a flight back to Charlotte. She hooked up her laptop and was able to get online and navigate to the website of the *Charlotte Observer*.

There it was:

Multimillion Dollar Heirlooms Stolen

The home of Henry P. Barnes III was hit by burglars. A diamond and ruby necklace, bracelet and earrings worth an estimated three million dollars were stolen from his posh Forest Hills home while he and his wife were on vacation. Nothing else seems to be missing. The police are

searching for Louis Ramundo, employee of Centurion
Locks & Security Systems.

Luís came back in the hotel room while she was folding up the
laptop and packing it in its carry case. "Find anything interesting?"
he asked.

"Well, you might call it that. The cops are swarming all over
Charlotte and the southeast looking for you," she replied.

"You're shittin' me!" he exclaimed. Then he read the article she
had copied down in longhand on a piece of hotel stationary. "I
wonder if he has noticed the money missing yet."

Felicity looked at him with disgust. "Think about it, boy
genius.... He'll collect the insurance money on the jewelry. As far as
the money goes, it's probably money he's not supposed to have or
hasn't reported to the IRS. Besides, after collecting on the jewels,
why would he care about a few hundred thousand? We're the ones
that made him millions, and we're fucked! By the way, I want out. I
want to go back to the good ol' USA, just as you suggested."

"No. I've changed my mind, you aren't going anywhere without
me. We are going to go to the Campo, talk to Carlos, and then decide
what to do next."

"Let me tell you something, you stupid asshole! I'll go with you
to the Campo because I want to see Carlos laugh in your face with my
own eyes. He'll *never* admit to taking the jewelry and you'll never
see a fucking dime. After that, I'm going back to Charlotte and
leaving your sorry ass here."

He grabbed her by the arm, jerked her around and sneered: "If you
think you are going back to dig up the rest of the jewelry and money
then hightail it out of my life, you are sadly mistaken. We go
together, or not at all. What did you think? You were going to just
waltz right out of here back to Myrtle Beach?"

Felicity struggled to get loose, but he held her firmly. Glaring
into his eyes she said, "After that article in the paper, it's obvious *you*
can't go back. So put that in your planning, Mr. Big Shot!"

He hesitated and then said, "We are in this together...forever. Do
you understand? Or do I have to spell it out for you? Together
forever, or else!"

91

She yanked free, and stormed out of the room. She was more convinced than ever that she needed to get out...the sooner...the better.

It was well after noon when Ty finally hit the sack. He blocked out the light with a soft velvet eye-pillow covering his eyes. He slept soundly for a few hours, but woke up when he heard a light tapping on his hotel room door.

"Ty, are you up? It's Raúl."

Ty removed the burgundy eye-pillow and opened his eyes. "Just a minute," he answered.

He felt like he'd only been asleep ten minutes, but after looking at the clock, realized it had been several hours. In his boxers, he opened the door for Raúl.

"Have a seat. I'll just take a quick shower," Ty said. "Where are we going to eat?" he asked from the bathroom.

"The Casa del Rio, we can walk there."

"Good, I'm kinda tired. After we eat, we'll stop by the amphitheater to make sure everything is okay."

Emerging with a towel around his waist, Ty went to the closet for light green shorts and a matching floral silk shirt. Raúl noted how meticulous Ty was. His trousers were all neatly aligned, then his shorts, then shirts, and all were grouped by color.

Ty straightened everything on top of his dresser. Lastly, he went into the bathroom and wiped down the sink, then folded the used towel neatly and placed it on the floor beside the bathtub. As they departed for the Casa del Rio, Raúl said, "You are extremely neat."

Ty laughed. "My brother calls it the 'drill.' I don't know...I've been doing it all of my life. It makes living in a hotel room more bearable if everything is neat and in its place. It also makes packing quick and easy."

"You have a brother?"

"Yes, T. J., and no, he's not as neat as I am," Ty added.

The girls were quite solemn on the ride back from the golf course. They'd lost to the guys and having to pay them ten dollars each was tortuous. Needless to say, the guys were rubbing it in at every opportunity. The duo began singing "We Are The Champions" in pathetic voices, and to make matters worse, other men gave them a "thumbs-up" when they heard them singing. Brianne and Robison countered by upping the bet for tomorrow's game. They had to win sometime, right? Why not tomorrow?

Back at the villa, Tom mixed some kind of fruit juice and rum drink. It tasted glorious even though Tom had no idea what he'd actually put in each glass. Thus he named it "Rum Surprise."

Tom offered a toast. "To the champions...now and forever!"

"I'll drink to that," Wade replied.

The girls retaliated by taking their drinks out back and sitting in the lounge chairs by the pool. They'd heard quite enough boasting for one evening.

Robison was tempted to tell Brianne about the handsome horseman, but she wasn't sure how Brianne would react—especially if Robison appeared to have been flattered and later alarmed by the encounter. Of course, Brianne hadn't seen the man bump into Robison at the bar, his display of charm, nor the horseman's "visit" in the fog while wearing a gun. Robison chose to keep silent under the circumstances.

"Hey, I'd love to sit here forever, but I think we need to get ready for dinner," Brianne said.

After they showered, Robison and Brianne made a grand entrance into the living room, modeling their new "dressy casual" clothes. Both wore short skirts, sleeveless tops and sandals, all of which were very tropical looking.

"Wow, you girls look great!" Wade said, whistling. "Robison, have I seen this outfit before?"

"No, darling. We bought these the last time we were in Myrtle Beach together. You know, getting tropical-vacation clothes for this trip."

"Hey, Wade, where's our coordinating 'tropical' outfits...?" Tom asked.

Brianne cut them off: "A waste of time! You two will never look as gorgeous as we do."

Wade shrugged his shoulders and switched the subject, now that they were ready to navigate to the El Pescador restaurant.

"Brianne, why don't you go first?" Wade suggested. "That way you won't get lost like last night."

Robison elbowed Wade in the ribs to shut him up. Too close to a raw nerve, in her judgment and there was no need to start dinner on a bad note.

But Brianne kept up the ribbing with: "Very amusing. And perhaps you noticed we didn't get lost on the way to the golf course today, did we?"

"Yeah, but that trip was in daylight," Wade retorted.

"And another thing, it didn't take me to get Tom lost. He did that all on his own!"

The bantering ended as they drove away. After they had parked side-by-side in the golf cart parking lot they entered the seafood restaurant, together. They were shown to a table on the veranda, just barely under the thatched roof. Below was the small beach and tidal pool—with the old boat anchored peacefully near the shoreline.

They all ordered drinks, including the customary big bottle of water. Brianne downed her margarita almost immediately and ordered another.

"Take it easy there, ol' girl." Tom cautioned. "I don't know how well margaritas mix with two Rum Surprises."

"But I love these margaritas! Besides, I'm on vacation."

"You're forgetting tomorrow's golf date," Tom reminded her. "It's not as much fun beating someone under the weather."

"Well, I have a personal doctor to fix me up," Brianne said, patting Robison on the shoulder.

Robison digressed by nodding in the direction of the art market and saying, "I would like to go over there after we eat, Wade."

"Sounds good to me. How about you guys? Want to walk over there, too?"

Brianne shook her head no.

"She's had one too many margaritas," Tom said. "But we may come back over here another day, if you find it worthwhile."

They finished their seafood dinners served under the stars, in a truly romantic setting. Afterwards, Tom and Brianne headed for their golf cart to return to the villa. Brianne was weaving a bit and giggling as they walked away. The margaritas were in control.

Wade and Robison, on the other hand, walked around the tidal pool, down along the beach, and over to the busy art market.

"Isn't this wonderful, Wade?"

"Yeah, and the weather is unreal. Maybe we should stay longer," Wade said.

"Now wouldn't that be nice!" Robison exclaimed. Spotting an interesting booth, she continued, "Let's go over there and buy something for the house and maybe my office. I really want something to remind me of this trip. Don't you?"

"Absolutely!"

TEN

L ate in the afternoon, Carlos went to his father's office in the south wing of the house. His father's signature was necessary to close the land deal, which he'd been working on for seven months. He also needed to report on the meeting with Luís, his cousin.

With two briefcases in hand, Carlos knocked and entered; his father was sitting behind his dark mahogany desk, talking on the telephone. Carlos hesitated at the door until Juan waved him in. Hanging up he said, "My son,...my son,...come in." Carlos walked over and gave him the obligatory kiss on each cheek. "Bibí and I missed you at breakfast this morning."

That last comment made the hair on the back of Carlos' neck stand on end.

"You know how I feel about her, Papá. And besides, I took the opportunity to ride Skyesrun this morning. What a wonderful horse she is! I'll never tire of riding her."

His father nodded. "Let's see the deal; lay it all out on my desk."

Placing the largest briefcase on the credenza, Carlos took out stacks of folders and neatly spread them out, taking up most of the space on the large desk. Opening a survey map with a large plot of land highlighted around the boundaries in yellow, Carlos launched into his explanation of the sale. It took three hours to go over every detail of the sale of government property needing the blessing and signature of the Minister of Finance.

"You have done well, my son. I see you are going to make a hefty six-figure commission on this deal."

"What are you complaining about? You're going to make a good six-figure portion under the table."

"Oh sí, sí. How else would I have all this...on my petty government salary? Being the Minister of Finance has its amenities; however, a huge salary is not one of them."

"As you have said, so many times. Anyway, I have the paperwork ready for your signature, Papá."

For the next half-hour, Carlos helped find all the different places Juan needed to sign or initial, then he checked to make sure they hadn't left anything out.

After everything was finalized, Carlos picked up the second, smaller briefcase he'd brought. He slowly turned around with a sly grin on his face. "And now...for the 'piece de resistance.' You absolutely won't believe it." He opened the case and laid the diamond and ruby necklace on his father's desk.

"Oh, be still my heart!" Juan picked it up gingerly, eyeing it with delight. "How much will it bring?"

"I have the fence coming day after tomorrow to look at it," he said. "Probably stone by stone, a couple million, maybe more. Naturally, we will disassemble the necklace. It's too traceable like this."

"I see. The switch obviously went very smoothly," his father commented.

Carlos laughed. "It couldn't have been better. Luís made it easy by knocking a beer out of my hand. It was perfect! It was so blatant, I almost didn't need Franco."

"How is Franco, anyway? Still doing his card tricks at that sleazy hotel bar?"

"Yeah. Believe me, this was the easiest five thousand pesos Franco ever made doing a sleight of hand trick. Hell, I could have pulled off the switch myself during all the commotion. Not only that, but Franco was so serious I could hardly keep a straight face. You should have seen the ratty little pin stripe suit he came up with...from God knows where."

His father slapped Carlos on the back in a congratulatory way, handing him back the necklace. Juan suggested a cocktail before dinner.

He walked over to the small wet bar, filled two glasses with three ice cubes each; Juan didn't believe in watering down expensive liquor. He then generously poured a single malt scotch for the two of them.

After toasting the new land sale and admiring the necklace, Carlos switched to unpleasantness. "Papá we need to discuss Bibí and the problem she poses for your campaign."

Elsewhere, Bibí was steaming mad. She and Juan always spent cocktail time together before dinner, but tonight the butler brought a martini while she sat alone in the parlor. After the second martini, she decided Juan had taken long enough and started down the hallway

97

towards his office. As she approached the door, she could hear Carlos and Juan arguing. Stopping short of the office door, she listened from outside.

"Papá, listen to me! How many times do I have to say it? Bibí is a threat to your presidential campaign. And, frankly, I'm sick of taking the heat for it from your publicist and security people. Her presence in your life is too goddamned dangerous!"

"I don't care."

"You don't care that I take the heat for it?"

"No. I don't care what those people think!"

"Stop being so stubborn. She's nothing but a whore! The only question is what to do about her?"

"What do you mean?"

"If you just dump her, she'll go to the tabloids. You'll have to arrange some sort of a deal to get rid of her. Or better yet, I will take care of her myself."

Juan paced around the office, shaking his head. "I'm very fond of her; she has been with me for years."

Carlos knew he was beginning to wear his father down; he couldn't stop now. "I know. But like I just said, your affair is too dangerous. You are putting too much in jeopardy. You could lose everything…and I mean…everything!" Carlos said with emphasis.

Juan let out a deep sigh. Clearly saddened, he began nodding his head. "I know you are right, my son. So go ahead…only I don't want to know the details," Juan whispered. He cared for her. But, his political future dictated he be pragmatic, not emotional.

"At least promise me you won't do anything to spoil this last weekend for me; my last weekend with her…please," Juan pleaded.

"It's a promise," Carlos agreed. He was relieved that after a few days he'd be rid of Bibí and all the complaints and problems associated with her. His father understood exactly what Carlos meant by "taking care of her."

And so did Bibí! She heard the butler approaching, so she spun around and departed. Furious at Carlos and disappointed with Juan, she made her way back to the parlor and poured another martini.

Well, if Carlos thought for one moment that he could offer her some paltry sum of money to keep her quiet until he could do away with her, then he was very much mistaken! She had assembled methods and opportunities, "weapons" in case something like this ever happened. Why all she had to do was screw the security guard, which she already had done on several occasions, and he would slip her a videotape of her and Juan in compromising positions. Bibí-the-bitch had a few tricks up her sleeve and she wouldn't hesitate to use them. She could make it too dangerous for Carlos to "get rid of her."

"Dinner is ready, Señores," said the butler to Juan and Carlos in the office.

Juan came from behind the desk and put his hands on Carlos' shoulders. "You're my only son. I love you more than life. You need to forgive an old man his dalliance. Please promise me you'll try to get along with her—only for a couple more days. For me, my son."

"Sí, Papá," Carlos whispered, then gulped down his last swig of scotch.

"Come, let us go into the dining room. We'll find Bibí along the way," Juan suggested. Juan felt a bit relieved that he'd managed to "buy" some time; he decided to think only of this weekend and nothing beyond. This would be his last fling with luscious Bibí.

As all three sat at the dining room table, it became more and more obvious the intoxicated Bibí was madder than hell. She berated the butler, she snapped at Juan, and she hissed at Carlos. At first, she felt terribly hurt, but now, only pure hatred! Especially towards Carlos. She truly realized what a precarious position she had placed herself in. She needed to act quickly!

When dinner was finished and while the butler poured the coffee, Bibí excused herself to use the restroom. "I'll be back in a few moments," she said. As she passed Carlos' chair, she said under her breath, "I'm sure you'll sorely miss me, you fucking asshole!"

Carlos pushed his chair back, stood up and threw down his napkin, and then started in her direction. But Juan grabbed his arm.

"Carlos! ...Please! You promised," his father said sternly.

Fuming, Carlos shouted, "Why should I mind my manners in front of a whoring pig?" He jerked his arm out of his father's grip and stormed from the room. He winked at the maid (who was obviously pleased at the word "pig" being used in reference to Bibí) as he left the room.

Juan's nerves were on edge. He went to the parlor, poured himself a cognac and lit a cigar—a hand rolled and imported Cuban Cohiba, which he kept in a large humidor on his desk. Puffing the aromatic cigar, he began thinking of life without Bibí, the upcoming campaign, the wife he didn't love, and back to Bibí again. Loud arguing from deep within the house interrupted his thought process. Shouts echoed down the long tiled corridor.

Carlos had been heading for his bedroom after leaving the dining room, when he noticed that Bibí hadn't gone to the guest bathroom. Instead, she was sneaking towards Juan's office on the other side of the house. He was tempted to follow her to see what she was up to, but then he recalled he'd promised his father to leave her alone.

Carlos went outside to clear his head and regain his composure. It was a glorious evening and he lit a cigarette. Contemplating the sky, Carlos suddenly had an eerie feeling about Bibí. She was going to his father's office when Juan wasn't there! ...And the necklace was so close at hand!

Changing his mind, he abruptly threw down his cigarette and headed to the office. He'd pack up the briefcase and papers they'd left strewn all over Juan's desk earlier, retrieve the smaller briefcase, the one with the necklace in it, and take it to a more secure location.

He'd already had enough of Bibí, but since he'd promised to do nothing about her until after this weekend, he made the decision to leave the estate altogether. Let his father enjoy her "pleasures" in the time remaining. There was too much bad blood between them to try to keep the peace for more than a few minutes, much less an entire weekend.

His mind made up, Carlos decided to hurry and get the hell out of there. But first he had to clear out Juan's office.

Carlos turned the knob and flung open the office door. Sure enough! There was Bibí with the wall safe open, holding a bundle of cash.

"What the fuck are you doing?" Carlos yelled at her.

She wheeled around as Carlos rushed towards her.

Quickly reaching back into the safe, Bibí pulled out a gun. Pointing it at Carlos, she sneered, "Come any closer, you son-of-a-bitch, and I'll blow your brains out!"

He paused...even took a slight step backwards. "You stupid little whore! You don't think you're going to get away with this, do you?"

"I'm blowing this joint. I overheard you and your pretentious father deciding to get rid of me. Right in this very room! And I don't need anyone to 'deal' with me. Especially,...you!" Bibí screamed back at him, trembling with rage.

Carlos tried reasoning with her. "Look. Let's talk this over. You misunderstood our conversation and..."

"Shut up, asshole!"

Still pointing the gun at him, she picked up the small briefcase and began putting the money into it. Bibí clearly hadn't seen the necklace, she assumed the briefcase was empty because it was so light. "I have always hated you," she continued. "I despise your sexual blackmail, too. If you were any kind of a man, you wouldn't have to use such tactics to get laid," she sneered. "Anyway, now it doesn't matter what tapes you have, because I'm leaving for good and taking this money with me."

Carlos spat on the floor. "That's what I think of you!" he said, edging closer. He didn't care about the money. But the necklace? No way in hell was she getting her hot sticky fingers on it! He took another step.

"Hold it! Hold it right there!" Bibí cocked the gun.

Carlos stopped.

The door opened and Juan stepped into the room. "What the hell is going on here? Bibí, what are you doing? Put the gun down!" Juan ordered.

Carlos spun around. "She's stealing your goddamned money!"

"Shut up!" Bibí shouted. "I loved you, Juan, and now you want to cast me out like that." She snapped her fingers. "And worse than that...you were going to let Carlos 'deal' with me. You traitor! ...You bastard!" she yelled.

"Bibí, take the money. Just put the gun down. I never intended for Carlos to..."

"Stop lying to me!" Bibí was shaking as she pointed the gun in Juan's direction.

"I'm serious my little pumpkin, take the money," Juan begged. "I don't care about it just put the gun down...please."

Juan didn't realize she was holding a lot more than just money.

101

"You're not leaving with that bag or anything else," Carlos growled, hoping his father would take the hint. It would be just his luck that his father would let her walk right out, briefcase and all, because she "deserved" a little compensation. Carlos didn't think she deserved squat, much less money and a two-million dollar necklace.

He could see she was considering Juan's offer to take the money and leave. Her gun hand was shaking, but she was determined to see this through. "Okay, I'll go. But I won't put the gun down until I'm safely out of that asshole's reach." She nodded, re-aimed the gun at Carlos and glanced at Juan.

Carlos seized the moment. It was now or never!

He lunged for Bibí and the briefcase.

Startled...she fired three times, in rapid succession. *Bang! ...Bang! ...Bang!*

Juan grabbed his stomach, staring in hazy disbelief. At the last minute he had stepped in front of Carlos, arms raised for protection.

Time stood still.

Juan was falling...falling. Carlos was staring in horror, first at Bibí and then at his father. They both saw the look on Juan's horror-stricken face. They watched as Juan slumped to the floor; his head hit the tile with a sickly "splat." Juan Alvarez lay motionless, the liquid of life seeping from his wounds onto the floor.

Bibí screamed terrifyingly loud, breaking the silence. She dropped the gun and briefcase and ran to Juan's side.

Carlos couldn't move. He was momentarily paralyzed.

"Juanito, no! No! Juanito!" she yelled, crouching over Juan.

Carlos could hear the bodyguards shouting and running as they approached the office. He came to his senses. Crossing the room in two giant steps, he pulled Bibí off Juan and threw her aside...her head hitting an antique table with a loud "crack." A small lamp fell and shattered on the floor beside her.

The guards burst into the office.

"Take her out of here! Lock her up!" Carlos shouted to the guards.

Bibí struggled against her captors as she screamed at Carlos. "You bastard! You made me do it....I didn't mean to shoot him.... You filthy bastard!" She was still yelling as they dragged her toward the door.

"Get that whoring murderer out of here!" Carlos called out as the guards took her from the room.

He put his head on his father's chest; Juan had a faint heartbeat. Turning to Donadio, his right-hand man, Carlos said, "We've got to get a doctor here immediately. No way can we take him to the hospital! There would be an investigation. How can I explain that his mistress shot him? Shit, this would be political suicide!"

Think…think…he needed a doctor…someone that could come here to the house. He grabbed a towel from the bathroom and hurried back to his father's side. He held it on his father's wound.

"Donadio, help me get him to the couch."

Ever so gently the huge bodyguard picked up the stout old man, carefully laying him down upon the couch. Juan was unconscious. Carlos dropped to his knees next to his father. Praying in silence, he asked God to save his precious papá.

"Papá! …*Papá!*"

No response.

Shit. Think…think. A doctor! Where was a doctor? A discreet doctor. A good doctor!

Then, he remembered…the call at the bar for "Dr. Murphy." The man with the attractive woman he'd bumped into. The woman he saw on the lounge chair by the pool…the villa key he'd picked up outside the restroom.

A plan began to emerge. He began issuing orders to the guards. "There is a Dr. Murphy at a villa on Cerezas. I think number fifty-seven or fifty-eight. Bring him here immediately! If he won't come willingly, bring him anyway—his wife, too. We may need her as insurance. Hurry! And don't mention this to a soul. Do you understand? Hurry!"

While Carlos waited for the doctor, he picked up the small briefcase on the floor near where his father had fallen. He hid it behind another couch across the room…out of sight.

Returning to his father's side, Carlos gently stroked his head. "Please don't die, Papá. I've sent for help. You are going to be fine. You'll see."

It was after nine forty-five that night when Luís and Felicity arrived at the Casa de Campo from Santo Domingo and checked into the hotel. Once they settled into their room and unpacked, they took a map of the resort and set out to find his Uncle Juan's vacation home. The two of them had hardly spoken to one another during the entire trip from Santo Domingo to the Campo. Luís hoped she would get over it, but so far she hadn't budged. She was being a pain-in-the-ass that he didn't need right now, on top of everything else.

Luís had decided to contact his Uncle Juan after his calls to Carlos had gotten him the big run around. It was becoming vividly clear that Carlos was in on the switch. Why else would he be giving Luís the cold shoulder? He wasn't sure what he was going to tell his uncle, but if Luís could get inside the house, he'd be in the vicinity of his swindling, two-timing cousin Carlos.

After winding down many roads in their golf cart, Luís and Felicity arrived at the guardhouse just as a car filled with four men flew past the guard. Obviously, they were in a big hurry.

Luís pulled up to the guard. "Is this the estate of Juan Alvarez?"

"Yes."

"I'm his nephew and I'd like to speak with him, please."

"I'm sorry; that is impossible. You will have to leave," the guard said, knowing all the chaos the shooting had caused.

His blood pressure soaring, Luís said harshly, "I want to speak with my Uncle Juan! Now!"

The guard retorted in a loud voice, "It is not possible! Please leave."

Luís got out of the golf cart, and approached the guard. "I insist on seeing…"

The guard drew his gun. "I said leave! This instant!"

Luís stopped dead in his tracks. Felicity began begging Luis to get back into the golf cart. Luís had no choice but to tuck tail and retreat.

~~~

The four bodyguards that flew past the guard and the golf cart with Luís and Felicity arrived at the Cerezas villa within two minutes. One waited in the car, while two others guarded each end of the house. Donadio went to the entrance of the villa and rapped loudly on the front door.

There was no answer. He waited and knocked again…louder.

Tom and Brianne had made an early night of it and were in bed. She had passed out after the two Rum Surprises and two margaritas. Tom heard the first knock and thought he was dreaming. Then there was a second knock…much louder. Hell, Wade must have forgotten his key. Tom got up and went to the door. "I'm coming…I'm coming. What the hell? Forget your key, did you?"

Tom, perplexed at seeing a large man standing in the doorway, asked: "Can I help you?"

"We have…emergency. We need doctor. A Dr. Murphy, yes?" Donadio was speaking his best English.

Tom arched his back to look at Wade and Robison's bedroom door. It was standing wide open. They clearly weren't there.

"Well, yes and no. They aren't back from the art market next to the El Pescador restaurant…"

Donadio turned to go before Tom finished, snapping orders at the three other men in a loud, commanding voice. All hurried to the waiting car. The doors slammed shut as the vehicle roared out of the driveway.

Tom closed the door, wondering what had happened. Normally when they traveled, Robison didn't want anyone to know she was a doctor, so how did they find out? Anyway, he was sure that Robison could handle it; the question was *would* she handle it.

Tom wandered back to bed and was soon snoring loudly.

Wade and Robison had bought two paintings and were looking at another. Wade was haggling with the salesman over the price, when a man called out, "Dr. Murphy? Dr. Murphy!"

Both Wade and Robison turned around. Two burly men came up to them.

"There has been…accident…we need doctor."

Robison naturally spoke up: "Well, I don't know who you are, but you need to find someone else. Go to the hospital."

Donadio ignored her, as if she didn't exist. He was expecting the doctor to be a man. Another guard stepped much closer to Wade and pressed a sharp object into his side.

"What the hell are you doing?" Wade demanded.

The bodyguards ignored his resistance and pressed the gun harder against his side. "Now we go...quietly to the car. ¿Comprende? ...Understand?" Donadio ordered.

When she saw the gun in Wade's side, Robison stifled a scream. The other bodyguard shoved her shoulder, to get her moving. Her purse and paintings dropped to the ground...but when she tried to retrieve them, a guard jerked her towards the waiting vehicle.

"Don't resist," Wade whispered. "Don't say anything! For some reason they think I'm the doctor."

"Shut up!" A guard ordered, shoving them from behind, creating a scene...but people only stared out of curiosity.

Why didn't anyone help them? All these people! Couldn't anyone see they were being abducted?

Wade and Robison were forced into the back seat. Before the doors had closed, the car shot forward, jolting them backwards against the seats. The car flew down the street, screeching around corners as they roared along the narrow two lane road.

They entered the estate without slowing at the guard gate and came to a halt in front of the main entrance. The house was all lit up and a cowering maid stood at the opened front door.

Donadio grabbed Wade by the elbow, hustled him out of the car, through the foyer, down the long hallway and into Juan's office. Robison wasn't far behind.

Blood-covered Carlos stood up when they entered the room. He was pale as a ghost; his eyes were puffy and red. Robison hardly recognized him as the poised gentleman she had seen on two brief occasions.

"Please, there has been an accident and my father is in need of attention," Carlos said as he approached Wade. "I need for you to help him."

Wade began, "Listen, we don't want any trouble here. I'm not a..."

The bodyguard twisted Robison's arm, she let out a small scream. When Wade turned around to look at her, she was being gagged.

"What the hell is going on?" Wade shouted, realizing they had been cast into a life-threatening crisis.

Carlos looked directly at Wade. "Clearly you don't understand, Dr. Murphy. So let me be direct. You *will* help my father or you will never see your lovely wife again."

Wade lunged at Carlos, but Donadio intercepted, and slammed Wade against the wall.

"You son-of-a-bitch! You don't understand!" Wade struggled to get loose, but when he looked at the gagged Robison he thought better of it. Wade needed to buy time so he could figure out what to do next. There were too many goddamned guards! It was clear that the two of them were not going to be able to overcome so many men. So if these thugs thought Wade was the doctor, then he would be the "doctor."

Wade relaxed, shaking Donadio off. "Okay, let me take a look at him," he said.

Robison was in total disbelief. How long could he fool them? She watched as he asked for a pair of scissors and cut away Juan's shirt. He was lying on a blood-soaked couch and Robison could see towels had been applied to the wound in an attempt to stop the bleeding.

"Okay, I'm going to need some clean towels, sterile water, and a place to wash my hands with soap," Wade ordered. He lifted one of Juan's eyelids as he spoke, not knowing what the hell he was looking for. "And I'll need some supplies."

"Make a list," Carlos snapped.

"Well, first, you must let my wife go. I mean to...home...to the villa...away from here," Wade said, looking at Carlos calmly, but sternly.

Carlos thought for a moment and then countered: "If my father dies, you die! He lives...then you live. I'm not sure about letting her go just yet."

"We are losing precious time," Wade said. "Let her go!"

Robison was desperately trying to signal Wade with her eyes. She knew he didn't have any idea how to "save" Juan. He hadn't even looked at his wounds...only under his eyelids, for God's sake! She knew he was trying to save her but...oh God! He would be a dead man for sure. She had to tell Carlos *she* was the one who could save his father. Then they might have a chance.

"The list. What is on the list?" Carlos demanded.

"First, I have to go to the bathroom and wash my hands, so I can examine him thoroughly," Wade said, trying to buy more time. "And I must see my wife alone...now!"

Carlos nodded. One of the guards showed them the way to a bathroom, shoved them both inside, then slammed the door.

"Listen," Wade whispered as he untied her gag.

"Wade, no, Wade...you listen to me. You can't save him. Maybe I can."

"Shhh...just give me a list of instruments and stuff to give to them."

"Wade..."

He covered her mouth with his mouth. He could taste her salty tears.

"You've got to get away. I'm just trying to buy some time. If they'll let you go then you can get the police. But you're not staying! More could happen to a beautiful woman than getting killed."

She nodded, took a deep breath, and began composing a list.

"But, Wade," she pleaded. "If I go out and help him, maybe they'll let us both go. This is crazy!"

"Let's go, in there!" The door burst open just as she finished writing.

Wade grabbed the list, handed it to Carlos and said, "Here's the list. Now let her go."

Carlos nodded, and handed the list to Donadio. No one seemed to notice Robison was no longer gagged.

"Clearly you take me for a fool, doctor," Carlos said as he paced near his father. "It was pointed out to me that you didn't even take a look at his stomach! Now do something, don't just screw around!" he shouted.

Carlos drew back and punched Wade in the gut as hard as he could. Robison let out a scream, broke free from the guard and rushed to Wade's slumped over body. While he was coughing and trying to regain his composure, Carlos kicked him in the side, sending him careening across the tile floor.

"Stop! Stop it! Robison screamed. "I'm the doctor, not him!"

They all stared at her in disbelief. She turned to face Carlos, a sense of strength welling within her. She was now in charge. "I will help your father, but not until I help my husband," she announced and headed towards Wade.

Carlos crossed the room in two long strides; grabbed her by the arm, and spun her around. "I am the boss here!" he yelled. "You will do what I tell you and my father comes first!"

Staring back defiantly, she said, "I'm your father's only hope...therefore, *I'm* in charge here." Jerking her arm out of his grasp, she continued toward Wade. He was coughing and beginning to breathe normally again and looked no worse for the beating.

"Are you all right, honey?" she asked as she brushed back his hair.

Wade managed a reassuring nod.

Robison stood up and turned her attention to the comatose figure on the couch...her patient. She eventually found a pulse; it was barely palpable. She looked at his pupils and then the wounds.

"He's in severe shock. Hurry with that list," she ordered in a professional manner, which thrilled Carlos—even under these circumstances.

She rummaged through a first aid kit that came out of nowhere. Matter-of-factly she said, "And another thing. I want you to let Wade go. He can do nothing here."

"No problem." Carlos motioned with his head to a guard, who escorted Wade from the room.

Robison found two minor abrasion wounds to both forearms, where Juan had attempted to deflect the bullets. The third entrance wound was to the upper left quadrant of the abdomen and it was bleeding profusely. She packed the wound to slow the bleeding as best she could. Next she scrubbed the arm wounds, and applied an antiseptic followed by bandages. These wouldn't need any further attention tonight.

"We need to move him to...perhaps the kitchen. Someplace that has a large table and plenty of light. I'm going to operate as soon as the supplies arrive. I'll also need sterile water and clean white cloths."

In Spanish, Carlos relayed her demands to the guards. He summoned the kitchen maid to boil water and get the cloths. Robison heard the helicopter taking off from the helipad; Donadio was on his way to Santo Domingo to purchase the supplies. She hoped he would make it back before it was too late.

While waiting, a conciliatory Carlos asked, "Is he going to be okay?"

"I think so. Much depends on whether you get me the items on the list. And quickly, I might add. Then I'll have to locate the bullet and remove it. An x-ray machine would help, but that seems out of the question. At least I'll be digging around for only one bullet. By the way, what's his name?"

Carlos knelt beside his father. "Juan is his first name. Juan Alvarez." Stroking his father's head, he added, "I'm assuming you will do your best when you're digging around for that bullet. I wouldn't want to see anything happen to such a beautiful woman."

Consumed with thoughts of Wade's safety, she ignored Carlos' attempt at flattery. Being unaccustomed to rejection, he made another bid as he walked over to the bar and asked, "Can I get you a drink or something?"

"I don't think you want your father's surgeon under the influence at a time like this," she snapped as she paced back and forth. "After I operate, I'll be on my way. You *did* let Wade go, didn't you?"

Carlos smiled slyly, poured himself a scotch…neat, saluted her with his drink…then gulped it down in one motion. Carlos liked a challenge, especially when it came from a desirable woman.

She stopped pacing and raised her voice insistently. "I said you *did* let my husband go, didn't you?"

Refilling his empty glass; he turned, and charmingly said, "But of course, Madam Doctor. Anything you say…"

ELEVEN

By three o'clock in the morning, the cast and crew had rehearsed an entire run-through, and Ty was having a meeting with all department heads beside the rink. The wardrobe room was bedlam as skaters sought last-minute alterations before the opening performance. Patience was in short supply.

Looking at the choreographer, Ty said, "We had a couple rough spots, but I think it'll be fine." Next he turned to the exhausted stagehands. "Good job as always, guys. I'll go over some lighting notes later, but there's no use getting into all of that right now when everyone is beat. Go have a couple of beers on me and get some shut-eye." He handed them a wad of pesos to pay for the beer. Conveniently, the corner bar would be open all night.

As a second thought, Ty said, "Don't forget to include the wardrobe women. Hopefully, the skaters are satisfied by now. But some tend to go on and on, like the whole world revolves around them."

Raúl told Ty how wonderful the run-through had gone. The rehearsal had dazzled him, for he lacked the trained eye to see the little mistakes that kept the show from running "smooth as silk." But Ty had put Raúl to work, which made him feel special. As interpreter for the lighting director, Raúl translated the lighting changes into Spanish. Before Raúl came along, by the time the lighting director had chosen his foreign words, the cue was long past due.

Swept up by the aura of show business, Raúl now considered himself an expert lighting director...even though he'd been at the job less than two hours. Ty allowed Raúl to live his fantasy—so long as the job got done. The savvy Ty chuckled as Raúl called all his friends and family to boast about his exciting new career in show business.

"You know what they call lighting directors, don't you?" Ty asked Raúl.

"Do they have a special name?"

"They're L. D.'s," Ty said, slapping Raúl on the back. "So let's go get a beer, L. D."

Raúl gave Ty a thumbs-up. He quickly climbed the steps of the amphitheater, and then headed to the bar with Ty.

111

"Yes, Señor Ty, since I am an insider now, could you just tell me how the magician makes that girl in the gold costume…umm…disappear? How does he do this?"

Ty laughed, shaking his head. "Sorry, L. D., I'm sworn to secrecy. But try to figure it out. You'll have plenty of chances to watch it while you're giving the lighting cues."

"I'll try my best, Señor Ty."

"At which? The lighting cues or the magic tricks?"

Raúl smiled, "Oh, both things!"

Ty laughed out loud.

"Really, I am serious. I am going to figure everything out, you will see."

⌒ᘉᘉᘏ

When Donadio returned with medical supplies, Juan lay naked upon the kitchen table, covered by a sheet. He had not regained consciousness.

"I need something to tie my hair back," Robison said to Carlos.

He mumbled something in Spanish to the maid, who soon returned with a fabric covered pony tail holder and some large bobby pins. Robison gathered her long, silky blonde hair, and brought the ponytail upwards, off her neck. She then laid out the supplies on the sideboard to see what she had to work with. Some of the instruments were quite rudimentary, but they would have to make do. Surely they were better than trying to operate with a kitchen knife and ice cube tongs!

"Tell the maid to boil these instruments in water, pronto!" Robison said, handing them to Carlos. He followed her instructions, seeming to respect her professionalism…and charisma. She went to the sink and washed her hands with hot, soapy water.

Walking around Juan, she began talking as if she were speaking to her staff. "Juan is diaphoretic and he is extremely pale. Respirations are labored at thirty-six." She held his wrist and checked her watch once again. "His pulse is one-sixty and barely palpable."

"What does that mean?" Carlos asked anxiously.

112

"It means he's going into shock. He's lost a lot of blood, as you know." Robison checked his pupils; they were pinpoint, consistent with the shock state.

"What is taking you so long?" Carlos growled. "You've checked his eyes and pulse a hundred goddamned times!"

"You're in my arena now. Be quiet!" she said irritably. "Bring that oxygen tank over here, if you want to be useful."

It was challenging enough, to operate without any professional medical assistance and now she had lusty Carlos breathing down her neck. God help her! At least Wade was out of this miserable place.

Applying a mask to Juan's nose and mouth, she began administering oxygen. She grimaced at the outdated anesthesia machine. She enlisted Donadio to help her get it in place, praying it still worked. The maid reappeared with the sterile instruments in the pan of hot water.

"Tell her to put the pan down over there on the table," Robison ordered Carlos.

Spreading out one of the sanitized cloths and using a disinfected pair of tongs, Robison lined up the instruments in the order she would need them during surgery. All the while, she was contemplating how she was going to accomplish this alone. She needed an assistant for this type of surgery, but she'd tackle that shortcoming later.

Robison managed to concoct a rapid infusion system with a bag of saline solution and a blood pressure cuff. She took a few minutes to ponder her course. Walking over to the sink, she scrubbed her arms and hands once again and motioned for the maid to do the same. Then the maid helped Robison put on a pair of sterile rubber gloves.

Once Robison had reestablished an acceptable blood pressure with intravenous resuscitation, she started a small amount of nitrous gas. Leaning over the instruments, she retrieved a Bard Parker blade.

Turning to her patient, she said, "Okay, here we go! Anyone faint of heart better leave the room, because I don't have time to deal with someone else once I start. And, by the way, I'll need someone to hand me instruments and things."

Carlos translated and two of the guards opted to leave. Robison smiled; they must have been "faint of heart."

"I guess I'll have to assist you," Carlos said. "I seem to be the only one left."

"Then go scrub and hurry up! All the way to your elbows."

The increasingly compliant Carlos grimaced a bit, but kept his mouth shut. He had little choice, if he was to save his father. What a convoluted dilemma!

Taking a deep breath, she opened the abdomen in one smooth slice…and was met by a flood of dark, warm blood.

"Oh, my God!" Carlos exclaimed, turning away from the table.

"Don't faint on me now. Hand me those pads," she ordered.

Steadying himself, Carlos produced the pads as directed.

She quickly packed all four quadrants. Once Juan's blood pressure stabilized, she carefully removed the packing from the other three quadrants and exposed the injured site. She recognized a typical spleen injury after removing the last pack.

"How are you doing?" she asked Carlos without looking at him.

"I'm trying not to look or breathe," he said, meekly. "The smell makes me want to vomit."

"Think about something else," she suggested. "Your horse, perhaps. The beautiful animal you ride so well. In any case, *do not* vomit on this table. Leave the room if you have to."

"So, you remember watching me ride by your villa?" he asked egotistically.

"Actually, I was watching the horse," she lied. How could she have acted so school girlish that day? Thoughts that she may have been thrilled at the sight of Carlos now made her ill.

She clamped and cut the vessels feeding the spleen. When the bleeding was under control, she was ready to remove the organ.

"Hand me that saucepan from the stove," she instructed.

Carlos translated to the maid, who nervously brought the pan over and held it out.

"Hold still," she said to the maid. Carlos interpreted.

"What is the pan for?" Carlos asked.

"I'm going to throw his spleen in it," Robison said nonchalantly, without taking her eyes off her work.

Robison had the spleen out in a matter of minutes and dropped it into the pan. They heard the ring of metal on metal when the organ hit the bottom and sloshed around.

"Well, there's your bullet," she said.

She turned in time to see Carlos hit the floor with a thud....He was out cold! There was no time to bother with him; she let him lie there.

For a fleeting moment, she thought of bolting out the kitchen door, but there was no way she could leave a patient lying with his abdomen wide open. She went back to the work at hand. After further inspection, she discovered a through-and-through injury to Juan's stomach, which she repaired and finished by suturing the wound.

In the meantime, the maid had placed a rolled-up towel under Carlos' head. When she found time, Robison placed a wet cloth on his forehead. He muttered something in Spanish, so he was coming around. She took a certain delight in saying under her breath, "Maybe the fall knocked some sense into him!" It was incredible to think that this egomaniac had once turned her head—if only for a moment.

She and the maid cleaned up, washed the surgical instruments, and wiped down the table and counters. Every few minutes Robison would stop and check Juan's vital signs. So far so good! She couldn't in all good conscience leave her patient just yet, even though she was anxious to join Wade and the Winsteads back at the villa.

Carlos finally made it back to the land of the living, with one hell of a headache and a lump on the back of his head. At his insistence, Robison probed the spot and informed him he would be fine.

"Take two aspirins for your headache," she said coldly. She could barely be civil to him.

Two guards had escorted Wade from the brutal scene in Juan's office. While Robison thought—hoped!—they had released him, they actually held him in the living room area of the house where they waited for further instructions from Carlos. Wade alternated between pacing the floor and sitting in various chairs around the room. He tried talking to the guards, but they weren't listening, much less comprehending. He couldn't be sure whether they didn't understand English or if they simply weren't allowed to talk. The few magazines on the coffee table were all in Spanish, but of sheer boredom Wade browsed through them anyway.

Three hours had passed when Carlos finally entered the room. He walked briskly towards Wade. He'd changed out of the blood-soaked shirt and now wore a T-shirt. Besides looking pale, his worry and apprehension were obvious to Wade.

Carlos took a long drag on his cigarette. "Okay, here is the deal. I'm not going to let you go; however…"

Wade jumped up from his chair. "You *are* going to let me go!" he shouted. "That was the deal! Where is my wife?"

Two guards lunged towards Wade, but Carlos raised his hand for them to back off. He blew smoke into the air and continued, "I'm not going to let you go…*yet*. However, I want you to stay in the small guesthouse we have on the property. Surely you understand I can't release you until I know that your wife…excuse me, the doctor, has performed the proper procedures on my father. I need to verify that he will make a full recovery. Even *you* must be intelligent enough to figure that out. Therefore, you will be my *guest* here. Fair enough?"

That Wade would be a "guest" didn't seem all that unreasonable, at least he wouldn't be a prisoner! He began nodding his head at Carlos. Perhaps this would work out for him and Robison after all.

"Surely you understand my predicament," Carlos continued in a reasonable tone. "My father is running for the presidency and no one must know that his mistress shot him." He took another drag on his cigarette. "I must add one thing: you will have guards at all times, so escape is quite out of the question. Of course, you wouldn't do anything stupid enough to jeopardize your wife's safety, now would you?"

On second thought…maybe Wade was a prisoner. But…how long could it last? A few hours, a day perhaps? No problem.

"Has she performed the surgery yet?" he asked.

"No, she is getting ready right now," Carlos lied.

If Wade thought the operation was over, he would want to leave…and with his wife! Well, that wasn't going to happen now…or ever.

Carlos had to plan a way to get rid of Wade and Robison when they were no longer useful. He would arrange an "accident," but the "accident" couldn't happen until Juan was a whole lot better than he was at the moment—lying on the kitchen table barely alive!

Wade watched Carlos' every move. He put out his cigarette in the ashtray and immediately reached for another. Without another word, Carlos walked to the door, and motioned for Wade to exit in front of him. Nudged by a guard, Wade went through the doorway and into another room with sliding glass doors leading out onto the pool deck. The guesthouse was secluded by flowering oleanders and swaying palm trees. It provided a breathtaking view of the ocean rippling in the moonlight. But Wade couldn't enjoy the ambience, because Robison wasn't there.

At the guesthouse, Wade was ushered inside, but the guards stayed outside. Wade looked about: two bedrooms, two bathrooms, kitchen, den and library. Making his way to the kitchen, he looked in the refrigerator and plucked out an ice-cold beer. He opened it and took a big swallow. After a few minutes, he decided to stretch out on the couch in the den and let his thoughts drift.

Robison would be joining him after she completed the "bullet removal." Presumably, both would be released and they would go back to the villa to resume their vacation. For all of about two minutes, he felt guilty about closing his eyes....But what else was there to do? Sleep soon overtook his indecisiveness.

Carlos returned to the main house with his right-hand man, Donadio. "Are you going to let him just wander around in the guesthouse?" Donadio asked his boss in Spanish.

"Why the hell not? If he thinks he's a captive, he'll try to escape for sure. On the other hand, if he thinks he is just waiting until his wife finishes her job, he'll be a much more agreeable prisoner."

"Very clever. But what about Bibí? Your mother will be arriving soon from Miami to care for Señor Juan."

Carlos glanced around before whispering to Donadio. "I'm going to get rid of the bitch once and for all.... What I want you to do is..."

His ringing cell phone interrupted the instructions. "¿Bueno?"

"You two-timing son-of-a-bitch! Did you really think you could get away with exchanging the real necklace for a fake one?" Luís snarled.

"I don't have your necklace. I don't know what you are talking about. You heard the guy...the expert...it's a fake. So take my advice and go back home. We have nothing more to say to each other." Carlos clicked off his cell phone.

Carlos regretted he hadn't looked at the incoming number before he'd answered it. He didn't normally answer calls without recognizing the number first. All this chaos had caught him off guard.

The phone began ringing again, so Carlos turned it off completely. He would change his number tomorrow so Luís, his slime-ball cousin, couldn't reach him. Carlos knew Luís was in over his head in a foreign country, playing way out of his league, so Carlos had the edge. Just as planned!

"Donadio, forget about Bibí for the moment. I have another thorn in my side I need you to deal with."

"Who, boss?"

"My cousin, Luís. I think he may be staying at one of the hotels here at the resort. Look on my cell phone, the number is probably still on it. I'll just get a new phone tomorrow."

"How do you want me to do it? And when?"

"Find him. Or them! He has a girlfriend with him. Felicity is her name. Take care of them both...permanently...the sooner, the better."

After three hours of post-op vigilance Dr. Murphy let them move Juan off the kitchen table, not the most comfortable place for a patient.

Daylight was breaking when they finally settled him into bed. Robison checked Juan's "vitals" one more time and was encouraged enough so that she could leave for the villa in good conscience. There was no fever and his blood pressure was good. Robison breathed a sigh of relief.

A guard held the bedroom door for her as she left Juan's room. She felt relieved to be getting out of this place and back to Wade. In fact, even though she had been up all night, she thought she could still make their tee time. It would definitely be a new way of getting the guys to give her more shots! "Dead tired due to surgery." That should be worth at least...two more shots a side, she mused.

What a night! What thugs! She smiled, thinking this would be the last time she'd let Brianne make any foreign vacation plans. After this disaster, a bed and breakfast no farther away than Georgia would suffice.

As Robison headed down the hall towards the winding staircase leading to the front door, Carlos grabbed her arm, forcing her through a nearby doorway into another room.

"What are you doing?" Robison shouted. "I'm going back to my villa! That was the deal!"

"Yeah, right! So you can go to the authorities or the newspaper?" Carlos asked sarcastically as he shoved her into a guest bedroom.

He drew her closer to him; she could smell the alcohol on his breath. Robison struggled. Carlos tried to kiss her, but she broke free and slapped him hard across the face. He threw back his head, laughing. Then he turned, grabbed the door handle and slammed it shut behind him. She heard the key turn in the lock.

What the hell was going on?

She looked around the room...this couldn't be happening! She started to cry hopeless sobs of exasperation. Without any tears left, Robison sat on the bed and leaned back on the pillow as thoughts whirled through her head.

Perhaps they were detaining her until Juan regained his strength. But what about Wade? He would be sick with worry when she didn't return to the villa right away. On the other hand, maybe he'd gotten away and would no doubt be back with the police any minute now.

Since she'd been up all night, and with the stress of operating with archaic instruments and on a goddamned kitchen table no less, Robison was past the point of exhaustion. Seeing a nightgown the maid had left on the bed, Robison opted for a long, hot shower. She grabbed the nightgown, went into the bathroom, and started the water running.

So many thoughts were running through her mind, it was hard for her to make sense of any of it. Why hadn't Wade come back for her? Finally concluding she was too tired to think, she decided sleep would probably help her more than anything else. No! ...Snap out of it! It was time to get the hell out of here! This was a dangerous place with dangerous people. Being torn between possible solutions made clear thinking impossible for Robison.

While toweling herself off and slipping into the nightgown, she caught the aroma of food. Sure enough, a tray of hot tea and sweet

119

rolls had been placed on the small table by the bed. The food smelled delicious. She never realized how good a sweet roll could taste.

On a whim she checked the door—still locked.

Someone had turned the covers back. Settling between cool, clean sheets, would enable her to plan an escape after some much needed sleep—if Wade had not shown up by then.

Dead tired, Robison crawled into bed and soon began to doze.

What was that?

Robison sat up. A strange noise! Perhaps it was Wade, but then…the sound was more like a moan.

Her heart was beating so hard, it felt like it was going to fly right out of her chest. Pounding…pounding. The blood was pulsating through her veins, creating a vibrating sensation in her ears. She concentrated very hard, tried to listen…. Hearing nothing more, she reclined on the pillow again.

She chastised herself; this was ridiculous, she should just go to sleep. She fluffed the pillow, and closed her eyes.

There it was again…a moan…or…weeping.

It sounded like a woman, perhaps in the room next door. This time she listened intently. The noise was coming from the direction of the bathroom. Getting up, she walked into the lavatory; standing by the sink, her knees felt as weak as two wet noodles.

Another muffled sound…. A sick moaning…. Oh, God, what next?

In the reflection of the mirror, she noticed another door that must lead into an adjoining bedroom. Cautiously, she twisted the bathroom door handle and opened the door.

The room was dark.

Robison stood still…listening.

Nothing…she heard nothing. She hesitated, at first, but then slowly stepped into the room.

"Hmmm…hmmm." A woman, gagged and tied up was sitting on the floor, in the corner. Robison saw that her eyes were swollen almost shut. Blood dripped from her mouth. Numerous other cuts had crusted over with dried blood. She looked up with terror in her eyes as Robison approached.

"Shhh,…I'm a doctor," Robison whispered. "I can help you."

Robison crouched down, and managed to remove the gag from her mouth. Next, she untied the woman's hands, and worked the rope off of her ankles. Robison helped her to the bed and put some pillows under her head. In the bathroom, Robison ran cool water on small towels to clean this poor woman up. Although Robison was gentle, the woman winced in pain. After a cursory examination, Robison concluded there were no broken bones or serious injuries.

"Do you speak English?"

Weakly she answered, "Sí,...yes. My name is, Bibí." She hesitated. "Are you the doctor Carlos brought here for his father?"

"Yes," Robison answered.

"You must get out of here." She continued, "They will kill both of us. I am a dead woman, but you may still be able to save yourself."

"Why would they kill me?" Robison asked. "And anyway, Carlos and I have a deal. He let my husband go, so I should be leaving soon."

Bibí ignored her comment. "I am the one who accidentally shot Juanito. He is a very important but dangerous man. His son, Carlos, is a madman. But he loves his father. So he will kill me as soon as he has a chance. Is Juanito going to live?"

Robison didn't know what to say; after all, Bibí had just admitted to shooting "Juanito."

"Well, I took the bullet out," Robison said. "And, unless he develops some kind of infection, he should be fine."

"I shot three times. He only took one bullet?"

"Yes. Thank goodness you're not a very good shot."

Robison went back to her room, then returned with a cup of hot tea and a sweet roll for Bibí. She wolfed it down and asked for another. Revived somewhat, Bibí continued their conversation. "Let me guess...Carlos promised that if Juan lives he will let you,...how do you say? ...let you go lickety-split?"

"That's right!" Robison assured her. Carlos promised to let me go if Juan lived. He already let my husband go, like I said. Carlos promised."

"Wrong! Don't be a stupid bitch! Do you think Carlos will let you or your husband go, when you could tell anyone about this? The scandal of all scandals? Juanito is the Minister of Finance, he's also running for president, you know, and I'm his mistress. And getting

121

shot by his mistress doesn't fit into that scenario at all. Don't you see now? You will both end up dead, whether Juan lives or not. You better get the hell out of here!"

"How could I escape alone in broad daylight?" Robison asked. "Why don't you come with me? We will escape together! Perhaps then we'll have a chance."

"Let me rest for a few minutes," Bibí said weakly. "By tonight, I'll have the strength to escape. Then we will go. Better to leave at night, when it's dark." Bibí closed her eyes, letting her head fall back upon the pillow.

Robison went back to her room. Taking stock of the situation, she quickly came to the conclusion it was imperative she get out of this place fast, even if it had to be in broad daylight. Everything Bibí had said made sense. And if Bibí was right, Wade was probably confined somewhere on the premises, but she dare not risk searching for him. Her best bet was to escape and go for help alone. Still…she hoped to find that Wade had been let go.

Changing back into her clothes, Robison quietly checked Bibí's outside bedroom door. It was unlocked. Robison guessed with Bibí's feet tied, they saw no reason to lock it. Seeing no one, Robison slipped silently down the hall, hurried down the long staircase and out the front door as if she owned the place. Where was everyone? All of this security and she had walked right out. Lucky her!

Running as fast as her legs could carry her, Robison came upon the guard posted at the end of the long driveway. He was in his little guardhouse reading a magazine. She surveyed the fence nearby, hoping to climb over it, but it was too high. She had to pass the guard; there was no other way out.

She hid in the bushes nearby, until she heard a car coming down the street. As it slowed to turn into the driveway, the guard stood up and went outside to chat with the driver. His back was to her now.

This was her chance. Run, girl,…run!

Ducking underneath the wooden arm that stretched across the driveway, she made it to the other side of the road just as the car started to pull away and the guard went back into his little house.

Apparently he'd heard something, because he called out, "Who's there?"

She pushed herself backward as far as she could into the vegetation growing up the high fence. Trying desperately not to be obvious, she held her breath and didn't move a muscle.

"Who is there? Anybody?"

An agonizing moment crept by...then he went back inside, sat down and picked up his magazine. His back was to her, but he was squirming around. She waited.

After a few minutes, she slid inconspicuously down the wall and out of the guard's immediate sight. She began running up the road...faster...she needed to go faster!

She had to get to the villa.

Finding Wade and getting off this island were her only thoughts.

Thank God, they could fly out on Tom's plane as soon as they could get to the airport. Forget packing; they needed to just get the hell out of here!

Robison finally came to the road leading to the villa. Now she slowed to a walk, trying not to appear out of the ordinary. Her thigh muscles were burning. She made a mental note to get into better shape once she returned home. Rounding the corner, she spotted the guard at the entrance to their cul-de-sac.

Safety...safety.

Cars were speeding up and down the road; life seemed normal all around her.

She took up a casual gait, trying to catch her breath as she approached the guard. Robison was so relieved she wore a big smile, as she brushed her blonde hair back out of her eyes. She was almost there!

"Señora, it is very dangerous to be out alone," the guard cautioned.

"Yes, I know. Thank you. I'm just in a hurry to get to my villa, if you don't mind."

He put his arm up and stopped her. "I will need to see your key."

"You don't understand; I don't have my key." Robison felt her composure slipping away. "I lost my purse. Just call the villa if you need to or the front office and ask for Angelisa."

"Okay." He stepped inside and dialed a number.

Robison was exhausted, impatient and scared, and she thought he was taking too long to call. Something wasn't right! Suddenly panicked, she started to dart. He grabbed her by the arm, and hauled her back.

"Stop it! Let me go!" she yelled out. "Help me! Someone…please…help me!"

A car approached at high speed.

Thank God; now he'd have to let her go to tend to this vehicle.

The car screeched to a halt. All four car doors opened at once.

Carlos stepped out, followed by his guards.

The guards hustled her into the backseat screaming and struggling. "You bastards…. You filthy bastards!" she yelled, half crying. "Help me! Somebody… help me!"

The car jerked backward, with doors slamming shut. It turned around, tires squealing, and sped back to the estate.

After passing the guard gate through which she'd just escaped, they slowly pulled up to the front door. Donadio yanked her out of the car. She was kicking, screaming and clawing at Donadio's face. One guard held her while Donadio tied her hands. They pushed her roughly forward. Carlos led the way, ignoring the chaos behind him.

"First, we are going to my father's room. I'm sure the beautiful doctor wants to check up on her patient. Doesn't she?" he stated sarcastically.

"I don't give a rat's ass about you or your father," she said defiantly.

Carlos spun around in the hallway, just at the foot of the staircase. "It would be in your best interest to give more than a rat's ass of concern, believe me. Your life may depend on it."

"I'd rather be dead."

"Clearly, I can accommodate your preference, but I still require your services while my father recuperates," he said coldly. His mind was no longer clouded by romantic yearnings. Carlos started up the stairs; the guards and Robison followed.

They entered through the large double doors at the end of the hallway. Carlos shoved her rudely towards the bed where Juan was sleeping. In open rebellion she simply stood there.

"Check him out," Carlos ordered. She said nothing and made no attempt to examine Juan. Carlos crossed the room. "I said look at him!"

"He's sleeping," she replied in a sarcastic monotone.

"I can see that much for myself, you bitch!" he yelled, slapping her hard across the face. She fell to the floor, hitting her head on the tile.

Everything went black.

TWELVE

Brianne awoke to the sounds of the maid rattling the breakfast dishes in the dining room. Tom was already in the shower. Forty minutes later, she emerged from the bedroom dressed and ready for a day of golf; Tom was standing out by the pool, alone.

Brianne decided to knock on the Murphy's bedroom door to make sure they were up and moving. It was getting late and she'd noticed their two coffee cups were still sitting on the tray untouched, not to mention that Robison was usually the first one up.

"Hey, are you guys up yet?" There was no answer so she knocked again. Still no response. Thinking they might have gotten up early and gone for a ride, she walked over to the front door and checked the carport. Both golf carts were there. She went back and knocked again.

"Hey, sleepyheads, it's almost tee time." Still no response. Brianne went out to the pool. "Tom, have you seen Wade?"

"No, I haven't seen either of them. But come to think of it, someone came to the door late last night needing a doctor, so perhaps Robison is doing her 'doctor' routine."

"I find that difficult to believe. Surely there's a hospital near by." Brianne turned and marched over to Murphy's bedroom. She turned the knob, and slowly opened the door. Their bed hadn't been slept in and their clothes from the day before were still lying on the bed.

"Looks like they didn't come home last night," Tom ventured as he peeked over her shoulder.

"Yeah, well, it's odd to say the least."

"Look, she may have had some emergency," Tom rationalized. "If Wade didn't know our number here he couldn't call...I bet they plan on meeting us at the golf course, so let's eat and go hit some practice balls."

Brianne looked worried all the same. "I don't have a good feeling about this," she said.

"Look, honey, if anything were wrong, one of them would have found a way to contact us. Since we haven't heard anything, we have to assume everything is fine. Let's just go and have a good time. After all, we only have one more day."

Brianne kissed him. "You're right, dear. Doctors have emergencies come up all the time," she agreed. "I'm just being silly, I guess. Let's go."

"Yeah, let's relax and enjoy another day of golfing in the tropics," Tom added.

"Well, I'd enjoy our day in the tropics a lot more…if we were all together."

Wade stopped his pacing and picked up the phone in the guesthouse, on the outside chance he could call out. The line was dead.

There was plenty of food, drinks and wine in the kitchen, but other than looking out at the beautiful view of the ocean and the swaying palm trees, he could either pace or sit around. Television programs were all in Spanish and limited to soap operas, at that. Too bad there weren't any football games, or soccer; even cartoons would have been better than Spanish soap operas.

All the books in the small library were in Spanish, too. On a table beside one of the winged-backed chairs was a checker set, but Wade had already played himself at checkers for hours. Out of frustration Wade grabbed the bottom edge of the game, flinging the checkerboard and pieces across the room. When it hit the wall of books, the pieces went flying in every direction. Back at the window, he watched the salt water crash against the boulder that was the helipad. Once he had thought he could never tire of this fantastic view, but now he was beginning to fucking hate it. He nervously ran his hands through his hair to smooth it back. "God!" he roared. "I'm going stir crazy!"

He sat down on the couch, tapped his fingers on the armrest and stood back up.

What's taking her so long? It's almost two in the afternoon! Operate and let's get the hell out of here!

Finally, completely exasperated by being kept in the dark about Juan's condition, or to be more specific, information about Robison and their eventual departure, Wade decided to make some inquiries. He opened the front door. Immediately a guard with a gun in his hand turned to face him. Wade raised his hands. "I only want to ask a question, for God's sake."

The guard shook his head. "No hablo inglés."

Oh, just fucking fabulous! He got a guard that didn't speak any English!

Wade tried again. "Carlos,...I (pointing to himself) want to see (pointing to his eyes) Carlos. Understand?"

The guard shrugged his shoulders and looked at Wade like he was crazy. Then he turned around and stood there in front of the door turning his back on Wade. Wade slammed the door as hard as he could, then went over and kicked the couch—hard! Having had his temper tantrum, Wade reclined in a chair...his toes began to throb. Resting his arms behind his head, he stared up at the ceiling.

This was getting ridiculous. Robison would have performed the surgery last night. The old coot should be out of the woods by now. What if, God forbid, he didn't recover? ...No, he would have heard about that. If Juan had died, it would have caused a big commotion.

But how much longer could he just sit here and do nothing? He needed to see Robison....Was she okay? More importantly, they needed to get the hell out of here....He was going to insist that they leave the island as soon as they were released. Tom and Brianne would just have to accept that.

God, he missed her! If he could only see Robison, hold her in his arms, protect her...save her. What kind of a man was he? Just sitting here doing nothing wasn't cutting it.

Ultimately Wade decided if they hadn't been released by later that night, he'd break out of the guesthouse and sneak into the main house. He would break in, get Robison, and get the hell out of Dodge! He would take a nap now and get up in the middle of the night to carry out his scheme.

On second thought, perhaps he was being hasty planning to break into the main house and get Robison. He needed to take a day to see what opportunities for escape he could find and then have a go at it the following night. Yes, he needed to scope out the "lay of the land." If he broke into the main house and didn't know where to go next, it would be disastrous! Wade needed a good plan...a detailed plan. Closing his eyes once again...he was soon in la-la land.

◡ ૨ ᠭ ᠊ᴜ

Paired with another couple, Tom and Brianne finished their round of golf. The starter had arranged the foursome when the Murphys didn't show up. After the last putt on the eighteenth green, they shook hands and went to their respective golf carts. Neither Tom nor Brianne played very well; in fact, they were pitiful. Their minds weren't on golf, and they didn't want to discuss the crisis in front of strangers. Not only were they just going through the motions, but both wanted the game to be over. And wouldn't you know it; the round lasted almost five hours. It was excruciating. Even the effervescent Brianne was solemn, something that seldom happened.

"I hope the Murphys are at the villa," Tom said, as their cart passed the pro shop, the practice green, and out onto the main road. Approaching the villa, they could see the other golf cart had not moved. They walked in and Brianne immediately looked in the Murphy's bedroom. Nothing had changed! The maid and butler were gone...Tom and Brianne were all alone. The solitude made them uncomfortable...panicky!

"So now can I start to worry?" Brianne asked Tom as she came out of Robison's bedroom.

Tom glanced at his watch. It was four o'clock. "I think I'll call Angelisa," Tom said as he picked up the receiver on the table and dialed.

"Hello, this is Angelisa."

"Yes, this is Tom Winstead."

"What can I do for you, Sr. Winstead?"

"Well, this may seem a bit odd, but we can't find our friends. They didn't come home from the El Pescador last night and then later some Spanish guys came to our door looking for a doctor."

"A doctor?"

"Well, yes, Mrs. Murphy is a doctor. Anyway, we haven't seen them since dinner last night. Do you have any ideas?"

"Well...is the golf cart there?"

"Yes."

"Hmmm...perhaps they decided on a romantic getaway after attending to the patient. Although we have had no information of anyone requesting a doctor, I will ask around. We have guards everywhere; if something had happened, we would know about it. Anyway, don't worry, at least not yet. Try to enjoy the rest of your vacation. I'll check back with you tomorrow…or if I learn anything."

"Thank you, I'll wait to hear from you."

Brianne asked, "What did she say?"

"She said not to worry. They might be on a 'romantic' get-a-way." He crossed his legs, removed his glasses and rubbed his eyes; clearly he was deep in thought.

"Shit!" she exclaimed. "Romantic get-a-way my ass! Something's wrong…very wrong!"

Tom put his glasses back on. "It's definitely time to worry," he said.

"But what can we do?"

"Well, for starters we need to cancel our dinner reservations at the Casa del Río and reserve a table back at the El Pescador," Tom said. "Maybe we can piece the puzzle together. Remember, they went to the art market afterwards, so we'll head there. We'll ask around and see if anybody saw anything unusual."

"Okay. I'll call the Casa del Río," Brianne said. She also called the El Pescador to reserve a table for four. She was being optimistic; Tom frowned, but didn't say anything. Wouldn't it be great if Robison and Wade did show up?

"Another problem though," Tom added. "We play golf tomorrow early in the morning and then we're supposed to leave. We'll have to check out before we go to play…*if* we play. If they haven't shown up by morning, we need to think about packing up their clothes."

"Pack up their clothes? How can you sit there and be so nonchalant about all of this?"

"We can't leave their things here, can we?"

"Nor can we just leave Wade and Robison here!" Brianne retorted.

"But we have no choice about getting out of this villa. A new couple comes in tomorrow," he said. "I've already checked on extending our stay, but it's booked solid."

Brianne sat down on the couch beside him. He put his arm around her and held her…she started to cry. Something very bad had happened…they could feel it in their bones.

"Let's go shower and get going," Tom said after a while. "Sitting here moping isn't going to change anything. Or help find them."

"Tom, what if we don't find them and it's time for us to leave? Seriously, we can't just leave without them!"

"Let's not get ahead of ourselves yet," he replied. "They may walk in the door at any moment."

Walking towards the bedroom, Brianne turned and said, "Tom,…I love you."

He smiled, "I love you, too."

"I'm scared…and I just want you to know."

"Honey, I know. Try not to worry. Everything will work out fine, I'm sure."

Tom wished he could believe his own words, but doing so was getting more difficult with every passing minute.

The house lights in the amphitheater went out…right on cue. The musical overture began while the ice-skaters took their opening positions on the ice during the blackout.

"Ladies and Gentlemen, Kelly Productions is proud to present…"

The amphitheater was full. Opening night had been pre-sold to a large banking corporation in Santo Domingo, which gave the tickets to their wealthiest customers and stellar employees. The show would open to the public tomorrow night.

Before the show began, Ty had a request from the bank board. The president of the bank wanted to give a short speech and present a few company awards during the fifteen-minute intermission. Ty arranged for a microphone to be available backstage. He also alerted the skaters not to get ready until he called "five minutes." Ty suspected there would be other speakers besides the bank president, which might increase the intermission time to thirty minutes. In that case the skaters could take off their skates and rest their feet.

From all indications, the show was off to a great start! The hard work and attention to detail was paying off.

Robison opened her eyes to the sound of muffled voices. Staying perfectly still, she tried to look around without moving her head. Slowly things were coming into focus. Recognizing the intricate molding around the high ceiling, she assumed she was back in the same bedroom as before. This time, however, she was lying on the floor at the foot of the bed with her hands tied.

Slowly, she managed to get up. By the way her head was pounding; she knew she had a concussion. Robison made her way to the door, but as she expected…it was locked.

Bursting into tears, she turned and leaned back against the door. Totally deflated now, she slid down and slumped to the floor. Her situation was absolutely hopeless.

Wade…where was he? Why hadn't he come back for her?

She tumbled over sideways and now lay in fetal position against the door, sobbing.

Several hours must have gone by when she again opened her eyes. The room was dark. She struggled to get up and make her way to the edge of the bed. She was a zombie!

Robison didn't respond to a light knock on the door. If they wanted her, they could just bust the door down and come in. So why should she accommodate them with manners? For that matter, why were they even taking the time to knock?

Another knock…but Robison said nothing.

She heard the key turn in the door…and it slowly opened.

It was the meek little kitchen maid bringing her some soup. The same little maid who had assisted her in surgery and did a mighty fine job taking over after Carlos hit the deck.

She put the tray of food down on the dresser and turned on the light.

Robison took heart. "¿Como se llama? What is your name?" she asked.

The maid replied, "Maria."

"Maria, could you get my hands untied?" she asked, holding up her hands. No answer came forth, so Robison repeated the question softly. Clearly, the maid didn't understand English, but surely she would get the drift when she saw Robison's bound hands extended in front of her.

Maria looked around the room, then went over and closed the bedroom door. Quietly, she went to Robison and untied her hands.

"Gracias," Robison whispered, rubbing her wrists.

The maid went into the bathroom to straighten up the towels, as if nothing were unusual. Suddenly, the adjoining bathroom door into Bibí's room flew open. When Bibí spotted Maria standing there, she began yelling at the maid. Although Bibí spoke in Spanish, Robison could see Maria cower under the obvious insults. When the maid bolted from the bathroom Bibí flung a glass, hitting Robison's bedroom door, just as the meek girl slammed it behind her. Shards of glass flew everywhere.

Robison sat stunned, watching all this commotion coming from a woman who could hardly move a few hours before. "Why on earth did you do that? What are you thinking?" Robison inquired in a shrill voice.

"That little bitch left me lying there in that room all tied up. She never came to rescue me and she is going to pay. You'll see."

"Aren't you being a bit harsh? Carlos is the one who tied you up, and he did it because you shot his father. Hell, I'd tie you up, too!"

Bibí spun around and directed her venom at Robison. "I don't need a lecture from you, the great doctor! ...Who is too fucking stupid to know that everyone in this resort owes all they have to the great...Juan Alvarez," she sneered. "No one will help you get away. And you think you are so smart...you are nothing but a fucking idiot! A soon to be...*dead*...idiot! I had a plan to get away from here, but you couldn't wait for my help...you had to try it on your own. You stupid bitch! Now, they will be watching your every move."

With that, Bibí was out the door. Robison collapsed onto the bed crying, heaving and sobbing for what seemed hours. At last, drained of all energy, her tears subsided. She was a mess! Her face and eyes were puffed and swollen. Her nose was so stuffed up she couldn't breathe. She went into the bathroom, ran cold water on a washcloth, and buried her face in the comfort of the cool rag.

She thought about Wade but there were no tears. There was nothing...no feeling at all.

Worse...there was no hope for escape. No hope at all.

She made her way back to the bed, lay down, and placed the wet cloth on her forehead.

Then she spotted something. Warily, she reached out for the small black book on the bedside table. It was a Bible in both Spanish and English. Robison opened the Bible at random with her eyes closed. With her forefinger she pointed to a place on the page. Then she opened her eyes and read:

> Rescue me and deliver me from the hand of foreigners,
> Whose mouth speaks lying words,
> And whose right hand is a right hand of falsehood—
> *Psalm 144: 11*

With a gasp of astonishment, Robison slammed the book closed and held it to her heart. She whispered a prayer: "God, help me. Please show me the way to escape this horrid place and get back to my beloved Wade and home to Murrells Inlet. God, please…I'm begging you…please."

To survey an escape route, Wade sneaked out of the guesthouse through the back bedroom window. He made his way as close as he dared to the guard gate. Spotting the high wall, he knew if they stayed up against it the guard might not see them and they could possibly get by him undetected. This particular Barney Fife (as Tom so fondly called them) was sound asleep at his post. So tomorrow night, if the guard was a creature of habit, there might be a small window of opportunity for their escape.

Making his way back to the guesthouse and around to the other side, he checked out different ways to get into the house. Oddly enough, the least protected entrance was the front door. Satisfied with the plan he had tentatively developed, he would try implementing it the following night—if they hadn't been released in the meantime.

He climbed back through the window and into the bedroom of his "guest" quarters. He felt he had accomplished something—at least a little something. Anyway, it was better than sitting around going stir-crazy.

Wade frittered the day away, anticipating his break-in of the main house, how he would find Robison once inside, and what they would do once they had escaped. His plan would begin around one in the morning, when all was quiet in the compound.

﹋﹌

It had now become routine for a guard to come and get Robison after every meal and take her to Juan's room. Today, Juan was sitting up in bed reading the paper after finishing a bland breakfast of soft scrambled eggs.

Robison checked his blood pressure, removed the bandages, and looked at the wounds. Then she put clean dressings on his abdomen. His arm wounds were fine; they could be covered with Band-Aids. He smiled, speaking to her in Spanish. Robison smiled slightly, nodding every once in a while. Tossing the covers back, he got up to use the bathroom. He had to walk crouched over with the maid assisting him. Robison waited for their return, and tucked him in again. Then she was escorted back to her room until after lunch, when she would once again go to his bedroom to check on Juan.

She knew that Juan was getting better by the hour. In fact, he wouldn't need her medical assistance much longer. And if she could believe anything Bibí had said, she had to admit that her life, indeed, was in impending danger.

She also wondered what had happened to Bibí. She wasn't in the adjoining room any longer and Robison hadn't seen nor heard her. Was she already dead? Did Carlos kill her himself? A cold shiver ran down Robison's back, goose bumps popped up on her arms and neck.

Yes…she had to get away. And it had to be tonight!

After eating dinner, she was taken on her usual sojourn to Juan's bedroom. This time, Juan wasn't in bed, but in the adjoining sitting room talking on the telephone with a blanket over his legs. He hung up and motioned for her to come to him. Checking his wounds once again, she found everything fine.

This confirmed that he was recuperating very quickly…and with every passing minute, her time on this earth was running out. She was convinced of it. Not only that, but it was obvious they had not released Wade, because he would have come with help. Where was he?

She couldn't allow her mind to delve into any more dark possibilities. Emotional numbness and an instinct for survival were keys from here on out. She would be more cautious…a lot more cautious!

Walking back to her room with her escort, she reiterated to herself the necessity to escape sooner rather than later. It would be better to die trying than just sit here like a pig waiting for slaughter! But this time she would plan more carefully. If nothing else, she would avoid the police and guards.

∼

While Brianne was packing Wade and Robison's suitcases, tears streamed down her face. The Winsteads had canceled their morning round of golf and would be out of the villa after breakfast. Tom was talking on the phone.

"But I'm telling you, Angelisa, they aren't anywhere. We have looked everywhere."

"I know that, Sr. Winstead. And I have checked with all of our accommodations in case they decided to stay somewhere else on their own. And I have checked with all the security stations and restaurant managers. Nothing! Are you sure they didn't go home?"

"At the moment, I'm not sure about a goddamned thing, except that our tourist visas expire today. They've pulled my airplane out and are refueling it as we speak—and two of us are missing!"

Silence on the other end of the phone, as Angelisa pondered the dilemma.

"What do you want me to do, Sr. Winstead? I have checked with the police, as well. This is a small resort. They would know if something was wrong."

"Thanks! I'll be talking to you again soon, or when you get here with the shuttle." Tom closed the discussion abruptly.

As Brianne brought the Murphy's luggage out of their room, the butler hurried over to help.

"Shit, I don't know what the hell to do!" Tom said tersely.

He stood and began pacing out of frustration.

"I've been thinking that perhaps the best thing for us to do is to go back to the United States," Brianne said reflectively. "I can't

136

accomplish anything through the legal system here, especially when I can't even speak the language. Maybe I can get something going through the Senator's office in South Carolina, or the State Department. Wade and Robison have their passports and money, so they could catch a commercial flight home. It's not like they can't leave the country, you know."

"Are you sure about their passports?"

"I saw them in her purse before we left for dinner that night."

Brianne drew in a deep breath and expelled it. She felt like they were abandoning their friends, but, realistically, they had no resources to help them unless they returned to the United States.

"There's no other choice," Tom agreed. "Let's wait, though, until the last possible moment before liftoff just in case they show up at the eleventh hour."

Angelisa arrived in the van to take them to the airport. The maid scurried over to answer the doorbell and let Angelisa in. Angelisa marched right by the maid and held her hand out towards Brianne. That's when Brianne noticed she was holding Robison's purse.

"Where did you find it?" Brianne asked.

"Someone found it on the ground at the art market," Angelisa said solemnly. "That's all we know. No one saw or heard anything."

Tom stood up. "So something *has* happened!"

Angelisa quickly responded, "Well, not necessarily. Like I told you before, no one has reported anything to us or to the police. As far as we know, Robison lost her purse and someone turned it in. So what does that prove?"

Tom turned slowly and shook his head. "You're right. A recovered purse doesn't prove anything." He looked around the room, then at his watch. "We'd better get to the airport."

On the ride there, Brianne whispered to Tom, "Their passports are still in this purse. Now how will they leave?"

"I don't know, but we can't leave the purse here. That much I *do* know."

Luís and Felicity had another heated argument back at the hotel. Once again, she told him she wanted to take her chances and return to the States, retrieve the buried goods, and haul ass out of the country. But he would have none of that scheme. He no longer trusted her. She might haul ass out of the country with the money and jewels, all right, but it wouldn't be back to him in the Dominican Republic. That much he was certain of.

Of course, she didn't trust him either, so they were at a stalemate on that subject.

Luís was more determined than ever to go to the estate, break-in, and find the necklace. Felicity thought it was a ridiculous idea because the house was so big. The necklace could be anywhere. And not to mention, the place was crawling with armed security. How would he even get by the guard at the gate who had pulled the gun on him before? Not to mention all the other guards surrounding the house. What if the necklace were in Santo Domingo? Luís wasn't in any mood to listen to her opinions, and she had concluded he was a complete idiot.

Luís was well aware that his uncle was running for President; therefore he would be under heavy security and there was no doubt that Carlos was taking advantage of all the security…that lily-livered, chicken shit coward! In any case, Luís had to do something.

One way was to circumvent the guard gate by water. The only other possibility was to accost Carlos outside the estate and demand restitution. Luís decided on the first option, so he spent the better part of the day scrounging up a gun and trying to hire a make-shift boat. The gun proved a lot easier to acquire than any type of water craft. No one wanted to get too close to the Alvarez estate or near the helipad, whether in their own boat or in one they'd rented to Luís. Unfortunately, Luís had closed doors by divulging his intended destination.

Out of luck with a boat acquisition, Luís would play the "waiting game" with Carlos. Using a gun to get the necklace back or get money instead was high risk to say the least—but what other choice did they have? Without enough money to begin their long anticipated new life, and without being able to go back to the United States, Luís and Felicity would be destitute. So there was no way they could leave the estate empty handed. It was do-or-die time for Luís and Felicity!

THIRTEEN

Returning from Juan's room after his evening meal, Robison decided to take a nap while waiting for the hours to tick by. It was after midnight when she woke up, went to the bathroom, and began getting ready to escape. She opened her bedroom door, which she found unlocked, they must have concluded she'd learned her lesson about running away. Robison waited, standing quietly in the hallway, listening for any movement in the house. The only sound was her own heavy breathing.

Gathering resolve, she slipped down the curved staircase, across the foyer, and out the front door. She hid momentarily behind a tall planter beside the grand entrance and held her breath.

She waited again...no one seemed to be following her. Thank God! ...So far so good. No one had spotted her.

She was mistaken, however. Someone sitting in the dark, in the parlor off to the left of the foyer, had seen her. But the observer made no move to stop Robison.

Taking another deep breath, Robison flew down the front steps and across the driveway, creeping past the guard. This time she paid more attention to the sweeping video cameras perched all over the exterior of the house. Timing her move, she ran when they were taping in the opposite direction.

God, she had been incredibly stupid the last time she tried to escape. What had she been thinking? That she could just run down the driveway and out through the gate? Being wiser this time would surely pay off.

The moon was so bright it almost turned night into day. Still, Robison managed to hug the high wall around the mansion to remain hidden from view of the guard—if he stayed in his little guardhouse. This was not the case, however, and she heard him approaching.

Why did he have to take a goddamned walk now?

She held her breath. The guard passed so close she could have touched him, but she didn't move a muscle. Only her eyes moved, tracking his every step. The breeze began to blow the palm trees, changing what had been a dead-still night. She glanced up and saw clouds approaching the big yellow moon.

Yes. Cover it...cover it!

The clouds ultimately obscured the moon completely, making it terribly dark.

The guard walked back to his little shelter. Still waiting in the darkness, Robison felt more secure; however, he still hadn't settled down. She had no choice but to wait while the minutes ticked by at a snail's pace.

A stronger breeze began blowing, followed by the first sprinkles of a light tropical rain. She was getting wet, but there was nothing to do but wait.

Finally, he sat down. After a few minutes she saw his head bob backwards; his mouth dropped wide open. Yes...he was snoozing....This was her chance! She watched the sweeping cameras, waiting for them to turn away from her intended path. It began to rain harder, and at the opportune moment she bolted.

Running down the road she turned right on Avenida Minitas—every step taking her closer to safety. Suddenly...a car approached from behind. She ducked into the trees and foliage along the side of the road. Once the car had passed, she continued her journey. The rain was still pouring down. She wound around, ended up on Avenida Central, and knew exactly where she was. Very close to freedom!

More vehicles approached, but, thankfully none of them were Carlos and his men...so far.

Her clothes were wet and muddy. Her stomach ached, but she put that out of her mind. Now on the main road, she encountered so much traffic that dashing into the bushes every few minutes wasted precious time. It took her over an hour to make her way to the guardhouse at the entrance to their little neighborhood street. Last time it had only taken fifteen-minutes after she'd left the estate, but then she hadn't been as careful.

Not taking any chances with the snitching guard who had called Carlos previously, she walked the long way around the group of villas and down the path between the back of the house and the golf course. It was the same path she'd seen Carlos riding on that morning while she was leisurely sipping coffee...so long ago. So much had happened. How could she ever have been intrigued by someone as insidious as Carlos?

140

The closer she got to the villa, the more her mind turned towards thoughts of complete escape—thoughts of returning to Murrells Inlet. She would need the Winsteads' aid in rescuing Wade. God, she couldn't wait to see them. Then they could all get the hell out of here!

A stabbing pain in her stomach doubled her over. She paused. She tried to ignore the pain, tried to push ahead. Then she spotted the house and to her complete delight, the lights were still on.

Tears came to her eyes.

She looked around...still no one was following her. Glancing ahead to the villa, something seemed odd—too many lights for this time of night. She couldn't see her watch in the dark, but it had to be around two in the morning. Filled with excitement over the prospect of seeing the Winsteads and the thought of safety, her heart began to pound with joy.

She brushed the wet hair out of her eyes, and hurried on with renewed strength.

She heard voices, but couldn't quite make them out. Oh, God! Her legs were numb from running. She didn't want to trip and fall. "Just a little farther," she kept telling herself.

Robison stopped dead in her tracks. She listened...not moving a muscle. Something was wrong! What she was hearing?

The voices from inside the house were speaking Spanish.

Could it be Carlos and his men already? God, no!

Crouching down, she crept around the pool to look into the windows. Her heart plunged to the pit of her stomach. It wasn't Tom or Brianne, but a Spanish family. It appeared to be a mother, father and three children, one of whom was a teenage girl.

She choked back a sob. Where could her friends be? Surely they wouldn't have left without her and Wade!

With her mind whirling, Robison tried to make sense of everything she was seeing. Family members drifted into their respective bedrooms, turning off the lights as they went. It was now dark inside and the rain was still falling.

Another stabbing pain seared her stomach.

Shit! She had to lie down; she needed to rest and sort everything out. Robison crawled under the awning that was attached to the side of the patio. Hugging her chest, she tried to overcome the chill—but

141

she couldn't stop shaking. She got up; there had to be something she
could cover up with. Rummaging around the storage shed, she found
a discarded lounge chair cushion and covered her shivering body.
Lying on her side with knees drawn up, she sought to make the aching
go away. Mercifully, she soon fell asleep.

A droplet landed on Robison's forehead; startled, she sat up. A
couple of hours must have passed, but it was still dark. The rain had
stopped though Robison's neck had stiffened on one side. She ached
all over. And then she remembered where she was. She wiped her
eyes; she needed to control her emotions and get on with her escape.
If this family had been American, she might have risked trusting
them. But she had learned the hard way she could trust no one. For
all she knew, this family was associated with Juan or Carlos like
everyone else on the island.

Questions came to mind: who could she turn to now? And what
about Wade? Was he still a prisoner at the estate? There seemed
little doubt, for where else would he be?

A window by the pool was open. Since there were no screens, she
decided to chance going inside. Dry clothes might help her feel better
and look less conspicuous. Looking around the living room, she saw
some clothes thrown in a heap by the front door, a sweater over one of
the chairs and several towels strewn about.

Thank God for messy teenagers!

Rummaging through the pile by the door, she found a pair of low-
rise blue jeans, obviously the teenager's. Undressing and towel
drying her body and hair, Robison slipped the jeans on in place of her
wet, muddy skirt. They fit fairly well and would be much better than
a skirt for traveling. She put on a dry T-shirt and grabbed the sweater.
Entering the servants' toilet adjacent to the kitchen, she spotted a
toilet paper roll and decided to take it. Her stomach ached, because of
incipient diarrhea. With a splitting headache, burning eyes, and
chills, she realized she had a fever. Nonetheless, she needed to get
supplies and hightail it out of this place…now.

In the kitchen, she found a plastic grocery bag to keep the toilet
paper dry. Eating was the last thing she felt like doing at the moment,
but not knowing what her future might hold, she grabbed an apple,
some cookies, and a bottle of water. She placed those in the bag with

the toilet paper. It felt good to have dry clothes on, at least for the moment.

When she looked outside, she saw it was raining...harder. She found a plastic garbage bag, tore a hole in the bottom of it, and pulled it over her head for a makeshift poncho. At the last instant, she grabbed a small serrated knife, and concealed it in the back of her borrowed jeans. She looked at the clock glowing above the oven; it was three-thirty in the morning.

Ready to go, she made her way back through the dining room, into the living room and was about to leave when she spotted a telephone on the living room table. Slowly and quietly she picked up the receiver and dialed her home number. It was ringing...abruptly the operator came on the line: "Your credit card number, please." Startled, Robison panicked and hung up. Her head was pounding and she felt queasy—another sharp pain in her stomach! Next to the phone was one of those maps of the resort showing the way to Altos de Chavón. Yes, that's where she would go!

God she felt weak, and she would have to walk all the way there to find an American. Surely she could find someone willing to help her. Maybe at that ice show they'd seen setting up at the amphitheater. If only she'd have the strength to get there...*if* she could find her way. She should have paid more attention to Brianne's instructions when they were riding in the shuttle to the little village. Robison stuffed the map into her plastic bag; there was no time to waste.

Back through the window she went, up the path, and towards the main gate leading out of Casa de Campo.

Half past midnight, and Wade was ready to escape. Going to the back bedroom window, he opened it and was just about to crawl through when he noticed the rain...pouring in fact. He went back to a closet in the hallway and pulled out a rain jacket. He was more than a little aggravated that they hadn't been released as promised. Surely, something had gone wrong. Climbing out of the window, he was soon on his way to the front entrance of the main house. Turning the knob, he carefully opened the front door and slipped inside. With so many guards, he supposed it wasn't necessary to lock the doors. He waited and listened…as he dripped rainwater onto the expensive Oriental rug. The grand house seemed quiet.

Hearing nothing, Wade quietly walked up the darkened hall towards the big curving staircase.

"Psst. Hey, you," a woman's voice called out to him in a coarse, raspy whisper. He looked to his right through the large archway. It was a dark room, perhaps a parlor. He could just barely make out the shadowy figure of a woman.

He moved towards the shadow.

"Well, it's like grand central station in here tonight. And I thought I was sneaking up to have a little martini," Bibí said in a low voice as she slowly walked out of the shadows and into the hallway. She saluted him with her drink.

Wade had no idea who this lady was, but she spoke English, a welcome change, and she seemed friendly, also a welcome change. "I'm looking for Robison," Wade whispered. "It would make things a lot easier if you tell me where I can find her."

"Why should I make anything easier for you?" Bibí shot back. "I don't even know who you are, or give a damn, for that matter."

Sipping her martini, she eyed him up and down seductively—the only way she could look at a man, really.

"Please, help me," he pleaded. "I'm desperate. I'm her husband."

They heard footsteps…she grabbed him by the sleeve, pulling him into the shadows and around the corner of the archway. Soon the footsteps disappeared deep into the house.

She let go of him, took a step back and eyed him cynically.

"All I want is to find Robison and get out of here," Wade continued.

"Well, big boy…you're too late."

Wade felt a "hot poker" plunge deep into his belly; he fought to remain standing. In a whisper, he asked, "They've killed her?"

Bibí, always with a flare for the dramatic—or in this case sadistic—didn't respond in a hasty fashion. Appearing to ignore his question, she walked over to the bar and refilled her glass.

"Tell me, goddamn you!" Wade demanded.

"No, she's not dead…yet. Not that Carlos won't kill her eventually, you understand. What I mean is you're too late. She escaped, right through that door." She pointed to the front entrance. "Oh, thirty minutes ago. That's when I decided to make myself a martini and watch the fireworks once they found out she had escaped again."

"Again?"

"Oh, yes. Your darling little doctor is quite the elusive prisoner. And I might add she puts up a pretty good fight. They brought her back kicking and screaming."

"Holy shit!" Wade exclaimed. Beads of sweat popped out on his forehead; he ran his hand through his wet hair. Then he spun around and took off.

Bibí watched him rush back through the archway. He looked up and down the foyer hall, then darted out the front entrance into the dark and windy rain. The door slammed shut, but no one inside the house noticed.

Bibí had put on a good show for Wade, looking like the tough woman of the house. Instead, she was on her third martini, bolstering her courage to go back to Juan's office, before making her escape. She had even considered sneaking into Juan's bedroom to tell him she was sorry, to try to explain everything, especially her hatred for Carlos and his sexual blackmail. The more martinis she consumed, the braver and easier and more appealing her plan seemed.

She was as good as dead if she didn't get out of the country, but she needed money to leave the Dominican Republic. Bibí also knew time was running out—Juan's wife was due to arrive anytime. So it was now or never for tough ol' Bibí.

Lucky for her, she had a lusty bodyguard on her side. She persuaded him to remove her from the adjoining bedroom with Robison and place her in the wine cellar. She even managed to "talk" him into leaving the door unlocked, accomplished by giving him a couple of well administered blowjobs. Not a bad price to pay in exchange for freedom!

Trying to be inconspicuous, Robison wound her way towards the resort's main gate. She'd forgotten how brightly lit it was. Of course, no other pedestrians were walking around in the rain at this time of night; those out were in vehicles. Even at this hour, the gate was a three-ring circus, with the trucks and cars coming and going. The guards weren't sleeping either…they were actually working. So with guards checking everyone who came through, she had to find another exit.

Doesn't anyone ever sleep around here?

To keep out of sight, Robison headed east through deep grass and a thick stand of palm trees. As she struggled along, she eventually heard cars speeding by on the two-lane highway. Since they didn't slow down to go through the gate, she concluded she was safely away from the main entrance. Her plastic poncho was in shreds, having snagged on so many bushes and branches, she finally ripped it off and tossed it aside.

To make better time, Robison moved on to the road, and walked close to the vegetation.

What was that noise? It was getting louder…closer. It was the sound of a scooter.

Oh, God! …That's all she needed, goddamned "scooter-man" to rape her or worse! She jumped into the bushes.…The driver was going too fast to see her in the dark.

Dizzy and cold, she stopped and hid behind a clump of palmettos. She sat down, thinking she might vomit. Her stomach was killing her. The pains along with the sudden urge to go to the bathroom confirmed her worst fear. Dysentery had set in! Her fever was rising so the chills worsened. She congratulated herself for having "borrowed" the toilet paper, even managed a weak smile at the thought of it. There was little else to smile about. What had her life come to? An overwhelming wave of nausea struck her. She threw up violently.

Recovering temporarily, she pushed on another mile before stopping to vomit…again. As she straightened up on the small embankment, she slipped in the mud and just barely missed the spot where she'd vomited. Robison wiped her mouth with the back of her hand. What a mess she was! Mud had been added to the blood from the small cuts on her face. Her hair was wet, matted and cruddy where she'd tried to brush it back with her hands. Robison was too exhausted to worry about how she looked; she was more concerned with staying alive. Shit...she could die of dehydration before she found help.

Weak, hot then cold, shaking and sweating, she pressed on in the darkness. Robison could barely keep her eyes open... unconsciousness was creeping up on her. She couldn't let that happen...not yet.

Hold on!

At last, the small village appeared in the distance.

Only a little farther...I'm almost there.

Robison eluded the gatekeepers by taking the long way around, making her way to the amphitheater. And then she was there! She looked down at the stage.

God, if only she could lie down...but not yet!

From the top entrance to the amphitheater, she staggered her way down the steep stairs. Dehydrated from dysentery and vomiting, weakened from exhaustive running, she stopped to rest several times. But she couldn't stay among the seats; they didn't provide any cover. She was right out in the open. After all she had been through she couldn't just sit here waiting for Carlos to find her. After another pause it was even more agonizing for her to get up and continue down the steps. She struggled to maintain her lucidity, things were becoming blurry. She just wanted to lie down, even if it was on the bare cement. She couldn't go on—not another step. So what if they found her?

More dry heaves racked her body; there was little strength left within her.

She stretched out full length on the cool cement, her body burning with fever. She didn't care about living or dying anymore. In fact, dying might be easier.

An hour later the sun was beginning to light up the sky. A fly buzzed around Robison's head. She wanted to swat it away, but realized she could hardly move her arms. Her lips felt parched and cracked.

How long had she been here? She had to get up...get going!

First she pushed herself into a sitting position, then made it to her feet. Whoa...she almost fell over. Limply, she pressed on downwards past the front row of seats. Arriving at the edge of the stage, she grabbed it for support. Looking around she saw no one.

In a weak and uncertain voice, she pleaded, "Hello? Hello? Is anybody here?"

She passed the refrigeration truck, and tried the door to the dressing room—locked! She yanked on the handle with all her strength, but finally dropped her hands. Leaning against the door, Robison slid to the ground sobbing uncontrollably.

She buried her hot, sweaty head in her hands. Gathering herself after a few minutes of sitting and crying, she looked up and noticed the back door of the refrigeration trailer was slightly ajar. Why not hide in there until she could talk to someone? ...An American perhaps. She weaved her way towards the trailer and managed to pull open the heavy, metal door. Just inside was a small ladder, which she pulled out and used to climb inside.

To her amazement, Robison saw a dim light, a small cot with a pillow and blanket, and, best of all it felt cool near the humming compressor.

Was she seeing things? Was this a mirage, delirium from her fever?

She blinked in disbelief.

When tears ran down her face, she wasn't sure they were from hopelessness or relief. Now she could rest in this secret hiding place for awhile.

She pulled the ladder back inside, shut the door, and sat down on the cot. From her plastic grocery bag she took the toilet paper, unwound several sheets and dried her tears. She felt the damp streaks trailing down through the mud and blood caked on her face. Although she wiped vigorously, Robison knew her face had to resemble a filthy road map. She didn't have the strength to care anymore.

Robison looked around the interior of the container, taking notice of the loud machinery, the different panels with colored buttons, and a large frost-covered hose leading out of the truck. She wondered how long she would remain unnoticed, for surely an engineer was nearby. She could only pray that he would be an American...not Carlos nor his men.

As she leaned back on the cot, she saw a small cooler beside a blue toolbox. Robison pulled the cooler closer and opened the lid. Bottled water! She had long ago finished the bottle she'd pilfered from the villa. She managed to open the plastic screw top and quenched her dehydrated body with the cold liquid, while silently thanking God for this miracle.

Dropping her plastic bag on the floor beside the cot, Robison leaned back on the pillow. The knife concealed in her jeans prodded her back, but she hesitated...measuring her discomfort against the effort needed to remedy it....Resolutely, she pulled the knife from her waistband. Shivering, she gathered the blanket around her quivering body and fell asleep—with the knife in one hand and the roll of toilet paper in the other.

Wade had gotten lost trying to find the villa. Once he'd arrived at Avenida Central, he'd turned left instead of right and wound up at the main hotel. Going into the lobby, he asked the front desk to connect him to the villa by telephone. The people that answered were definitely not Brianne and Tom and didn't speak English; he hung up quickly. Maybe that was Carlos at the villa...shit!

Next, he phoned the Winsteads in North Carolina, but there was no answer; because their machine was full, he was unable to leave a message. He had no way of knowing that they were in-flight...on their way home. If only he had memorized Tom's cell number instead of having it on his speed dial.

Wade was hoping the Winsteads had stayed an extra day and the plane was still at the airport. If they had to move out of the villa, maybe they were staying somewhere else—waiting for the Murphys to surface. He needed to ask someone if the Winsteads had registered in the hotel. All the clerks were busy; he waited as patiently as he could.

Wade wasn't sure which day it was, nor when they were to leave for home. Still waiting for help at the front desk, Wade started to make a call to his parents when one of Carlos' guards walked through the front entrance, obviously searching for him or Robison. Dropping the receiver, Wade mixed in with some tourists going out the front door, and eluded Carlos' posse.

Hailing a cab, he was soon on his way to the airport. Wade needed time to think, time to figure out where Robison would have gone. If Tom's airplane was there, it meant the Winsteads were still around. He knew Robison had no money; he remembered her purse dropping to the ground when Carlos' men had grabbed them in the art market. Neither one of them had their cell phones on them. Where could she have gone? She had no means to buy anything, not even food. Oh, God!

When he arrived at the airport, he could see the Winstead's airplane was gone. Then he thought perhaps Robison had made it out in time to leave with the Winsteads. His only consolation was that she was still alive. Now he prayed that she was in safe and caring hands.

But what was he to do? He couldn't stop looking just because Robison *might* be on the Winstead's plane. Then the thought struck him: If Carlos had his men searching for them; Robison must still be here somewhere. The big question was…where?

<hr>

"Hey,…buenos días, Manolo. Up and at em, boy!" Ty yelled, throwing open the refrigeration truck door and bounding up the ladder bright and early, ready to greet his night watchman. It was a beautiful sunny morning and Ty felt great.

Robison shot straight up from the cot like a scared wolf backed into a corner. Her eyes raged from fever and fright. He could see that she was covered with dirt and blood, and her blonde, filthy, matted hair was all askew. Letting out a loud scream, she pointed the knife at him with a trembling hand. The sound of the compressor muffled her outburst.

"Hey, hold on…hold on…I'm not going to hurt you," Ty said, holding his hands up while he stood perfectly still. He could see pure fright deep within her glassy stare. Upon reflection, he decided her blonde hair was disgusting and her clothes smelled. Where in the world had this animal come from? Clearly she was desperate, traumatically so.

Trying to ease the moment, he said, "So what are you going to kill me with? The knife or the toilet paper roll?"

She glanced at her hands, not realizing she was still holding the toilet paper. Suddenly, she leaned over and vomited all over the floor.

"Whoa,…that wasn't what I was expecting," he said, instinctively backing up a step or two. "Let me go get some help…"

"No!" Robison shouted as she shook her head. Her eyes were filled with fear and she shivered uncontrollably. She wiped her mouth with more toilet paper and took a deep breath. As she observed Ty, her glassy stare slowly began to change. Something in his manner reassured her; this man could be trusted…perhaps.

"Please…help…help me," Robison pleaded. "I need to hide…I need to…" (sobbing now)…"I'm in trouble…. Please…I beg you."

At this point, she passed out. The knife and toilet paper roll fell to the floor of the truck.

Rushing to her side, Ty felt her forehead. Just as he had suspected, she was burning with fever.

He stood up to take stock of the situation. With his hands on his hips, Ty looked down at this dirty, sick, smelly, strange woman who had just begged for his help. And what a time she picked! "Shit!" Ty exclaimed. "Everything was going along just fine today and bam! Out of the blue…I come across a vomiting, fever-crazed woman with a knife and a toilet paper roll…passed out in my refrigeration truck! And where the hell is Manolo, anyway?"

Manolo, the night watchman he'd hired from Raúl, had been drinking most of the night and had passed out in one of the dressing rooms…luckily for Robison.

Not far from the Alvarez estate, Luís and Felicity sat in a nondescript rental car waiting for Carlos. They were tired and bored, but they seemed undeterred. Or at least Luís felt undeterred; Felicity was ready to go home and forget this whole disaster. They saw a car filled with men leave the estate heading towards the hotel. Carlos, however, was not among them.

"I just had a horrible thought, Luís."

"What now?" he whined.

"What if Carlos doesn't leave by car?"

"What do you mean?" he asked, as he straightened up in his seat and turned towards her. "What if he takes the helicopter to the airport and just leaves? Gone! …Adios! …Good-bye!"

"Hell, I hadn't thought about that," Luís said. "For that matter, he could already be gone, couldn't he?"

Luís decided to find out if they'd been outfoxed. He dialed the house of his uncle on his new cell phone. A woman answered, "¿Bueno?"

"Is Carlos available to speak with, please?"

"No, he is in a meeting. May I take a message?"

Luís covered the speaker and whispered to Felicity. "She says he's in a meeting."

"Meeting my ass," Felicity said. "It's just another lie!"

"Do you know when he is leaving the estate?" Luís asked over the phone.

"Not for a few days."

"This is his cousin, Luís, I need to see him. Do you know where I can find him? Perhaps when he's out to dinner?"

"I don't know. Good-bye." She hung up abruptly, probably having heard the background comments of Felicity.

"They're all covering Carlos' ass," Luís said.

They sat in silent frustration for a while, then Luís added, "Well, that conversation didn't tell us jack-shit about his coming or going. We need to get closer and see for ourselves. We can't park the car that close to the house, but we could get close with a golf cart," he said.

Felicity looked at him scornfully. "Oh, great! Carlos comes driving out in his big high-powered car and then what, smart-ass? We run him down with our golf cart? Get real! He'd plow over us like road kill and never look back."

Felicity had no idea how close to the truth she was.

FOURTEEN

Bibí wanted to sneak upstairs to see her Juanito. She desperately wanted to speak to him and apologize. At the landing of the back staircase leading up from the kitchen, she could see there was no way for her to pass by the guards. She also noticed Juan's wife had arrived with a ton of fanfare after the long flight from Miami. Naturally, she would be full of questions for Carlos and the servants, regarding Juan's condition and the mysterious "shooting," as soon as she could get everyone assembled. Already many people were gathering in the upstairs hallway.

With no other options, Bibí turned her thoughts to planning her escape before Carlos killed her. She silently thanked Mrs. Alvarez for keeping everyone so occupied; now she would have a chance to make a run for it.

Bibí began making her way back down the stairs and into the office where the shooting had taken place. She needed to find the money she'd put in the briefcase earlier. Thinking Carlos might have put it back in the safe, that was the first place she would look. With all the commotion, surely he hadn't had time to change the combination. Besides, she was fairly certain Carlos didn't know how to do anything that technical himself, and no outsiders had been allowed into the house.

Looking at the bloodstained couch and carpet caused Bibí's stomach to somersault. She hesitated, but made her way across the office. Quietly, she crept behind the desk and over to the safe. Just as she expected, he hadn't changed the combination. Upon opening the safe door, she saw it was empty. Bibí searched the room, and eventually came across the briefcase hidden behind the small couch. She cracked it open and found the money still inside. Perfect!

As she hurried out of the office, Bibí looked at her watch; it was four-thirty in the morning. With the briefcase concealed under a sweater draped over her arm, she made her way to the servants' entrance of the house. Hanging by the door were the chauffeur's hat and coat and the keys to the limousine that Mrs. Alvarez had just arrived in.

No doubt, as soon as Mrs. Alvarez heard the whole story of the shooting, they would come looking for her in the wine cellar. She'd better get the hell out of here while she still had the opportunity. She put on the chauffeur's coat and hat and made her way to the garage. Knowing this was one car no guard would stop, Bibí got behind the wheel and took off. Her calculation was correct—the guard only waved as she drove nonstop through the gate. Now she would go to the airport in Santo Domingo and get on the first airplane that would take her out of this country—and away from her ruthless pursuers!

Bibí wouldn't be able to live forever on the seventy-five or eighty thousand she'd just snatched from Juan, but she would have a good start. As long as she kept her body in fantastic shape, she'd have no trouble creating a new life...with somebody! Preferably, the next somebody would be another rich old fart.

Bibí kept glancing in her rearview mirror to see if anyone was following....So far so good! Mrs. Alvarez was keeping all of them busy—too busy to follow the runaway mistress.

Felicity was fed up with sitting in the car waiting for the elusive Carlos to appear. And even if he did drive by, what was Luís going to do? This whole situation was ridiculous! In the middle of the night they were idling their time away by the side of a road, hoping to recover a valuable necklace from Luís' deadbeat cousin. Felicity was exasperated, to say the least.

"Look, here comes a big Mercedes." Luís pointed out to her.

They strained to see if Carlos was in the car.

"It's only the chauffeur," Felicity said. "No one's in the back seat."

The Mercedes screeched around the corner, flying by Luís and Felicity's parked car in a blur. They watched it swerve around the line of cars, exiting the main gate of the resort without so much as slowing down. The guards had ignored it.

"He's sure in a hurry!" Luís observed, craning his neck to see who it might be. He watched the car disappear from his rearview mirror, not realizing their precious necklace had just passed within ten feet of them—in the hands of the fleeing mistress!

"I'm sick of this. I can't do it anymore! My back hurts and I need to go to bed. In a real bed, not the backseat," Felicity complained. "Plus, I'm hungry and I have to go to the bathroom."

Without a word, Luís started the engine and drove to the hotel. Felicity was a real pain in the ass!

Meanwhile, Bibí pressed hard on the accelerator of the limousine, speeding through the dark of night...to freedom. To a life richer than even she could have imagined.

~∿~

In the throes of delirium, the dreams had been bad at times. Someone was forcing fluids down her throat...water...it was water. Or was it medicine? She could feel herself choking, coughing. Tossing her head from side to side, she tried to stop the intake of liquid. After a struggle, her breathing returned to normal and she relaxed.

Strong arms lifted her gently—she was being carried! She tried to hold her head from bobbing up and down but she had no control. She couldn't wake up. A warm spray poured over her from head to toe, and she smelled flowers. Robison tried to reach out for one of them, but it disappeared when she felt a terrible pain in her stomach.

More liquid—no she wasn't going to drink it! She tried to slap at it. Someone grabbed her arm, and tried to calm her down. Robison couldn't make out the words. It was all so jumbled!

A cool cloth was placed on her forehead; a caring touch brushed the hair off her face.

The tossing and turning lasted several hours. Once the fever broke, however, she fell into a deep sleep, sinking sumptuously into the comfort of the cleanliness and warmth.

Much later, Robison roused herself from the feverish slumber. She turned over in the roomy bed; the scent of the clean sheets and the hum of the air conditioner seemed like a slice of heaven. It had been such a safe sleep she had to force herself to wake up. Abruptly, she heard a sharp noise...someone was stirring in the room. She didn't dare move a muscle, or even open her eyes.

Where was she? She couldn't remember. Was she a prisoner once again in that horrible house? Was that Carlos? Everything seemed so blurry.

She made herself take a deep breath to relax. She needed to think for a minute…to retrace her steps. She was sure she'd made it away from the estate but couldn't remember much else—except feeling so sick she wanted to die. She remembered struggling with all her might before finding a small cot in a truck somewhere. But she wasn't there now; she was in a big, luxurious bed. How had she arrived here? Vaguely she remembered the kind touch and strong arms that carried her somewhere—it must have been to here. But where was here?

Hearing the clicking of computer keys, she decided to take a little peek around the room. Just barely cracking her eyes open, feigning sleep, she looked around. She was in a hotel room. Another double bed next to hers was neatly made-up. Lined curtains were drawn back to reveal a large window overlooking the Chavón River. The bathroom was to the left and a closet to the right. She could see male clothing hanging there. The clothes were hung neatly, all in a row, separated by color. Odd, she thought, that she would be noticing such a trivial thing in such desperate times. There was a stuffed chair with a floor lamp, brightly tiled floors and a desk with a small chair.

Continuing to look slowly around the room, she saw the back of a man with broad shoulders in shorts and a T-shirt working on his computer. She stared at him, trying to recall who he was…anything about where she was…or what had happened.

She stared at his back. He was not an acquaintance, nor was he a stranger. His hair was a dirty blonde, so, thank God he couldn't be Carlos or one of his men. This man was definitely not Spanish!

She closed her eyes once again to take stock of herself. No, she'd decided she didn't feel scared; in fact, she felt fairly secure. Her stomach didn't hurt like knives stabbing through her anymore and her fever was gone. She even smelled good. Or was it just the sheets?

The stranger's cell phone rang; she peeked through one eye, watching him grab it off his belt. He answered it—in English! She could understand every word! What a beautiful sound. She closed her eyes tightly, turning on her side to listen to the conversation.

"Sam, my man. How the hell are you? And where the hell are you? Are you still working on Crazy Horse?"

156

"Listen, Ty, you need to see this. I'm telling you...you just wouldn't believe it; it's awesome! But alas,...I'm leaving for Florida today, old buddy. I also have my ticket to Greece and my visa is all set. By the way, wait 'til I tell you what I found on the mountain."

"Just wait 'til I tell you what I found in the refrigeration trailer!" Ty exclaimed, glancing over at Robison, supposedly sleeping. "We'll compare notes in Greece."

"Great. Who do I contact when I get to Greece? I assume I'll be arriving before you, correct?" Sam inquired.

"I'll have to get back to you on that. I think it's a Vladimir somebody. They should know at the Stuart office. I plan to go to Greece as soon as the show is over here, so I'll be a few days behind you. At the moment, I'm not sure if I will fly from here or go back to Stuart first and then fly out. But I'll let you know," Ty said.

"Okay, I'll talk to you soon. Adios and good-bye, my friend," said Sam.

Ty shook his head from side to side, picturing Sam on the Crazy Horse Monument. He really did want to see it some time. Ty's biggest problem with that was when he wasn't working, the last thing he wanted to do was travel anywhere. He didn't even want to go out to a restaurant when he was home. In any case, he figured one day his work would bring him into the vicinity of the monument, then he'd get a look at it and perhaps Sam would be with him to show him the ropes. Hopefully, they wouldn't be blown to smithereens.

He took a steno pad out of one of his briefcases. Robison could see he had written "Russia/Greece" on it very neatly. Ty made a few notes, then tried to call the Russian ice show office, but there was no answer. They kept strange hours over there.

Clicking the phone off and replacing it on his belt, he turned towards Robison, and said, "Well, did you finally decide to join the land of the living? Or do you still want to kill me with a knife and toilet paper roll? Of course, the vomiting on my shoes was a nice albeit unexpected touch." He was smiling as he talked.

She opened her eyes, seeing her savior's face for the first time in the light of day. He looked vaguely familiar. Then she remembered...he'd found her in the truck, but she was so dizzy she really couldn't remember what he looked like.

After leaning over, and returning the pad to its assigned place, he said, "Tyler Kelly is my name, by the way."

She sat up in bed, glancing down at the nightgown she had on. She grimaced because she was still sore all over. Her diaphragm still ached from all the vomiting.

"I'm Robison Murphy," she announced, and then the questions poured forth: "How long have I been here? Where am I? I need to get out of here, I need to make a call, I need..."

"Hold on a cotton pickin' minute! Not so fast....And with that southern accent, I'd think you'd be a little more laid-back. Not to mention a 'thank you for saving my ass' would be a nice touch."

She dropped her head. "I'm sorry, Tyler...and you're right. I should thank you before I ask for more help." She brushed her hair out of her eyes. "Thank you. Really...thank you."

"You're welcome, and just call me Ty." He stood up, turned about and sat back down on the small office type chair straddling the backrest. "First I'll tell you what I know. Then you can take your turn. You have been here in my room...oh...about thirty hours and you've had Montezuma's Revenge. Luckily, I had pills for that problem. It just wasn't easy trying to get them down your throat. You put up quite a fight.

After I found you in the container, I brought you here. None of the maids have come in, so no one has seen you. And yes...I gave you a shower; mainly because there was no way you were getting into one of my beds covered in vomit, blood and dirt."

"How did I...?"

He interrupted, "Go to the bathroom? Well, I helped you do everything, including go to the bathroom....Okay, your turn."

"I'm embarrassed," she said. Even though as a doctor she was used to such experiences, she felt herself blushing. That Ty was good looking and suave didn't make things any easier for her.

"Oh, for crying out loud! Do you think you're the only woman in the world I've ever seen naked? Besides, no offense, but...you weren't the least bit sexy. I was afraid you'd vomit on me again. You had a few 'touch-and-go' moments of dry heaving in the shower," he said with a mischievous smile and a shrug of his shoulders.

"Were you with me...in the shower?" she ventured.

"Of course," he answered. "But don't worry. I had my hands full scrubbing you down. Nothing happened I can assure you."

"I'm sure it wasn't the least bit sexy," she agreed. She stretched then sat up. "God, I ache all over," she groaned.

"Try to forget about it!" he said. "Think about something else, like are you hungry?"

"Starving!"

"Okay, let's go get something at the restaurant. That is...as soon as you take a shower, which I assume you can probably do on your own now."

"You assume correctly," she added, raising an eyebrow as she spoke.

Ty had made her feel so secure that she overlooked her predicament. Panic returned: "Oh! I can't go out. Carlos may have guards looking for me. I can't..."

"Hold on! Holy smokes...chill, why don't ya? Look, I've already thought of that, but we have to eat. I have this dark short-haired wig from the show and here's a pair of sunglasses. No one will ever recognize you. We'll get something to eat, and you can fill me in on what's going on. Maybe I can help you get back home. Okay?"

She nodded, then added, "But, I have no money and my clothes...by the way where are my clothes?"

Ty turned back around in his chair with his back to her. "Oh, those things. I threw them out. You'll find new clothes in the drawer over there," he motioned with his head as he punched computer keys.

"The way I figure it...if you have enough money to be vacationing down here, you're probably good for the cost of a breakfast. The clothes are a 'get-well' present. But no more outbursts, agreed?"

"Yes, agreed and thank you, again."

"By the way, I did try to wash your clothes, but they were such a mess! What were you doing, rolling around in the mud?"

"Something like that. Actually they weren't mine...I stole those clothes," she added, pushing the covers back. Standing up in a fetching nightgown, she opened the drawer and was taken aback by her new things.

"What a great selection!" she said, milling through the clothes.

"Yeah, well at least I didn't steal them," Ty said, noticing that Robison was very attractive—once cleaned up! "Just don't make a big mess in the bathroom. And whatever you do…don't touch my toothbrush. I bought the pink one for you."

"Wow! You think of everything, don't you?"

The warm water beat down upon her head and it was glorious. He'd put body wash and a disposable razor in the shower for her use. Yes, she felt safe and comfortable with Tyler Kelly, ice show impresario. She thanked her lucky stars that fate had brought them together. She contrasted Ty with Carlos, who would be glad to kill her just to shut her up. What a difference in two handsome men! One she could lean on, the other she must avoid at all costs.

Thank you, God, for Tyler Kelly!

Toweling off, she looked into the mirror and noticed small scabs on her face from the sharp branches. Otherwise, she wasn't looking too horrible. He had purchased all kinds of toiletries for her and had placed them in a small basket on the other side of the vanity—near his shaving kit. She selected some pear-scented body lotion and smoothed it all over her body. Now she began to feel like a human being again. Yes, Ty was so thoughtful and quite charming.

Down the elevator and out into the sunshine, they strolled, window-shopping as they walked to the restaurant. She placed her hand on his arm; after all, they had to affect a disguise, didn't they? It was nice not to be running for your life.

At the open-air café, he held the door for her to pass. "Let's eat inside," he suggested. "No use in hanging out here for someone to spot you. You're not unattractive you know. You do draw attention."

"Oh? Well, thank you, but perhaps it's the black wig."

"I think it's more than that," he said, smiling.

They found a small table in the back of the crowded restaurant. With so much hustle and bustle going on at every table, no one noticed them.

"I'm so hungry I could eat an elephant," she said. "But I think I want oatmeal…no pancakes."

"I have news for you. You can't have either one."

"Why?"

"Because, you may feel a hundred percent better, but your system still isn't hunky-dory. So you'll be having toast and hot tea."

"Toast and hot tea? Are you out of your mind? I'm starving!"

"I'll make a deal with you. You eat what I order for you and if after an hour, you're still hungry and haven't had anymore stomach pains, I'll bring you back for pancakes *and* oatmeal. Deal?"

"I'm a doctor, you know," she pouted. "I can decide what I can eat or not eat."

He looked up from the menu. "I don't give a damn whether you're a doctor or not, I know about eating in foreign countries. I've had experience with dysentery and know how your system is going to react. It's doubtful whether living in the cotton fields of the Deep South has afforded you as much 'hands on' education about Montezuma's Revenge as I've had. So, do we have a deal? Or are you going to be upchucking pancakes from here to eternity?"

Reluctantly, she nodded. "Deal," she replied, somewhat flattered that he was looking after her so zealously. Still she couldn't let him get off scot-free. "For your information, 'hunky-dory' isn't exactly medical terminology, you know."

He didn't respond, apparently he didn't appreciate her little dig. She was sorry she'd said it. But it had been a long time since she'd eaten anything…long before her escape. But how could he have known?

"I know what you're thinking," he said, not looking from behind his menu.

"Oh, really? What, pray tell?"

"That you feel fine and I'm out of my mind. Am I right?"

She stared at the backside of his menu. Reaching over, she pulled it down so she could see his face. "As a matter of fact…I do feel fine."

He raised his menu back up, adding, "We'll see."

She ordered the tea and toast. He ordered eggs, steak and fried potatoes. She eyed every bite he took, but ate her toast, and against his better judgment, his toast, too.

Ty listened to her story about their vacation, and about the older gentleman running for president who had been shot by his mistress. She explained how Dominican hoodlums had coerced her into treating Juan and how his son, Carlos, was out to silence her. She told of her missing husband and best friends, her first attempt at escape and finally the escape that brought her to his doorstep…literally.

161

"I don't understand. How could your husband and friends leave without you?"

"They wouldn't have left without me. But to be honest, I'm not certain where any of them are. Wade may still be imprisoned at the estate, or maybe he escaped like I did. I do know the local authorities would never help my husband or my friends rescue me! They all are tied-in with the Alvarez family. The Winsteads may have gone to a hotel and didn't leave. On the other hand, they may have returned to the states to ask the American government to intervene...she's an attorney you know.

Nothing makes any sense," Robison continued. "I tried to call home when I was at the villa, but I couldn't get through. I needed a credit card, which needless to say, I didn't have. I lost my purse when they abducted me the first time."

"Why call home if you thought your husband was still here?"

"I just thought the decorator might answer and I could find out if Wade had called." She thought a moment. "I have an idea. I'll call all of the hotels at the resort and see if he or Winsteads are registered at any of them."

"Oh, yeah! And while you're at it, send up some flares so this Carlos guy knows exactly where to find you."

He handed her his cell phone. "Try calling home and see what happens."

While he paid the bill, she dialed her house, hoping beyond hope that the decorator would answer. As it rang, she formulated the message she planned to leave on the answering machine if he didn't. Ty returned to the table. He sat down and watched her listening.

The ringing stopped; someone picked up.

"Hello," said a deep voice with a thick Spanish accent. This was definitely not the decorator. Her eyes opened wide with fright; all color drained from her face, the cell phone started to slip from her hand. Ty caught it. Putting it up to his ear, he listened.

"Hello...Who ees calling? Hello..." the thick accent yelled. Ty switched off the phone.

She looked up at him, bewildered. He stood up saying, "Let's go back to the room and call the U.S. Embassy in Santo Domingo. At least that's a place to start."

162

They left the café and headed back up the street to the hotel. On the way, Ty stopped to buy a newspaper to make sure the ads were running for the show as planned. He folded the paper under his arm, and they continued to the hotel.

She felt a little pang in her stomach. God! He must have been right. She was hoping she'd at least keep the toast down until they got back to the room. How embarrassing…if she were to upchuck right here on the sidewalk. Not to mention Ty might add an "I told you so." She reflected how buoyant she'd been just an hour ago. Robison was not out of the woods yet, not by any means.

Morning, and chaos was rampant at the Alvarez home. It was bad news from one end of the house to the other. The maid came in first to tell Carlos that Bibí was not in the wine cellar or anywhere in the house. Next, a guard came in to tell him that Robison was missing and a third to tell him Wade had escaped. Exploding into a tirade, Carlos immediately called for all the guards, including the one who was watching the gate. Meanwhile, the chauffeur came in to tell him his clothes, keys, and Mrs. Alvarez' car, were gone. He wondered which one of the three had stolen them? And how far away were they by now? Were they all together or separate?

A scream came from deep within the house, a shrieking that wouldn't stop, followed by the sound of dishes slamming to the floor breaking into a million pieces. The high-pitched outcry was from Maria, he could tell.

Rushing two steps at a time up to the first floor landing, Carlos ran into his father's room. He couldn't believe his eyes.

A knife protruded from his father's abdomen. Blood covered the sheets, bed and his pajamas. His mother was standing over her husband, the Minister of Finance, the presidential candidate, the cheating bastard!

"Mamá! What have you done?"

Slowly and deliberately she pulled the knife out and turned to her son, Carlos. "He informed me that he was going to marry Bibí. I couldn't stand the thought of it. I've put up with his shit for thirty-eight years…and I will put up with it no more!" She was shaking violently.

"But that wasn't the plan," Carlos yelled in agony. "I was to get rid of Bibí permanently!"

"Is that what he led you to believe? Funny, he just told me a few minutes ago that I was to go hire an attorney. That he had changed his mind. And that he wanted a youthful presidential wife…he said…a sexy 'trophy' wife, not a fat old woman." She dropped the knife on the floor. "He said he loved her." She began to sob, burying her face in her bloody hands.

"I don't believe this, Mamá!" Carlos turned to Donadio. "Where the hell were you?" he screamed at him.

"Señora Alvarez told me she wanted to be alone with her husband!"

Carlos hurried to close the bedroom door. He was trembling.

"My mother is not taking the blame for this murder. Understand?" Carlos was talking to the maid, Maria, and Donadio. "I will take care of everything. Meanwhile, take my mother to another room; she needs rest. And find a sedative to give her."

Carlos gently helped his mother make her way over to Donadio who led her out the door and down the hallway. Walking over to Maria, he grabbed her by the throat and said, "You open your mouth about this…and you are dead! ¿Comprende?"

All the maid could do was nod in agreement. He shoved her away and she hurriedly began picking up the broken dishes that were strewn all over the room where the tray had fallen from her hands.

He turned towards her again. "And by the way, Maria, make sure to get the bloody clothes my mother has on, and burn them!"

Without looking up, she answered, "Sí, Señor."

When Maria had finished cleaning up, she left as quickly as she could.

He stood staring at his beloved father. Alone…he was totally alone. Carlos broke into hysterical sobs, throwing himself on the body.

"No, God, please no!"

After a few minutes, he rechecked his father's pulse…but the body was already getting cold and clammy. He knelt by the bed and said a silent prayer.

Rising, he went to the phone to call the police and then to call a priest. He needed to manufacture a story before the police arrived. He had a lot to do—a lot to think about. Whatever the story was—it had to be ironclad. Hurrying from the room in deep frustration, Carlos slammed the bedroom door behind him.

Back in the hotel room, Ty was looking up the phone number for the U.S. Embassy in Santo Domingo when Robison emerged from the bathroom and flopped down in one of the chairs beside the bed. She hadn't gotten sick, but her stomach wasn't feeling too steady.

"I shouldn't have eaten your toast," she said.

Ty ignored her comment. "Looks like there are two locations for the U.S. Embassy; that's kind of weird. Oh well, here's one on Calle Leopoldo Navarro."

"What's a Calle Leopoldo Navarro?" she asked as she removed her short black wig, and began running her hands through her long blonde hair.

"Leopoldo Navarro Street. Calle means 'street' in English," he answered.

She reached for the folded newspaper on the bed, not that she could read Spanish, but at least it was something to do for a few minutes.

Opening it, she stood straight up with a gasp and dropped it on the bed. Her hands flew up to cover her mouth. Her stomach turned upside down.

"What the hell is it now?" Ty asked. "You're such a drama queen."

She was pointing to the large color picture of an elderly gentleman on the front page under the headlines. Her pointing finger was shaking.

"That's him....That's the man I took the bullet out of. You must tell me what this says! ...What are the headlines?"

Leaving the phone book open on the desk, Ty walked over and picked up the paper. She watched him read the headlines and then he began reading the story below Juan's picture slowly and deliberately to himself.

"Read it out loud, for God's sake!" Robison demanded.

He dropped the newspaper and looked at Robison.

"Let me ask you something. You said, and correct me if I'm wrong, that you took two bullets out of this man and he was recovering when you left?"

"There were three bullets fired, but only one hit him in the abdomen. The bullet lodged in his spleen, which I took out. And yes, he was resting quietly. And barring any unforeseen complications, he was recovering very well. In fact, he was up and eating scrambled eggs. He was in street clothes, for God's sake. He was fine, I'm telling you. Is something wrong with him now?"

"He's dead. Murdered! He was stabbed several times with a knife. His son walked in on the perpetrator. But they say it was such a shock, he passed out. Blood was everywhere, it says in this article."

"Oh, my God! Who would do such a thing? He was under such unbelievable security it would almost be impossible to get away with anything like that," she said, sitting back down in the chair.

Her mind was racing a hundred miles per second, trying to figure out how this could have happened. Why would anyone do this?

"This may come as a shock to you, but Carlos named a Dr. Robison Murphy as the killer he saw standing over his father."

Shooting straight up out of the chair, she yelled, "Me? I didn't do it! I saved his life, for God's sake!"

"Calm down and lower your voice before we have the goddamned cops swarming all over the hotel," Ty ordered.

"I'm sorry, but you've got to believe me," she said, her whole body shaking. Grabbing the arms of the chair to steady herself, she gingerly sat back down. "You don't believe I did it. Do you? I was here. How could I be there?"

He turned and walked slowly over to the table where the open phone book was and said, "No, Robison, you weren't here. This happened the night I found you…and you *were* holding a knife."

She stared at him in disbelief and shock. Now it seemed the one man who could help her might not want to. Ty didn't believe her! How could she convince him of her innocence? It was all too much. She buried her head in her hands and sobbed.

He sat down and rested his arms on top of his head, contemplating the doctor's dilemma. It was a few minutes before he said anything.

Then Ty walked over and knelt on one knee in front of the hysterical Robison.

"Look, I'm sorry I yelled at you," he said quietly. "Yes, I believe you. And by golly as sick and weak as you were, there is no way you could have stabbed anyone. Shit, you couldn't even sit up."

Her hands fell into her lap and she looked into his blue eyes.

"Besides, it says in the article that blood was everywhere, including all over you. Well, I have to admit you were covered with a lot of stinky shit, but not a lot of blood. Just some drops from the brush cuts on your arms and face," he concluded with a smile, wiping her tears away. Their eyes locked...saying more than words ever could.

The shrill ringing of the hotel phone eased the tension in the room. Ty quickly stood up and walked to the desk. "¿Bueno?"

"Ah, Señor Kelly. L. D. here. (Raúl) We have a small problem, but nothing that you cannot handle in a few minutes. Have you heard about the murder of Señor Juan Alvarez?"

"Sí...yes. I read about it in the newspaper this morning." Ty said as he put his finger to his lips, motioning for Robison to be quiet.

"Well, the authorities would like all the cast members in the show to be down in the lobby at two o'clock with their passports to verify and identify themselves. It is only a precaution, you understand."

"No, I don't understand," Ty begged to differ. "Do they think one of them did it?"

"Oh, no, Señor Ty. They know an American doctor did it. It is only a matter of finding her. They think she will try to get help from someone in your company or from other American tourists. She escaped on foot and must be close by."

"I see. Okay then, I'll have everyone in the lobby at two o'clock."

"One more item. They are going to search the entire area, the rooms and the amphitheater.... In case she is...how do you say? ...hiding."

"No problema. See you at two," Ty said, hanging up the phone.

He sat at the desk not saying anything. Picking up the pen, he fiddled with it between his fingers, bouncing it on the desk in a rhythmic fashion. He glanced at his watch. It was noon. He had two hours.

"Well, that explains the Spanish speaking person that answered your home phone," he said.

"What do you mean?"

"They already have someone from *here* looking for you *there*," he said.

"I guess he was important, running for president and everything," she said. "Are you going to call the embassy?"

It was as if he didn't even hear her. He just kept rapping the pen on the table, thinking. Maybe he was thinking about ditching her, or turning her in.

"Hello?...Are you going to call the embassy?" she repeated.

"No, we aren't going to call the embassy," he said calmly. "Neither of us knows the laws in this country regarding the treatment of American murderers who supposedly killed a presidential candidate. They may just turn you over to the local authorities instead of informing the American Embassy and execute you. Who the hell knows? It may turn out to be one of those deals where they 'throw away the key' and no one ever sees or hears from you ever again. Meanwhile, we have a more immediate problem. We've got to get you out of this hotel and hide you for awhile—until we can get something figured out."

"Do you have a place in mind? Or am I on my own?"

Pursing his lips, he answered, "Yes, I have the perfect place to hide you. Hell, after all this, do you think I would just let Carlos waltz in and take you?"

After another maddening pause, he looked up at her. "Shit, everything was going along hunky-dory, and now I'm harboring a damned murder suspect in a foreign country with no papers, no money, a captive husband and no answers."

"A captive husband?"

"Well, surely you don't think, from what you've told me, that this...Carlos guy...would just let your husband walk out of his house, just because *you* told him to. Do you?"

"I...I wish I knew..."

"Yeah, well, let's just assume that he's still in their possession," Ty said, handing her his cell phone.

"Try calling your friend's house and see if they are home. But don't say anything, just hang up, okay? There is no telling who might be listening to all the cell phone transmissions."

She dialed Brianne's house. After three rings, Brianne picked it up.

"Hello? ...Hello? ...Who is this?" Brianne asked.

Robison switched off the phone as instructed. She ached to speak to Brianne...to bring her up to date. To tell her that she was desperately trying to find Wade. That she was just plain desperate...but she obeyed his instructions.

"It was Brianne. Perhaps Wade is with them...maybe they all stayed together." She was grasping at straws and Ty knew it.

"Well, at least Carlos doesn't have your friends," Ty said. "That's two people we can eliminate from our 'missing' list. Besides, do you honestly think that your husband would leave the country without you? Or maybe I'm not asking the right question. Does your husband love you enough to stay and look for you?"

"Stop it! Stop it! Of course he loves me!" she shouted. "Why, he would give his life for me!" A tear rolled down her cheek.

"Maybe he already has," Ty said under his breath, turning back to the desk.

His words made her stomach do a flip flop. Covering her mouth she ran for the bathroom.

"I think I'm going to be sick..."

He tossed his pen at the closed door and raised his voice: "And that's another thing to add to my trauma list over finding you..."

In a few minutes, she opened the bathroom door, wiping her mouth with a towel. "You don't have to worry about taking care of me. I'm a doctor, remember?" she reminded him.

"Yeah, well. The only doctoring that's been going on so far has been mine, if you'll recall."

"And a mighty fine job you've been doing, too, I might add," Robison said, attempting a smile. She was truly grateful; she knew she could count on him to see her through this.

He handed her a pink pill. "Take this; it will settle your stomach."

"What am I taking?"

"A pink pill. What the hell does it look like?"

"What's the name of it?"

He looked at her, puzzled. "Hell, I don't know; the pink ones are to settle your stomach and the little white ones are for Montezuma's Revenge and they both work. What else do you need to know? If you don't want to take the goddamn thing, then put it back."

Swallowing the pill, she said, "Your bedside manner could use a little adjustment."

"Get your wig back on glamour girl; we've got to get you out of here, pronto."

She tossed the towel towards the bathroom where it landed on the floor.

"Well...now see...that's another problem," he admonished. "Did you see any towels thrown on the floor before you went in there?"

"Sorry," she said picking up the towel and walking it into the bathroom. She wiped the sink, folded the towel and put it on the floor next to the tub, then ceremoniously turned off the light.

"If you're going to live with me, and I might add you have no choice at the moment, you'll have to learn the drill: A place for everything and everything in its place."

"Yes, sir!" Robison said, saluting as they walked out the door. "Maybe you need a wife around here to change your values."

"Yeah, well,...you learn the drill, and I'll work on my bedside manner. And I sure as hell don't need a woman complicating my life right now...I have you for that," he said. "On second thought, you're probably right. I should be more hospitable towards vomiting, runaway doctors on the lam whom I may find in one of my containers who just happens to be indicted in the murder of a presidential candidate of a foreign country."

"Are you always so sarcastic?" she asked.

"Only when I'm trying to 'aid and abet' someone. I hope you realize I could also be thrown in jail. That'll be two keys they'll throw away, thank you very much!"

"I hadn't thought about that," she said pensively.

"Yeah, well, I think it may take more than some goddamned white and pink pills and a great bedside manner to get us out of this predicament...unfortunately."

He was hurrying her down the street, guiding her by the arm. They weren't far from the amphitheater now. As they passed the café, he asked her, "Want some pancakes and oatmeal now?"

"Ugh, no." She shuddered, remembering she'd just tossed her cookies into the toilet. "You delight in torturing me, don't you?"

"Yep. It's part of my new bedside manner. How do you like it so far?"

"It's not exactly hunky-dory," Robison fired back.

"That wasn't quite the reaction I was after," he said as gave her arm a gentle squeeze.

Despite his occasional sarcasms, she found his touch reassuring. Intuitively, she knew Ty liked her…and would never desert her.

FIFTEEN

Making their way down the street, Ty and Robison saw police swarming all over the village, they had arrived earlier than Raúl had predicted. Instead of two hours, it hadn't been forty minutes since the phone call from Raúl; Ty had delayed only to call his cast and crew to tell them to be in the lobby in a couple of hours. That the police were already searching indicated they were under heavy pressure to find the female fugitive.

Evading the "policia" by mingling with tourists, they looked straight ahead and walked steadily towards the amphitheater. Fortunately, the police didn't appear to be well organized yet; they were doing quite a bit of talking amongst themselves. Ty was hoping they didn't really know what Robison looked like, which would give her a little extra time.

As they descended the steep stairs of the amphitheater, Ty and Robison could hear the police behind them.

So much for a little extra time. Shit!

"I thought they were going to search the hotel first," Robison said under her breath. She appeared calm, but Ty could sense her underlying fear.

"Obviously, they have more than two or three cops out looking for the presidential candidate's assassin."

"*Alleged* assassin let me remind you," she corrected him.

He ignored her comment and picked up the pace, occasionally slowing to look behind them. So far it didn't appear they were being followed.

"We don't have much time, so listen up," Ty said. "I'm going to hide you inside one of the magic props that has a false bottom. You'll have to stay all crunched up for a little while. Okay?"

"I'll try my best," Robison said, trying to keep up with Ty's long stride. "But I'm scared to death."

"Once you're inside, the only time you come out is when you hear three knocks. One and a pause, then two short knocks together. That's our signal. Don't come out if you hear or feel anything else. Understand? Not even if you feel like you're moving or someone is tapping on the glass or on the bottom of the prop. Got it?"

"Yes."

"Only come out on my signal."

"I heard you the first time. I'm not deaf, you know."

They reached the empty shiny glass box edged in chrome. It had a beautifully sequined piece of cloth draped over one side.

"I can't hide in that clear box," she exclaimed. "Are you out of your mind?"

"Out of my mind for aiding and abetting you, yes! Anyway the box has a false bottom, so don't worry, you'll fit."

She scrutinized the prop closely when he removed the cloth. "But I can see quite clearly; there's only about two inches below the glass!"

"That's the illusion, trust me. I built it myself. It's not roomy, but you'll be able to stay in there a few minutes."

"Okay, stuff me in," she quipped, noting the police were nearing the top of the theater.

Ty lifted the false bottom, she climbed in, and Ty explained how to fold her legs to adjust to the cramped quarters. Already the police were entering the amphitheater's upper level. He closed the prop and asked, "Are you okay?"

"As good as any sardine, I suppose."

"I'm leaving now, so no more talking."

He draped the beaded cloth over to one side, leaving the glass box totally revealed. Ty smiled to himself. "She's a pain in the ass but she's got a lot of guts!" he muttered.

Ty walked away from the prop, and went over and unlocked the ladies' dressing room. The police would want to search it, of course. Then he went to find his inebriated watchman; Ty had a score to settle there.

Ordinarily, Ty would have had one of his own ice engineers with him, but they were all busy somewhere else and Sam was on his way to Greece. So that's why he'd hired Manolo upon the recommendation of Raúl, but Manolo turned out to be more of a problem than a helper. Still, everything seemed to be going smoothly...at least in the ice freezing department...so Ty would let it ride—unless he now caught Manolo drunk again.

"Manolo? Manolo?" he called. Manolo wasn't in the ice truck. Then Ty saw the door to the male dressing room was ajar. Damn it to hell, he must be in there smashed! And if the wardrobe lady knew Manolo was in her domain, she would have a flying-hissy with pink tassels. And that really would be something to write home about!

Ty opened the door and stepped inside. It was dark, so he waited for his eyes to adjust.

"Manolo? Manolo? Where the hell are you? This is the last straw, my man. I told you before not to do this…"

Someone grabbed Ty from behind and held a sharp skate blade to his neck.

"¿Que quere? (What do you want?) Manolo…let's talk man!" Ty said in Spanish.

"I don't speak Spanish, I'm not Manolo but I need your help! Aren't you an American?" the man asked in a pronounced southern accent.

"I have a news bulletin for you," Ty responded. "This is no way to get help, trying to slit my throat with a goddamned ice skating blade."

Wade released Ty.

"Sorry, I just wasn't sure…"

Ty turned around and saw the police nearing the ice rink. He could also see Manolo out cold, snoring in the corner. Ty made a mental note to fire him after he'd slept off the booze and returned to the land of the living. Enough was enough!

Ty turned to Wade. "Look, I know who you are and the police are on an all-out manhunt for Robison."

Wade's eyes brightened. "You know my wife? Is she all right? Tell me where she is."

"Yeah, she's all right and I'll tell you everything later. But right now you need to hide in the bottom of this costume crate. And listen, if they discover you…you'd better do the best imitation of a gay skater you can muster or you'll blow this whole deal for you and your wife. Her life may depend on it literally! By the way, Manolo over there hasn't seen you, has he?"

Wade was trying to get into the crate as quickly as he could. "No. He's been a lump."

"Good, well you can claim he's your lover," Ty suggested. When he noticed Wade's outraged expression, Ty said, "Don't worry, Manolo will deny it, of course, which will make it all the more real."

"Gee, thanks," Wade said, settling in his hiding place.

Ty covered him up with several costumes, and grabbed a jock strap and threw it on top for good measure. He doubted the police would touch it.

Excited at having located Robison, Wade was frustrated nonetheless. There was a never-ending amount of shit to plow through just to get to her. And how did a gay skater behave, anyway? Hopefully, he wouldn't have to conjure up a "queer act" of any kind. And claim Manolo as his lover? Holy shit! Wait until the Winsteads heard this one.

When Ty went back outside, the police were coming out of the female dressing room, giggling and smirking. They stopped at the ice rink and peered inside the tent.

"Go inside the tent if you want to," Ty said in English. "At least it's cool in there." If they knew he spoke Spanish they might interrogate him...and that's all he needed.

One policeman held the tent flap open while Ty and another went inside, where they felt the frozen surface.

"Is really ice, no?" one asked, looking at Ty.

"Yes, it is real ice."

Another policeman looked at some of the magic props. Walking over to the one Robison was hiding in, he jerked back the beaded cover draped over the edge and looked inside. He knocked on the bottom—Ty held his breath, hoping she would remember.

Thank God, she didn't appear!

The policeman wheeled the prop around, obviously looking for a trapdoor. Then he stood back, peering through the glass.

"Is no possible to hide anywhere in this box. I see this in the show but I no understand," said the policeman. "First, the magician is standing on top of this box, then he raises the cloth and immediately drops the cloth and a girl is standing there instead. And they have ice skates on, too!" he explained to the other policeman. "Tell me, how they do this," he demanded of Ty.

"Sorry, I'm sworn to secrecy," Ty said, smiling. He began to walk away, trying to draw them away from that particular prop. Obviously satisfied with Ty's answer, they followed him towards the male dressing room.

"We saw you coming out of here before. What's in there?" One policeman asked.

Ty laughed. "It's just the men's dressing room. Go right in and you'll see my night watchman drunk in the corner. Be my guest and wake him up so I can fire him," Ty said.

All the policemen laughed, although they probably hadn't understood what Ty had said. It didn't matter; it was a diversion. One stepped briefly inside. He looked around and came right back out. Ty guessed he'd rather look at female underwear, than at gross jockstraps lying around.

After inspecting the ice trailer, the police sauntered back up the steep stairs of the amphitheater. Ty followed to see where they were going next and to make sure they didn't leave a guy behind as a "look-out." Panting when he reached the top of the theater, Ty stopped to catch his breath. Well, at least he was getting his exercise running up and down all the stairs.

Ty went through the entrance and out onto the sidewalk, where police were searching in stores and restaurants. Others were interrogating tourists, obviously asking if they'd seen the American fugitive. He was satisfied the "policia" wouldn't be coming back anytime soon.

Ty went back down the steps to the backstage area—to the prop hiding Robison. He gave the three-code knock and Robison abruptly appeared.

"Phew! I thought you were never coming back!" she exclaimed.

"How'd it go? A little cramped in there, huh?" He lifted her out of the prop and set her down gently.

Hearing strange voices, Ty placed his finger on his lips. Then he took her by the arm, and led her behind the refrigeration container. There they waited until all was quiet.

"Get into the ice truck and stay there," he advised, leading her up the ladder. "I'll be back for you later, but I'm going to lock it from the outside so you'll be safe. There's water and stuff in there, as you already know."

"Yeah, I'll feel right at home," she joked. "This time I'll try not to puke all over the floor."

"Your kindness is overwhelming." He laughed and patted her shoulder. She smiled back. Then he went down the little ladder, before sliding it back inside.

After locking the door, he went and uncovered Wade.

"Where's Robison?" Wade asked.

"There's no time for conversation now," Ty warned. "Go straight up that street (pointing north) about two blocks to the Ponce de León hotel. Here's the key to my hotel room; just stay there, don't make any phone calls and don't open the door until you hear me knock three times. If you pass policemen or detectives on the stairs just act as though you belong here. If they ask you what you are doing, tell them you work for Tyler Kelly."

"What about Robison?" Wade insisted. "I want to see her!"

"She's okay, but she's in a shit-load of trouble and can't be out in the open right now. So get going. We'll meet you at the hotel later, after dark."

Wade grabbed the key out of Ty's hand and said, "Thanks, man."

"And don't stop for anything!" Ty reminded Wade as he walked towards the stairs.

"Felicity, honey, wake up. Felicity…wake up!"

It was no use; she was out like a light. Luís couldn't sleep; he'd paced the floor all night after they'd gotten back to the hotel.

He'd ordered a small breakfast for the two of them. Room service had just arrived and still she hadn't stirred. He ate his muffin and drank two cups of coffee, then covered the rest, leaving it for her to eat later. He was hoping she would wake up with a better attitude than she'd gone to bed with.

Next, he found a piece of paper in the small desk and wrote her a note. He was going to get a golf cart and go back to stake out the area near the estate. He would return later to pick her up.

When he left the room, she still hadn't moved a muscle.

Wade made his way towards Ty's hotel. He was walking on air. It was unbelievable how good his luck had turned, running into the man who knew where Robison was hiding and learning she was safe and well. Now, if they could just get the hell out of here and back to Murrells Inlet! He was also thankful that Ty seemed like the kind of guy that would help them. Unfortunately, Wade lulled himself into complacency—and courted disaster.

Ignoring Ty's instructions, he stopped along the way to buy toiletries, underwear, a T-shirt and shorts. He even went to the small café, ordered a beer and some food. It slipped his mind that Ty had told him to get to the Ponce de León as quickly as possible without raising any suspicions. So it was much later that Wade arrived at the hotel room and hopped into a hot, steamy shower.

He retraced the events in his mind while the water beat down. With Ty looking after Robison, what was there to worry about? Invigorated by the hot, flowing water, Wade thought of Robison soon being free of her captors...and of their impending reunion and all that it promised. There was indeed, a light at the end of the tunnel.

It was evening now and people started filing into their seats at the amphitheater. Unlocking the refrigeration container, Ty climbed the small ladder and went inside.

"Listen, it's too dangerous for you to go straight to the hotel by yourself," he told Robison. "So I think the best idea is for you to sit out in the audience and watch the performance. 'Blend-in' if you know what I mean. Then when everyone leaves after the show, you intermingle your way out of here with the crowd and back to the hotel."

"I don't know," Robison said. "I'm scared to be out in the audience alone, much less go back to the hotel without you."

"I have a lot of work to do and I don't want to raise any suspicions by not being where I'm supposed to be. You'll be just fine. When all the lights and spotlights are shining on the stage, it's dark in the audience. But listen: when you leave, don't make a beeline for the hotel. Go the other direction and double back. Take your time. And when you get there, knock three times."

"So you'll beat me back to the hotel?" she asked. "Why can't you just go with me?"

Ty smiled, "Because they may be watching me. You'll be okay, I guarantee it."

"How do you know how to do all this…all this 'evasive maneuvering' stuff?"

Ty smiled again and said, "I obviously read *way* too many detective novels. Anyway, we'll have to wait and see how good my 'evasive maneuvering' stuff works."

After he'd gone she climbed out of the truck, noticing the hustle and bustle of the backstage area. Ice skaters were warming up; a pair team was doing overhead lifts on the ground and one lady was showing three girls a few dance steps over to one side. While the crew rolled up the tarp that had covered the ice, Ty sat on a small tractor-like machine resurfacing it. Other stagehands were setting up props behind the stage curtains. Over by one of the dressing rooms a man was sharpening skates on an electric grinding wheel, throwing out sparks in the process. She watched him hold up the blade, look down the length of it, touch it, then reapply it to the wheel once again. Soft music was playing over the speakers, as the amphitheater filled up with people.

Robison sat on the ladder steps for a while, watching all the pre-show preparation. Not one person seemed to notice her. All were too absorbed in getting ready to bother about an onlooker. What she didn't know was that Ty had told them Robison was a friend of Raúl's and didn't speak English. So why attempt to speak to someone who didn't speak English?

After awhile, Ty came over and spoke confidently. "It's just about show time, so you'll need to go find a seat. Don't go too high up. You don't want to be the first one out of the theater afterwards. Aim for the middle. Okay, Doc?"

Robison smiled at that last bit. It was kind of nice to be kidded even under dire circumstances.

"Okay. Then, I'll see you back at the hotel, right?" she asked.

"You worry too much! Just watch the show, ease out with the crowd and double back to the hotel. Simple as that," he said, patting her on the back.

Eventually, the lights blacked out and the announcement began: "Ladies and Gentlemen, Kelly Productions is proud to present…"

The show was starting right on time, which always pleased Ty. Raúl was calling the light cues, the ice was firmly frozen, no wind was blowing, none of the skaters were sick, the theater was filled and the crowd was extremely enthusiastic. Yes, Ty was happy!

He looked out over the audience and spotted Robison sitting up midway, towards the back of the theater. It appeared she was squished next to a huge family with several children.

Good girl! She blended right in. One good thing about Robison: she followed instructions—most of the time anyway.

Ty was anticipating Robison's reaction when she discovered Wade in the hotel room. Ty would give them space and sleep on the cot in the refrigeration truck tonight. He'd return to his room the next morning, and the three of them would figure out an escape plan. Better yet, since Robison was now Wade's responsibility, Ty could duck out altogether and concentrate on the ice show.

Yes, they could fly back to South Carolina and Ty would be rid of them and all of their problems…forever. In any case, he wouldn't have to worry about Robison anymore. Not even think about her. What a huge relief for Ty! He had about run out of escape ideas and "evasive maneuvering" tactics. Still, a sense of pending loss nagged him.

"What the hell is wrong with you, Kelly? Shake it off, man, she's nothing," Ty said to himself. Still, he couldn't help looking up at her, watching the show.

The audience was roaring with laughter at the antics of the little comedian now onstage. He was skating alongside a "straight man" who towered over him by a foot. From Argentina, Little Lito stood only five feet three inches tall, but he had vim and vigor that made his presence much more imposing…and appealing. For over ten years, Little Lito had traveled with Ty's shows.

A Charlie Chaplin look-a-like, he did a stupendous job of imitating the legendary comedian in one of his routines. He was especially popular in Latin American countries where he spoke the local language. In fact, Little Lito's English was terrible, even though he had been around Americans for many years. One exception though: he knew all the cuss words perfectly; the stagehands had seen to that.

Ty glanced up at Robison again. She was laughing! For a moment—just a moment, she'd forgotten all of her troubles. Good! "She deserves a break," Ty told himself.

An hour and a half sped by for Robison, but as the finale began she started looking for the exit. Instinctively, she checked out people milling around the top of the amphitheater. She could only glance back furtively; she didn't want to be conspicuous. She counted eight policemen; at least, that's how many were in uniform. She was suspicious of every man she saw, and decided a life on the run was not for her. Even the stress of her job as a doctor paled in comparison. She craved a return to normalcy...and Wade.

As ten girls costumed in solid sequined gowns skated intricate patterns, the adagio team appeared from the wings. A handsome skater grabbed his partner by the ankle and began spinning her very fast, her head barely skimming the ice. The audience squealed each time her head brushed the snowy surface. The white snow shone brightly against her dark hair. Next the leading lady stepped into a flying camel spin while the male star performed a double axel around her.

The last performer to take a bow was Little Lito who evoked loud cheers and much clapping from everyone. The audience yelled to him in Spanish and, of course, he "thanked" them in Spanish, through mimicry and miming. Everyone cheered louder.

The climactic ending was a shower of fireworks, raining down like a huge waterfall of silver and gold. Music accentuated the visual effects. The audience sprang to its feet in a prolonged ovation. The stage went black, the ice skaters exited, and the lights in the amphitheater came on. Everyone started filing out, moving slowly toward the aisle where they could walk up the steep climb to the top. Robison turned back to see if she could see Ty, but he was no where in sight.

Ty was observing Robison's every move from behind the ice tent. Some eight uniformed policemen scanned each person as they exited, but Robison managed to sneak out behind a tall man carrying a screaming child. It seemed the child wanted to dance to the "exit" music playing over the sound system. Robison never thought she'd be thankful to a screaming child, but now she was.

On her way to the street, Robison fell in step with the family she'd been sitting next to—a natural and timely coincidence. Fortunately, they all turned in the opposite direction of Ty's hotel. As they made their way down the cobbled sidewalk, the family paid little attention to her in their midst, as they chattered away about the show. Incidentally, the screaming little girl was now a radiant child, singing and dancing on the sidewalk, pretending to ice skate her way along.

What a happy family! Maybe she and Wade would have a family one day. Wade…Wade. Oh how longed to see him! Tears welled in her eyes, but she brushed them away quickly. This was no time for sentiment—this was a time for complete objectivity, like that of the most serious surgical procedure. She had to stay focused!

She crossed the narrow road, turned back up a parallel street, and finally made it to the hotel. She thought it might be smart to go in a back entrance—if she could find one. However, when she walked up the rear alley, she could clearly see a policeman watching the back of the hotel. Damn! Now what could she do?

Robison retraced her steps, crossed over to a different street and waited for the skaters who would be returning to the hotel. She fell in behind them, walked straight by the policeman at the front door and into the elevator. Thank God, none of the skaters asked who she was or where she was going. Had Ty arranged that as well?

If only Ty could arrange for Wade to come and get her: that would be the miracle for the ages! No use dreaming…it only made her weepy. Why, she had been choking back tears all the time lately. She was so edgy…so nervous…so scared.

She knocked three times. No answer.

Oh, God! Ty wasn't here yet. Why hadn't he given her a key? Now what was she going to do?

She waited a few minutes and knocked again. Still no answer. Then she put her ear to the door. He was in the goddamned shower! And here she was standing out in the hall, for God's sake! Wait until she got hold of him.

Looking up and down the hallway, she could hear the elevator doors open. Nervous and afraid to stand in the hallway any longer, she went to the exit stairs, opened the door, sat down and waited ten minutes.

Surely to heaven Ty was clean by now.

Then she remembered it was Ty and gave him an extra five minutes for good measure.

She went back and knocked three times. She could hear him fiddling with the chain lock on the other side of the door. Then it opened, but just barely a crack.

She pushed the door open wider and stepped inside—the room was pitch black.

Reaching for the light, an arm slid around her neck from behind. She let out a small scream—a hand covered her mouth.

Wade snapped on the light.

"Oh, my God!" Wade exclaimed.

"Wade! Oh,...Wade!" Not believing her eyes.

He slipped her wig off; caressing every feature of her face.

They kissed passionately...tears streaming down their faces.

"I'm sorry I grabbed you like that," he whispered. "But your shadow didn't resemble Ty's and that black wig fooled me." He rocked her gently back and forth.

She stood back to take a good look at him. "I'm not crying because of that, silly; I'm crying because I'm so glad to see you!"

She wiped away tears with the back of her hand.

They embraced again.

Static from the walkie-talkie on the desk interrupted their kissing.

Startled, Wade asked, "What's that?"

"Oh, that's the walkie-talkie to the refrigeration truck. In case the ice melts or something, the night watchman can reach Ty here."

"Hey, this is Ty. Don't answer; I just want to let you know I'll stay here tonight. You can have the room to yourselves. If you need me, have Wade call me on this. But we might not be alone, if you get my drift. And Doc, you know the *drill!* Sweet dreams."

Robison wanted to rush to the walkie-talkie and thank Ty. But she knew better than to talk over the airwaves now. Surely, she would see him tomorrow.

Ty fluffed up the pillow on the cot. He'd fired Manolo after the show and was certain Manolo wasn't the least bit surprised. In fact, Manolo appeared not to give a damn one way or the other—typical.

With the show off to a good start, Ty began thinking beyond Altos de Chavón. He would soon be on a plane to Greece so he had to organize his thoughts. He missed his steno pads with all his lists and contacts; however, they were in his briefcase back at the hotel. Ty was a stickler for note taking; it kept him organized, especially with business in so many different parts of the world.

With only the weekend left and four performances to go, it was time to plan the load-out. Ty would see Raúl tomorrow morning about hiring local manpower for the job. He would have to tell Raúl that Manolo would not be rehired under any circumstances. And, oh yes, he must find a chassis driver to haul the containers back to the port. Without any paper to jot it all down, Ty had to rely on his memory. He closed his eyes on that thought—and the nagging realization that Robison still "complicated" his life. "Time will take care of that," he told himself.

"The drill?" Wade asked Robison. "What's the drill?"

Without a word, she walked to the bathroom and snapped on the light. "Yes, the drill." She pointed to the towel Wade had thrown on the bathroom floor.

"The drill is you don't mess anything up and you clean up after yourself. Did you look in the closet? Ty's a neat freak. Everything is in precise order and for heaven's sake...don't ever touch his toothbrush! Believe me, he hangs it in a particular way so he'll know if it's been touched."

She picked up Wade's towel, wiped the sink and counter, then neatly folded the towel and put it in the corner.

"Wow, he really *is* a neat freak," Wade said, looking in the closet.

"Since he saved both of our lives, I'd say that's not too much to ask. Right? And consider this: he doesn't even get to sleep in his own meticulously organized room tonight," Robison said with a twinkle in her eye. "But we do!"

"You're right, darling."

Wade walked up and put his arms around her.

"My God...you feel so good." Wade said softly, blinking back tears.

"I've been so frightened for so long," she whispered in his ear. "And we're still not out of danger. Not with the police swarming all over the place."

"Shhhh," he put his finger over her lips. "We do have tonight."

He carried her to the bed—and tenderly laid her down. He brushed back her blonde hair and looked into her eyes. "We're together now," he said. "Everything's just fine. We'll get out of this country tomorrow. I promise."

They melded together then, tearing at each other's clothing, touching familiar parts, until they managed a needed and frenzied reunion.

SIXTEEN

Carlos had no time to grieve. The police were on their way and he made a beeline to the security room to make sure there wasn't anything on the videotapes to incriminate his mother. There were no cameras in the bedrooms, but there was one in the hallway. Carlos needed to see exactly what *was* on the tapes. He didn't want to overlook anything…especially in his frenzied state of mind.

Alone in the security room, he put a tape in the machine and pressed Play. It picked up Robison on the front steps, then, again, running towards the guard gate. Time: 12:20 AM.

On the next tape he saw Wade approaching the main entrance of the house. It was raining. Time: 1:02 AM. More pictures of rain. Then Wade running from the front steps of the house towards the guard gate. Time: 1:10 AM.

What in the hell was the guard posted at the gate doing? Sleeping, Carlos figured. Steaming mad, he contemplated going out and firing him on the spot. But he had a couple more tapes he wanted to look at first. He still had Bibí-the-bitch missing and perhaps he could tell if she'd helped the other two escape.

Third…fourth…on the fifth tape he saw Bibí in the wine cellar. She was removing her clothes. He could only see the back of the guard and couldn't make out which one. He watched her go down on him; the guard throwing his head back in obvious ecstasy. Then he zipped up his pants and walked shakily towards the door leading back upstairs. Carlos still couldn't make out who the guard was, but he now knew how she had coerced her way out of the cellar.

Sixth tape…Bibí was running across the driveway to the garage. She was carrying something under a sweater. He rewound the tape and played it again in slow motion. God Almighty…it was the briefcase! Fuck! He continued to watch her back up the Mercedes and speed away from the guard gate.

"I don't fucking believe it!" Carlos screamed, banging his fist on the table.

He jumped up and ran down the hallway into the office. Yanking the sofa back, he stared at the empty space where he had hidden the briefcase.

186

He was pacing wildly...up...and down. Nervously he ran his hand through his pitch-black hair, then he went over and poured himself a scotch-neat and chugged it in one swallow. Pouring a second, he slammed it back as well.

"You fucking bitch!" he yelled, throwing his glass against the wall. It shattered into a million pieces, with shards of glass scattering all over the tile floor.

Upon hearing the commotion, Donadio entered the office.

"Find that fucking bitch; she left in the Mercedes and has the briefcase with the necklace in it. She must be heading for the airport. Call ahead and have her stopped!"

Carlos hadn't noted the time on the tape of Bibí's departure. By the time Donadio was calling the airport near the resort and then the airport in Santo Domingo, Bibí-the-"sly"-old-bitch, was on an airplane sitting in first-class, flying to Rio de Janeiro. With the briefcase safely tucked in the overhead storage bin...she was euphoric. After taking off, she had opened the briefcase to discover the multi-million dollar heirloom stashed along with the money. Luck had finally come her way. Placing the necklace around her neck, she reveled in thoughts of her newly elevated position as one of the nouveau riche of Brazil.

"Can I serve you a beverage?" the stewardess asked Bibí.

"Why, yes, thank you. I'll have champagne, please. Your most expensive bottle, if you don't mind."

The stewardess poured her a glass of bubbly. Leaving the small bottle, she continued down the short aisle.

Bibí saluted Carlos in absentia. "Here's to you, asshole. I finally had the last laugh."

Gulping it down in one swig, she poured another. Admiring the bubbles flowing from the bottom to the top of her cold glass, she felt the warm richness of the diamond and ruby necklace around her neck. Yes, she was now going to have the luxurious life she felt she deserved. Fuck 'em all!

After waking up in the refrigeration container early Friday morning, Ty relaxed on the cot for a moment. His thoughts drifted to the lovebirds in his hotel room. "Wade's a lucky guy," he said aloud.

So much for that! He needed to go back there, take a shower, get clean clothes on, and talk them into leaving…today. He wanted them out of his hair. Out of the country would be even better! Even he was a bit taken aback by this outburst. "She's gotten to you, ol' boy," he mumbled. "Get over it."

Ty checked his cell phone messages. Thank God, there were only two…but it was still early. He'd have many more before long.

The first was from Sam; he had arrived in Florida and was calling from the Stuart office. He was ready to leave for Greece tomorrow and wanted to call in case there were any last-minute instructions. Ty made a mental note to call him later on after he'd double-checked everything with the Russians, and then with the promoter in Greece. He also needed to give Sam the bill-of-lading information on the ship arriving with the ice equipment, and those copies were in his briefcase at the hotel. Again, Ty needed to get to his computer, briefcase and steno pads.

The other message was from Raúl; Ty was to meet Raúl at the outdoor café for breakfast at seven thirty. He looked at his watch; he had fifteen minutes. The shower would have to wait. He guessed they were meeting to discuss the load-out scheduled for Sunday night. Raúl hadn't really been specific in his message and sounded a bit rushed. Anyway, if he went to meet Raúl first, it would give Robison and Wade a little more time to get their act together. Nonetheless, he decided to give them a wake-up call on the walkie-talkie.

"Hey, boys and girls…rise and shine! I'll be there in about forty-five minutes. Just giving you a heads up."

He wasn't expecting an answer, so he cut off.

Ty started for the café and arrived before Raúl.

"It's good that we meet this morning," said Raúl after sitting down in the booth with Ty.

Ty noticed how fidgety he was.

"Have you seen the news?" Raúl asked him, as he sipped the strong coffee.

"No, I didn't have the TV on last night."

Ty didn't want to go into details with Raúl. Ty let him assume he'd spent the night in his hotel room, not in the refrigeration trailer. As for the "news," he was hoping it wasn't any more bad news concerning the search for Juan's assassin, Dr. Robison Murphy, although that's what he fully expected to hear.

"What's up?" Ty asked nonchalantly.

"We may need to think about loading-out after the show tonight," Raúl said.

"What? And cancel Saturday and Sunday?" Ty inquired, totally caught off guard.

"Where have you been?" Raúl was surprisingly sharp with his words. "There's a hurricane coming to this island. It may hit us Sunday evening, maybe sooner. 'Francis' is a category three, they say on the news, maybe a category four by tonight. The government is issuing a warning to all the tourists. I am sure there will be a mandatory evacuation by Saturday— tomorrow! We must get the ice skaters off the island, don't you agree? And back to Miami while we can still get seats on an airplane. The airport will be full of tourists very soon. We must hurry!"

Ty let out a low whistle. "Son-of-gun! What next?"

Raúl looked puzzled, but Ty quickly added, "You're right. I've got to get my people off this island. Can you make the flight arrangements for the skaters for late tonight or early tomorrow morning? Maybe there's a red-eye flight the stage crew can leave on after we load-out. I have to get to the hotel and try to notify everyone." Ty got up to leave, having barely touched his eggs and toast.

"I will go to the airport right now and get the tickets," Raúl added. "I am sure it will be busy, but I have some influence with people who will help me."

They paid the bill, tipped the waitress and were out onto the hot sunny street. Their meeting had lasted a whole twelve minutes. It was hard to imagine a hurricane in such beautiful weather.

Raúl headed to his car and Ty started back to the hotel on foot; it was only a couple of blocks away. He'd just have to surprise Wade and Robison earlier than he'd mentioned on the walkie-talkie.

As he walked he was formulating a plan for the cast, the load-out, and the crew. He still needed to make his overseas calls. Shit…time was running out.

Of all the damn times to not be in his room! Well, they would just have to get out on their own; Ty had too much money on the line to worry about Dr. Murphy and husband anymore!

From the front desk, he called the cast and crewmembers to come to a meeting in the lobby, in thirty minutes. Next, he took the elevator to his floor, but as he walked down the hall, he noticed his door standing slightly ajar.

That's odd. Why would they leave the door open like that? Jeez, how thoughtless can they be? My computer and all of my records are in there. With the door wide-open…perhaps it's already gone. Holy shit!

Maybe Robison and Wade had seen the news, panicked and rushed off. On second thought, if they'd left for good—it was good news for him. But…at least they could have closed the damned door.

The closer he got to his door, the eerier he felt.

The hair on the back of his neck stood up.

He stopped—listening…

Silence.

Shit….He was really getting paranoid. This was ridiculous.

He touched the door and slowly pushed it open. His hotel room looked like hurricane Francis had already hit; lamps lay broken on the floor, the bed was torn apart, and some of the sheets were piled by the door of the bathroom. A large bloodstain blotted the bedspread of the second bed. No one was in sight.

Then he noticed Wade, unconscious and bleeding on the floor between the beds.

Wade wasn't bleeding profusely and he was breathing regularly, but he'd taken a brutal beating. Thank God, he didn't have to worry about racing Wade to the nearest hospital for stitches. He hurried into the bathroom, "Robison! Robison, are you here?" He looked out on the balcony and in the closets.

Dr. Robison Murphy was gone!

Shit! Shit! Shit! Of course, she was gone, and it didn't take a genius to figure out what had happened—and the thought sickened him.

Ty leaned over Wade, and slapped his face lightly, trying to bring him around…to wake him. No response.

Ty needed to be downstairs in a few minutes for the meeting. But Wade needed his attention. And what was he to do about Robison? The load-out, the evacuation, Wade, the Doc, the hurricane—what a fucking mess!

He stood up and looked around. The television, on the floor standing on its side, was showing the radar picture of the approaching hurricane. A weather lady was pointing to the "eye" of hurricane Francis. Ty placed the television set back on the dresser—upright. Francis was heading directly towards them and she looked huge!

Fuck!

As he listened to the weather updates, he went into the bathroom, wet some towels, and placed them on Wade's forehead and neck. Next, he put a pillow under Wade's head, although he hadn't regained consciousness. Wade began stirring—so Ty was encouraged. Pulling the bloodstained bedspread off the other bed, Ty grabbed the sheet and covered up Wade. "He'll have a headache and a bruised face…but he'll make it," Ty reassured himself.

This doctoring shit was getting to be too much. First the wife and now the husband! And who the hell had time for this? But God…where was Robison?

Ty picked up paperwork from the floor, grabbed a yellow legal pad and wrote Wade a note. "Stay in the room and keep quiet until I come back." He added the time on the bottom of the note, which he propped up against the bathroom mirror. Surely, Wade would check his wounds before going anywhere. He hung the "Do Not Disturb" sign outside the door and hurried out for his evacuation meeting.

On his way downstairs, he searched though his "Russia/Greece" steno pad for numbers and began dialing the Russian ice show office.

Shit! When it rained it came in torrents!

~~~

Carlos knew if they found Wade they would eventually get Robison, and, sure enough, one of Carlos' guards spotted Wade on his way to Ty's hotel room. Wade hadn't been as inconspicuous as he

191

thought, so by not following Ty's instructions he'd led Carlos right to his doorstep.

The guard had waited until he saw a dark-haired woman enter the room an hour or so after Wade. He phoned Carlos several times, until he finally got through. Carlos instructed him to make sure the two people in the hotel room did not leave before he and Donadio could get there. Carlos figured if that dark-haired woman wasn't Robison in disguise, Wade would know where she was hiding. However, Carlos was willing to bet the farm Robison was wearing a dark wig; and now he had her trapped. His plan was still intact!

He called downstairs for Donadio who had left the estate on an errand but was expected back shortly. Not ten minutes later, Donadio called Carlos from the kitchen.

"Donadio, bring the car around; we are going to go get our little murderer," Carlos promised.

"Sí. But why didn't you just blame Bibí?"

"Because, as far as the country knows, Bibí never existed and the shooting never happened. And I sure as hell am not going to let anyone put my mother in jail. That's *why*."

Donadio hurried out to get the car; his boss was edgy!

Carlos' mother had left with the priest, along with the body of his father, and was on a plane back to Santo Domingo. Carlos promised he would join her as soon as he cleared up some of his father's business matters.

Carlos, too, had watched the Weather Channel while getting dressed and he now decided to ready the house for the approaching storm. He called the stable to take Skyesrun to his ranch inland with the other horses. And Skyesrun was to have priority treatment in traveling comfortably. Then he instructed the staff to prepare the house according to a set plan.

Once in the car, he, Donadio and another guard sped by the guard at the gatehouse.

Luís was sitting in his golf cart hiding in the bushes, where he'd been for the last hour and a half. He'd seen a small car leave and return with a couple of big guys inside, which raised his suspicions. Now he saw the car carrying Carlos and the same two men whiz by the guard gate. Damn, Felicity was right! How was he going to catch up with Carlos while sitting in a stupid golf cart? If he hurried, maybe Luís could get back to the room before Felicity read his note. He didn't want to admit she was right. Why add fuel to the fire?

∽

It was six-thirty in the morning when guards burst into Ty's room with guns pointing at the horrified couple, naked and asleep. Carlos marched into the room behind the guards and stood there smiling. He was very amused by his "conquest."

"Well, well. What do we have here? A murderer and her husband!"

"I'm not a murderer…," Robison started to say.

Carlos interrupted, "Shut the fuck up!" He gestured to the guards. "Get her."

Wade jumped out of bed and lunged at the guard. Robison grabbed the sheet, instinctively wrapping it around her body, and backed into the corner of the room near the bathroom.

"You goddamned son-of-a-bitch!" Wade yelled at Carlos. "Leave us alone!"

Carlos smiled again as Donadio punched Wade in the stomach; Wade doubled over and slid against Ty's desk. The collision sent papers flying, and the lamp crashed to the floor. Gasping for air, Wade was trying to avoid the broken glass, when an uppercut to the jaw landed him back on the bed. Next, Donadio hit him across the head with the butt of his gun. Blood spurted onto the spread as Wade rolled to the floor between the beds, face down.

Robison continued to scream: "Stop it! For God's sake, stop it!"

Carlos crossed over to grab Robison by the arm and clamp his hand over her mouth. As she struggled to get loose, Robison bit two of his fingers, causing him to release her. "Let go of me! I didn't kill your father," she shouted. Then she spit in his face.

The television flipped over on its side when he flung her against it, yelling, "Why, you little bitch!" He stood momentarily, wiping spittle from his face and contemplating his bleeding fingers. Clearly, the doctor was a hellcat when aroused. Well, he would show her—and enjoy the action!

Carlos grabbed the sheet, and yanked it off. She stood there stark naked while Carlos sneered. He turned and walked slowly away in

193

taunting fashion…just daring her to move. He crumpled the sheet, threw it down by the bathroom door and walked to the other side of the room. "I've seen enough, get some clothes on. We're leaving."

When Robison hesitated, the guard put a gun to Wade's head and cocked it.

"Get your clothes on or you're going as you are. I don't give a rat's ass either way, but these guys may prefer you naked," Carlos said, nodding towards the leering guards.

Robison hurried over to the other side of the bed and picked up her clothes. She went into the bathroom—door ajar—and put on her things as fast as her trembling hands would allow. She came back out shaken and teary-eyed, and, ignoring her tormentors, rushed towards Wade still passed out cold on the floor.

Donadio pulled her back and pushed her towards the other guard, who held her as Donadio cuffed her wrist to his.

Carlos approached, getting up close in her face. "You will not get away from me again!" he taunted.

She turned her head away, but the guard grabbed her chin and forced her to face Carlos. He slipped his hand beneath her T-shirt, toyed with her nipples, and fixed on her with a lusty stare as he fondled. Robison stared back unflinchingly, hatred pulsating from her eyes like bullets.

Withdrawing his hand, he bent over and ran his lips up her cheek towards her ear. "Defiance is a quality I find irresistible," he whispered. "I knew when I first saw you that you harbored passions." Abruptly he turned to Donadio and said, "Let's go!" snapping his fingers. It was the signal for all of them to leave.

"Attached" to Donadio, Robison looked back at Wade. Maybe her feminine wiles were still in play after all. She would give it a try: "Carlos, please let me go! I didn't kill anybody," she pleaded. "I'm begging you, please! I'll do whatever you want, just let me go."

Ahead she saw Carlos' disappear through the door. Never hesitating in his gait, her appeal to reason had fallen on deaf ears.

Luís quietly entered their hotel room. Felicity was still asleep and it was almost eight in the morning. She hadn't even touched the breakfast tray. It was time to go. She needed to get up and get moving if they were going to catch Carlos when he returned. They needed to be blocking his way back into the estate so Luís could force Carlos to listen to him. With the hurricane looming offshore, Luís figured Carlos wouldn't be gone long.

Luís turned on the television to get an update. While he waited for the commercial to finish, he jerked open the curtains and bright sunshine beamed across the king-size bed. Maybe that would wake Felicity.

"Felicity, for goodness sake, get up! You've been sleeping long enough. We have to load the car and get out of here."

He began packing his clothes. Once they met with Carlos, made a deal one way or the other, they'd go back to Santo Domingo and figure out their next move. Either he would have the necklace...or some money in lieu of the necklace; then they could start a new life.

"Felicity, I'm not playing games. Get the hell up! There's a huge hurricane coming, and Carlos should be returning to the estate and that's when we'll have our opportunity to confront him."

She didn't answer.

Luís went over to the bed and shook her by the shoulder. She didn't move. He shook her hard. "Felicity!"

Her head fell backwards—she was dead. Her neck had been broken.

He took two steps back. Holy shit! He had to get out of here!

Hurriedly, he finished packing. As he closed the hotel room door, Luís heard the man on TV repeating the order for a mandatory evacuation. Luís hung the "Do Not Disturb" sign on the door, then rushed down the back stairway to the car. There was no doubt in his mind that he would be the primary suspect when Felicity's body was found.

Dazed and in a state of shock, he couldn't make sense of any of it. Surely Carlos wouldn't stoop to murder. Or would he?

Fuming over Carlos, Luís started the engine and drove over to the estate to wait. Yes, he decided, Carlos would kill to keep the necklace. Things were quickly falling apart for Luís. If Carlos didn't come along soon, a maid would find Felicity's body and the police would be combing the resort to find him. Luís didn't have much time, and he had a lot at stake. One question kept popping up: Would he now be trapped for Felicity's murder by his own greediness?

In the lobby, waiting for everyone to assemble for the meeting, Little Lito was entertaining the cast and crew with jokes and miming routines. It was all made funnier by his broken English and nonsensical words he made up when he was at a loss for the correct words. His humor was much needed, for many of the cast were nervous over the impending hurricane. Why stay and do one more show? Why not get out of here immediately?

"Look, I can't cancel tonight's show," Ty explained. "That's Raúl's call. He's the one who has to refund the money to ticket holders."

Still waiting for the few who hadn't readily rolled out of bed, Ty took this opportunity to put in a call to the Port Authority in Miami and another to Greece. He needed to find out where the cargo ship, heading to Greece, was at this moment and if it was out of the hurricane's path. He didn't really expect the Greeks to have any information, but it was worth a shot, especially if he couldn't get through to anyone else. After seeing Francis on TV, Ty wasn't sure how long his cell phone would continue to work; thus, he needed to make all his important calls while he still could.

Back in Hickory, North Carolina, Brianne was relentlessly pursuing every avenue open to her. She was now trying to call Senator Michael Moore in Washington, D.C., and at his office in Columbia, South Carolina. But all she was getting was the royal "red-tape" runaround. Under her breath, she cursed all politicians! What a slippery bunch!

In the beginning, no one would help her because Brianne didn't have proof that Wade and Robison were actually missing. All that she accomplished was to get transferred from one office to another. Everyone wanted more information before they would help her. Or at least that's how she was put off. Now into the weekend, nothing would happen until Monday.

After dinner, Tom turned to the third page of the newspaper and noticed a small article.

"Holy Moses!" he shouted.

Brianne turned. "What is it?"

"Looks like you have your proof that Robison is missing," he said.

She grabbed the newspaper and read aloud. "The Finance Minister of the Dominican Republic, Mr. Juan Alvarez, will have an official state burial today. The government is still trying to find suspected murderer, Dr. Robison Murphy." Brianne gasped. "According to reports, Carlos Alvarez, his son, saw the doctor stab his father three times with a large kitchen knife. Dr. Robison Murphy escaped and continues to evade police."

Brianne sat down heavily beside Tom on the couch. "Holy crap!" she whispered.

"And how does Wade fit into this picture?" Tom asked. "Where the hell is he?"

The doorbell rang at that point. "Who could that be?" Tom wondered as he went to answer.

Two men were out front. They presented their credentials—FBI.

"If you don't mind, we have a few questions we would like to ask you and your wife," one agent said. "I believe she's been in contact with Senator Moore's office."

"Yes,…yes. Come in." Tom led the way into the den.

After describing their entire trip, including the strange men at the door of the villa trying to find a doctor, followed by Robison and Wade's disappearance, there was little else to offer them.

"Have they been in contact with you?" asked one of the agents.

"No. We're worried sick," Brianne replied. "But let me say this: there is no way on earth that Robison could do this. She's devoted her life to helping and healing. She's been framed. You must do something to help her."

The two agents thanked the Winsteads and left a business card with instructions to call them if they heard from the Murphys. They offered Tom and Brianne no encouragement whatsoever.

"What do we do now?" Brianne asked Tom.

"I haven't the faintest idea," Tom said, tapping the business card on the end table.

"Perhaps I need to fly to Washington and meet with Senator Moore in person," she offered out of desperation.

"What good would that do? She's a wanted criminal in a foreign country. You don't think they're going to let her go on Senator Moore's request, do you?"

Frustrated, Brianne stood up, turned towards her husband and asserted, "But we have to do something, for God's sake! Perhaps we should go back down there and look for ourselves. Maybe arrange for an attorney from Santo Domingo. Something—we must do something!"

"Well, let's think about it some more," Tom said.

Reluctantly agreeing, Brianne went upstairs to take a long, hot bath. Tom soon brought her a cold glass of Chablis to sip while she soaked in the tub. He could see that she'd been crying; her eyes were puffy and her face was splotchy red.

"More bad news, I'm afraid," he said, handing her the glass.

She sipped the wine, saying afterwards, "How could it get any worse?"

"Here's how," Tom said. "There's a monstrous hurricane heading directly into the southeast coast of the Dominican Republic. So flying there right now is out of the question...even if we decided to go. They're evacuating that side of the island."

Brianne held the cool glass to her forehead, as if to relieve a pain. "Well, if the hurricane doesn't kill her, maybe it will buy her some time."

"Where in the hell could Wade be?" Tom asked again. "He must be with her, surely...surely she's not alone."

"God, I have no idea. We can only pray."

Ty had finished his calls and let Little Lito finish his last joke when Raúl popped in, apparently just coming from the airport. He went over to Ty and said, "No show tonight either. The hurricane has picked up momentum. I have the skaters leaving on various flights this afternoon. And the crew is booked later this evening on the last plane out. Make sure they don't miss it."

Passing along that information to the performers, Ty then told his crew to eat and start tearing down the show as fast as they could. He passed out the payroll even though it was two days early.

"Here are your checks, but you won't be able to go to the bank because they are all closed for evacuation. So I'm arranging for T. J. to have some cash at the airport in Miami in case you need it to get home," Ty explained.

"Don't get in a big panic; just get your belongings packed, go to the rink, pick up your skates, and get to the airport. You may not all be on the same flight. It will be chaotic at the airport with all the tourists trying to leave too, but please...just be patient. Everything will be fine."

Ty listened as Raúl gave them the particulars on their flights and handed each of them a ticket. Then they headed back to the lobby. "What about getting some local guys to help take out the rink?" Ty inquired of Raúl.

"I believe the American expression is 'are you pulling my leg?'" A bit smugly Raúl continued, "No, seriously. Everyone is trying to get their homes boarded up and their families moved inland. In fact, I must do the same. I am very sorry, Señor Ty, but you are on your own with the rink and equipment."

"Gee, thanks. Your helpfulness is overwhelming!"

"I suggest you get out of here as well," Raúl added, somewhat apologetic for leaving Ty high and dry. "Here is a ticket for you...it's the last seat out."

Ty refused the ticket: "I won't be leaving my equipment behind. But don't worry, I can take care of myself. This isn't the first time I've been in a hurricane or some other kind of shit...come to think of it."

They shook hands and Raúl made a beeline for his car. Ty didn't blame him for putting his family first. He would have done the same.

Slapping his yellow legal pad against his leg, Ty went to catch the elevator back upstairs.

His cell phone rang; it was the Stuart office: "Ty, there is a hurricane heading your way."

"No shit, Sherlock," Ty answered, still waiting for the elevator.

"Anyway, your brother wants to talk to you."

"Okay, thanks," Ty said to the warehouse supervisor.

"Hey man, got yourself in a little pickle, haven't you?" T. J. announced. Not waiting for an answer: "Anyway, the ship to Greece is fine and out of danger. Do you need me to come down there and help you?"

"Well, at least that's a piece of good news," Ty responded. "No, you stay put. Francis may be heading your way after it hits this place and there's no use both of us being here. Thanks anyway, and by the way, the cast will be arriving in Miami tonight and the crew early tomorrow, probably after midnight. I paid them but they have no way of cashing their checks; none of the banks are open. So you'll need to bring some cash to the airport."

"No problem; I'll be there," said T. J. "Listen, be careful."

"Thanks, I'll talk to you later. Oh, and tell Mom I'll be fine, and not to…" Ty was in mid sentence when his cell phone went dead.

Well, hell,…"there's no business like show business" all right. Damn! He needed to get into a different line of work; anything had to be easier than this turmoil.

Ty was heading for the elevator but questions from performers detained him along the way. Finally, they all settled into the evacuation schedule and went to their rooms to finish packing. The veterans, of course, had bags packed and out in the hall for pickup. Why couldn't they all be like that?

Hurricane Francis was picking up strength as it traveled over the warm waters of the Caribbean. Now upgraded to category four, the winds were exceeding one hundred forty miles per hour. The storm spanned some two hundred and fifty miles in width. It was on a collision course of mass destruction, and its swirling fury was less then twenty-four hours away.

SEVENTEEN

Carlos, Robison cuffed to Donadio, and the other bodyguard piled into the car and began heading out of town. Robison, up to this point, had not uttered a single word since she'd been kidnapped from Ty's hotel room. With her last memory of Wade lying beaten and bleeding, she didn't know if he was dead or alive. Everything had happened so fast. Her prevailing despair was overwhelming. Surrendering to the realization that her destiny was in the hands of this lying, conniving asshole, Carlos, was dismally morbid. This time she saw no way out.

The road from Altos de Chavón, which normally saw minimal traffic, was now bumper-to-bumper with local people evacuating all coastal areas. Many had most of their belongings strapped to the roofs of their cars; all were overloaded with adults, children and pets. Chaos was rampant, tempers were short, and the evacuation time was going to be long and tedious for several thousand people.

Robison, however, still didn't realize a hurricane was bearing down on them, nor was she aware of the congested traffic. She wasn't cognizant of anything going on around her, except her present dangerous situation, and her thoughts about Wade...the love of her life. Would she ever see him again? Would he ever hold her in his arms again?

Carlos was constantly snapping instructions to his driver, while he was continuously on his cell phone making one call after another. Finally, when there was a break in his calls, Robison asked, "Where are you taking me? Back to the main house?"

"Yes. I have to make sure they are boarding up the estate and securing it before we leave. Surely you know a big hurricane is heading this way. That's why the traffic is so bad and it's taking us so long to get back there."

My God, what else? Feeling that she could now forgo any hopes of getting back to Wade and Ty amid the traffic and now the storm, Robison was completely despondent. Silent tears trickled down her face. Ty would have found Wade in his hotel room by now, unless Carlos had done something with him. Even if they never found her, at least Ty would help Wade she was certain.

Then there was her probability of escape…which was not high. Bound to Donadio was going to make flight difficult, if at all possible. And if she could get away, Altos de Chavón would be the first place they would look for her. But where else could she go? Every person and policeman would be searching for her as the assassin of Juan Alvarez. There was probably a reward on her head. She tried to settle her nerves down. There was no use in worrying about where she would go until she could figure out a way to gain her freedom.

Summoning a little courage, she said, "I didn't kill your father. Why are you doing this to me? Why can't you just let me go?"

Carlos, still staring out the window said, "I saw you stab him and that's what I'm going to tell the police and the judge. Isn't that right, Donadio?"

"Sí, Señor!"

"You killed him, didn't you?" she asked, quietly.

"No, I loved him. Now shut up! I don't want to talk about this anymore," he said abruptly. He was clearly upset by this line of questioning.

Turning into the Casa de Campo's main gate, they headed for the Alvarez house. When they reached the street the estate was on, the driver saw a car blocking the entrance. With an outburst of Spanish among the three men, Carlos told his driver to continue past the vehicle so he could see who was in the car. After they drove by, Carlos' driver kept looking in the rearview mirror. Robison turned to look out the back window, but Donadio forced her to face forward. Exasperated, Carlos was mumbling under his breath. But she couldn't make out what he was saying or even whether it was in English or Spanish. All she knew for sure was that it wasn't directed towards her…for a change.

Once they were well past the parked car, Carlos had his driver pull over to the side of the road, out of sight. All three of them checked their weapons.

God Almighty! What was she getting into now? A sick feeling plunged to the pit of her stomach. Was this how she was going to die? Amid a shower of flying bullets, none of which were meant for her?

Donadio unlocked his cuff and reattached it to the inside car handle. With Robison now cuffed to the car, there was still no possibility of escape.

They slowly turned the car around. Donadio's gun was drawn, but he kept it low and out of sight. Stomping on the accelerator, they rounded the corner, and squealed to a stop, blocking the other car. Donadio hopped out so fast Robison hardly knew he was gone. Carlos then stepped out cautiously but stayed positioned behind the open door.

"Get out in the open, cousin," demanded Carlos in English.

Robison could see everything going on through the side window, but, better yet, she could understand the language. The driver's car door opened and out stepped a man. Apparently this Luís guy didn't seem too worried about approaching Carlos. Nor did he seem to be worried about gun-toting Donadio. What could this guy be thinking? She surmised he was just plain stupid.

"I want my money or the necklace," Luís demanded. And I'm not leaving until I get one or the other."

Carlos answered, "I already told you, I don't have the necklace. I gave it back to you."

"You lying son-of-a-bitch!" Luís said, stepping closer. "I know you made a switch at the hotel. What do you think I am, fucking stupid?"

Carlos coolly lit a cigarette. "You said it, not me. What's that saying in America? If the shoe fits…wear it."

"You son-of-a-bitch! I want to speak to my uncle."

"That is impossible," Carlos said sternly.

"I want the necklace or money, one or the other!"

"Look, Luís, you stupid asshole. Turn your puny ass around and get the hell out of here and forget you were ever part of this family…or else."

"Or else what? You will have your men kill me like they killed Felicity?"

Carlos didn't respond. He took a long drag on his cigarette.

"You had Felicity killed, didn't you? Didn't you?" he screamed at Carlos.

Carlos nodded to Donadio who aimed his gun and shot Luís four times. His body fell to the ground with a sickening thud; his skull hit the pavement with a "splat." Blood poured out of the bullet holes in Luís' body and onto the road.

Robison let out a scream, covering her eyes with her one available hand. This was too much. How could this happen? What was in store for her? She couldn't even imagine. They were all cold-blooded murderers.

The guard behind the wheel of the car got out while Carlos and Donadio got back in. This time Donadio drove. With the sound of rubber squealing against the pavement, he drove into the estate.

"You can't just leave him lying there like that!" Robison screamed.

"Shut the fuck up, or you'll be next," Carlos snarled.

"He was your cousin; how could you?"

Carlos grabbed her arm, pulling her roughly towards him. "I said…shut your fucking mouth or you'll be next!"

He let go of her with a shove. She began to tremble uncontrollably.

The car halted in the circular drive out front. She could see several workmen boarding up the windows and doors; others carried suitcases and boxes with paintings and crystal, carefully loading them into several vans. They were working furiously, trying to cover the boxes and tie down those already in a pickup truck over to one side. Men were pulling out parked cars from inside the garages. One was the black limousine used by the presidential nominee.

Carlos got out and began shouting instructions to several of them. He had to holler loudly so they could hear him above the wind. His black hair was blowing into his eyes; nervously he kept sweeping it back so he could see.

A trailer carrying the large horse she had seen Carlos riding past her villa that morning was hooked to a truck, ready to travel. Carlos walked over to the driver motioning towards the gate. The driver immediately fired up the engine and began slowly pulling out with the trailer in tow. Several other horse trailers were leaving also, but they each had more than one horse inside. Clearly this particular horse was receiving "star" treatment, so a man like Carlos, a cold-blooded killer, could actually care about something…even if it was a four-legged animal.

She stayed in the car while Carlos rushed inside the house. Donadio re-cuffed himself to Robison and decided to entertain himself by putting his hand on her breast. She jerked away as best she could; he only laughed. She could hardly catch her breath, as the trembling was so severe. The worst part was…not knowing what would happen next.

She couldn't rid herself of the vision of Donadio shooting down the man in cold blood. Or of the "thud" of his body hitting the pavement and the sight of blood splattering all over the road. There was no doubt in her mind that they'd killed Felicity…whoever she might be.

She was praying Wade hadn't met the same fate. She felt like vomiting, but she had to hold on and not let her imagination run wild. For the sake of her own sanity, she tried to remember all the events after they left the hotel room. Yes, all four of them had stayed together. Neither one of the bodyguards ever left, to her recollection, to go back and harm Wade further. Hopefully, other henchmen had not been instructed to kill him once Carlos had left the hotel. She prayed her husband was still alive.

Inside, Carlos was making sure everything of value was being evacuated. The entire staff was busy running back and forth in pandemonium. Making his way into his father's office, he closed the door behind him. He needed a short respite to collect his wits. Things seemed to be spinning out of control and he couldn't let his men see him in this state. They wouldn't respect him if he showed frailty.

Standing there amidst the naked walls where once great paintings hung seemed sad and surreal. Snapping out of it, he made his way over to the minibar and poured himself a stiff libation. He hadn't meant to envision the shooting of his father again, but the bloodstained couch and carpet were sad reminders. Two stiff drinks bolstered his courage and settled his nerves, or so he thought. He made a mental note to have the room redecorated before he returned again.

It was time to go. He slammed back one more scotch and was out the door.

After what seemed like an eternity, but couldn't have been more than about fifteen minutes, the driver reappeared. Carlos came out carrying a suitcase and the driver opened the trunk for him. With a few last-minute instructions from Carlos to the workers, the driver sped their vehicle about and down the road.

Robison could see the angry sea churning and crashing onto the beach as they roared up the driveway and out through the gate. They were approaching the place where that man, Carlos' cousin, was lying—dead. She closed her eyes; she didn't want to see the body again. But her curiosity got the best of her and she opened them.

The body was miraculously gone. So was the car. So was the blood.

She didn't want to know how or where, so she just remained silent as Carlos babbled on to Donadio in Spanish. God only knew what they were planning next. Sickeningly, she could smell alcohol on Carlos' breath. Pig!

The wind was beginning to pick up velocity. The palm trees were bending over, the fronds ripping around like rags in the oncoming storm. Scraps of paper and pieces of boxes used in packing were swirling in the wind, hitting the sides of the car or anything in their path.

Heading out of the Campo, they found the main gate was open for all to pass. There were no guards to check papers or passes. They, too, must have gone home to prepare for the storm.

Surprisingly, the driver turned right toward Altos de Chavón, not left toward Santo Domingo. They were only able to navigate the road by traveling on the shoulder (what there was of one) as both lanes of traffic headed away from the coast. And here they were…going in the opposite direction!

She couldn't figure out what Carlos was planning and, for obvious reasons, didn't really care anymore. It all seemed so futile. There was all this commotion, honking, hollering and even hand gesturing, as they headed against the traffic flow.

A couple of times they got stuck on the sandy shoulder, then they would back up and try again. Several times the other guard and Donadio leaned against the back of the car and pushed so they could continue.

All three men were sweating profusely, although it didn't seem that hot to Robison. She figured it must be their nerves or their excessive drinking the night before—probably the drinking. She already knew Carlos had been in the bottle. Why would the other two be any different? At any rate, there was nothing she could do about it.

She got her hopes up when they were approaching Altos de Chavón. She hoped for a miracle that would release her from her manacle to Donadio, who always made sure to re-cuff himself when he returned from pushing the car. She prayed for a knight in shining armor to come along and pluck her out of this incarceration. She thought of Ty...handsome, resourceful Ty.

Robison watched in silence as they passed the turn to Altos de Chavón and kept heading east. Just seeing the road sign to the small village prompted a stabbing pain in Robison's stomach and a lump to rise in her throat.

Yes, hopefully Ty would have found Wade in his room by now. Good old Ty, she was sure he would "doctor" Wade, as he had "doctored" her. The thought brought a trace of a smile to her face. All she dared hope now was that Wade would get away and save himself. She had resigned herself to the probability that her life was over...

She prayed his was not.

The street narrowed to barely a two-lane road and soon they were riding parallel to the Chavón River. The traffic was moving slowly and progress was difficult against the oncoming flood of evacuees.

"Where are we going?" Robison asked again.

To her surprise, this time Carlos answered in a reasonable tone: "We're going east, then we will take the ferry across the river and go north to a ranch I have there. Taking the ferry will cut off five hours of driving, perhaps even more with this traffic. Don't worry. The ranch will be out of the hurricane's path."

"I don't understand," she said. "I thought you were turning me in to the police?" Robison's fear now lay in Carlos sequestering her in some remote location. Then Wade would never find her, even with Ty's help. Perhaps the police and a murder charge would have been easier to handle—safer in many respects. Carlos didn't answer. Confused and tired, she sank into deep depression as they beat a sluggish retreat ahead of the storm.

A long line of cars and trucks were queued up to board the ferry across the Chavón River. After waiting in line for two hours, they didn't seem to be any closer to the ferry landing. They progressed at a snail's pace…a few feet at a time.

The radio was blaring incessantly in Spanish and Robison knew it must be reporting on the hurricane, but she didn't have the curiosity to ask about it. In between the quick chatter, the station played music that always featured loud trumpeting. It was enough to give any sane person a splitting headache. None of the others noticed the loud music; they only paid attention to the news portions of the program.

What difference would the ravaging storm make to her anyway? Trapped is what she was, with her murderer to be sitting next to her. Robison had gotten away twice before, but there was no apparent way out this time. She was doomed.

After another hour, the men decided they needed to take a leak, so like many of those in front of them they just got out of car and urinated on the side of the road. To Robison's disgust, her cuff-mate took her along when he relieved himself. She tried to turn away, but Donadio jerked her around and said, "You like what you see?"

"You are a pig!" She spit on the ground.

Donadio laughed.

Back in the car, Carlos asked her, "Do you have to go?"

"Yes, but I won't go on the side of the road with everyone watching. And how can I go cuffed to this…this gorilla?"

Carlos laughed at the "gorilla" and translated to the other men; they all chuckled.

Rattling off in Spanish again, Carlos motioned to the "gorilla" to unlock the cuff.

"I will go with you," Carlos said. "And I am going to watch you. There will be no running away this time. Do you understand? I will shoot you if you try anything." Carlos held the door for her and the two of them marched over to the dense foliage.

After relieving herself, they walked back towards the car while he held her arm tightly. No one observing would have suspected she was a prisoner.

"How far is the ranch once we get to the other side of the river?" Robison inquired, as Carlos seemed to be more reasonable now.

"It's not far to Caltengo…the ranch's name is Caltengo," he replied calmly. "Anyway, there's no hurry to turn you into the police. I'm the star witness since I saw you stab my father. And the courts and the police are busy with the hurricane right now. You might slip out of their grasp and I don't want anything to happen to you. Also, Donadio is going to back up my story. This will be an open-and-shut case. No further investigations. Assassin hunted, captured and convicted!"

"But I didn't do it!" Robison cried as they reached the car.

"Shut up!" He squeezed her arm hard this time. "As far as the world is concerned, you did do it!" He shoved her into the backseat of the car.

The "gorilla" walked ahead to see if the line was getting shorter. He was wondering what kind of timetable they were facing to get on the ferry. With Donadio gone, Carlos strapped the cuff to his wrist and hers. Leaning his head back on the seat, he closed his eyes. It would be a couple more hours before it would be their turn to board the ferry…if they made it at all!

Wade opened his eyes and realized he was on the floor between the beds. The light on the ceiling was blurry. He blinked several times to clear his vision. Slowly he began to sit up. His ribs and stomach hurt so badly it made him catch his breath. Finally on his knees and leaning against the bed with his elbows, he was able to push himself up to a standing position.

Glancing around the room, trying to bring things into focus, he closed his eyes and took a deep breath. He grimaced from the sharp stabbing pain in his ribcage. "Robbi? Robbi?" he called weakly, hoping beyond hope she'd been left behind.

Hearing nothing, he slowly began walking towards the bathroom. Turning on the light, he was shocked at his reflection in the mirror. He grabbed a towel and wet it, trying to dab off the crusted blood that was partially covering his face and head. The room started to spin and he grabbed the edge of the sink for support. He knew he must have a concussion. It took a few minutes to get the spinning under control.

Then he found Ty's note directing him to stay put. Where the hell was he going to go, anyway? He could barely make it from the bed to the bathroom. It was all he could do to hold himself together.

Looking back up into the mirror he noticed writing on the wall behind him. He turned, leaning back on the sink for support. The message was scribbled in lipstick:

"W - I'll always love you. R."

He held his head in his hands and sank slowly to the floor. The message was so final. His complete and utter helplessness only added to his overwhelming despair. How would he ever find her now? Sobs racked his body.

When Ty returned to his hotel room, he could hear the shower running and was glad Wade was up and around. Quickly, Ty began to pack his clothes and belongings.

Wade staggered out of the bathroom. "Oh, my God, I'm glad you're here. Do you know anything about Robison?"

"No. You tell me," Ty said.

Wade explained what had happened when Carlos and his men broke into the room and kidnapped Robison. Ty kept packing while he listened to both Wade and the weather report, not looking at either one.

"I need to go back to the house in the Campo and find her," Wade said. "I can't think of any other place to start looking, can you?"

Ty stopped, looked up. "Well, they won't be at that house. Isn't it on the ocean?"

"Yes."

"Don't you know there's a hurricane heading this way and everyone is evacuating?"

"Shit, no! Now what am I going to do? I'll never find her!" Wade threw the towel down violently, then started putting his pants on.

In a calming tone of voice, Ty said, "Look, I can tell you for certain that she isn't going to be at the oceanfront house. We don't know where she is now, but the best thing we can do is wait. This hurricane may buy her some time. So get your stuff together; you're coming with me. We're going to take the ice out and get those containers packed before Francis hits."

"You mean we're staying here?"

"For your information, we will probably be in the safest place possible. Down inside the amphitheater, we can stay in one of the two cement block buildings used for dressing rooms."

"I still can't believe this trumped-up charge of murder. That son-of-a-bitch, Carlos; I'd like to get my hands on him...," Wade exclaimed.

"Yeah, right! By the looks of your face, we know who got 'hold' of whom!" Ty said.

"God, my head hurts!" Wade exclaimed.

"Just hold on...I've got pills for that."

Finished with his packing, Ty took out his legal pad and made a small list. He tore off the sheet of paper and handed it to Wade along with a couple of Advils.

"Here, stop and buy these supplies on your way to the rink. I'll take our bags and a couple of pillows. It'll be a long night." Ty paused and turned at the door. "And hurry. We'll have plenty of time later to plan some kind of rescue operation. In fact, we'll probably have all night. And damn it, don't dawdle around; look what that cost you the last time."

Son-of-a-bitch! He was sounding more like a detective on television every time he opened his mouth lately. What the hell did Ty know about a goddamned rescue operation? Oh, what the hell! If it made Wade relax a bit...it was worth the police jargon.

"Do you think they are looking for me?" Wade asked while he hurriedly put on his shirt.

"If you were important to this Carlos guy, he would have taken you, too, when he took Robison...or killed you for that matter. Obviously, he doesn't give a damn about you.... Lucky you!"

"I guess you're right." Wade was standing in the middle of the torn-up room. He took the two Advils with a swig of bottled water that was on the dresser.

Ty took a last look around. "Gosh, what a mess! I hate it when people don't know the drill," he grimaced. And with suitcases in hand and a pillow under each arm he left.

Wade finally persuaded a shop owner who was busy boarding up his store to sell him some supplies. Flashlights, batteries, water and food; he bought as much as he could carry. The shopkeeper charged him an arm and a leg, but Wade had no choice. Outrageous prices came with hurricanes; part of the collateral damage.

At the top of the amphitheater, Wade paused to watch the scurrying below. Most of the show's sets and lights were already in one container and some crew members were breaking out the ice with sledgehammers.

The wind had picked up considerably, blowing the layer of air away and causing the ice to melt. Although Ty had lowered the temperature to around zero a few hours before, the chillers couldn't stop it from melting. The wind was gusting up to forty-five miles per hour, so the wet surface was slowing down the load-out. The stage crew was slipping and sliding trying to get the ice shoveled over the side and onto the ground. The bottom of workers' pant legs were soaking wet, as were their shoes and socks. Precious time was slipping away—all because of the wind. There was no time to take a break.

Hurrying down the stairs, Wade found Ty shouting directions over the howling wind. Dirt was blowing into Wade's eyes; he noticed Ty had sunglasses on.

"Where do I put this stuff?" Wade inquired of Ty.

"In that dressing room over there; that's where I've set up shop for us," Ty yelled.

Ty let out a loud whistle when he saw the shuttle driver appear at the top of the stairs. All the workers came to a standstill; it was time for them to head for the airport.

Knowing Ty was staying behind, the crewmen all shook hands and wished him well. Some even offered to stay behind, but Ty insisted they leave. Besides, he told them, he had a built-in helper and pointed to Wade as he emerged from the dressing room.

"No offense, Ty, but he doesn't look like he's in the best of shape," one man observed. The black eye and laceration on Wade's forehead made him look as though he'd already been through a violent storm.

"He'll do in a pinch," Ty retorted. "Don't you worry about us; just get to the airport. T. J. will meet you Miami in case anyone needs a ride or money. I'll call tomorrow and let you know how we manage."

The stage crew was quickly on their way, as the wind continued to pick up more velocity. Ty stood looking at the pipes that had yet to be loaded. The wind was whipping his pants and shirt around wildly, the sky was darkening. Time was running out.

"Well, Wade, my man, it's just you and I. So grab a pair of gloves over there and let's start loading these coils into the truck."

"Coils?"

"These pipes...God Almighty, where did you grow up?"

"In the goddamned south! Where there aren't a hell of a lot of ice rinks!"

"Just lift your end," Ty shouted.

"Son-of-a-bitch! How much does a coil weigh?"

"Oh, probably a hundred and fifty pounds a piece. A little out of shape, are we?" Ty cajoled.

Ty and Wade finished loading the last of the coils onto the truck just as huge drops of rain splattered them. They rolled up the tarp as best they could in the rain and wind and dragged it into the block building that had once served as the alternate dressing room. Perhaps during the eye of the storm, or after it had passed, they could lay the tarp out to dry, then fold it properly and pack it into the ice container. As it was now, soaked, there was no way the two of them could lift it into the truck; it was just too heavy.

A steady rain now evolved into a gusty downpour. Torrential sheets of water were sure to follow.

Inside the block building, they changed into dry clothes and rummaged through the food. Wade was so exhausted he sat down in one of the folding chairs and didn't move.

"A little whipped, are you?" Ty asked with a smirk.

"You know what? I've never worked so hard in my life!"

"Welcome to show business! What do you do for a living?"

"I'm a stockbroker. I sit in a chair most of the day." Wade laughed, clutching at a pain in his rib cage. "Well, at least I *was* a stockbroker. No telling what they'll do when I don't show up for work!" He paused, then added, "Show business is too goddamned much work, but I'm sure it's exciting at times."

Ty chuckled and shook his head. He was making a sandwich and opening a bottle of water. "Want something to eat?" he asked.

"Yeah, if I can get off this chair. I'm not shittin' you, my back is killing me," Wade said.

Ty handed him two sandwiches and a couple more Advils. The electricity flickered at that point and went out. Ty grabbed the mini-mag flashlight he carried on his belt, and shined it onto the plastic grocery bags spread on the floor. He located the larger flashlight and batteries Wade had purchased earlier, assembled it and soon had enough light to make two more sandwiches.

"Ain't this cozy?" Wade exclaimed, while the wind and rain roared outside.

Ty shined a light on the door; he could see water underneath…creeping towards their supplies. Ty picked up all the gear and placed it on the shelves overhead. He then shined the light on Wade who was still sitting in the chair but was beginning to doze off. Taking a couple of packing blankets, Ty made two pallets, one for the top of each table. Then he helped Wade out of the chair and onto the makeshift bed.

Ty lay in the dark with only the sound of the raging storm to fill the void. Beside him, Wade was now wide awake, worrying about Robison.

"So how did you get into this line of work?" Wade asked, as a diversion from his thoughts.

"I grew up in it," Ty began. "My parents owned their own ice show. In fact, when my mother was a girl, she skated in the Sonja Heine movies. Since skating wasn't my forte, I opted for the operations end of it. And 'voila,' here I am, in the middle of a category four hurricane on an island in the Caribbean, sleeping on a goddamned table with a dead-tired stockbroker whose wife is a missing doctor that's wanted for a murder she didn't commit. Shit! …What could be better than that?"

Wade guffawed! …Then groaned when his rib cage hurt from laughing.

The wind grew louder, obliterating any further conversation. But it didn't obliterate Wade's thoughts of Robison. Wherever she was…God! He loved her.

Despite the raging storm, sleep came swiftly for Ty…and mercifully for Wade.

EIGHTEEN

Robison woke up to the sounds of a heated Spanish discussion. The driver was speaking to Carlos from the front seat as he pulled forward a few feet and stopped. She vaguely remembered the starting and stopping of the car several times while she had been dozing. There was a camper and a furniture truck in front of them, blocking her view of the ferry, and making it impossible to determine how the line was progressing.

Robison thought surely there had to be a better way to get to Caltengo than this. But what difference did it make to her, anyway? Another route would only put off the inevitable. She let her mind wander, which turned out to be a mistake; all she could picture was that cold-blooded murder back at the estate.

A commotion began a few cars ahead. Carlos turned towards Donadio and they began talking fast and furiously with one another again. She could see the ferry operator making an announcement into a bullhorn, but she didn't know what he was saying. Even if she could have understood Spanish, it was very hard to hear above the howling wind. People were angry in line behind their car. They were shouting and honking; some got out of their vehicles and stormed past waving their fists.

Obviously, the message was that they were going to stop the ferry crossings and people were upset, to say the least. She wondered if it they would get onboard. Vehicles behind them started turning around and leaving, frustrated from wasting precious time necessary in getting out of the path of Francis.

Finally, the only vehicles waiting to board the ferry were the large truck, the small camper and the car carrying Carlos and company. Now Robison had a better view of the boarding procedures, which were not going smoothly.

The furniture truck was approaching the steel ramp; however, turbulent water shifted the ferry back and forth, causing the ramp to rise above the landing with every rolling wave. Those approaching had to wait for just the right moment, then the driver would "gun" his vehicle to shoot onboard before the next wave rolled in. Success in this loading tactic depended on the skill of each driver, who learned by watching others. Nerve-racking indeed, but Robison was certain there was no turning back for Carlos and company.

The driver of the large truck was having difficultly timing his move. The heavy load of three cars abreast and ten deep caused the ship to sink low in the water. Thus the ramp now slanted downwards instead of upwards. It appeared that the large truck was to park on the far left, the rickety camper in the middle and Carlos' vehicle on the right. Their car would be the last on…if they made it!

After several tries, the furniture truck finally got onboard. Now the driver was trying to pull as far left as he could, which took several minutes of seemingly fruitless jockeying. Robison wasn't sure the camper and their car would fit into the remaining space. But then she'd never been very good at judging the width of parking spaces.

Carlos must have reached the same conclusion, for he instructed the driver and Donadio to make sure that they got on the ship—even if it meant "convincing" the ferry operator to reject the camper in front of them. Carlos would not be left behind!

As the two guards got out and walked quickly towards the ferry, she noticed each of them pat his side, checking to see if his gun was in place. She wondered if they were aware of this habit, or if it was calculated to send a message.

The two men jumped onto the ship just before the ramp slid out of position once again. Donadio slipped, almost losing his footing. He cussed out loud as he straightened up his jacket. "Too bad he hadn't busted his ass!" Robison thought to herself. "It couldn't have happened to a bigger asshole!"

"What are they going to do?" Robison asked.

"They're making sure we get onboard, one way or another," Carlos snapped back.

"So what does that mean? If the ferry operator isn't agreeable, he gets shot like your cousin?"

"You need to mind your own business, Doctor. Besides, people are meaningless to me."

That was a truthful statement if she'd ever heard one.

Dusk was closing in. Rain was beginning to fall and the wind was gaining more strength now. From what Robison could see, it wasn't far across to the other side of the river. Hopefully, the trip wouldn't take long because waves were getting higher with every passing moment.

The camper pulled forward so Carlos needed to pull forward as well. Since the driver had not returned, and still cuffed to Robison, Carlos got out of the back of the car with her in tow. He shoved her into the front seat so he could get behind the wheel.

With the car in Drive, he idled forward as the camper struggled to get onboard. Carlos lit up another cigarette; he was clearly nervous. He pulled forward a few more feet while the camper, now on the ferry, jockeyed into its position next to the furniture truck.

It was now their turn. Carlos threw his cigarette out the window and prepared to drive the car onboard himself. He pulled up to the edge of the ramp, and was about to gun the motor when the ship started to list. He struggled with only one hand to steer: the other was cuffed to Robison.

The operator shouted at Carlos to hurry. Carlos cursed back as he unlocked the cuffs. With both hands now on the steering wheel, he leaned forward to gauge the opportune moment to shoot onboard. He had the added handicap of not being sure his car would fit into the space between the camper and the railing. How was he going to gun the car and still fit precisely into that little slot all at the same time? With the ship rocking continuously, there never seemed to be just the right moment for him to make his move. Robison looked at Carlos, who was sweating profusely.

In the meantime, the ferry operator was telling Donadio that Carlos couldn't make it and he should back off the ramp. Carlos lowered the window and started yelling in Spanish at the operator, insisting he was coming onboard come hell or high water. The ferry operator was just as determined to stop Carlos. Ultimately, the "gorilla" and other guard went over to the operator and shoved him up against the railing.

It was now dark and raining, so none of the other passengers could see what was happening. However, they didn't like the delay, so several began hollering for the ferry to get moving before it was too late. Others screamed at Carlos to back off and let the ferry proceed.

Carlos doubted his driving skills at that point. What if he hit the railing or the camper and totaled the car? What if he was stuck half on and half off the ramp? Because he had been chauffeured so much, he was out of practice as a driver. Still not giving up, he gave Robison instructions:

"Put down your window and see how much room I have on that side. Don't let me hit the railing!"

She did as he asked and reported, "There are only a couple of inches on this side."

She left the window down, so she could warn him as they proceeded. Besides, the outside air was a welcome relief from the second hand cigarette smoke.

Carlos eased slowly between the camper and the railing to Robison's right. The side-view mirror of the camper was almost touching his window on the left. Ironically, it was such a tight fit the "gorilla" and other guard could not get back in the car; they would have to endure the ride across standing in the rain. Delighting in their misfortune, Robison let a tiny smile cross her face.

The ship was still rocking turbulently from side to side. Someone had mentioned the ride would take about fifteen minutes, perhaps twenty with the waves and rain. That was the good news; the crossing would be over soon. The bad news was what might be in store for Robison on the other side when they arrived at Caltengo. She tried to put that out of her mind.

Carlos put his window up, shut off the motor and lit another cigarette. Thank God she'd left her window open! She felt like the ferry had become a "floating prison," with everyone trapped in their vehicles.

The boat lunged forward with a start. There was a loud clanking of the motor straining to engage its gears, followed by the squeaking and groaning of the old ship getting under way. She looked down at the murky, swirling, brown water; it wasn't the beautiful blue river she had seen from the restaurant at Altos de Chavón along with Wade and the Winsteads. Trees surrounding the little cove obscured the landing and blocked the wind. Soon they would be out in the open water, beyond the dense foliage.

"I hope we don't sink, we'd never be able to get out of this car," Robison noted.

"It's a short ride, twenty minutes perhaps, no more," he said, motioning with his cigarette.

"I know."

"Well, aren't you just the 'little miss know it all.'"

She ignored his comment.

The ferry cleared the trees, and headed into a fierce wind. The waves rocked the boat from side to side ominously. The river was white capping in its rage, so Robison gripped the car door handle.

"I don't like this rocking," she said.

"Well, if you're going to vomit, stick your head out the window. I don't need the smell of puke in my car."

"I'm not..."

She stopped when the large furniture truck shifted towards the camper and them...before settling back down.

"Did you see that?" Robison exclaimed.

"Don't be such a sissy," Carlos said trying to be casual. "We're almost across."

But she saw through his façade. He was as scared as she was! And they weren't "almost" across; they weren't even halfway yet. The rolling waves were more violent. She felt queasy.

Carlos flicked his cigarette out the window in front of her face, sending a message that he couldn't care less. She watched him take out yet another cigarette, but decided not to say anything about his chain-smoking, nor to mention that the acrid smoke added to her seasickness. At least the cuff was off, a relief from being connected to the "gorilla."

Donadio, soaking wet, was trying to light a cigarette in the wind and the rain. He finally gave up and threw it in the river. Water was dripping off his nose.

The ferry operator was nowhere to be seen. Hopefully, he was still alive.

Another surge of the boat sent Robison's stomach to her throat. Again the weight in the large truck shifted to the right on the wet slippery deck. It touched the camper beside it ever so slightly, with a clanking of metal rubbing against metal. It gave Robison the sensation of hearing fingernails being dragged down a blackboard.

With her window open, she could hear the driver of the camper yelling at the truck driver to his left. Several other vehicles had slid and banged into one another, sending temperaments soaring. Everyone was hollering, cussing and throwing hand gestures to one another. Robison was certain a fistfight would have broken out if any of them could have opened their doors and gotten out. Thankfully, they were parked tightly together; no one could move. A giant brawl is all they would have needed now. She tried to ignore the unpleasantness by looking in the other direction, out her window where there was fresh air…mixed with blowing rain.

With her mind racing, Robison glanced at Carlos, who was still chain smoking to conceal his nervousness. Soon this trip across the water would be over. Then what? What was he going to do with her in Caltengo? Oh, God, Wade! Where are you when I need you so much? She prayed for God to help her.

Another huge wave tilted the ferry, shifted the loaded truck, and brought the excruciating noise of metal grinding against metal. In fact, the furniture truck rammed the camper sideways with such force that it pushed into Carlos' vehicle. The side view mirror of the camper broke through the car window and pinned Carlos' head against the seat. He grabbed the mirror with both hands, and tried to push it away. More screeching sounds of grinding metal as the mirror threatened to choke the life out of him. Carlos reached for the electric button on the side of the seat to let the seat back, and to relieve the pressure on his neck. Straining…straining…he couldn't reach it.

The camper leaned sideways, and was now slightly on top of the car. The lady on the passenger side of the camper was almost touching heads with Carlos, separated only by the glass of the camper window. She'd cut her face; blood was oozing out onto the transparent surface.

Carlos continued squirming and struggling to free himself while not looking at the screaming face of the lady. He called for Robison to help him…but what could she do? She stared at the lady on the other side of the bloody glass; the woman's head so close to Carlos; so surreal in a horrendous way!

The wave passed underneath them and suddenly the entire load shifted back to the left as the ferry righted itself. The mirror retracted from Carlos' neck. The lady in the camper was no longer suspended over Carlos, but now she was crying and covered her eyes with her hands. Blood flowed down her face from the cut on her forehead.

Furiously, Carlos grabbed Robison's hair and jerked her closer. "You bitch! Why didn't you help me?" he screamed, their faces almost touching. "I could have died!"

Staring defiantly back, she replied, "Go to hell, you son-of-a-bitch!"

He slapped her hard across the face, adding venomously, "I could kill you right now."

"Then who would you frame for your father's murder?" she sneered back.

Shoving her back to her place in the front seat, he said, "You can stay where you are, but I'm getting in the backseat so that fucking mirror won't trap me again."

He climbed into the back, quite a feat for a man so tall, and then he lit another cigarette.

Her face stung, where he'd slapped her. With tears welling up in her eyes, Robison gazed out her open window, trying to recall Wade's face...so loving, so serene. Trying to remember when life was simple...and life was safe. Brimming over, the tears rolled down her cheeks.

Where is God now? What did I ever do that was so horrible? Why has God let me go through this nightmare? Why?

She began thinking of the Bible verse she'd read at the estate and more of the prophetic Psalm came to mind:

> *Stretch out Your hand from above;*
> *Rescue me and deliver me out of great waters,*
> *From the hand of foreigners,*
> *Whose mouth speaks lying words,*
> *And whose right hand is a right hand of falsehood.*

The sky was darkening to pitch-black, wind gusts were getting more turbulent and the rain was now coming down in torrents. Most of the time the wind was blowing away from her open window, so Robison wasn't getting too wet. In any case, it was still better than sitting in a smoke-filled car. She glanced at her watch; forty minutes had gone by, twice as long as it should have taken...but no matter, they were almost to the other side.

Her head rocked to the left and then to the right over and over. She felt like a cork bobbing up and down and side to side in a ride she couldn't stop. What if they didn't make it across? Then it calmed, for the moment. Tears continued to trickle down her cheeks.

From the backseat, Carlos suddenly grabbed her around the neck, pulling her tightly against the headrest. "Crying doesn't become you, Doctor. I thought you were much tougher than that."

Grabbing his arm with both hands, she tried to loosen his grip, but to no avail. Struggling, she yelled, "Stop it! Let go of me!"

Pulling her tighter, he licked her ear, which sickened her. He whispered, "You know, I'm attracted to spirited bitches like you."

"Go to fucking hell," she screamed, still struggling to get loose.

He let her go then. She was coughing and trying to catch her breath, as she wiped her ear with her sleeve.

He leaned back and took another drag on his cigarette. "You'll like Caltengo; it is peaceful out in the country."

"And I suppose it has a wall around it, too," Robison said coldly. "Is that where you customarily shoot people, or do you just drop them in their tracks wherever it's convenient?"

He ignored her. "Caltengo is a working ranch; there are sixty employees. And yes, there is a wall around the main house. But no matter, it is too far away from anywhere to run. And no, we don't drag people there to shoot them. It is a place of family...of respect."

"You wouldn't know what respect is. You don't even respect human life." Then she asked, "How long do you plan for us to stay at Caltengo?"

"Until the storm passes. Then we will take a helicopter to Santo Domingo and turn you over to the police."

"I know you don't have any qualms about incriminating an innocent person, but doesn't it bother you to shoot people in cold blood?"

"If I have my reasons...no. No, it doesn't bother me in the least."

"Well, at least you're truthful about it. I'll give you that much," she said.

Abruptly, the ship listed violently to the port side, causing Robison to again grab the door handle to hold on. Harrowingly loud sounds of metal against metal erupted once again, but this time Robison heard sounds of screeching and the horrible screams of human beings. The ferry then tilted far to the right, and the camper slammed heavily against their car again. More terrified shrieking.

The camper's mirror once again plunged inside their car, but Carlos was safely in the back seat. Robison closed her eyes. She didn't want to look over at the woman smashed up against the glass again...blood oozing out of her head wound.

This time, the screeching didn't stop. With another violent jolt, the big furniture truck shifted one last time, crushing the camper against the car.

Carlos was yelling at her in Spanish, which she didn't understand. Then he began stammering in English, but she couldn't make out what he was saying. Her mind was racing, he was yelling...and they were all tilting...tilting.

With a final pitch of the ferry to the right, the truck and camper crushed Robison's car door against the steel railing. She was suspended over the turbulent river, no longer was she able to see the horizon, she saw only water...dark, swirling water. The pull of gravity made her feel like she was falling out of the car, so she held on to the seat and the door handle with all her might. She was dangling over what would be sure death in raging waters. In the background, people were screaming. Carlos was yelling...

She was being drawn towards the water; gravity was pulling her out. She prayed the ship would tilt back and right itself as it had all the other times. She couldn't hold on much longer.

The truck continued to slide; the camper was steadily crushing against them. The steering wheel was slowly being pushed to the center of the car, almost touching Robison. The bloody woman on the other side of the glass was coming closer. Robison came to the frightening realization she may be squished to death.

The loaded vessel listed to the right even more; the screeching continued, the steering wheel kept getting closer...

In a split second decision, Robison started to climb out the window. Carlos lunged forward, grabbed her by the hair and yanked her back. She screamed, pulling her hair loose from his grip, as he grabbed her arm. "Come back you bitch, you're not getting away!"

"Let go of me you bastard!" Robison turned and scratched his face, then pounded him with her fist. Carlos yelled and loosened his grasp. Again she started to climb out the window, hesitating as she looked down at the steep drop to the water. Would she die from the fall? Robison glanced back; the steering wheel was coming closer! She lunged out the window and over the railing with the upper part of her body...he grabbed her foot. He was bent over the front seat, hollering at her to come back, as he held her suspended over the churning water. Robison kicked him with her other foot as hard as she could.

He let go!

Falling…falling. She could hear Carlos screaming until she hit the water and plunged deep into the murky, swirling Chavón River.

Silence!

The water was cold; she was stunned from the shock. Robison opened her eyes to see how far it was back to the surface, but it was no use—everything was black. She swam as far as her breath would take her underwater…

Reaching her arms high over head and pulling down, she worked her way up through the murky river consumed by one thought: getting as far away from the ferry as she could.

Her lungs were aching when she finally broke the surface, gasping for air. Treading water, she brushed the hair out of her eyes. She had to get her bearings, but the waves kept pounding her in the face. Bobbing up and down, she spun around towards the sounds of humans screaming, and metal creaking and splitting. The ferry listed even farther to the starboard side and was about to roll over.

She saw Carlos crushed up against the glass in the backseat. His window wouldn't open; he was pounding on the glass…screaming. The first row of vehicles on the right side of the ferry slid first…. Trapped in his falling vehicle Carlos plunged deep into the churning abyss. Robison watched him silently screaming all the way down.

The second row of vehicles continued sliding towards the demolished railing. People opened their car doors trying to escape, but could not fight against the pull of gravity on the rain-soaked surface of the ship. They slid over the side, arms flailing wildly as they hit the water.

Sounds of splashing, yelling, crying, begging…drowning!

A huge swell of water was coming towards her, energized by the plunging vehicles.

Once the vehicles began sliding, nothing on earth could stop them. The second row continued to slide closer to the edge of no return. She watched as the camper with the screaming woman plunged after Carlos' car, followed quickly by the furniture truck sliding on top of the camper with a gigantic splash. Thus, Carlos lay crushed beneath the vehicles in the depths of the Chavón River, along with all the other people trapped onboard.

Another surge of water was created by the falling vehicles, floating Robison atop ten-foot waves. Still gasping for breath, as she rode the huge waves with the wind battering her face, Robison desperately tried to tread water. She watched in horror as the ferry steadily rolled over—capsizing!

Boom! The explosion ripped through the night sky. The orange ball of flames shot high into the air throwing debris flying in every direction, before raining down in a fiery shower. Soon flames covered the surface of the water...above the graveyard of so many human beings. The lives of so many innocent people had ended in a split second. All except one—Dr. Robison Murphy—who had been spared from murderous prosecution with the death of "eyewitness," Carlos.

Boom! ...A second explosion! The wind carried the burning remnants of the ferry towards Robison. She dove beneath the water and began swimming as hard as she could towards the shore. More explosions from the ship...the force of the turbulence rippled through the water, propelling her forward violently. Coming up for a breath, she regained momentum and continued swimming back to the shore where they had boarded the ferry.

She didn't see anyone else swimming, or anyone that she could help. An angry wave smacked her in the face. It stung! Fiery floating debris riding oncoming waves headed towards her as she gathered herself.

Although tired beyond tired, Robison submersed and continued; she found it easier to swim underwater than to fight the surface wind and rain. Coming up only to establish that she was on course, she continued beneath the surface. When she came to the surface yet again, it seemed she was no closer to shore than before. Oh, God! What if, after all she'd been through, she didn't have the strength and endurance to make it? She had come too far to drown now! No way! No matter what, she would escape this time!

Down below the surface once again, she was swimming, fighting...thigh muscles burning. Abruptly...swimming became easier...much easier. She came up for air and saw why. She'd gotten into the cove where the wind was partially blocked by heavy foliage.

Treading water, she looked at the empty shore; there would be no one there to help her. So what? She would make it back to the village by herself. Back to Wade!

But when her head bobbed forward and she swallowed water, Robison realized she was losing it. Choking and coughing brought her back, however, and she shook her head to refocus. She stretched her legs downward...and felt sand beneath her feet! She caught a wave, rode it in, and crawled ashore up the riverbank and onto solid earth.

Her legs and arms were numb beyond belief. The rain struck her body like bullets and the wind blew her slight body from side to side. If she stood up, the storm would surely hurtle her back into the sea. So she lay there exhausted in the midst of the storm.

A palm frond from a nearby tree glanced off her forehead, scraping the skin over her right eye. Lifting her head, she began looking around in the dark. She could barely keep her eyes open against the raging wind so she closed them again tightly.

What to do now? She couldn't stay where she was; she would need to find shelter from the storm. But where?

She got up on her hands and knees, but immediately had to drop back to the ground. So she began creeping up the narrow road, but even then the wind blew with such intensity she feared she would be slammed against something and killed outright. She inched forward until she reached more foliage and more cover. She clung to a tree for support. Deadly debris was flying through the air, borne on the winds of Francis.

Robison looked back towards the burning water. Yet another explosion rocketed pieces of ship and vehicles high into the air, with the wind blowing particles towards shore. Surely, human remains were included. Bile rose to her throat, but she swallowed hard to fight off vomiting.

She forced her exhausted body onward, stumbling, crawling, creeping. It all seemed so hopeless! How would she ever make it all the way to Altos de Chavón? As the storm strengthened, her hopes of being rescued evaporated. But...this wasn't how Robison wanted to die.

Through the downpour she made out the outlines of an old pickup parked off the road, near a small brick wall that once had been a building. A tarp securely tied down covered something in the back, with bricks and logs weighting down the edges as an extra precaution.

"Hello? Hello? Is anybody here?" she screamed at the top of her lungs.

No one answered.

Making her way to the bed of the truck behind the wall she loosened the tarp in one corner. When Robison climbed under the covering, she discovered the truck bed was filled with tools and dirt. Wonderful! In fact, the dirt felt warm and soft. Now she would rest and let the storm pass.

Tears trickled down her grimy face. Her body was wracked with fatigue and aching pain. The truck was rocking from side to side and the sound of the wind was roaring in her ears, but all that bedlam couldn't shut out the recurring sounds of screaming people as they slid, fell, and splashed to a watery grave. Nor would the echoes of metal crushing metal stop. Robison squeezed her eyes tightly shut, and began to hum a childhood tune her grandmother had taught her when they were at her Edisto beach house so long ago.

Mercifully everything eventually went black...and thankfully silent.

NINETEEN

From up above, Donadio saw Robison fall into the swirling river. He was desperately trying to reach Carlos, when he watched his beloved boss plummet to his death in the murky water. Donadio himself was in a life-or-death struggle trying to hang on, trying to avoid slipping into the river amid the plunging vehicles.

Unable to stop the inevitable, he balled up his body and braced for the impact. He plunged deep into the river, hit a submerged van and catapulted to the side...out of the way of the next falling vehicle. Donadio began swimming as fast as he could...away from crushing debris and away from the sinking ship. Explosions were spewing towards the sky, as he came up for a deep breath of air. Once he got his bearings, Donadio began to swim towards shore...the shore leading to Caltengo.

The steadfast bodyguard was so weak he barely made it to the embankment. There he rested and caught his breath. Blood oozed from cuts on his head and forearm. They didn't appear grave, besides there was nothing he could do about them now anyway.

He headed up the road on his way to the big ranch of Caltengo. He frequently heard screaming voices, saw flailing bodies, and thought he caught a brief glimpse of Robison lying on the bank of the opposite shore. Donadio waited for illumination from another explosion. Yes! He saw it was Robison...and now he knew what he must do.

Donadio didn't see any other survivors...just he and Robison. Carlos was dead. He replayed the vision of the camper crushing Carlos' car over and over again in his mind. Donadio must carry on in the absence of his boss; it was the least he could do out of loyalty to Carlos.

Donadio now saw three missions: First, and most important find Robison. The ever-loyal servant would pursue the "murderer" of his boss's father and exact revenge. Second, get to Santo Domingo and inform Señora Alvarez that her son was dead. Third, he would go after Bibí no matter where in the world she'd gone. He would eventually find her and do away with her as well. He swore to God that he would accomplish these things, or die trying.

The pummeling of the island by the hurricane continued for several hours. With winds exceeding a hundred thirty miles per hour, Francis pulverized many of the homes and businesses along the coast. The poorest of the homes, not more than hovels in many circumstances, were swept away by the high winds. The sturdier constructed buildings had windows broken, or parts of roofs blown off, with torrential rain soaking the contents. After the eye passed, a backlash would surely follow. Ultimately, the surge would inundate low lying areas.

Down inside the amphitheater, the winds were beating and swirling against the stone walls with almost horizontal sheets of water. There was no power or cell phone signal. Ty and Wade were out of communication with the world, with no idea of how they stood in relation to Francis. All they could do was ride out the storm. Both prayed silently for Robison's survival.

Robison's eyes shot wide open when the truck roared to a start.

Oh, my God. Should I jump out?

A sick, panicky feeling welled up inside her. Before she could decide what to do, the truck jerked forward and began moving cautiously ahead.

Water was dripping through the tarpaulin that was just inches away from her face. It must have pooled up on top and was now seeping through as the truck twisted and jolted up the narrow, rocky road. With each jolt of the truck, she sank deeper into the dirt "bed." A big bump sent tools falling towards her face, but she managed to duck just in time.

The wind had dropped in velocity; they were probably in the "eye." She thought the rain had subsided as well, but it was hard to tell from under the wet, dripping tarp. Soon the ride was smoother; they had finally reached some pavement. Traveling faster now, she dared a peak from under the tarp.

The driver appeared to be going up the road towards Altos de Chavón. Her heart beat with excitement at the prospect. This was better than she ever expected! Soon she would be back with Wade and they could leave this place…forever!

Her hopes were dashed when the driver slowed down and made a sharp left turn, slinging tools to the right side of the truck. Now they were on another bumpy gravel road. Dejected, she fell back onto the pile of dirt. The constant bouncing up and down over the rough road was hurting her back. She tried to squat under the tarpaulin and hang on for dear life, but she was tossed from side to side and eventually ended up back in the pile of dirt. She decided to remain in the dirt pile. It was easier.

The truck suddenly stopped, the driver got out and slammed his door. Not having the strength to face any more jolting realities, she closed her eyes and prayed for God to give her the strength to carry on.

Perhaps he wouldn't return for a while and she could steal a few minutes of tranquility before facing what was to come next. Whatever might be, she was too scared and tired to imagine. But how could anyone be as bad as Carlos and his men? Unless the driver of this truck was in cahoots with Carlos, she had to be better off. She took a deep breath and waited. All she could hear was the sound of her heart beating. Afraid, wet and exhausted, Robison had to collect her wits and persevere.

Awakened by the absolute stillness, Wade opened his eyes in the dark room. He was trying to remember where he was. When he moved slightly, his aching body reminded him he'd been sleeping on a table in a dressing room riding out the hurricane. He tried to sit up but a stabbing pain took his breath away. He felt his rib cage and it was still sore to the touch. Wade leaned back on his elbows, trying to catch his breath and gain relief from the throbbing, aching pain. A slight breeze blew the dressing room door ajar.

"Ty, are you here?" Wade asked. But there was no response.

Wade swung his legs over the edge of the table and sat up. He groaned out loud. There wasn't a bone or muscle in his body that didn't hurt. He stood up and grabbed the table to steady himself. He was standing in a shallow pool of water that had been blown under the door during the first half of the storm. Sloshing over to the dressing room door, he peered cautiously outside. He wasn't sure what to expect.

Ty was across the way, sitting halfway up the amphitheater seats, leaning back on his elbows and looking up at the starry sky.

"Hey, Ty, what are you doin'?"

Wade was standing outside the dressing room with a large flashlight in his hand, shaking the water off his feet.

"I'm just gazing at the stars. Getting a little fresh air," Ty said. "Come on over and pull up a seat. I have about nine hundred and ninety-nine of them to spare."

Wade smiled and limped by the stage. He started to climb the stairs up but stopped halfway.

"Son-of-a-bitch! I can hardly move. What the hell time is it, anyway?"

"About three in the morning. Let's go up and walk around the city and see if there's a bunch of damage," Ty suggested. "We're in the eye of the storm, so we'll be holing back up in that block building again after awhile. And we don't want to go stir-crazy in there. Besides, the walk will do you good; loosen up some of those sore muscles."

"I'll try to make it up but...I don't know....Aren't you sore at all?" Wade asked, wincing in pain.

"Nope. You're really out of shape, man! Obviously you sit around in your stockbroker's chair too much," Ty said, laughing as he watched Wade.

"Yeah, well let's not forget the ass-beating I took, too."

Wade had started up the steep climb when Ty's phone rang.

"Who in the hell is that in the middle of night? In the middle of a damn hurricane! I thought you didn't have any signal?" Wade asked.

Ty shined his flashlight at his cell phone. "I don't have any signal. But it's Russia! Who the hell else could get through at a time like this?"

It was a reassurance call from the secretary of the Russian ice show confirming the cargo ship was fine and still on its way to Greece. They had managed to rent a chassis trailer that would meet the ship at the docks and transport the containers to the local amphitheater. The secretary had no idea that Ty was in the eye of a hurricane; he was incredulous as he listened to her—as if it was a call from aliens!

After hanging up, Ty tried to call out, but there was no signal. "Go figure!" Ty shrugged.

"Don't they know it's the middle of the night over here?" Wade inquired.

"Most of the time…no. I keep telling them there's a big time difference, but I don't think they really care to tell you the truth."

The two men walked out of the amphitheater, across the cobblestone street, and about Altos de Chavón. They found it eerie, like a ghost town or deserted movie set, with no one staying behind. The streets were wet and several shops had inventory soaking in the mud. From what they could see, most buildings hadn't sustained much damage other than by minor flooding.

Strewn everywhere were leaves, trash, limbs and pieces of roofing from faraway hovels. Some of it covered the cobblestone streets and sidewalks in places. The awning outside the breakfast café had been ripped in half and was plastered against a building down the street. They tried the door, but found it locked.

Actually there was little for Francis to destroy, since this sixteenth-century knock-off city was built like the stone fortress it was meant to resemble. Fortunately, the little city was quite high above the backlash and surge of the hurricane. However, Casa de Campo was a different story entirely. The surge that was certain to follow would be devastating to all those expensive homes. But at the moment, in the eye of Francis, the village was dead still—not a single leaf was moving.

"What am I going to do to find Robison?" Wade asked as they walked along.

"As soon as we have a phone signal, we need to start calling some people," Ty said. Not really knowing what else to tell Wade, Ty felt he needed to say something encouraging.

"Like who?" Wade persisted.

"Like…well…your friends for starters. Perhaps they've heard from her. If not, then our next option is to plead our case to the U.S. Embassy. That's about the best I have to offer at the moment." Ty checked his phone signal again...nothing. He continued, "On the other hand, we need to be careful when dealing with someone as powerful as Juan Alvarez was. They'll probably be tracking all cell phone calls, so we just need to be very cautious."

"By her possibly calling the Winsteads, you sound like she has a hope in hell of escaping again. Shit, we don't even know if she's alive, much less calling friends, for God's sake!" Wade was getting worked up.

"She escaped before; hopefully she will again," Ty said calmly.

"Well, you can bet your bottom dollar Carlos will be more leery of that and guard her around the clock. I'm sure he's having her watched like a hawk, don't you think so?"

"Yes. I suppose so."

"It's my fault. If I hadn't stopped in town, and instead just went to the hotel like you told me to, they wouldn't have found us, would they?"

Ty sensed the agony in his voice. "Look, you can't keep going over that again and again. We'll have to keep a positive outlook, and after we get through the next part of the storm, we'll work on finding her. Then we can work on getting the charges dropped or escaping this country or whatever." But he couldn't resist a timely jab: "I must tell you, though, your wife follows instructions a hell of a lot better than you do!"

Wade nodded agreement as he and Ty made their way up to the hotel, which had been boarded up with plywood over the doors and windows. Walking around to the far side, they looked down upon the Chavón River—now a black hole...churning far below.

On the banks were several relocated boats, thanks to Francis. Some looked fine and others were smashed to smithereens. There weren't any people in sight down there; all was quiet. Everyone had either evacuated or was too scared to come out until Francis had run its course. Ty was sure this wasn't the first hurricane to hit here.

In the distance, perhaps a couple of blocks away, they could hear voices echoing through the back alleyways. It sounded like two men. In the darkness, Ty and Wade could make out the beam of an oncoming flashlight reflecting off the buildings.

"I think we'd better get back to the theater," Ty suggested. "I don't know what the evacuation policy down here is."

"What do you mean?"

"Well, my guess is that they might be looking for looters or loiterers, or some other stupid thing. They might even think we're vandals."

"Yeah, and arrest us! Then who's going to find Robison?" Wade added.

"That's a good question...even if they don't arrest us!"

Walking quickly and keeping close to the buildings, they made their way back to the safety of the amphitheater.

"Hey, maybe *those* guys were vandals! Did you ever think of that?" Wade asked.

Ty shook his head. "Either way, it's best we avoid meeting strangers in the dark, under these circumstances," he said.

The wind was picking up again; meaning the calm was running out. Ty checked his signal and four bars popped up.

"Holy shit! I've got a signal," he exclaimed.

He handed the phone to Wade, who tried to call the Winsteads...but all circuits were busy. Ty tried his Stuart office...all circuits were busy.

They continued down the stairs and Wade tried the phone one more time, while he still had a signal, and before the storm returned in full force. The call finally went through.

"Hello?" Tom answered as he looked at the clock beside the bed: 4:42 AM.

"Tom...it's Wade. I can't stay on the line too long; this call might be monitored or traced."

"Son-of-a-bitch! Thank God you called! What the hell is going on? Where's Robison? Is she there with you?"

There was a long silence, as Wade realized they hadn't heard from her.

"Wade, are you still on the line?"

"Yes."

Tom could hear Wade's voice choking up, followed by a clearing of his throat.

"Yes, I'm here...I don't know where Robison is though," Wade said with obvious dismay.

"Listen, Wade, you're breaking up."

Wade blurted out Ty's cell phone number.

"I gotta go. The storm is getting worse and Ty and I have to get into the dressing room. Thanks. Bye."

"What did he say? Tell me!" Brianne demanded.

"He's fine. A bit choked up because Robison is still missing. He couldn't talk for long because he was afraid the call would be traced, anyway, the connection started to break-up and he was on his way to a dressing room with Ty."

"Who the hell is this Ty?"

"I don't have the faintest idea. Should we call the FBI?" Tom asked.

"Not yet."

"Okay," he said as he turned off the lamp, pulled up the covers, and tried to get back to sleep. Neither of them wanted to continue the conversation, especially about the "missing" Robison.

Wade and Ty half ran, half jogged the rest of the way to the dressing room, just as it started to rain. Once again, Ty fixed sandwiches as they talked awhile.

"I don't know what I'll do if I don't find Robison," Wade said dejectedly. "She's my life....She's everything to me. If she's dead, there's no reason for me to live."

"Whoa, man! First, there's no reason to think she's dead. That woman doesn't ever give up! Don't worry; we'll find her, you'll see." Ty wasn't as certain as he pretended, but he had to prop Wade up to get through the storm. Then maybe they could do something to find her...or find out *about* her.

They both stretched out on their respective tables, settling in for the rest of Hurricane Francis. Neither of them said another word.

~~~

It was an excruciating scream of a woman. Startled, Robison raised up and accidentally hit the top with her head. The tarpaulin was abruptly thrown back and a small Spanish man stared at her in disbelief. He was also pointing a gun at her.

Dear God in heaven! Am I the only one that doesn't have a gun in this country?

She stayed perfectly still, not daring to move a muscle. Several agonizing seconds ticked by. Slowly, a smile crossed his face and he lowered the gun. Then he offered his hand to help her out, but before she could comply, another scream came from inside. He dropped his hand and ran towards the house. He stopped short of the front door, turned and motioned for her to follow. He quickly disappeared inside, not waiting for Robison's response.

Robison slowly climbed out of the back of the pickup, and stretched her dirty, wet body. When she brushed the matted hair back from her face, she saw all the mud on her clothes. What a sight she must be! Maybe in the house she could take a shower and wash her clothes. Or was she hoping, once again, for too much…

Her watch was waterlogged; she looked up at the stars which told her nothing about the time. However, she came to the conclusion that they were in the "eye" of the storm. She wasn't looking forward to the backlash, but at least she wouldn't be in the back of a pickup truck—or lying on a river bank outside.

Robison peeked inside the front door. The man nervously ran to the kitchen, muttering under his breath in Spanish. First he leaned against the kitchen sink for support and then he wiped the sweat from his forehead with a towel. Robison looked around in the dark; she guessed the electricity was off…if this house even had electricity.

It was a plain house, or a more suitable description, a "shack" with one bedroom, one bathroom, a tiny kitchen and very small living room. A candle was flickering as she walked to the window over the sink, her muscles aching with every step. There was nothing to see outside, but it didn't really matter—everything was dead still. Not a wisp of wind.

She watched her "host" go to a cupboard and take out a clean towel and soap which he handed to her. He lit another candle and gave it to her while pointing down the hall that led to the bathroom. There was a shower and although the water was only lukewarm, she felt marvelous and, for the first time in a long while, felt pangs of hunger. She scrubbed her body and hair vigorously, even made a stab at washing her clothes under the running water. She hoped to get some of the dirt out, but her clothes came out anything but clean. She hung the wash on the shower rod, and wrapped herself in the towel. Then she headed to the kitchen for something to eat. Surely, the man wouldn't mind.

Holding the candle, she rummaged around inside the circa nineteen-fifty refrigerator and found some cheese and a soft drink. There were some cookies on the counter in a clear jar that looked homemade. Robison hadn't thought about food in a long time and although cheese and cookies weren't gourmet, they filled the void.

When she sat down at the tiny kitchen table, she spotted a telephone. Picking up the receiver, she found the line was dead. Robison had almost become used to the fact that she would always face doom and gloom...nothing would be easy. So the dead phone only confirmed her supposition.

The wind began to pick up again, and since there wasn't anything she could do or anywhere to go, she decided to sleep. The little man didn't appear to be predatory, so she lay down on the sofa, and covered up with a big crocheted blanket that was there. She would ride out the rest of the storm all snuggled up; hopefully, her clothes would be dry by morning and she would be on her way to find Wade.

Another scream brought Robison to a sitting position. It took a minute for her to get her bearings, and to realize where she was. This time yelling in Spanish followed the scream. Robison made out the voices of a man and a woman.

Robison got up from the sofa, readjusted the towel and wrapped the crocheted blanket tightly around her. Then she walked slowly down the short hallway to the room across from the bathroom. She knocked, but they couldn't hear the knock above the yelling and screaming.

What in the world?

When the woman screamed again, Robison cracked open the door and she saw at once what was happening. She was in labor! Robison pushed open the door and took over. The man stood up and started jabbering to her in Spanish. But Robison shook her head and said, "Me a doctor...doctor..."

Shit. What's the Spanish word for doctor?

Seemingly, the man understood or at least out of desperation came to the decision that he needed help...anyone's help. Even from the strange blonde woman stealing a ride in the back of his truck and who was now standing in their bedroom wrapped in a blanket.

Robison pulled the sheet back to reveal the extent of the woman's labor.... The baby was crowning...it wouldn't be long now.

Hurriedly, she ran to the kitchen to find some towels and wash her hands. The father-to-be was going to be of no help at all since they couldn't communicate with one another; Robison was on her own. She hadn't delivered a baby since medical school and hoped it would all come back to her. She motioned to him to find her something to wear while she continued to gather supplies. He returned with a brightly colored dress that was about four sizes too big. No matter; it would suffice better than a blanket.

Two hours later, a little boy was born with all ten fingers and toes. Robison cleaned him up and left the newborn suckling at his mother's breast. All three of them, mom, dad and baby were deliriously happy—especially the "proud papa." The parents couldn't thank her enough.

Padding off to the tiny living room carrying her candle, Robison reclined once again on the sofa. Snuggling the blankets all around her, she blew out the candle and fell asleep as the second half of the storm raged on. It felt good to rest in a place that was clean and safe. She felt like she could comfortably close her eyes and not worry—at least for the moment. What a welcome relief.

As soon as the storm passed, she would get "proud papa" to drive her to Altos de Chavón…back to Wade. After she had delivered the baby, Robison knew he would be more than happy to drive her anywhere. Yes, everything was looking much brighter for Dr. Robison Murphy.

The backlash of the hurricane brought winds in excess of a hundred sixty-five miles per hour. The mighty storm pounded the beaches and towns of the southeast Dominican Republic. The destruction to homes and businesses was in the millions of dollars. The large estates at the Casa de Campo, those lucky enough to remain standing, suffered severe damage. Several of the golf holes on the Teeth of the Dog course were completely obliterated. The ocean's surge reclaimed sand from sand traps and consumed houses that had once stood as monuments to wealthy vacationers. Only the "H" painted helipad boulder and parts of the high wall once surrounding the infamous Alvarez estate were all that were left of the presidential candidate's palatial retreat.

Hurricane Francis now turned its stormy rage towards the Bahamas and was predicted to hit the East Coast of the Carolinas within thirty-six hours.

TWENTY

Cut off from all outside communication, Caltengo stood like an isolated fortress. It was still raining, but with the thrust of the storm over, Donadio drove back to the ferry landing. A rescue team dispatched earlier had a barge with a large crane on it that was pulling up cars and trucks. Divers were searching for bodies in the now smooth flowing Chavón River. The salvage operation was an excruciatingly slow process, especially for relatives waiting for some news of their loved ones. Apparently, there were no survivors other than he and Robison, and it was a sure bet no one standing here…was looking for either one of them.

Soon the rain subsided altogether and the sun shone brightly. Donadio arrived just as they were pulling Carlos' car up with the crane and he could see parts of his body humped over inside and an arm hanging outside the crushed vehicle. It turned his stomach; the tough man that he'd always considered himself to be, ran to the closest bush and vomited. He wasn't so tough after all.

Several small crowds were gathering, some to console those who had lost loved ones, others who were just curious and…the ever-present press. Television cameras and reporters were swarming all over the landing. With the screeching metal from the tangled vehicles and the voices yelling directions from the barge, coupled with the crying and moaning of people in agony over the carnage, Donadio felt like he was watching a horror movie. Nearby, an attractive young reporter was telling her story on camera, giving it dramatic emphasis. He was in a nightmare that he couldn't control—that he couldn't wake up from.

Deciding there was nothing he could do here and still feeling queasy, he climbed back into his truck and wheeled around, peeling rubber as he started up the steep hill. In all the commotion, no one seemed to notice the screeching tires.

He was taking the long route over to the other side of the river…to find Robison. There would be no ferry crossing for a few days, until after the salvage operation was complete. In fact, the thought passed through his head that he might not ever be able to take the ferry again. He didn't know if he could stomach crossing over the spot where he'd just seen what was left of Carlos' mangled body dangling in the wind. He tried shaking those thoughts out of his head for the moment. Back to the matter at hand: find Dr. Murphy…fugitive from justice.

After the long trip to the other side of the river, Donadio decided to wait near the road leading into Altos de Chavón. Robison would have to pass this way either on foot or by hitching a ride. There was absolutely no other way out of this desolate area unless it was by helicopter, and Donadio doubted that she had rustled up a helicopter from the poor people who lived in this vicinity. Either way, he would spot her and finish his job.

His plan was to take her to Santo Domingo and turn her over to the police for the murder. After all, he still needed to protect Señora Alvarez. Then he would go and give Carlos' mother the bad news regarding the death of Carlos, if she hadn't already heard about it. Chances were she'd probably hear about it on the news from one of the insidious news commentators at the ferry landing, before he could get to her. In any case, he had a job to complete in memory of Carlos.

Then there was the problem of locating Bibí, although it was doubtful she would still have the necklace by the time he caught up with her. At least he could finish the job that should have been done the day Juan Alvarez was shot. His plan was to shoot Bibí exactly as she had shot Juan. That's what Carlos would have wanted; he was sure of it. An eye for an eye was the only way Donadio operated.

As he drove along, he was gradually feeling better physically and mentally. He had three big jobs to complete and he was going to get them done!

Waking slowly out of a deep sleep, Robison could smell bacon and coffee. Delicious! She opened her eyes and saw "proud papa" at the kitchen stove, busily scrambling eggs. Fresh squeezed cantaloupe juice was in a large pitcher on the table, the spent melon halves still on the counter. Glancing out the window, she could see the sun was shining gloriously and there wasn't a hint of wind. Francis was gone. Thank goodness!

Collecting her thoughts for a moment, she sat up and then walked into the kitchen. She poured a large glass of the cantaloupe juice and drank it all. It was delicious; she'd never had that before. But then, in the tropics, cantaloupe was so plentiful and sweet.

He pulled out a chair for her to sit down, poured more juice, then returned to his cooking.

"Como se llama?" Robison asked him.

He turned around, still holding the pan and spatula. Robison pointed at herself. "I,…Robison."

"Rodolfo," he replied, rolling his "r" with great flare.

"Rodolfo." She repeated it, but didn't quite get the same rolling "r" thing happening. She laughed and tried pronouncing it a second time.

The eggs and bacon were the best meal she'd had in a long time; after finishing the first plateful, she had another. Now she was anxious to get to Wade, and although she still felt sore, she also felt clean, rested and well fed.

After many hand gestures accompanied by her broken twelve words of Spanish, she was quite certain Rodolfo understood that she wanted to go to Altos de Chavón, and go soon…pronto.

She started to look around for her clothes and motioned to him. He nodded as if he understood and rushed from the kitchen.

Reappearing, he brought her tattered and muddy clothes in the one hand—apparently the washing hadn't gone so well—and held a pair of thongs in the other. She opted for the thongs, which were also several sizes too big but were a no-brainer, since Robison had no shoes. Still dressed in the bright red dress, she'd at least found a piece of rope to make a belt that drew a good portion of the fullness in around her waist. Robison made a mental note to send them some clothes and baby items when she arrived home. This housedress might have been one of the few the poor woman owned. And wouldn't Rodolfo have given her his wife's "best" dress to wear since she'd delivered their baby? Probably so, she surmised.

She picked up the telephone; it was still dead as a doornail. Then she went to check on baby and mother and to say good-bye. After lots of hugs and kisses, Robison was able to work herself out of the bedroom and towards the front door. She wondered what kind of life the baby boy would have in this jungle. She had to admit, though, mama and papa seemed very happy…albeit poor…but happy.

Rodolfo was waiting in the rickety old truck for her. When she approached the passenger side, he hopped out and held the door for her. Climbing into the pickup, she was elated at the prospect of surprising Wade with her reappearance. Now that Carlos was dead, he couldn't indict her in the murder of Juan Alvarez, or at least that was what she was thinking. All she needed to do was to call Tom and ask him to fly over and pick them up as soon as possible, hopefully, today. God, it would be wonderful to be in Wade's arms again!

Looking down at her oversized thongs, she made another mental note to ask Brianne to bring her some clothes or to send some with Tom. It didn't matter what they were, as long as they were clean and fit better than this red tent and the snow-ski-length flip-flops she was wearing.

The windows were down in the small clunky truck and the breeze was blowing through Robison's blonde hair. It was a sensation that was exhilarating and made her feel totally free. They bumped along slowly through the small village not far from his house. Every so often they'd pass someone Rodolfo knew and he would stop. They were obviously asking about the baby. Between the hand gestures and smiles, Robison would end up waving when it was her cue to wave.

Rodolfo was boasting about God sending him his very own doctor that had arrived in the back of his pickup. "It was a miracle," he told them, pointing to Robison. This made for a very long trip over a very short distance. But how could she begrudge this man who was driving her towards salvation his few moments of braggadocio? She continued waving and smiling on cue.

Passing the empty stage, Raúl could see the two containers all packed and ready to go. He knew Ty must be in one of the cement block dressing rooms and began knocking on the one to the left.

"Señor Ty, are you in there?"

"Yeah, hold on."

The door opened and both Ty and Wade made their way outside into the warm glowing sunshine. Ty put on his sunglasses, while Wade squinted into the sun.

"I see you have survived," said Raúl.

"No sweat. How about you? Is your family and house okay?"

"We had some roof damage, but nothing compared to some other families. By the way, I have the chassis trailer coming in two hours," Raúl said, not paying any attention to Wade.

"Great!" Turning to Wade, Ty said, "Let's get that tarp out, unfold it, and let it dry in the sun."

"What about Robison? Fuck the tarp!" Wade yelled.

Raúl seemed shocked at this outburst. He took Ty to the side. "Does he know Dr. Robison Murphy? The doctor wanted for murder?"

"Yes. And did *you* know Carlos Alvarez kidnapped her out of my hotel room?"

"Your hotel room? What was she doing with you?" Raúl asked incredulously.

"Just hold on...she wasn't exactly with me; she was with her husband," Ty explained, motioning towards Wade. "That's her husband, Wade."

"So, she was kidnapped by Carlos just before the hurricane hit. And you say she was with Carlos? Are you certain?" Raúl asked seriously, with a knowing look of doom and gloom on his face.

"Yes, why? What do you know? What have you heard?" Ty inquired, not certain he wanted to hear what Raúl had to say.

Raúl took Ty by the elbow once again, edging him further away from Wade. He whispered, "Carlos was in an accident; he is dead. His car is at the bottom of the Chavón River. It was crushed by other vehicles when the ferry...how do you say? ...tipped over. And as far as the rescuers know right now, there were no...umm...survivors."

Ty had to catch himself as he started to sway. He looked over at Wade, who had overheard the conversation. Apparently Raúl's whispering hadn't been too quiet. Wade was in shock and was standing as still as a statue. Ty waited.

"Jesus! Sweet Jesus! ...No! ...No!" Wade screamed out as it echoed through the amphitheater. He turned, knees buckling; he leaned against the stage for support. Ty went over and put his arm around him. What could he say? Wade began to sob; his chest was heaving with every breath.

"I am sorry. I did not mean for him to hear me," Raúl tried to apologize.

Ty motioned with his head for Raúl to get out of there and let them be, while Wade slowly collapsed to the ground, grabbing his head in his hands. Ty sat down next to Wade, trying to analyze his own feelings about Robison.

Ty closed his eyes. "Fuck! ...It wasn't supposed to end like this!"

⁓

Finally away from all of Rodolfo's friends and neighbors, the rickety old pickup bumped along. Rodolfo could manage very little speed, but at least he was going in the right direction. There was a lot of other activity along the road as people began to reclaim their homes and lives after the storm. The traffic was heavy, but they continued to move forward. This was the happiest Robison had felt since she was at dinner with the Winsteads before this nightmare began.

Although that evening felt like it was a hundred years ago...a different lifetime, thankfully now there would be many more lovely dinners to come...thanks to Ty and Rodolfo.

Her thoughts lingered on Ty. He'd been a lifesaver...her lifesaver. No telling where she'd be if he hadn't helped her get well and hide from the authorities. It felt good to know she wouldn't be running and hiding anymore. The nightmare was just about over.

Interrupting her thoughts was the voice of the guard as they pulled up to the entrance to the quaint little city. Robison began looking around excitedly. Her heart was pounding once again, but instead of beating from trepidation, it was beating with excited anticipation. She was safe and Wade couldn't be far away now. She could almost feel him, he was that close!

But so was Donadio!

The gun-toting guard fell in line two vehicles behind Rodolfo and followed—after he'd spotted Robison in the truck! With only one street in and the same street out, there would be no escape for Dr. Murphy this time. In an unconscious gesture he felt for his gun, making sure it was in place. The "gorilla" was sweating, excited that he'd found his prey, anticipating a job well done. His heart was beating rapidly. This would be for Carlos!

The guard gave Rodolfo the signal to proceed through the gate and into Altos de Chavón. Robison was directing Rodolfo towards the amphitheater. Since there weren't many tourists in town, there were plenty of parking spaces.

Now the only worry to cross her mind was what if Ty wasn't here? How would she find Wade? What would she do then? She guessed her second option would be to see if the Winsteads would fly back down and help her search for Wade. She held her breath, praying Ty was here. Surely, Wade had recovered from that terrible beating in the hotel room and had stayed with Ty throughout the storm. She was positive she had seen him breathing when they dragged her away.

Pulling up to the curb, the little man stopped the truck. They exchanged hugs and thanked one another profusely. It wasn't a long good-bye because of the language barrier. As she walked away, he watched her pass through the entrance of the amphitheater, where she turned to wave at him one last time. He waved back, smiling the smile of a happy and content man.

From the top of the theater she could see Ty folding up a large tarp, but Wade was nowhere in sight. She started running down the steep stairs as best she could in her oversized flip-flops. She finally took them off and held them in her hand. The skirt of her oversized housedress was flying behind her, like a big, red-plaid balloon.

"Ty! Ty!" she yelled, waving her flip-flops over her head.

He looked up startled at first, then waved back at her. "My God! It's you!"

Ty dropped the tarp and ran to the dressing room where Wade was lying down on one of the tables. He'd been trying to gather the strength to call Robison's parents and the Winsteads to tell them of her apparent death.

"Wade, you'd better get out here!" Ty yelled, running as fast as he could towards the dressing room. Ty found Wade curled up on his bed-table, shutting out the world. "There's someone here to see you and she's very much alive!"

Wade sprang from the table and rushed out the door, his heart pounding.

Could it be? Could it be...her?

"Oh God! ...Oh, God Almighty!" Wade was running towards her, relieved and astounded.

"Wade! ...Wade, darling...," she called out, as she made her way across the grass towards the stage...towards her soul mate.

Wade held out his arms: "Oh, Robison, Robison," he repeated.

He picked her up and spun her around with kissing...hugging...crying. He gently put her down and stared into her blue eyes, as tears streamed down his cheeks. He caressed her face with both hands, then swept back her blonde hair from her eyes to see her better.

"I can't believe it's really you," he whispered. "I thought you'd drowned!"

"Oh, Wade. I love you so much," she said, hugging him tightly. "I was so worried about you."

They'd both survived; they'd beaten the odds. Two people bound by endless love.

Ty watched the reunion silently, then went around to the back of the dressing room to call Raúl and tell him the good news. Was he being discreet? Or did he just not want to see them together, he wasn't sure. But he was happy to know Robison was alive. In any case, perhaps things now would get back to normal for Ty—the normal chaos of show business!

Crack! A gunshot rang out...echoing through the amphitheater. Donadio was at the top of the stairs...his gun aimed at the couple. They ducked, he missed! Donadio started deliberately down the stairs, the gun pointed at them.

Wade stepped in front of Robison.

When the shot rang out, Ty had hung up on Raúl. He heard a man with a deep voice yelling in Spanish. What the hell? He crept around the container, making his way to the stage. Wade and Robison didn't understand Donadio, but there was no mistaking his intent. Ty standing some distance behind them began translating: "Come on, Doctor...you are coming with me. You can't get away now."

Donadio was nearing the bottom of the stairs.

Wade ever the hothead, shouted, "You filthy bastard...you aren't going to get her."

Ty didn't bother to translate this to the angry man. Not only would it piss him off more, but the guy probably gathered what Wade meant by the tone of his voice.

"I'm taking her to the authorities for the murder of Juan Alvarez," Ty translated, as he walked across the grass towards the couple.

"She didn't do it!" Wade shouted. "You know that!"

Donadio stopped and started speaking in broken English: "I no care. Carlos is muerto (dead) and I...bodyguard saw...saw she stab him."

Ty began edging closer to Wade and Robison.

"Stay where you are, Señor," Donadio ordered Ty in Spanish. Looking back at Robison, he said, "Come here, Doctor, or I will shoot your husband."

"Go ahead! Shoot me...you ugly bastard," Wade shot back. "She's not going with you!"

"Wade, stop!" Robison pleaded, struggling to get around him. "Please, stop!"

Ty spoke in Spanish: "Listen. Let's all calm down and talk this over. There has been a mistake..."

A second shot rang out—Wade dropped to the ground and didn't move.

Robison screamed and knelt on the ground beside him.

"Oh, my God! ...Wade...Wade!" she yelled.

"For God's sakes, man! Stop it!" Ty hollered in Spanish at Donadio.

Donadio ignored Ty and spoke again to Robison. "Now get your ass over here, or I'll shoot this other man next!"

Ty had to translate.

Robison, still bending over her bleeding husband, did not comprehend Donadio's orders, so Ty spoke up: "Robison! Robison...I really don't want this guy shooting me. Okay? Pay attention to what I'm saying and look up towards the gunman. Will ya?"

She couldn't believe Ty wanted her to go running over to Donadio just so he could save his ass. She glared at Ty contemptuously, but he was nodding his head towards Donadio...one, two, three times. She turned her head to look at what Ty was seeing; then she understood why he wanted her to look in that direction.

She stood up a little shakily and began to swoon; Ty took a giant step towards her and grabbed her arm. Without moving his lips he whispered, "Come on! You can do this. I'm here to help you. When I holler 'ahora' (now) you duck. Understand?"

"Let go of her!" Donadio hollered, sending another bullet into the ground near their feet; dirt flew into the air beside them.

"Goddamn it...all right," Ty said in English and then in Spanish, as he pushed her away.

She began walking towards Donadio, like a zombie, barely able to put one foot in front of the other. She couldn't go through anymore. This was it, the last straw. "Okay, I'll go. Don't shoot anymore...no mas (no more)," she said softly. "No mas."

Slowly she made her way across the grass—her heart heavy with worry.

Just as she was about to reach Donadio, Ty yelled "Ahora!" as loud as he could. Both Ty and Robison ducked simultaneously as Rodolfo pulled the trigger of his rifle from where he stood at the top of the amphitheater. He had aimed directly at the back of Donadio's head.

The bullet dropped Donadio where he stood. He hit the ground next to Robison with a loud thud and a groan. But he had brushed against her as he fell, knocking her over. Hysterical she tried to get up...but he was lying on part of her dress. Pulling...and...pulling. Crying...and screaming...she couldn't get disentangled. Grabbing more material, she tugged with all her strength, shouting: "Get off me! ...Get off me, you filthy bastard!"

His bloody hand grabbed her by the throat! Donadio slowly brought the gun up and placed the cold steel against her forehead. As he rose up to shoot her, she could see blood oozing from his nose and mouth.

She trembled with fright. Would Donadio lose consciousness before he pulled the trigger?

Another shot rang out...echoing throughout the empty amphitheater.

Donadio's body collapsed from the impact of the second bullet, dropping his full weight on top of Robison.

She couldn't stop screaming. "Somebody help me. Please help me!"

Donadio, the "gorilla" would never, under his own power, move again.

Rodolfo ran down the stairs, towards Robison as she tried to claw her way from beneath the bloody body. But Donadio was too heavy, she couldn't budge him. As Rodolfo reached her, he dropped his gun to the ground, and, with all of his strength rolled the dead man off Robison.

He clutched her in his arms, and rocked her back and forth to calm her down. He whispered, "Is okay. Is okay." Then he lifted her up…and carried her towards Wade. Rodolfo put her down near her husband and Ty. All were covered with splotches of blood.

When the second bullet ended Donadio's rampage, Ty ran to where Wade had hit the ground. Since he hadn't moved, Ty listened for a heart beat.

"Wade! Oh my God, Wade!" Robison cried out, as she collapsed on the ground next to him.

TWENTY ONE

Ty and Rodolfo carried Wade into the dressing room and carefully placed him on the table. Meanwhile, Robison was using the hose pipe and some of Ty's industrial cleaner to wash the "gorilla's" blood off her hands.

Raúl had heard something that sounded like a gunshot over the phone while talking to Ty about the chassis trailer. When Ty hung up, his final words being, "Holy shit!" Raúl called the police and an ambulance. Raúl didn't know what had happened, but figured it must have been an accident.

Wade was still unconscious…and Robison, now surprisingly cool in her bloody, red, plaid dress and giant flip flops, began tending to him. "Ty, could you find something for me to put under his head, please?"

He returned with some rolled up material and helped her get it positioned.

"Is he going to be all right?" Ty inquired.

She was busy taking his pulse. Then Robison examined the gash on his head where he'd hit the ground and looked at the bullet wound in his shoulder.

"I think he'll recover, but we need to get him to a hospital right away. Meanwhile, I could use a first aid kit or something with some alcohol and bandages."

"Sure thing," Ty said as he disappeared into the container and returned with a small white and red box that he handed to Robison.

She heard the welcome sound of sirens blaring in the distance.

Ty immediately dialed Raul; he hadn't paid attention to the sirens. "Raúl, I need…"

"An ambulance," Raul interjected. "We are on our way. I am almost to the amphitheater. What happened?"

"I'll explain when you arrive." Ty hung up and looked towards the top of the theater.

He stepped outside to talk to Rodolfo who was very concerned for Robison and Wade. After Ty told him they both would be fine, he thanked him for saving Robison's life, first at the landing and then by killing Donadio. Rodolfo smiled and told Ty all about Robison delivering his new baby boy. Ty congratulated him and shook his hand; Robison was something else!

Ty's cell phone rang. "Ty, here," he answered.

It was Tom Winstead.

"Can I call you right back? We've got a lot going on here and Wade needs to go to the hospital to get a bullet taken out of his shoulder," Ty said, hanging up without giving Tom a chance to say anything.

Tom looked at Brianne. "Son-of-a-bitch! Now Wade has a bullet in his goddamned shoulder! What the hell is going on down there?"

"How could you let him off the line without finding something out?" Brianne yelled furiously.

"He hung up! I can't get information from the damned dial tone, you know!" Tom and Brianne were on edge, clearly reflected in their testiness to each other.

Policemen and medics rushed down the stairs, carrying emergency equipment and stretchers. The police surrounded Donadio's body while Rodolfo explained what had happened.

By this time, Wade had regained consciousness and was conversing with Robison.

Ty took the opportunity to call Tom back. "I believe you can get ready to come and pick up your friends now," Ty said. "They thought you might be willing to fly down."

"You mean they're both there?"

"Yeah, they can't come to the phone because Robison is doctoring the bullet wound in Wade's shoulder."

"God Almighty. What are you talking about, man?"

"I'm telling you, she's working on Wade who was unconscious until about a minute ago. But after the ambulance gets him to the hospital and they perform surgery, I'm sure they'll be ready to leave here for good. Robison doesn't think it's too serious, so he should be able to leave by the time you get down here."

"Thanks for the info. Give them our best and we'll get there as soon as we can."

"Okay, we'll meet you at the airport."

Robison was waving at Ty, to get his attention.

"Tom….Hold on a minute…" Ty listened to Robison and then continued, "Oh, Robison says to bring her some clothes and shoes. She also doesn't have any…uh…underwear."

"Holy shit! How do you know she doesn't have any underwear on? Is she naked?"

"Not exactly, but you'll see when you get here." Ty chuckled and hung up.

Robison smiled upon overhearing this. "I guess I've worn some ridiculous outfits around you," she said.

"Yeah, some times nothing at all!" Ty replied as he walked over and placed his arm around her while the medics placed Wade onto the stretcher.

"Are you going to be okay?" Ty asked her softly, handing her one of the skater's robes to put on in place of her bloody red, tent dress.

"I'm great now…thanks," she answered looking into his eyes. She gave him a quick hug before leaving to follow the stretcher up the stairs to the ambulance.

Ty and Raúl soon had the tarp loaded and the containers were ready to be sealed. Raúl went to the hospital while Ty waited for the chassis driver to arrive and haul the containers to the port. Meanwhile, he began returning the dozens of voice mail messages on his cell phone from people all over the world. Listening to Sam and the Stuart office made him feel reassured, and relieved to get back to his normal, hectic lifestyle. Enough of Doc and company!

In between calls and talking to the driver, Ty had a call from an unknown number. In light of all that had happened, he thought he'd better answer. "Hello, Ty here."

"Hi," Robison said quietly. "Raúl gave me your number. He's gone to check and see if Wade and I are free to leave the country. The police haven't questioned me at all. Don't you find that strange?"

There was a long pause. "I don't know what's strange anymore. How is Wade?" he asked trying to keep the conversation on the right track.

"He's sitting up, albeit a little groggy, but he'll be fine. At least the local doctor agreed to discharge him since I'm a doctor." There was an awkward pause. Robison continued, her voice quivering, "Ty,

I...I just want to tell you how much you mean to me, and tell you...I..."

He interrupted her, "Listen, I have another call coming through. I'll see you at the hospital in a few minutes." He clicked his phone off and closed his eyes. Taking a deep breath he climbed the amphitheater's stairs for the last time, and hailed a taxi.

Ty's cell phone rang as he entered the hospital. It was Brianne and they'd just landed at the airport. Ty suggested they stay put so they wouldn't have to go through customs and immigration. She also told Ty she had Wade and Robison's passports; therefore, they should be all set to leave whenever Wade was ready.

While they waited on Wade's discharge from the hospital, Robison made Ty promise he would fly back with them and not wait on a commercial flight to Florida. They would have to stop in Fort Lauderdale anyway to go through U.S. Customs. Ty could get off there. He somewhat reluctantly agreed, although during this conversation he tried not to be left alone with her. Besides, a day of rest and doing laundry before leaving for Greece would be a welcome respite, he rationalized.

Raúl went to the gift shop, bought a newspaper and began translating an article to Robison. On the second page were two large pictures side by side of Juan and Carlos. A smaller picture below the one of Carlos featured the crane pulling vehicles out of the Chavón River. Under the picture of Juan was a picture of an older woman in handcuffs going into what looked like the police station.

Raúl explained the woman was Mrs. Alvarez, who'd turned herself in to the police. In her quote to the press she admitted to stabbing her husband in a jealous rage, so with her husband and son both dead, she had nothing to live for.

"So, that's why the police weren't interested in questioning me!" Robison declared.

The hunt for the American Dr. Murphy was officially over.

"I owe so much to so many people. I only wish I'd seen Rodolfo before he left," she said to Raúl and Ty.

Ironically, Robison wasn't the only one who owed her life to Rodolfo. Unknowingly, Bibí owed her life to him, as well. Otherwise, Donadio would have hunted her down like a relentless bloodhound in his quest for revenge. Instead, at this moment, Bibí was sipping a Piña Colada on the veranda of her new oceanfront condominium on Copa Cabana Beach in Rio de Janeiro, barking orders at the maid. Some things would never change.

Arriving at the airport in Raúl's car, Ty helped Wade out of the backseat and Raúl opened the trunk. Ty was the only one of the three who had luggage.

Brianne rushed to embrace Robison, saying: "Look at you! I don't even recognize you. And those clothes!" Brianne was looking at the robe and over-sized thongs flapping with every step Robison took. "Here's something decent to put on, including panties." Brianne handed her the small carry-on.

"Oh, this outfit is pretty form fitting, compared to what I wore before," Robison explained. "Now if I could just find a shower."

Raúl directed her to a VIP facility, where she bathed, applied cosmetics and put on a casual but comely outfit—with dainty underwear beneath.

As Raúl told Ty goodbye, he said, "Señor Kelly…it has been very exciting being around you."

Ty clapped Raúl on the back and said, "More exciting than you know. Thanks for all your help and expertise. Maybe we'll work together again some time. Hey, Tom's waving at me, so I'd better get going. I only have a day or so to do my laundry and get organized before I leave for Greece."

"No problema," Raúl answered as he watched the five of them march down the tarmac and onto the airplane. Ty turned and waved at Raúl, promoter, lighting director, Casanova.

The King Air landed at the private airport in Fort Lauderdale where the Murphys, the Winsteads and Tyler Kelly went through U.S. Customs and Immigration. Then they refueled and returned their rented Life Raft Kit to the local aviation company. They also unloaded Ty's luggage; this is where he was parting company from the rest of the group. Tom and Brianne were going to drop the Murphys off in Myrtle Beach and then continue home to Hickory, North Carolina.

Robison turned to Ty. "Care for a drink while they refuel? You can spare a few minutes, can't you? I'm buying."

"Oh, you have money now?" Ty kidded.

"No, but…Tom does."

"Just one beer," Ty said as he looked at his watch. "Any more than that and I may say something I'd regret later."

"That'll be the day," Robison said saucily. "Besides, I'd like to see you out of control just once."

Affectionately, she took his arm and walked him into the small private bar. Wade and Brianne were already sliding into a booth, Brianne questioning Wade about everything that had happened. When Tom joined them they ordered beer all around.

"I still can't believe all that stuff happened to you guys," Brianne gasped.

"Well, we wouldn't be here if Ty hadn't helped us," Robison responded.

"Yeah," Wade agreed. "There's no way we can ever repay you, Ty, but we can invite you to visit us in Murrells Inlet and cook a hell of a meal for you. Tom and Brianne can fly down, too."

Ty seemed interested, asking, "Do you steam crabs? …Over vinegar?"

"Just about the best you'll ever eat!" Tom exclaimed. "Wade's a great cook!"

"Well, hell! Why weren't you making the sandwiches during the hurricane?" Ty asked.

"Shit, I couldn't get off the chair!" Wade laughed.

"I have a couple of really good friends that live up your way," Ty said. "I may just stop by some time," he added, not sounding very sincere as he looked in Robison's direction. Ty continued, "Well, I've got to run along now, so here's the deal. I'll be in Greece for a month. Just promise me Brianne won't plan a vacation there until I leave! My heart couldn't stand much more of this kind of excitement anytime soon."

When everyone laughed, Brianne carped, "Very funny, butt heads."

Ty shook hands all around. When he came to Robison, she took his hand and stood up. The two of them walked towards the door arm in arm. They melded together in a touching embrace. "Don't get into any more trouble, Doc," he whispered.

"I'll miss you. There's so much I want to say…," she said softly.

"This is goodbye, Robbi. Let's leave it at that." He felt her nod on his shoulder. Pushing her gently away, their eyes locked for a long moment. Then he turned and walked away.

During the awkward minutes that followed, Robison sat down and took a sip of her beer—not daring to look in Ty's direction. She contemplated her glass as the others watched.

"Well, that was one hell of a 'handshake,' Robison," Tom ventured.

Brianne arched an eyebrow, and said nothing.

Robison's shifted slightly, and started to reply. But Wade interrupted, "Everything is okay," he said, gently stroking Robison's arm. He looked up at Tom and Brianne, "We owe our lives to that man, we're both alive, and that's all that matters now." Wade looked back at Robison. "I love you."

"I love you too. Let's go home!" Robison said with a smile.

ABOUT THE AUTHOR

Patrice Leary began a career as a professional ice skater when only a child. She performed as a solo and pair skater for twenty-six years with *Holiday on Ice* and *Ice Follies* skating in such famous venues as Madison Square Garden and Radio City Music Hall. She also performed in fourteen foreign countries during her touring years.

After retiring from skating full time, Patrice went into producing and directing ice shows. Leary Ice Productions still provides ice rinks and ice shows for companies all over the world.

Threaded throughout her novels are the experiences, places, and characters she encountered along the way, providing a unique perspective, that comes from having grown up on the road. Her real-life adventures make her writing believable and exciting.

Patrice and her husband Ed enjoy fishing and are avid golfers. They split their time between homes in Murrells Inlet, South Carolina, and Jensen Beach, Florida.

Dire Crossing will be followed by *Flight of Lyons*.

For more information and pictures visit:

www.patriceleary.com

Printed in the United States
16477LVS00005B/58-153

9 781414 028484